Barefoot

Published by: Michelle Holman
First published 2010
Second edition published 2024

ISBN:
978-1-0670071-5-7 (Printed)
978-1-0670071-4-0 (eBook)

Produced by: Indie Experts Publishing
www.indieexpertspublishing.com
Cover design by Ammie Christiansen
Cover artwork by Katie Fisher
Typesetting by Fast Forward Design
Typeset in 10pt Georgia

National Library of New Zealand Cataloguing-in-Publication Data
Holman, Michelle. Barefoot / Michelle Holman

Barefoot

MICHELLE HOLMAN

Chapter 1

G ood girl, sweetheart — not long now,' Dan Brogan murmured. Sherry watched her sister, Lisa, collapse again into her husband's arms and wondered how much longer he could lie through his teeth. She couldn't fault Dan: he'd been by Lisa's side from the moment her waters broke (how was it possible for a woman's body to hold that much fluid?) and the contractions began, rubbing her back, wiping her face, telling her jokes (earlier on, when Lisa could still smile), and stoically accepting the two times she screamed at him that he was never going to get her naked on the hood of a car again. Sherry laughed, but their mother, Jill, pretended not to hear.

As the hours passed and Lisa grew more tired, Dan's face got more haggard and he gritted his teeth each time a contraction began. Sherry had to admit that in his own way he was suffering, too. He was a doctor and had seen women give birth before, but it must be hell watching the woman you loved in so much pain and knowing you'd played a big part in causing it. The baby was very much wanted, but Sherry wished — she winced as Lisa screwed up her red, sweaty face, reared up again and began to push — it would get its shit together and get the hell out of her sister. It seemed like hours since the nurse had said Lisa could start pushing, which Sherry had naïvely assumed to mean the grand finale was close, but all there was to show for Lisa's pushing, panting and swearing was a round circle of wrinkled skin covered by a few strands of dark hair. Sherry wasn't impressed that her new niece or nephew appeared to be sporting a bad comb-over. At home in New Zealand she was a police officer; when there was a problem, she was used to doing something to resolve it, not standing by watching.

She checked the clock on the wall of the delivery room; she checked her mother's face where she stood opposite Dan at the head of the bed holding Lisa's hand; she checked the face of the nurse who calmly repeated that everything was progressing normally. Sherry shook her head in disbelief. There was nothing normal about something the size of a juggernaut — relatively speaking — being forced through an aperture the size of a lemon. No bloody way. In Lisa's shoes, Sherry would have gobbled down every drug available and offered up any part of her anatomy the hospital staff cared to have if it meant missing out on the pain and degradation of the birth process. Better to be stoned or unconscious. Given a choice between celibacy and pregnancy, she'd settle for option A and buy a vibrator.

Earlier, there'd been some discussion about Lisa having a caesarean because the baby was big. Sherry set the blame for that firmly on the shoulders of her six-foot-five-inches brother-in- law but relented when she saw that Dan had reached the same conclusion. Lisa had turned down the caesarean, insisting she wanted to try to do things naturally, although she had accepted some pain relief. Sherry wished she could have some, too. She didn't think she could stand by for much longer watching her sister be tortured by the 'natural birth process'. The fact that her mother and the others considered what was happening normal horrified her.

She took some slow, deep breaths. When she'd arrived two days earlier with her mother, she was already tired because of the amount of overtime she'd put in recently at work, and jet lag hadn't helped make her feel any better. Sherry was a detective constable in a family violence unit. She loved her job and had her sights firmly set on passing her sergeant's exam and promotion. In a crisis she was usually level-headed and clear-thinking, but right now she felt like she wanted to faint or throw up. She was as healthy as a horse — not the kind of woman who fainted.

'The head is delivering,' the midwife announced. 'Take a deep breath and give me a big push, Lisa.'

Sherry checked what was happening between her sister's legs and the doughnut she'd eaten an hour earlier began reversing its way up her throat.

Jill noticed her eldest daughter's pallor and asked sharply, 'Are you alright?'

Sherry was transfixed by what she was seeing and unable to speak or look away. Lisa strained, grunted, strained again, and collapsed back against Dan's chest while everybody peered ecstatically at the small pink bowling ball covered in black hair between her legs. Sherry's stomach roiled. That was a head?

'Sherry!'

She started and looked at her mother. 'What?'

Jill was torn between watching the birth of her first grandchild and keeping an eye on her increasingly pale elder daughter. 'Are you alright?'

Sherry fanned her face. 'Of course I'm alright! It's just

hot in here!'

'If you're going to faint, please do it over there by the beanbags,' the midwife said in a Midwest American drawl. 'Maybe you should go outside.'

Lisa screwed up her face and struggled upwards, and the midwife's attention was diverted back to her patient and the bowling ball.

Sherry gulped and tried to slow her breathing. She was not going to faint. She saw worse things when she attended car accidents and suspicious deaths. There was a flurry of activity around the bed, and she was grateful when the midwife blocked her view; this was one gig where it paid not to have ringside seats. She kept her eyes on Dan's taut, anxious face as he lifted Lisa and supported her while she pushed and grunted and — Sherry gulped again — screamed.

Sherry's vision went fuzzy around the edges and she swayed. She focused desperately on Dan's face as he stared down at something on the bed with an awestruck expression. A huge smile replaced the tense, drawn look he'd worn for the past few hours, along with what Sherry could only describe as a look of wonder. Sherry knew she would never forget how Dan looked the first time he saw his baby. Suddenly, she was glad she'd stayed in the birthing room.

There were some snuffling noises. Dan turned his head and kissed Lisa on the cheek where she lolled against his shoulder like a rag doll. 'Lisa, honey— it's a girl!' he cried hoarsely. 'We've got a little girl!'

Lisa reached up and wrapped a shaky arm around Dan's neck; he kissed her dry, chapped lips. Sherry's nose stung and she swallowed. Watching them and knowing how hard they'd fought for their happiness made everything, even Lisa's ordeal, worth it.

'Oh, she's beautiful!' Grandma Jill sobbed as the baby began to cry.

The midwife stepped back and Sherry got her first look at her new niece. Her eyes widened in dismay. She was no expert, but it looked to her like the baby's head was lopsided and had a point. She ventured a few steps closer and tilted her head to get a better view as the midwife handed Lisa the squalling infant. As the baby was turned to fit into the crook of her mother's arm, Sherry gasped.

Her sister had given birth to a cone-head.

She looked at the midwife, Dan and her mother, but none of them seemed worried; they were acting like everything was fine. Sherry guessed now wasn't the best time to ask if it was OK that the baby's head looked like the tip of an HB pencil. There was definitely nothing wrong with Sherry's eyes, she had perfect 20/20 vision. Her niece had arms and legs, little fingers and toes, and her lungs seemed to be in good order, but there was no getting away from that lopsided, pointy head. Oh dear God, what if she was brain-damaged?

Sherry felt like the blood suddenly gurgled from her head and down the drainpipe provided by her neck. She wilted some more.

'Sherry!' Jill ordered. 'Go out!'

She straightened her shoulders and licked her lips. 'I'm fine.'

'You are not!'

Dan looked up from his rapt contemplation of his new daughter's tight little fist wrapped around one of his fingers and cast a professional eye over Sherry. 'Would you mind going out to the waiting room and letting my folks know, Sherry?' he asked.

She knew she was being given an excuse to escape. Dan was like that — observant, thoughtful, tactful — but Sherry was contrary and stubborn. 'Are you sure you don't want to tell them yourself?'

His gaze drifted back to his wife and daughter. 'Tell them that as soon as Lisa's ready I'll come and get them.'

Ready to do what? Sherry wondered, and on cue, Lisa pulled a face and squirmed.

'The placenta is delivering,' the midwife announced.

Sherry bolted from the room. She made her way unsteadily along the corridor to the cosy, sunny lounge where Dan's mother, Molly, his father, Kell, and brother, Glenn, were waiting. Molly and Kell lived in Boulder, but they had come to stay for the week before the baby was due. Sherry liked Dan's parents; they'd welcomed Lisa into their family and taken her under their wing when Dan was offered a job as a paediatric surgeon in Denver and he and Lisa had moved to the States from New Zealand. His brother, Glenn, however, was a different matter.

Glenn was a retired pro-basketball player with a ruined knee and bad attitude who'd earned himself the nickname of 'The Blitz' thanks to his uncanny ability to sink three-pointers. He and Sherry had started off on the wrong foot when Glenn had arrived at Auckland airport for Dan and Lisa's wedding with a banana in his golf bag and Sherry had almost arrested him for breaching New Zealand bio-security. She was ferociously protective of her family and concerned about how Dan's relatives would react to Lisa, considering the weird way she and Dan had met. It soon became clear that Glenn felt the same way about his older brother and wouldn't be slow to voice his opinions if he thought Lisa wouldn't make his brother happy. Sherry thought Glenn was an emotional lightweight. Glenn thought Sherry was a ball-breaker.

Two years ago, aged thirty-four, his career as one of the top shooting guards in the NBA had ended due to his injured knee, leaving Glenn with more money than he knew what to do with and too much time on his hands. He was a regular visitor at Dan and Lisa's house, and when he wasn't visiting or travelling, he seemed to spend the rest of his time playing golf or posing for advertisements with bikini-clad models to endorse Blitz sunglasses, shirts or whatever else he'd agreed to attach his name to. Lisa had shown Sherry a magazine advertisement of Glenn wearing a white ski hat and jacket and sleek, black wraparound sunglasses with a stylized lightning flash and 'Blitz' written in pale blue on the side. Two models were snuggled either side of him, wearing ice-blue ski jackets and Blitz sunglasses. They had their backs to the camera and their heads turned to press voluptuous, open-mouthed kisses to Glenn's cheeks. Even with his eyes and hair covered, Sherry would have recognized that one-cornered smirk.

Get Blitzed This Winter — You Know You Want To the advertisement urged. Lisa had said that the photos for the new summer campaign were on billboards all over the country, and either failed to notice or ignored the way Sherry's upper lip curled. The photo had confirmed her first impression of Dan's brother:

emotional lightweight.

Sherry took her time making her way to the waiting room to give herself a chance to regain her composure. Glenn Brogan would enjoy finding a chink in her armour, but Sherry would like to see just how chipper he'd feel if he'd just watched Lisa doing — Sherry shuddered — what she'd just done. As she turned the corner into the lounge, Molly and Kell jumped up. Glenn was on the other side of the room looking out the window. Despite the air conditioning, Sherry felt like the heat of the Denver summer had invaded the room. She brushed at her sticky forehead and forced her rubbery legs across the carpet towards Dan's parents.

Her pale face alarmed Molly. 'Is everything alright?'

Glenn joined them, the slight hitch in his gait the only indication of the ruined knee that had ended his career. Sherry flicked him an impatient look. His hands were buried in the pockets of his jeans and a lock of black hair tumbled across his brow like Superman.

Dan had quiet silvery-grey eyes but his younger brother had a bold golden stare and sulky bad-boy mouth. Sherry was five foot eleven inches in her bare feet and used to looking down at people, but Glenn was six foot seven inches tall. She resented having to look up at him, and thought it was dishonest that somebody with so many personality defects had that mouth and those eyes. She smiled at Dan's parents. 'You've got a granddaughter.'

Molly gave a cry and hugged Sherry, Glenn and Kell. Kell hugged Glenn, Sherry and then Molly, which left Sherry and Glenn face- to-face. They automatically reached for one another before their arms fell to their sides.

Under the cover of his parents' chatter, Glenn said, 'Congratulations, Auntie Sherry. I'd hug you but I haven't had all my shots.'

Sherry replied in a hollow voice, 'No need to apologize, Uncle Glenn. Although I really think that vet should be reported.' The heat beat at her. She blinked as the room seemed to darken and her ears began to buzz.

'Is Lisa OK?'

'How much does the baby weigh?'

'Can we go and see them?'

They sounded a long way off and their faces began to waver like a mirage in the desert.

'What does she look like?' somebody — Molly? — asked.

Sherry pictured the baby's pointy head and the buzzing in her ears became a roar. She managed to say, 'She's got a really pointy head.'

And then she crumpled.

Chapter 2

Glenn sat beside one of the waiting-room couches looking down at Sherry Jackson's pale face and closed eyes. Strictly speaking, she wasn't beautiful. Her jaw was too square, her nose a shade too long and her dark-blue gaze too challenging. Lisa was the pretty sister; she had black hair and big cornflower-blue eyes set in a heart-shaped face. Sherry was handsome rather than pretty, and her body ... well, that centrefold body made up for the long nose and the ice-box personality.

His mother called Sherry 'statuesque'. Glenn preferred 'voluptuous' or 'stacked'. She was a big girl with full breasts, broad shoulders and round hips that made her waist look even smaller, and she had long, long legs that ended somewhere near her ears. Sherry knew how to dress, how to make the most of her height, and with that siren's body looked like she should be stalking a catwalk instead of criminals.

They'd met twice before, the first time when Dan and Lisa were married in New Zealand, and the second when Sherry and her mother arrived in Denver a couple of days ago. It took only five minutes in each other's company for Glenn and Sherry to realize that things hadn't changed between them — their mutual antipathy was matched by an equally strong desire to jump one another's bones. In New Zealand they'd dealt with it by ignoring each other, and when they absolutely couldn't avoid contact — like at the wedding when Sherry was maid of honour and Glenn was best man — making snide comments that upset Lisa, Jill and Molly, and to a lesser extent, Kell and Lisa's father, Brian. Ben (Sherry and Lisa's brother) and Dan had both guessed the real reason Glenn and Sherry argued.

After Dan arrived in the lounge and backed up Sherry's assertions that she was just suffering from jet lag, Glenn agreed to stay and supervise the patient while Dan took their parents to see Lisa and the baby. Sherry wasn't keen on the arrangement, but Glenn knew his mother wouldn't leave if somebody didn't stay with Sherry. Even so, although Molly was dying to see her new granddaughter, she seemed doubtful about the wisdom of leaving Lisa's sister to Glenn's tender ministrations. If the positions were reversed, Jill would have been just as reluctant to leave Glenn in Sherry's care.

Molly looked hard at Glenn. 'Are you sure she'll be alright?'

Glenn interpreted this as: *Are you sure you'll behave and not embarrass me?*

'She'll be fine, Mom. Go see Lisa and the baby.'

When Molly continued to hover, he picked up Sherry's hand and tensed at the awareness that crackled beneath his skin at the contact. Sherry flinched and tried to pull away, but Glenn refused to let go and gave her hand the kind of brisk pat doctors and nurses administered when they were trying to bring up a vein to draw blood.

Sherry's face was as white as paper. 'You go,' she said, as she tried to retrieve her hand, again unsuccessfully. 'All of you. I'll be fine, I'm just jet-lagged.' It sounded so much better than shit-scared after watching her sister give birth.

Molly sighed and sat back down. 'I'll wait until Jill comes out.' Glenn was confronted by the collective might of family disapproval. A smart player knew when it was time to change from offensive to defensive mode. He stroked the back of Sherry's hand to reassure his mother he wouldn't strangle Lisa's sister in her absence. Sherry dug her nails into his palm and Glenn tightened his grip. 'You go ahead; I promise I'll take good care of her.'

'You'd better,' Dan said. 'Lisa wants her to be godmother.'

It was on the tip of Glenn's tongue to say *Are you serious?* But he kept quiet in case Molly the Martyr insisted on staying.

He watched Dan and his parents leave the room and continued to absent-mindedly stroke Sherry's hand. Dan looked terrible: watching Lisa give birth seemed to have aged him ten years. *How hard can it be to sit and hold your wife's hand?* Glenn wondered. Over the years, he'd looked at plenty of photos of his team-mates' offspring and listened patiently while they explained how their son or daughter was a certifiable genius because he/she moved his/her ear, nose or eyes a certain way two hours after they were born. He'd nodded and hadn't shared his observations that newborn babies' eyes were either crossed or rolled in opposite directions, and that their ears and noses were squashed so flat that the locations on their heads was the only way of telling what they were. When any of the guys talked about the physical aspects of birth, Glenn tuned out; there were certain parts of a woman's anatomy that he preferred to associate with pleasure. He didn't want to know what went on at the business end. He liked children and wasn't opposed to having some of his own but was less keen on the idea of settling down with one woman.

'Can I have my hand back?' Sherry's face was turned towards the back of the sofa so her voice came out muffled, but there was no mistaking her annoyance. She tugged. 'Let go of me.'

'But, sweetheart,' Glenn drawled. 'I've dreamed of this — you and me, alone, holding hands.'

Her hand went limp. She spoke with exaggerated patience: 'It's obvious that you've taken one too many hits in the head from basketballs over the years, so I'll say this slowly, let go of my hand or I'll deck you.'

He wished just once she'd crack and really lose her temper instead of always being so controlled and self-possessed. Dan claimed that Sherry had once manhandled him out of her house, but Glenn didn't believe it; he couldn't imagine Detective Constable Sherry Jackson losing her cool or managing to shove his brother out a door. When she got annoyed, her eyes and voice iced over — Glenn had good reason to know this, because she looked like that a lot when he was around her. He'd take a woman who threw things and yelled over one who looked down her nose and had ice cubes in her eyes any day, or at least he had believed he would until he met Sherry Jackson.

Glenn took Sherry's wrist between his thumb and forefinger and draped it across her thigh. She tucked her fist beneath her chin and refused to open her eyes. She was no lightweight. He knew this, because he had caught her when she'd swayed and lifted her onto the couch. The contact had confirmed what he had always suspected: that Sherry was a combination of lean muscle and luscious curves.

The first time Glenn had seen her, Sherry was wearing a police uniform, a bulletproof vest and a ponytail. Every nerve in his body had leapt to attention. He couldn't recall having such an instantaneous physical response to a female since the tenth grade when Lori Rathbone had shown him what was beneath her Wham T-shirt. The sight of the black-haired cop with the sexy little mole beneath her left eye made him forget about his argument with a customs officer over the banana in his golf bag. Glenn had
given the cop the smile that had bowled over countless women, but instead of smiling back she'd looked down her nose and explained that, unless Glenn paid more attention to the customs officer, she might just have to arrest him for breaching New Zealand bio-security.

Women in bulletproof vests had never figured high in his personal fantasies, so Glenn was pissed when he began dreaming about Lisa's sister wearing her Kevlar vest and not much else. She shared the distinction of being one of his least favourite people; along with several NBA referees and his physical therapist, who was always on his case about not taking better care of his knee. All that silky black hair and white skin made her look like Snow White. Glenn's gaze lingered on the tiny black mole beneath her eye. He imagined painting it with the tip of his tongue and frowned at his body's response.

Sherry cracked one eye open. Dan's brother was still

sitting beside her, glowering. Why'd he have to choose now to play Boy Scout? Obviously, the only way she was going to get rid of him was by proving she was OK. She grabbed the back of the sofa and sat up. The rapid change in position made her blood pressure plummet, and she would have fallen off the couch if Glenn hadn't caught her by the shoulders. Tiny shockwaves fluttered beneath her skin, adding to her disorientation. She knew Glenn felt it, too, because he nearly dropped her onto the couch. Sherry draped an arm over her eyes to block out his face.

'No need to throw yourself into my arms,' he crooned. 'I promise I'm not going anywhere.'

When Sherry didn't answer, Glenn decided she must be feeling really bad. The wide neckline of the silky green tunic she wore belted over a pair of skinny-leg black jeans was designed to leave one shoulder bare. She wasn't wearing a bra. The tunic and absence of a bra had been bothering Glenn ever since she'd come out of the delivery room earlier to get a drink of water. He was an expert on women's underwear, having dated several lingerie models and invested heavily in it as presents for former girlfriends, and he knew that a woman built like Sherry couldn't go commando. He'd bet money she was wearing a merry widow. In the long hours while they waited for news, Glenn had entertained himself imagining what colour the merry widow was and how Sherry would look in it. He'd decided it was probably black rubber with a place to hide a switchblade and would fire off a blast of liquid nitrogen if a man's hand ventured too close.

'Just keep your hands to yourself, OK?' Sherry

muttered.

Glenn sighed heavily. 'I'm doing my best, but they keep itching to find a way around your throat. The risk of freezer burns just isn't enough of a deterrent.'

She raised her arm and glared at him. 'You're enjoying this, aren't you?'

He smiled. 'Hell, yes.'

Sherry retreated beneath her arm again. It was bad enough having Glenn witness her humiliation, let alone have him gloat about it. Why had Dan turned out so nice and his not-so-little brother so horrible? Although to be fair, Dan hadn't behaved like a knight in shining armour in the early months of his relationship with Lisa, but he was still a big improvement on Glenn. Had all the good parts got used up first time around?

Jill Jackson came into the lounge carrying a washcloth. 'Molly said you passed out.'

'I didn't pass out,' Sherry insisted. 'It's jet lag.'

'Why didn't you go out when I told you to?'

Sherry gasped as the icy-cold cloth was slapped onto her forehead. 'What is this? Water torture?'

Jill held the cloth in place. 'Stay still.'

Glenn got to his feet. 'Be a good girl and listen to Mommy.'

'Thanks for looking after her,' Jill smiled at him. 'Go and see the baby. She's beautiful.'

'Really?' he said innocently. 'Sherry said she's got a pointy head.'

'She does *not*!' Jill looked at Sherry accusingly. '*You* were the one with a pointy head. I thought I'd have to keep a hat on you all the time.'

Sherry pulled the washcloth over her eyes to block

out the sight of Glenn's silent laughter.

'Hopefully, she'll get the best traits of her mother and both her grandmothers,' he said, so sweetly Sherry was sure he'd need an insulin injection.

Jill watched Glenn head towards the birthing rooms and said warmly, 'Molly and Kell did a wonderful job of raising those boys.'

Sherry spoke from beneath the washcloth. 'Personally, I think they broke the mould after their first attempt.'

Jill whipped the cloth away and folded it into thirds. 'Dan's a wonderful husband to Lisa, and he's going to be a wonderful father. Glenn will be just the same.'

Sherry snorted. If there was one thing Glenn Brogan *wasn't*, it was husband and father material. From what she'd seen, he had a lifetime membership to Playboys Are Us. 'I think polygamy is illegal in Denver, Mum. Lisa can't be married to Dan and his brother at the same time.'

Jill slapped the washcloth across Sherry's forehead. 'You know what I mean.'

'I think I'm going to be sick.'

Jill's concern evaporated when she saw Sherry's sneer. 'You ungrateful little wretch!' Only a mother could get away with calling her almost-six-foot-tall daughter little. 'It was good of Glenn to wait out here with you when he was probably dying to see Lisa and the baby.'

Not as much as he was dying to see me throw up all over myself, Sherry thought. 'He's a blot on humanity.' She shook out the washcloth and covered her face with it again.

'The baby weighs nine pounds.'

Beneath the cloth, Sherry grimaced. 'Now that,' she said faintly, '*is* disgusting.'

Of course *Uncle Glenn* was a pro at handling newborns.

He scooped up his little niece and cradled her against his wide, manly chest, pulled faces at her, stroked her cheek and basically made a complete prat of himself, while the baby stared back transfixed. The new parents laughed and the new grandparents beamed, while Sherry prayed her niece would throw up or, even better, crap on the front of Glenn's *Bona Fide Blitz* shirt — he had a range of menswear named after him, too. She tried to get out of holding the baby, but everybody looked at her like she'd just announced to a class of pre-schoolers that Santa Claus wasn't real. Sherry capitulated because she didn't want to hurt Lisa and Dan's feelings, but, unlike Uncle Glenn, Auntie Sherry held her niece stiffly across her forearms like she was a log of wood, and the baby began to cry. Of course that gave everybody a good laugh, *especially* Uncle Glenn, and Sherry handed the baby back to Dan.

In front of the family, Sherry and Glenn put on an act of beaming ultra-politeness that kept their mothers happy but, frankly, made everybody else nervous. Glenn's wide, white smile made Sherry think of *Jaws*, especially when he asked, 'Do you want me to give you a few pointers?'

She twinkled back. '*So* sweet of you, Glenn. I bet

there'll be three of them.'

'What are you going to call her?' Kell asked hastily.

'Georgia,' Dan replied.

There was a long silence while everybody digested the news and avoided looking at one another. Georgia was the feminine version of George. They all knew who George was — even though Lisa and Dan had told them the story only once, it wasn't something they were likely to forget. How could they, when Dan, a paediatric surgeon who dealt in scientific fact, and Lisa, a former teacher, explained that George was the angel in Heaven's waiting room who'd sent Lisa back into the wrong body after she had a near-fatal car accident and woke up to find she had a husband? Nobody spoke about it. It was easier to ignore it and just be thankful that Dan and Lisa were so happy together.

Kell spoke up again. 'Is that all? Just Georgia?'

Molly and Jill raised their heads expectantly, each thinking it wasn't unreasonable to expect their granddaughter to be named after one, or maybe even both, of her grandmothers. In a rare moment of accord, Glenn and Sherry's amused glances tangled, before sliding away again.

Lisa spoke up from where she was sitting in bed, leaning against Dan who was holding their daughter. The baby looked tiny against her father's chest. 'Georgia Sherry.' Lisa smiled at Sherry's shocked expression. 'After her auntie, who stood by me at a time when I needed her most.'

Sherry's nose stung for the second time that day as she remembered that horrible time when Lisa was trying to convince the family that she was their daughter and sister.

'Georgia Sherry Brogan.' Kell smiled. 'I like it.'

Chapter 3

Sherry wasn't surprised that Lisa needed some stitches after the birth. However, she was shocked when Lisa came home the day after Georgia's birth. 'Do you think you should?' Sherry asked.

'Of course I should.' Lisa's eyes were on her daughter asleep in her arms. 'Having a baby is a normal process. I don't need a nurse; I've got Dan and Mum and ... *you*.' She smiled wryly. 'And I want to be at home in my own bed, with Dan.'

Lisa did nothing all day but sleep and breast-feed and change and cuddle Georgia. Dan had taken paternity leave, and what with him, and Jill and Molly hovering over the new mother and baby, Sherry felt like a fifth wheel. She watched from afar, convinced that the best thing she could do was leave her sister and niece to the experts. She told her brother, Ben, as much when he phoned from New Zealand to check on Lisa and Georgia's progress.

'Babies have never been your thing; you'll probably feel better when Georgia's older,' he said.

Sherry imagined seeing Georgia at her sixteenth birthday and hearing her say, 'Auntie Sherry? I've heard about you. Aren't you the one who almost dropped me on my pointy head the day I was born?'

'So you haven't been offering to change nappies?' Ben asked.

'No. And neither would you if you saw the stuff that

squirts out her rear end. It looks like mustard but take my word for it when I say you wouldn't be in any hurry to put it on your sandwiches.'

'What does she look like?'

'A baby.'

'Is that the best you can do?'

'A squashed baby,' Sherry amended. 'She's got ten perfect little fingers and toes and she makes everybody feel good.' Even her; Georgia was so small and innocent — there were no thoughts of stealing cars or hoodwinking old ladies going on inside that fuzzy little head. 'It's nice to see Lisa and Dan so happy; they'll make great parents.'

'Yeah, they will,' Ben agreed. 'Dan emailed some photos.'

'So why were you asking me to describe Georgia?'

'There's nothing wrong with her head. She's gorgeous. Dad said your head looked a lot worse when you were born.'

'How was I to know it was normal?' Sherry protested. 'Dan called it moulding.'

'Yeah, I think I read about that.'

Ben was a notorious bookworm and would read just about anything he could lay his hands on. Sherry and Lisa had once told one of his girlfriends that if there wasn't a book or magazine handy Ben would read signs on walls or even the labels in his clothes — 'He's an expert on dry-cleaning; just ask him.' The relationship had ended soon after with the girlfriend citing Ben's weird sisters as one reason for breaking it off. But Ben hadn't been too concerned. He was never single for long, and the opportunity to get his own back on his sisters always presented itself if he was patient.

'The point on her head is starting to go down, but in the delivery room it was downright scary,' Sherry said. 'She looked just like Dan Ackroyd.'

Ben replied wistfully, 'Wish I could have been there.'

Sherry wished he could have been, too. She'd have changed places with Ben in a flash if she hadn't felt she'd be letting Lisa down. Ben was calm and centred. Just like Georgia, he made everybody feel better, whereas Sherry spent most of her time with criminals and there was little call to make them feel better. Even the baby card she'd bought had been wrong ...

The card had a cartoon image of a gormless idiot pushing at a door marked 'Pull' to gain admittance to a building marked 'School for Geniuses'. It was just the sort of thing Lisa usually laughed at, but motherhood and something called 'third-day blues' had apparently killed off her sense of humour because she took one look at the card, laughed and then burst into tears.

'I'm sorry, Sherry!' she sobbed. 'I think it's funny! I really do! It's just hormones and cracked nipples and ...' She turned into Dan's waiting arms and bawled.

Dan smiled over her head. 'Don't take it personally, Sherry.'

Of course Glenn was there to witness her humiliation again. According to Lisa, he was making himself scarce — Sherry had a pretty good idea why — but, once again, he'd managed to stop by between rounds of golf and whatever else it was retired basketball players and full-time playboys did. And he was there again when Sherry ventured closer to Georgia's crib and said, 'How's my favourite little Martian today?'

Lisa laughed, and then bawled her head off again. Molly looked disapproving, and Jill told Sherry she should be ashamed of herself. Glenn winked: 'Way to go, Auntie Sherry.'

She narrowed her eyes. 'Why don't you celebrate Independence Day by sticking a rocket up your bum and lighting it?'

His golden eyes glowed with mischief. 'Careful now, Mommy might hear and ground you.'

Both mommies did overhear, which prompted Jill to break out the 'Angora Sweater' story that supposedly explained why Sherry couldn't help being 'difficult'.

Sherry said stiffly, 'You are *not* going to tell everybody that ridiculous sweater story.'

'We're family,' Glenn urged. 'Feel free to share.'

A couple of years ago, Jill had bought Sherry a beautiful pale-blue angora sweater in a sale, not realizing her mistake until she'd given it to Sherry and Lisa said, 'Mum, have you lost your marbles? Sherry will ruin that sweater. I'm the daughter who knows how to hand-wash woollens; Sherry is the daughter who knows how to change fuses and spark-plugs.'

It was too late. Sherry had already thrown the sweater into the washing machine on the regular cycle, and Lisa had unwittingly landed them with the respective titles of 'The Daughter Who Knows How To Change Fuses And Spark-plugs' and 'The Daughter Who Knows How To Hand-wash Woollens'.

'And Ben?' Molly asked.

'He doesn't know how to hand-wash woollens either,' Lisa said.

'Ben?' Jill repeated blankly. 'Ben is Ben.'

Ben was like a river, he just flowed onwards, smooth and placid on the surface but with hidden depths.

There was nothing placid about Glenn Brogan, and Sherry was certain he didn't have any hidden depths. He walked into a room and owned it. The Angora Sweater story had obviously appealed to his warped sense of humour because he stopped making himself scarce. And started whistling. Sherry loathed whistling, especially when the whistler kept tweeting out the old Frankie Valli song 'Sherry Baby' like a demented canary. That Glenn could whistle in tune didn't help.

Dan and Lisa lived in a lovely old house near Washington Park. Sherry got into the habit of leaving her running shoes by the back door so that the moment Glenn drove up in his ice-blue BMW M6 convertible she could head for the jogging path in the park. In fairness, it wasn't only Glenn's presence that drove Sherry from the house; she hated being idle, and ran, cycled or played some kind of sport most days.

Her response to Glenn confused and upset her; it reminded her of how she'd felt when she'd started to develop breasts and men had started noticing her ...

Even after the rest of her classmates had stopped growing, Sherry kept on shooting up and her boobs kept on getting bigger. She finally stopped at the upper limits of a D-cup, but was all boobs and long, skinny legs. Sherry hated her height and curves, and the attention they got her, and asked her mother why she'd turned out so different.

Jill was as surprised as Sherry. 'I think your father had an aunt who was a — er — big girl.'

Sherry didn't want to be a big girl *or* a small girl. She just wanted to be a normal girl and fit in like everybody else, but that was impossible when she towered over every other girl and nearly all of the boys in her class. To make matters worse, people began suggesting she think of modelling as a career. She'd always been an above-average student, but it was as if her big boobs, height and face made her intelligence superfluous.

The other girls thought Sherry was a moron. 'Why do you want to go to university when you could get paid to have your photograph taken and wear beautiful clothes all the time?'

Sherry didn't know what to say and her silence gained her a reputation of being standoffish and snobby.

Since then, Sherry had stopped hunching her shoulders and had learned to use her height and looks to her advantage. She loved beautiful clothes and had great instincts when it came to fashion. She began wearing four-inch heels and uplift bras and gave any man stupid enough to talk to her breasts a cold, intimidating stare that made them sorry they'd struck up a conversation in the first place.

But Glenn Brogan reminded Sherry uncomfortably of those early adolescent days. She would step out of the shower at Lisa's house, catch sight of herself in the mirror — and wonder what Glenn would think of her body. If he walked into a room, it was as if she was a needle on a compass and he was true north and her body woke up and pointed his way. None of her boyfriends had ever made her feel like that, including Stuart Sherborne, the guy she'd just broken up with.

She'd finished with Stuart not long before she left for Denver, because he'd started talking about getting married and Sherry giving up her career to raise their future children. Any boyfriends who raised the subject of marriage and children were quickly shown the door, but even if Stuart hadn't gone that route, being introduced to his mother had been enough to set alarm bells ringing in Sherry's head. Stuart didn't live with his mother, but they spoke on the phone most days. The kindest thing Sherry could say about Mrs Sherborne was that she was weird — an impression confirmed when Sherry came across a rerun of *Baby Jane* on Turner's Classic Movies and realized Stu's mother was a dead ringer for Bette Davis, right down to the frilly, childish clothes and the big bow in her dyed blonde hair. Stuart had said he'd promised his mother he would never put her in a home and that when the time came, she'd live with him and his wife and children. When Sherry had found out that she'd been given the stamp of approval by Mama Sherborne, she couldn't get out of the house or the relationship fast enough. Stuart hadn't taken the break well, and kept texting and calling, asking for another chance.

'I don't know why you're always making snide comments about Glenn being on the phone to his agent when your ex-boyfriend is constantly phoning you,' Lisa remarked.

'It's not the same thing. I don't take Stu's calls, and I delete all his messages. Georgia's baby blanket went off the other day while Wonder Boy was walking around the garden, supposedly showing her the trees. He didn't have a pocket and had decided to tuck his BlackBerry in her blanket.' Sherry was miffed when Lisa only laughed.

Stuart worked in Information Technology and thought a cellphone, laptop and wireless connection were more important to life than a liver, heart and lungs, but even he'd draw the line at tucking his cellphone in a baby's blanket. Stuart was the opposite of Glenn. He was decent and adored Sherry; whereas Glenn was cocky and overbearing and enjoyed giving her a hard time. Stuart irritated and bored Sherry; Glenn just irritated her. She was certain that if she slept with him once, she'd discover he was useless in bed and they'd get along fine, but that wasn't going to happen because Glenn was Dan's brother and Sherry was Lisa's sister. She liked to date independent, career-focused men who understood there were women who felt the same way. Most of Sherry's boyfriends had started out as friends first.

'Does he always spend so much time here?' she asked Lisa when she got out of the shower after a run only to discover that Glenn still hadn't left. She knew because she could hear him whistling Coldplay's 'Fix You' in Dan's study. Sherry knew exactly who he wanted to fix.

Lisa looked at her hazily. 'Does *who* always spend so much time here?'

Sherry rolled her eyes — Lisa knew who she was talking about. Lisa might not get involved in the Molly/Jill strategy-planning sessions on 'How to deal with Sherry and Glenn', but Sherry was certain that Lisa and Dan discussed them in the privacy of their bedroom at the top of the house. She tilted her head in the direction of the study where Glenn was glued to his BlackBerry talking to his agent. He spent so much time on the phone to him that Sherry had asked why they didn't get married. 'Him — Wonder Boy.'

'Glenn?' Lisa repeated in the irritatingly vague manner she'd acquired since Georgia's birth. It was as if her brain had moved into her uterus and there was no sign of it reappearing any time soon. 'He wants to see Georgia.'

Yeah, and bug me, Sherry thought. 'Doesn't he have a job?' She was surprised when Lisa answered tartly, 'Sherry, Glenn doesn't need to work ever again.'

'Why doesn't he coach or something?'

'He does coach some of the younger Cougars players, but he isn't interested in taking it up full-time.' *Of course not, because he'd probably have to take orders from management.* 'He has contracts with sponsors to fulfil, like the advertising campaign for the sunglasses. Glenn dropped off a pair for Mum. Dan and I have a couple of pairs each. I know he'd get you some if you'd like.'

'I'll take a rain check,' Sherry said drily.

The night before, a new TV commercial for Blitz sunglasses had aired with Glenn and the same two models. The models were sitting on a beach, watching as Glenn roared across the water on a black and silver-blue jet ski, which he abandoned in the shallows. His ice-blue board shorts were the same shade as the models' bikinis. He sauntered slowly through the waves towards the beach wearing nothing but a cocky smile and the shorts riding low on his hips. A black arrow of hair descended from his navel and disappeared into the waistband of his shorts — all that was needed was a neon sign on his six-pack flashing the message 'All Roads Lead Here'. Somebody had been at him with the baby oil and his chest and shoulders glistened in the sun. As he stepped onto the sand and strolled towards the models, he looked so outrageously handsome that Sherry had felt like diving into the television and body-dumping him on the sand. But it was because Glenn did look so utterly gorgeous — and the reactions of the two models were so unexpected — that the commercial was raised from the standard hunk-meets-clueless-blonde-bimbos to laugh-out-loud funny. First one, then the other, girl sat up on her beach towel — ice-blue, of course, and decorated with the Blitz logo — and raised her sunglasses as Glenn stopped in front of them. He looked down at them through black sunglasses trimmed with silver, and a smile slowly unfurled across his petulant, bad-boy mouth.

One of the girls tapped the arm of her sunglasses against her bottom lip and frowned, 'Don't I know you?'

Glenn's lids dipped and the cocky smile climbed one cheek. 'We met last winter — on the ski field,' he drawled. (Sherry cringed. It was the worst case of over-acting she'd ever seen.)

The other model gasped. 'Of course! You were wearing Blitz Lightning Bolts — that's why I remember you!'

Glenn appeared stunned at being remembered only for his sunglasses, but brightened when the first girl stroked her hand up one of his bare calves, complimented him on his sunglasses and invited him to join them. He looked directly at the camera, gave a shrug and a smile, and sank to the sand between the models, accompanied by a voice-over of him murmuring, 'Get Blitzed this summer — you know you want to.'

It was corny and funny, and Sherry was surprised that Glenn had let himself be set up to play the fall guy. She wondered if it had been a calculated move, if he'd realized how much more appealing and attractive a man with a sense of humour was than some beefcake with a handsome face. Lisa said that the winter commercial had been the same, and that Glenn's agent had wanted him to go for a more 'traditional' approach, but Glenn refused and said that if he had to make a damned advertisement, he at least wanted to have some fun.

'How many acting lessons did he need before he shot the commercials?' Sherry asked.

'Stop being such a bitch,' Lisa retorted. 'Glenn would rather be playing basketball than making ads for sunglasses or speaking at benefit dinners. He wasn't ready to retire — he had to.'

'Wasn't he getting kind of old? I mean, how long do most players last at that level?'

'Up until he hurt his knee, Glenn had never had any major injuries. He was playing great basketball and had no plans to retire, and the team management certainly didn't want to lose him. Glenn was one of their veterans: he won games,' Lisa explained. 'Can you imagine how you'd feel if you got injured and had to leave the police?'

She knew how much Sherry loved her job in the Family Violence Unit. Georgia stirred, and Lisa lifted her against her shoulder. 'Have you noticed that Dan and his parents don't talk much about Glenn's knee?'

Sherry almost felt guilty.

'Glenn had more surgery last year in the hope that it'd make some difference. Dan didn't think it was a good idea and tried to talk him out of it, but Glenn wanted the surgery.' Lisa patted Georgia's back. 'It wasn't successful. Dan was the one who told Glenn that this was the best his knee would ever be and he needed to take care of it, but Glenn doesn't listen. Instead of running himself ragged on the basketball court, now he runs himself ragged on the golf course.'

'Or chasing women?'

Lisa's lips tightened. 'Apparently, it's got much worse since he retired. Before that, Dan said he had a few really nice girlfriends and that he even lived with a couple of them for a while.'

'Are you sure they weren't just homeless?' Sherry held up her hands. 'OK! I'm sorry! I'm sure they were perfectly nice women with homes and brain cells.'

Molly had confided to Jill that she couldn't keep up with Glenn's girlfriends and found out about most of them when she came across photos of him and strange women in magazines. 'He can't seem to find that special someone.'

Jill shared the information with Sherry in the wee hours one morning, when their body clocks were still out of whack and they were sitting in Lisa's dining room drinking hot chocolate laced with brandy to help them sleep.

Sherry splashed some more brandy into her mug. 'He's not looking for somebody special, he just wants to get laid.'

'Ever since you joined the police, you've got more and more cynical,' Jill complained. 'It isn't attractive, Sherry. Glenn has been hurt.'

'Who by? Cuckolded husbands?' Sherry took a swallow of hot chocolate and grimaced. Perhaps she'd overdone it a bit with the brandy. 'Joining the police hasn't turned me cynical; it's all those men I keep meeting who beat up their wives. And what do you mean, "Glenn has been hurt"?'

Jill sipped her chocolate. Sherry had slipped in another shot of brandy when Jill wasn't looking and was waiting to see how long it took before her mother's eyelids started drooping. The strongest thing Jill ever imbibed was a glass of sherry on her birthday and at Christmas. Sherry's arrival nine months after Brian and Jill's wedding day was the cause of a long-standing family joke about how she got her name, which Jill strenuously denied — 'I've always liked that name!' 'She obviously started hitting the sherry earlier than we thought,' Ben said.

Jill took a swallow of hot chocolate. 'This is nice. I must get you to make it for me again.' She frowned. 'Now where was I? Oh yes — one of Glenn's ex-girlfriends got pregnant after they split up and claimed he was the father. Her name was Amber. She sold her story for a lot of money and made Glenn's life *very* difficult—'

Sherry clutched her mother's arms across the table. 'Don't tell me! Amber's got an angora sweater that she ruined in the washing machine.'

'— until the baby was born and a blood test proved it wasn't his,' Jill continued crossly, shaking her off. 'Molly said Glenn was very upset.'

'About the ex-girlfriend selling her story or the baby not being his?' Sherry reached for the bottle of brandy. She'd had enough of listening to stories about Dan's brother.

Jill put her hand over her mug. 'I don't think I should.'

'It's medicinal, Mum — for the jet lag.'

She removed her hand. 'Just a little, then.'

Sherry added another slug and was helping her mother upstairs when Lisa drifted past in her nightdress on the way down. Dan came close behind, wearing a pair of pyjama bottoms and yawning. Jill and Sherry didn't make a sound as they passed by. When Lisa was stressed, she walked in her sleep. Dan was an old hand now at rounding her up and returning her to bed without waking her. Sherry guessed that Lisa's renewed nocturnal wanderings were due to her becoming a mother. She continued herding Jill upstairs to her bedroom.

Jill blinked at the ceiling above her bed as Sherry tucked her in. 'The room is going around. Did you get me drunk?'

'It's the jet lag.'

'It *was* mean, you know,' Jill insisted fuzzily.

'What was?'

'What that girl did to Glenn.'

Yes, it was, but the ex should be counting her lucky stars that Dan's brother wasn't the father of her baby. A tie like that would last a lifetime.

Sherry watched Lisa's hand draw slow circles on Georgia's pink stretch-suit.

'Did you get Mum drunk the other night?'

'Don't be foolish, Lisa. Our mother doesn't get drunk; she just gets tiddly and oversleeps the next day, which is why you and Dan only had Mother Molly to fight off when it came to getting your hands on Georgia this morning. Oh wait, I forgot — Uncle Glenn turned up for breakfast, didn't he?' Sherry added sourly.

Lisa sniffed, and Sherry braced herself for another one of her crying outbursts — they came with little warning — but it turned out that Lisa was suspicious about the contents of Georgia's nappy.

Sherry tried to be conciliatory, because for some reason Lisa was very fond of her brother-in-law. 'His leg must be feeling better — he's playing a lot of golf.'

'Playing golf is one of the worst things Glenn can do for his knee; he should stick to running straight lines in the park. The therapist keeps telling him that, but Glenn won't listen. He's always buying and selling houses, too, but that doesn't make him happy either.'

'If he owns so many homes, why does he insist on spending all his time here?'

'I said Glenn owns *houses* — not *homes*. His place in Aspen and the beach house in Malibu only get used for a few weeks each year. The one-time Dan took me skiing in Aspen, I wanted to run amok on the designer rugs and heartwood floors in my ski boots to mess it up a little. It looks like something out of an interior design magazine, and apparently the beach house is no better except, according to Dan, it's got lots of strategically placed driftwood and a full-size lifeboat in a corner of the living room. Dan hates Glenn's condo in Denver the most, whatever you do, don't get him started on it.' Lisa shifted Georgia higher on her shoulder and patted her padded bottom while Sherry watched the baby's fingers spread like starfish. 'Glenn's problem is he's got too much money and not enough to do. People are always wanting something from him. They treat him like their personal bank.'

Sherry was surprised. 'You mean he's stupid with money?'

Lisa shook her head. 'Dan said he was when he was first drafted, but he's more careful now. When he signed the deal for Blitz sunglasses, he waived his fee and got his agent to negotiate for a percentage of the profit from each pair of sunglasses to go to his favourite charities.'

Glenn was beginning to almost sound admirable. 'Professional basketball players earn a lot of money.' It was part question, part statement.

'Yeah, *a lot* of money.' Lisa unsnapped Georgia's suit; stuck her finger beneath the elasticated opening of the nappy and peered inside. 'She needs changing.' She held the baby out to Sherry. 'Will you take her while I get a nappy?'

They were alone in the living room, enjoying the sunshine streaming through the windows. Glenn was still in Dan's study. Dan and Kell were outside in the garden planting some trees. Jill was ironing, and Molly was hanging washing on the line. As usual, Sherry's offers of help had been brushed aside. She slowly unclasped her arms and extended them just as Molly walked in.

'I'll take her.' Molly whipped Georgia from Lisa before her precious grandchild could make contact with her evil aunt.

Lisa frowned.

Sherry shrugged. 'I'll get the nappy.'

Glenn was lounging in Dan's desk chair with his good leg propped up on the desk talking to his agent when the Ice Queen from Down Under walked into the study and closed the door. Considering the efforts she made to avoid him, Glenn was surprised. She looked fresh from the shower and was dressed in a gauzy burnt-orange top that left her arms bare and showed the lace on her balcony bra, which he knew was the brassiere of choice for well-endowed girls after dating one of the lingerie models in the Blitz advertisements for a couple of months. Clearly, Sherry appreciated sexy underwear as much as he did; it was probably one of the few things they agreed on. Her top was a few shades darker than her floaty knee-length skirt, sandals and — Glenn raised his chin to get a better view — the orange beaded anklet on her leg.

Sherry stopped on the other side of Dan's desk and studied Glenn. His gold shirt matched his eyes. She was sure it wasn't an accident; Glenn liked the good things in life and didn't stint when it came to spending money on himself or his family.

He stared back; only half-listening to Fraser

describing the house in Cherry Hills that Glenn was buying, as the air between him and Sherry began to do its weird vibrating thing. 'Can you give me a moment, Fraser?' He gave Sherry a pointed look. 'I won't be long.'

She was unmoved by the insult.

He pressed the BlackBerry against his shoulder. 'What do you want?'

'To talk to you.'

As usual, her cool-as-a-cucumber voice set Glenn's teeth on edge. He still hadn't managed to make her lose her cool — nearly fainting didn't count, she'd had no control over that. He had a feeling Sherry would rather eat dirt than get into a screaming match. 'What do you want to talk about?'

Her nose wrinkled. 'Us.'

His interest was piqued. He told Fraser he'd call back, and then sat back in Dan's chair with his hands tucked behind his head. 'I'm all ears, Attila.' He waited to see if the nickname he'd given her at Dan and Lisa's wedding would put a dent in her composure, but she didn't take the bait. He should have whistled instead.

'Lisa's upset that you're staying away from the house because of me.'

He was fond of his sister-in-law and didn't like the thought of her being hurt by something he'd done or, in this case, not done. 'I don't want to upset Lisa. Dan said she had a rough time having Georgia.'

Sherry grimaced at the memory. 'I don't want to upset her — or Dan — either, but I can go on only so many runs.'

'And I can play only so much golf.' Glenn didn't add, *before my knee cripples me*. He scooted closer to the desk and leaned on his arms. 'When are you going home?'

Sherry flattened her palms on the wooden surface and leaned closer. 'Day after tomorrow; I could only get a couple of weeks leave. Mum leaves next week.'

It was the closest they'd got to each other since she'd fainted. Glenn's eyes were drawn to the tiny black mole beneath her left eye. He wrapped his fingers around a paperweight on the desk and squeezed. 'Fine, I'll come back when you've gone. Your mother likes me.'

Sherry studied the insolent curl of his full bottom lip and drummed her fingers on the desktop. 'She likes orthopaedic inserts in her shoes as well.'

The distracting bottom lip bowed in a mocking smile. 'You know what your problem is?'

Sherry raised her brows. 'Apart from you?'

'You're a ball-breaker. You don't know how to have fun.'

'Oh really? You know what *your* problem is?'

Glenn leaned back in the chair again. 'Apart from the one standing in front of me?'

'You're an emotional lightweight.'

His mouth flattened. He dropped the paperweight on the desk and stood up. 'Satisfied?' he asked curtly.

Sherry picked up the paperweight and studied it. 'Yes. Are you?'

'Yes,' he replied tersely, but thought, *Not by a long shot.*

She looked up. 'One last thing.'

He might have known it was too easy. 'What?'

'If you whistle around me one more time, I will shove your BlackBerry up your bum...' Sherry paused.

Everything would have been fine if Molly and Jill hadn't interfered. 'Sherry likes to run a lot, doesn't she?' Molly asked as they fixed dinner.

She didn't approve of Lisa's tall, superior sister; there was something unnatural about a woman who didn't want to cuddle a newborn baby and who treated Glenn like he had some kind of social disease. However, Molly was fair-minded enough to admit that her youngest son's behaviour towards Sherry wasn't all that it should be. Perhaps if they spent some time together away from the house and their families, things would improve between them?

'I don't understand,' Molly complained to Kell. 'Why are they so rude to one another?'

'I can't say,' he replied, and Dan snorted.

Jill didn't understand how a woman as smart as Sherry could be so stupid about babies, but, like Molly, she thought Glenn was equally to blame for the tension between them. Being cooped up together in the house didn't help matters. 'Sherry's never been able to sit still for long; she was on the go the whole time I was pregnant with her. She started walking at ten months; by the time she was three, she was the height of a five-year-old.'

Molly added tomatoes to the salad. 'Glenn walked at nine months; he's never been able to stay still either. I felt like the inside of a washing machine when I was pregnant with him. Dan liked to sleep a lot and didn't walk until he was sixteen months old. Hauling him around was no fun because he weighed a ton.'

'Jesus …' Dan muttered.

'Well, it's true,' Molly insisted. 'Your father and I were beginning to think there was something wrong with you. I wonder how old Georgia will be when she starts walking?'

'Maybe we'd better let her learn to sit and crawl before we begin speculating about when she'll walk.'

He was making Lisa a sandwich after fighting off the determined efforts of both mothers to take over. It was no surprise Sherry lacked confidence with Georgia, it was hard getting hold of her with the two grandmothers hovering and offering well-meaning advice. Dan was seriously considering asking Sherry to do her hot-chocolate number on both mothers one night. Lisa had told him about Molly snatching Georgia away from Sherry. 'Promise me that if I ever get like our mothers, you'll shoot me.'

'Sweetheart, it's a given. And if for some reason I can't do it, I'm sure Glenn or Sherry will shoot you instead.' Dan thought it was time he spoke to the grandmothers. He and Lisa wanted to make sure Sherry got some time alone with Georgia before she left.

Jill took a block of cheese from the refrigerator and got out the grater. 'Glenn plays a lot of golf, doesn't he?'

'He and Kell always play when they get together. Dan prefers windsurfing or cycling.' Molly stopped slicing tomatoes and looked at Kell. 'Why don't you ask Sherry to join you and Glenn for a round of golf? You could play at that fossil golf course.'

Kell exchanged an uneasy glance with Dan. 'You mean Fossil Trace.'

'I don't think Sherry plays,' Dan said quickly. If everybody would just leave Glenn and Sherry alone instead of always trying to force them together, things would be a lot more peaceful around the place.

'I'm sure she'd love to play,' Jill insisted. 'She's always been sporty.'

Dan considered warning his brother or Sherry, or both, but decided they could take care of themselves. There were only a couple of days left until Sherry went back to New Zealand, and Dan had the grandmothers in his sights — he'd deal with them instead. Glenn and Sherry could fight their own battles.

A round of golf wouldn't do any harm.

Chapter 4

G lenn didn't know Sherry was joining them until Kell pulled up at Fossil Trace Golf Club with her in the car beside him. Sherry looked as surprised and unhappy to see Glenn as he was to see her. She was the reason why his father had chosen to play at a public course instead of one of the private clubs where Glenn had membership.

Fossil Trace was set at the foot of the Rocky Mountain Front Range not far from downtown Denver and was one of the most popular public golf courses in Colorado. The view of the Rockies was spectacular enough, but it was the sixty-four-million-year-old Triceratops footprints near the twelfth green that helped make the course famous; those and the sandstone pillars emerging from the fairways and the massive remnants of old clay-mining equipment scattered around the course.

'What a surprise,' Glenn said flatly when Sherry emerged from the car.

She slipped on a pair of sunglasses and turned up the collar on her blue polo shirt to protect her pale skin from the hot summer sun. 'Yes, like pulling a Christmas cracker and discovering that it's a hand grenade.'

'Blame your mothers,' Kell said. 'It's got something to do with you both starting to walk too early.'

He got their golf clubs out of the back of the car and led the way to the clubhouse to collect their cards and the golf cart. The thought of spending time in the close confines of the cart with Sherry wasn't appealing. Glenn dumped his golf bag in the back and said, 'I'll walk.'

Sherry smiled sweetly at Kell. 'OK if I drive?'

Glenn made a mental note to stay out of the path of the cart. Sherry said she hadn't played before, so he resigned himself to a day of chasing balls into the rough and hanging around while she took photos of the scenery. Glenn bought Lisa golf clubs as a Christmas present just before she found out she was pregnant, and she'd only used them twice because she'd had such bad morning sickness. He'd taken her out both times while Dan was at the hospital, and it soon become obvious that Lisa wasn't going to make a golfer because her hand–eye co-ordination was hopeless. They'd spent more time drinking coffee and swapping jokes in the clubhouse than on the course playing.

Kell had been briefed by Molly to make sure Glenn and Sherry got to know one another better. 'How do I do that?'

Molly had given him an exasperated look. 'Use your imagination!'

Kell slowed up play and pissed Glenn off by asking what made Sherry decide to join the police.

'When I left school, I did a degree in management and employment relations and politics, and when I graduated, I spent a year working in human resources at Auckland airport,' she explained.

Glenn pulled his driver from his golf bag. 'So that's where the fixation with bananas started.'

Kell wished Glenn wasn't too big to send to his room.

Sherry looked down her nose at Glenn. 'I don't have

a problem with bananas — just with the monkeys who bring them in.'

Kell soldiered on. 'Then what happened?'

'I went abroad for a year with some friends and did the backpacking-around-Europe and working-in-pubs-in-London thing. I'd always been interested in joining the police, and when I got back, I did a ride-along one night.'

'A ride-along?' Kell knew that Glenn's apparent inattention was a ruse and that he was listening closely.

'I went out in a squad car for one of the night shifts and I was hooked. Mum was horrified, but Dad, Lisa and Ben weren't too surprised.' Sherry fell silent while Glenn and Kell took their tee-shots, then answered Kell's questions about the Family Violence Unit as they walked to the women's tee.

There was nothing wrong with Sherry's hand–eye co-ordination. She was cool-headed and competitive, and it was clear that the person she most wanted to beat was Glenn. He was on a two handicap which meant Sherry didn't stand a chance, but Glenn enjoyed watching her try. He knew better than to give her any pointers and left it to his father to provide instruction and praise. She hit a few air shots and into the rough on several occasions but didn't lose a ball until she drilled her first two shots into the water at the tenth. However, her third shot had Kell and Glenn whistling in admiration.

'I think you've found your game,' Kell said, and Sherry laughed.

Glenn stared. He thought she didn't know how to play. He'd already played four rounds that week — way more than his therapist recommended. Walking and jogging straight lines was fine; it was twisting his knee when he swung the club that caused him grief. *That's what I do now,* Glenn thought bitterly, *play golf and sell sunglasses.* He kept in touch with his former team-mates and the Cougars management, and knew they'd take him back in

a coaching role, but Glenn didn't want that. He didn't know what he wanted, just that it wasn't what he had.

As they continued towards the eleventh, Glenn's limp got worse. Sherry wished he'd give in and get in the damned golf cart. Kell sat beside her with his arms folded, apparently watching the scenery. 'Don't say anything,' he said. 'He'll stop when he's good and ready.'

Sherry gripped the steering wheel. 'He's really angry about it, isn't he?'

Kell nodded.

Curiosity got the better of her. 'I don't know much about basketball, but whenever his name comes up people seem to want to fall on the floor and genuflect. Was he really that good?'

'He was really that good. When he retired, the Cougars retired his number three jersey.' Kell's smile held a mixture of pride and sadness. 'They only do that for the great players.'

Sherry frowned at his son's distant figure. 'Tell me.'

'Glenn started shooting baskets when he was four years old. Nobody made him, he just did it,' Kell explained. 'He'd beg for another few minutes outside when we called him in for bed and throw an almighty tantrum when we said "No". We never had to ground him, just threaten to cut his basketball time. Of course, with Glenn that happened fairly often. Later, he won a sports scholarship to the University of Wisconsin where he studied science and landscape architecture.'

Sherry raised her brows. 'Unusual combination.'

'Glenn never does what's usual,' Kell replied drily. 'The image of the "dumb jock" is a myth. Students on athletic scholarships have to maintain a certain grade-point average and do a mandatory number of hours of study each week or they have their playing time cut. Glenn attended classes, studied and had basketball practice as well.'

It made Sherry's time at university sound like a visit to Club Med. 'How did he do it?'

'No choice, if he didn't, he was out. And Glenn hates to lose. He was a standout player for the college team and caught the attention of the talent scouts,' he continued proudly. 'But Glenn held out and completed his degree before turning pro. The money and attention did make him a little crazy for a while, until he realized he had to work even harder if he was going to get on the court. His idol was Larry Bird, and, just like Bird, Glenn would spend hours before and after practice alone on the court shooting hoops. He did it every day - even in the off-season he would shoot between four hundred and six hundred baskets a day.'

Intrigued by the picture Kell was painting, Sherry stopped the cart to listen.

'Signing with the Cougars meant he could come back to his home state. He played the last three years of his professional career here. Glenn earned his third MVP title and his second championship ring when he landed a thirty-five-foot bomb that won the game for the Cougars in the last minute of the fourth quarter. He

could have run for governor on the strength of that shot,'
Kell joked. 'People still talk about it.' He paused and
finished sadly, 'But then a couple of blows to his knee
ended it all.'

Sherry watched Glenn stubbornly limp his way along
the fairway; she had a feeling that no longer being able
to mix it up on the court caused him more pain than his
leg.

At the twelfth green, Kell suggested that Glenn show
Sherry the Triceratops footprints in the sandstone walls
while he lined up his putt. Glenn looked on while she
took photos and thought what a contradiction she was:
spiky one moment, icy-cold the next, always elusive.
They stood side-by-side looking at the dinosaur prints,
aware that they were alone, that nobody could overhear
them — and that trying to ignore their mutual physical
attraction wasn't working.

'I don't like you, Glenn,' Sherry said.

'I don't like you either, Sherry,' he replied.

She took a deep breath and sighed, 'But ...'

'But ...' Glenn held his breath.

'I'm leaving tomorrow.'

'I know.'

She stared hard at the Triceratops footprints. 'We
have to put this thing between us to ...' Her voice trailed
away and she swallowed.

'Bed?' Glenn supplied. From the corner of his eye, he
saw Sherry nod and it was his turn to swallow. 'I'll pick
you up at eight for dinner.'

She looked appalled. 'Are you mad? If our mothers
find out, they'll be picking dates for the wedding.'

He grimaced.

'*Exactly*. We don't want to date — we just want to sleep with each other.'

Glenn felt the familiar warring urges to either kiss her or strangle her. 'Are you always this blunt?'

Her winged brows drew together. 'I don't have a lot of time left,' she said haughtily.

He was used to women throwing themselves at him, but this felt like booking an appointment at the dentist. 'You're sure you can fit me into your busy schedule?' he asked sarcastically.

'I'm visiting the cousin of somebody I work with, at one of the police precincts this afternoon. Her name's Roberta. She's taking me to a honky-tonk bar tonight.' Sherry mentioned the name of the bar and Glenn knew it. 'Can you meet me there at ten-thirty?' she asked. 'I don't want to be home too late.'

Now he was being given a time limit. 'Only if you wear your merry widow.'

Her jaw dropped. 'My *what*? How do you know I've got a merry widow?'

'Are you two coming to take your shots?' Kell called.

'Never you mind,' Glenn retorted. 'Just wear it.'

Sherry had removed her sunglasses to take the photos, and fumbled as she wrenched them from her pocket and jammed them on her face. 'I'll think about it,' she said, and strode away.

Sherry had deep reservations about spending the night with Glenn. A police officer was trained to look at a crime from every angle and find an explanation of the what, how and why. Sherry had looked at all the angles and was no closer to finding an explanation for why she was so attracted to Glenn when she found him so annoying. She'd tried ignoring him, but he wasn't the kind of man who was easy to ignore. She'd tried using her words — and told him to piss off — but that hadn't helped either. All that was left was option number three. Sherry was prepared to be disappointed; in her experience, great-looking men were too self-absorbed to make good lovers, which was one of the reasons she avoided them. Glenn's unexpected arrival at Dan and Lisa's as she was preparing to leave for her visit to the precinct made her heart leap. Sherry watched him let himself in through the front door. He was dressed to go out in a white dress shirt with a pleated front with the top button undone, jeans, a denim jacket, a black cowboy hat, and the biggest pair of cowboy boots Sherry had ever seen. The shirt should have looked out of place — it belonged under a tuxedo — but on Glenn it looked just right. His black hair shone, and his guinea-gold eyes glowed with mischief. The rakish tilt of the black hat did odd things to Sherry's stomach; she could almost believe he had a horse tied up outside. If he called her 'Ma'am' she wouldn't be held responsible for her actions.

She was sitting with one knee tucked beneath her chin, wrestling with the tiny ankle strap on one of her purple sandals. They matched her silky, sleeveless wrap dress, which had ridden up her thighs and pooled in her lap. 'What are you doing here?' she demanded.

Glenn took his time enjoying the view as he closed the door. He spoke to Sherry's endless legs. 'I came to say goodbye and wish you a safe journey.'

'Oh.' At least one of them was thinking straight. The thought of the night ahead was tying Sherry's nervous system into knots. Glenn wasn't in any better shape — he didn't think he could last out until ten-thirty. He checked to see if anybody was in the lounge or dining room and murmured, 'Are you wearing your merry widow?'

A bolt of heat seemed to strike Sherry in the groin. She clamped her legs together and licked her lips. 'I … might … be.'

Glenn's eyes closed briefly. He swept the hat from his head and tapped it against his thigh a time or two before dropping it on the hallway table. 'You'd better be.'

Sherry was transfixed. 'Say *Ma'am*,' she whispered.

'What?'

She glanced quickly at the lounge and dining room and urged, 'Call me *Ma'am!*'

A smile tugged at his lips as he caught on. He dropped his voice an octave so that it rumbled up from the depths of his chest and murmured, 'You're looking mighty pretty … *Ma'am.*'

Sherry gulped.

He took a step closer to the stairs and drawled, 'You'd better be wearing that damned merry widow, *Ma'am.*'

She fell back on her elbows and stared up at him.

Glenn covered the remaining distance between them and said grimly, 'I don't think I can last until ten-thirty, *Ma'am.*' He looked at her sprawled on his brother's staircase, one knee bent high, the other long, beautiful leg extended, the silky purple dress showcasing that X-rated body, and frowned. 'Do you really think you should wear that dress to a police station?'

The spell was broken. Sherry remembered she was draped across the stairs with her dress wrapped around her thighs and that her mother or Glenn's could walk by any moment. She sat up and tugged down her dress, and Glenn almost groaned when her cleavage rose up like twin pillows from the V-neck of her bodice.

Sherry bristled. She wasn't used to her taste in clothes being challenged. 'What's wrong with my dress? I'm going out dancing afterwards.'

'To a honky-tonk,' Glenn said tightly.

Her eyes snapped. 'What *is* a honky-tonk?'

'The music at the one you're going to is predominantly country and western, and the dancing is done in long lines.'

'You mean, like Billy Ray Cyrus? "Achy Breaky Heart"?'

'Things have moved on since Billy Ray, but you've got the idea.'

Sherry looked at her purple dress and Glenn's jeans and cowboy boots and felt herself get all hot and bothered again. Ten-thirty seemed like a month away. 'I don't own a pair of cowboy boots or a hat.' She latched onto the boots like a skydiver to a parachute. 'What size are they? They're huge.'

'Size fourteen and I wouldn't worry, I'm sure somebody will lend you a Stetson.' Glenn studied the purple dress. It was held together by two little buttons at her waist. Two little buttons — it was criminal.

'A Stetson?'

Jill walked by carrying an armful of baby clothes. She smiled when she saw Glenn and Sherry appeared to be having a civilized conversation. 'Hello, Glenn.'

Sherry watched Glenn schmooze her mother and Jill melt. 'I just came by to wish Sherry a safe journey.'

'That's very thoughtful.' Jill gave Sherry a meaningful look. 'Wasn't that nice, Sherry?'

'Yeah, lovely.'

Glenn turned his megawatt matinee smile on Sherry. 'I hope you have a great night.'

'*So,*' she said pointedly, '*do I.*'

'*I'm certain,*' he said emphatically, '*you will.*'

'Sometimes, when things are too planned, they lack spontaneity,' Sherry retorted.

'Sometimes, a little planning can result in a whole lot of spontaneity,' Glenn shot back.

Their gazes locked.

You'd better not be a waste of space, Brogan.

I hope you live up to that Sports Illustrated body, Officer Jackson.

Jill looked from one to the other in bewilderment.

'Is Georgie asleep?' Glenn asked her.

'No, Lisa's giving her a bath.'

Sherry plastered herself against the banisters as he followed her mother upstairs to see Georgia. On the way out, she stole his Stetson.

Lisa lent Sherry her car. Sherry made her visit to the police station via a hair and nail salon, thinking a manicure might give her time to calm down a little before she met Roberta, only to discover that Glenn had followed her. First on the billboards dotted around the city showing him wearing his blue board shorts and holding the models in the string bikinis in the same pose as they'd struck for the Blitz winter ads, and then when she walked into the nail salon there was an autographed photo of him pinned to the wall beside the reception desk. This time he was wearing a turquoise-blue and white singlet with a leaping yellow cat and the word *Cougars* written beneath it. A big yellow *3* decorated the front of the singlet. Both Glenn's feet were off the ground, one arm extended gracefully above his head, eyes intent as he launched a ball towards the basket. He looked hot and sweaty and the muscles in his arms bulged. *Blitz Brogan — Colorado Cougars* was printed beneath the photo. Sherry checked the other photos and saw they were all of Cougars players.

The nail technician noticed her looking at Glenn's photo and said, 'We're big Cougars fans. Blitz did a free personal appearance earlier this year to help us raise money for a literacy programme for kids.' She stroked a hot-pink nail decorated with a yellow daisy along Glenn's sulky bottom lip, and Sherry got the feeling good ol' Blitz had raised more than money on his visit. Apparently, Lisa was right. He did do something besides play golf and model sunglasses. Sherry got her nails painted purple like her dress and allowed the nail technician to put tiny diamond chips in the centre. She didn't usually go for something so colourful, but figured they were perfect for a woman planning a night of hot sex with a man she hardly knew and didn't much like. Not only were the nails more colourful, they were a lot longer than Sherry was used to; she was glad it was the northern summer, because putting on a pair of pantyhose would have been beyond her — she'd poke a hole in them just taking them out of the package. The nails would have to go when she got home.

Roberta was a wiry blonde in her late twenties with big blue eyes. She seemed a little surprised when a woman wearing a purple dress, high heels that made her a towering six foot three inches, and with the body of a centrefold pin-up sauntered into the precinct claiming to be a fellow officer. Sherry realized Glenn was right, she should have worn jeans and a sweatshirt. She swapped police memorabilia and work stories with Roberta and some of the other cops and discovered that they had the same gripes and dealt with the same assortment of wackos and strays — bad, ugly, mean and the downright sad.

'Do you still want to go out?' Roberta asked.

'Love to,' Sherry said, 'but I have to leave at ten-thirty. I've got a plane to catch tomorrow.'

Chapter 5

Denver was situated over five thousand feet above sea level on the Rocky Mountain Platte, which is why it was known as The Mile High City. Its residents skied, hiked, went camping, and played in the city parks, sports stadiums and amusement parks. Each year they enjoyed over three hundred days of sunshine, and in the winter regular falls of snow. Sherry could understand why Lisa loved living there. She'd fallen in love with the restored downtown historic area and 16th Street Mall, and visited the aquarium, zoo and museums, including The Molly Brown House Museum, home of the colourful woman who had survived the sinking of the *Titanic*.

The honky-tonk bar Roberta took her to was painted pale blue on the outside and had a picture of a saloon girl and a cowboy by the door. Sherry wore Glenn's hat and followed Roberta and her friend Shawna past the cowboy bouncers. The inside of the club was huge with a big, hardwood dance floor, arcade room, pool room, mechanical bull, and a trough full of beer just inside the front door. It was loud and smoky and packed with people having a good time.

'Are you hungry?' Roberta asked when they'd found a table and the waitress had handed them menus.

Sherry ordered a salad and a vodka and tonic; she ate her salad when it arrived and chatted. She watched the line dancers and listened to the country and western band who all wore cowboy boots and hats. Every so often she touched the brim of Glenn's hat, checked her watch, and scanned the crowd for a towering figure and familiar black head, but he wasn't there.

'Do you know how to line dance?' Shawna asked.

Sherry shook her head.

'Want to try?'

It was another two-and-a-half hours until ten-thirty; she had to do something or she'd go mad. Sherry picked up the steps easily enough. She attracted attention because of the purple dress and because she was easily the tallest woman in the room. Someone told the band she was from New Zealand and going home tomorrow, and they played a song especially for her. She'd just returned to the table to grab a glass of iced water when Glenn walked in on the dot of nine-thirty, accompanied by two men, one of whom was at least seven foot tall. The fact he was an hour early put Sherry's insides into a spin, and from the look on the faces of the rest of the women she wasn't the only one feeling that way. She watched as shoulders were squared and breasts displayed more prominently, as hair was flipped and compacts were whipped from handbags to reapply lip gloss.

Roberta nudged Sherry excitedly. 'That's The Blitz — Blitz Brogan. He's an ex-pro basketball player, one of the best shooters in the game.'

'Yes, I know,' Sherry replied, and Roberta looked surprised.

Shawna couldn't take her eyes off Glenn. 'I was there when he sank that thirty-five-foot bomb right on the buzzer that won the championship final,' she said reverently.

'If you hadn't already guessed, we're big Cougars fans,' Roberta explained. 'Blitz retired a few seasons ago because of a ruined knee.'

A ruined knee is the least of his problems, Sherry thought. *There's also that pesky personality defect.*

Roberta continued, 'The Cougars still haven't found a shooting guard to replace him.'

'They're never going to do that.' Shawna sipped her drink and nodded at the shorter of the two men accompanying Glenn, 'That's Jay McCosh. The Cougars hope he'll eventually replace Blitz.' She sniffed and added, 'From what I've seen, he's more cocky than talented.'

Jay was a few inches shorter than Glenn, and had rich, dark brown hair and — Shawna was right — a cocky grin. Sherry didn't see how Blitz's two disciples could complain about Jay being cocky when their hero suffered from a surplus of it himself, but wisely kept this observation to herself. 'He's shorter than Gle—, I mean Blitz.'

'The Blitz is taller than average for a shooting guard,' Roberta said.

'Made him harder to defend,' Shawna added.

Glenn and his companions took a seat at the bar and ordered drinks.

Sherry stirred her water with a straw. She didn't know what to make of Roberta and Shawna's particular brand of hero worship, or how she was going to extricate herself and leave with Glenn at ten-thirty without coming to blows with them. They acted like they owned him.

'He's got Chopper with him.'

Sherry had just figured out that Shawna was talking about the seven-foot giant with Glenn when he turned on his seat, leaned his elbows on the bar behind him, and searched the crowd until he found Sherry. Glenn smiled, pointed his beer bottle at his Stetson and mouthed 'Nice hat' before turning back to his friends.

Sherry tensed as Shawna and Roberta's eyes locked onto her like heat-seeking missiles.

'You *know* him?' Shawna demanded indignantly.

She shrugged a shoulder. 'His brother is married to my sister.'

'You mean *your sister* who just had the *baby*?'

'Yeah,' Sherry nodded casually. 'I borrowed his hat.'

Her cheeks heated as their eyes rose to Glenn's Stetson. What was happening to her? She didn't get flustered, but Glenn Brogan was like a rogue power surge overloading her internal wiring and making it short-circuit. It was mortifying. Sherry hastened to nip the speculation she saw in Roberta and Shawna's eyes in the bud. 'He knew I was coming here tonight and loaned it to me.'

Add *lying* to flustered.

Shawna stared at the Stetson as if it had the winning numbers to the lottery printed on it. 'I wouldn't mind borrowing Blitz Brogan's hat.'

'Especially if he's still wearing it,' Roberta added.

Because it would look suspicious if she ignored Glenn, Sherry showed mild interest as men and women approached him and his companions for an autograph or chat, but for the most part people left them alone to enjoy their beers in peace and quiet. When she commented on it, Roberta said, 'We respect our sports celebs' privacy here. People tend to leave them alone if they see them out and about. Of course, it's different when they're playing — then they belong to us.'

Sherry stopped feeling flattered by Glenn's early arrival as he became engrossed in a conversation with his friends, and with some of the women who approached him and seemed predisposed to linger.

'Out-of-towners,' Roberta sniffed. 'They don't know how to behave.'

Sherry glanced at the smile on Glenn's face as he talked to a brunette with sprayed-on jeans who kept rubbing her breasts against his arm like she thought a genie might pop out of his bicep. From what Sherry could see, Glenn didn't seem to have a problem with the behaviour of the out-of-towners. She didn't know what she'd expected, but it certainly wasn't to be ignored. When a man offered to teach her how to do the 'two-step' she accepted and spent the next half-hour in the arms of different men, all of them shorter than her. She was used to it. It was unusual for her to get a dance partner as tall as, or taller than, her, especially when she was wearing high heels. Her eyes strayed again and again to Glenn's broad back and his long legs hooked around the bar stool. Even if she was wearing high heels, he would still top her by at least four inches, and after ten-thirty he was supposed to be all hers. Well, maybe she'd changed her mind. She splashed iced water onto her hot cheeks, put Glenn's Stetson back on and headed back to the dance floor.

By ten-thirty her hair was stuck to her forehead and her dress was stuck to her back. Her make-up had melted, and her favourite Chanel No. 5 perfume was just a distant memory. A trip to the women's restroom confirmed Sherry's suspicions, she looked a mess and stank of sweat — hardly conducive to acting out the big seduction scene she'd imagined. She washed her face and shoulders, brushed her hair, and went back outside with the intention of telling Glenn she'd changed her mind; that she was tired; that she'd just got her period — any excuse would do. She wasn't prepared to find him leaning against the wall opposite the restroom, waiting for her.

Glenn sat at the bar keeping a discreet eye on Sherry as she danced with a long line of — he was pleased to note — *short* dance partners and waited impatiently for ten-thirty to arrive. He'd managed to palm off the brunette who kept rubbing herself against his arm to Leonid Chopiak, the Cougars' big blond Russian forward who was nicknamed Chopper because of his ability to annihilate the opposition offence. Leonid was twenty-seven and had a head shaped like a bullet, which made him look mentally challenged, but he was extremely smart and spoke excellent English. He'd perfected an act of speaking English badly and telling any woman he was attracted to, 'I like American vomen very much' or 'You are vonderful' in a heavy Russian accent. His stumbling attempts at English meant that he didn't have to make an effort to talk to women, just sit there and pretend to listen. Even better, they didn't expect him to understand them.

The brunette's name was Desiree, and she said she

was twenty-one. She'd had too much to drink and kept looking at her friends who were watching her and giggling on the other side of the bar. Glenn was an old hand at being hit on by tanked women out to impress their friends by getting off with a basketball player. When he looked sceptical about Desiree's age, she produced her ID to prove it. Either way, Glenn wasn't interested — she was too young and he was too old to be hanging out in bars drinking beer with over-sexed, rookie basketball players. If it weren't for Sherry, he wouldn't be here. Desiree was soon sitting in Chopper's lap telling him all about her job in a pet shop in her hometown in Michigan, while Chopiak told her at regular intervals, 'You are vonderful.' He had better manners than McCosh and wouldn't take advantage of Miss Michigan's inebriated state, so Glenn didn't feel too bad about redirecting Desiree's attention to him. She climbed off Chopiak to pay a visit to the restroom with a promise that she'd be back soon.

'I wish I was Russian,' Jay said when Desiree had gone. 'I've never had a women tell me it was OK that I didn't understand her.'

'Being Russian wouldn't help you,' Chopiak replied. 'Women would still know you are too dumb to understand them.'

'Wait 'til she sees the size of your ass when you stand up,' McCosh retorted. 'She might change her mind when she realizes you've got a head shaped like a round of ammo and a big ass.'

Chopiak's big, muscular butt earned him plenty of ribbing from the rest of the team. All the team apparel was custom-made to accommodate larger-than-average men, but Chopper's big ass was the stuff of legend. The Cougars team manager was positive that Chopper had the biggest butt in the NBA.

Jay turned and watched the crowd restlessly. He'd been given the eye by women since they'd sat down but hadn't wanted to take up any of the offers. The Cougars head coach had asked Glenn to work with McCosh one-on-one to improve his game and attitude. The young shooting guard was a bundle of raw, restless talent who sometimes forgot that teams — not individuals — won games. Jay didn't always acknowledge the work his team-mates did to feed him the ball when he was open so that he could score flashy three-pointers, and he paid for it by not always being named in the starting line-up. His ambition was to be better than The Blitz. Glenn knew that he should feel flattered, but instead he just felt old.

McCosh suddenly spoke up. 'Now *that* I like, stacked *and* tall. Bet she's a swimsuit model.'

Glenn looked over his shoulder and saw that McCosh was staring at Sherry. He wanted to deck the younger man. Glenn knew exactly what Jay was imagining doing to Sherry, because he'd imagined doing the same things himself. The Cougars coach had asked him to spend some time off-court with McCosh, too, and, because he was a friend of Jay's, Chopiak often came along. Jay and Leo were into basketball groupies and the lifestyle that went with them, and for a while after his last knee surgery Glenn had slipped back into habits, he thought he'd outgrown years ago. He wasn't proud of it. Most players, when they were Jay and Leo's age, had their heads turned by the beautiful young women who hung around professional basketball teams. The smart ones got over it, got married, and walked the other way when pert young things made themselves available.

Glenn said in a pleasant, warning voice, 'She's not a model, she's a cop.'

Leo and Jay stopped looking at Sherry and looked at Glenn instead.

Jay frowned. Blitz Brogan seemed to know every good-looking woman in a one-hundred-mile radius and had a reputation as being a real hell-raiser, but so far, off the court, Jay had been disappointed in him. To be honest, he was annoying on the court, too, because all he talked about was discipline, and Jay was pissed that Blitz could still outshoot him.

'You know her?' he asked.

'She's my brother's sister-in-law.'

That sounded promising — she wasn't a current or ex-girlfriend. Jay took another cautious look at the tall goddess in the purple dress but was nailed to the bar by a glare from his mentor. Jay raised his hands in surrender and turned around. 'OK!'

'At home in Russia, I dated a girl from the Ukraine who was six-foot-ten-inches tall,' Leo announced.

Jay moodily spun his empty beer bottle on top of the bar. 'That was no woman, Chopper.'

Glenn sucked a drop of beer from his lip and nodded. 'It was a man in a dress.'

Chopiak glowered.

Miss Michigan Pet Shop, aka Desiree, reappeared. 'I'm back! Did you miss me?'

Chopiak's high, bony forehead smoothed. He stretched out an arm and gathered her in. 'You are vonderful.'

Women and men kept coming over to talk to them. Glenn chatted and kept one eye on his watch. He introduced a tough-looking Asian girl who wanted his autograph to Jay because the girl looked like the type who could handle herself. He watched as they hit it off, and wondered if he should start a matchmaking business for basketball players and fans. He rested his chin in his hand and nursed the same bottle of beer he'd bought when he first walked in. At ten-thirty, he watched Sherry excuse herself from her dance partner, tilt her head imperiously, and disappear in the direction of the restrooms without so much as a glance in his direction.

Glenn sat up. He had the ominous feeling that Queen Sherry was pissed at him. He signaled the barman and ordered a round of drinks for everybody in the club, and, under cover of the whoops and yells of approval, escaped to the restrooms, leaned against the wall opposite the Ladies and waited.

'What were you doing in there?' Glenn demanded when Sherry eventually came out. 'Redecorating?'

'If you don't know why people visit the restroom by now, then you're beyond help.' She didn't mean to sound so frosty, but whenever she got angry or upset, she slipped into what Ben called her 'Headmistress act'.

Glenn's eyes drilled into hers. 'You're pissed at me. Don't tell me you've changed your mind.'

She stepped aside to let a group of curious women

into the restroom, and jumped when Glenn caught her arm to draw her away from the door and back her against a wall. He braced his hands above her head but left her plenty of room to escape if she wanted to. 'Tell me what the problem is.'

She would rip out her tongue before she'd admit she was jealous of the women at the bar. 'I'm a mess.'

He looked her over. 'No, you're not.'

'I'm all sweaty.'

Glenn leaned closer and inhaled. 'I don't smell sweat, I smell woman.' He shot her a mischievous look and drawled, '*Ma'am*.'

Sherry's heart bounced like a tennis ball. 'That's cheating.'

'I prefer to think of it as shortening the odds.'

He looked so smug she struggled not to smile. 'I'm too tired.'

'You can just lie there; I promise I'll do all the work.'

She closed her eyes and the smile blossomed. He was incorrigible, an irresistible mixture of self-deprecating wit and arrogance. Sherry's breath caught and her eyes opened as she felt something brush against her cheek.

Glenn gently stroked the little mole beneath her eye with his thumb. Sherry clasped his wrist. 'What is it? Have I got something on my face?'

He looked at her long fingers wrapped around his wrist, at the contrast between her pale, pink-tinted skin and his darker bronze, and knew that was how they'd look entwined naked on a bed. Heat burned a path from his wrist to the pit of his stomach. Sherry was still waiting for an answer to her question. Glenn pulled himself together. 'Yeah, you do have something on your face. Thankfully, it doesn't come off.' He bent his head and touched the tiny, black mole with the tip of his tongue. 'Are we through with this nonsense?' he asked huskily.

'We're through,' Sherry whispered, and went to make her excuses to Roberta and Shawna.

Glenn had just sold his house in Cherry Hills and was buying a new one in the same area for no better reason than he felt like a change. In the meantime, he was living at his condo downtown. He wanted to take Sherry there, but she refused.

'Motels are the place for hot, dirty sex.'

Glenn wasn't pleased but didn't argue. 'We better find somewhere not too far from Dan and Lisa's place so you can find your way back in the morning.'

'Not too close; we don't want to take a chance on somebody seeing us.'

'Nobody is going to see us,' he said shortly. 'Follow me in Lisa's car.'

When they reached the motel, Sherry waited in the car while Glenn paid for the room and arranged to park his BMW somewhere out of sight. The drive from the honky-tonk bar to the motel had shredded her nerves like lettuce leaves. The feel of her clothes against her skin was torture. She wanted to tear them off and weld herself to Glenn.

Glenn unlocked the door to the motel room and would have held it for her if she hadn't told him to go ahead. He waited while she followed him inside and closed the door. Sherry leaned back against it, clutching her bag, and watched as he removed his denim jacket.

They stared at one another.

'So, here we are,' Glenn said.

'Yes,' Sherry agreed. 'Here we are.'

He dropped his jacket.

Her bag hit the floor.

'Is that shirt a favourite of yours?' she asked.

'No.'

'Good, because I've always wanted to do this.' She curled her fingers around the edges of his shirt, tugged once, then twice, and ripped it open. There was a ping as a button hit the television in the corner. Sherry didn't notice; she was mesmerized by Glenn's bare chest, and watched it expand as he took a slow, deep breath.

'Not bad for a first effort.' He dropped his gaze to the front of the purple dress. 'Is that dress a favourite of yours?'

Her blood seemed to slow in her veins. She shook her head.

'Watch and learn.'

Glenn reached for the buttons at her waist and yanked the purple dress apart. He opened the two sides and gave her near-naked body the same close attention she'd given his chest. She was so pretty it hurt to look. Her white cleavage spilled over the merry widow, which was black with silver embroidery; she was wearing matching French knickers. She was shaped like an hourglass — like a woman — all luscious breasts, tiny waist and round hips with long dancer's legs below. Glenn placed a thumb against the white curve of her breast above the merry widow and gently pressed. A pale pink nipple crested the material. Sherry shivered as he reached for her other breast and did the same thing. His expression was so intent she murmured uncertainly, 'Glenn?'

'I've imagined this so many times, I'm just savouring the moment,' he said unevenly.

She took a step forward, linked her arms behind his neck and stood on tiptoe in the purple sandals. Her breasts glided over his naked chest as she whispered against his lips, 'Savour this instead.'

Their heads tilted and their tongues tangled.

The first time, they had hot, dirty sex against the motel door. It was fast, furious and totally lacking in finesse. It was glorious.

'Where's the condom?' Glenn asked when they'd got their breath back. 'I took it off and put it on the wrapper. I want to check that it's OK.'

'Of course it's OK.' Sherry ran her palms down his back and cupped his buttocks — they were as hard as rock. 'I put it on; you took it off.'

She was a wonderful lover: enticing, demanding, erotic, yielding — and abundantly feminine. Glenn was moody, masterful, funny, tender — and good at games. They took turns wearing his cowboy hat, and Sherry couldn't recall laughing so much while she was having sex.

'On the bed, wench, on your hands and knees.'

She did as he asked but put her own stamp on it by tilting her hips and looking over her shoulder through slumberous eyes. 'Is this what you had in mind, master?'

Glenn felt like a sausage on a grill; he was sure his skin was about to burst — or at least something was.

'No,' he replied hoarsely, 'it's better.'

Sherry's gaze trickled down his body. Lisa had let slip that Dan was well-endowed; it seemed to run in the family. She rotated her hips in silent invitation. Glenn dived onto the bed and grunted when he jarred his knee.

'Are you al—'

'Forget about it.' He caught her hips.

Sherry pushed against him and was surprised, and then furious, when Glenn held her off. She glared up at him through her long, black hair, her face flushed with temper and passion, and pressed harder. Glenn tightened his grip and she hissed like a cat, 'What're you—'

'Wait!' He growled and closed his eyes. 'Just — wait, dammit ... we've got all night.' He moved and Sherry sighed as the tension dissolved from her body and then began to build again.

It was a night of firsts.

The first time Sherry had sex with a man tall enough and strong enough to make love to her against the wall or a door. The first time Glenn made love to a woman who could match him for stamina and had a sense of humour and imagination, too. They devoured one another, petted one another, laughed when one of their more energetic performances resulted in Glenn's elbow colliding with Sherry's eye and they fell off the bed taking the bedside lamp with them.

Sherry sprawled across Glenn and gasped, 'Is it broken?'

'I'll buy them a new one.' His arms closed around her. 'Come here.'

In between they dozed and talked, even about the

taboo subject of how Dan and Lisa met.

'Do you ever think about what happened?' Glenn asked.

'Sometimes,' Sherry admitted. 'But it's too weird.'

'I know.'

'I'm just grateful I got my sister back.' She rested her chin on the edge of her hand and rotated her foot in the air behind her. 'What about you?'

Glenn wound a strand of her hair around his finger and studied it. 'I'm glad Dan is finally happy. You know he'd given up on having kids before he … met … Lisa.'

She dropped her chin to his chest. 'Lisa had endometriosis. She never thought she'd be a mother.'

He stroked her hair back from her face and smiled. 'Georgie's great, isn't she?'

'She definitely looks a lot cuter now than she did the day she was born.'

'You're supposed to say she was beautiful.'

Sherry snorted. 'Babies are *not* beautiful when they're born. Remember, I was there — you weren't.'

'It can't have been that bad.' Glenn stroked the mole on her cheek. 'Lisa's already talking about having another one.'

She ran her hand across the muscles in his chest. 'She must have fallen and hit her head when she got up in the night to feed the baby. Given a choice between giving birth and having the hairs pulled out of my nostrils one at a time, I'd opt for the latter.'

He looked at her curiously. 'Don't you want to have children one day?'

'Maybe when I'm eighty. What about you?'

'I wouldn't mind some kids; I'm just not so keen on

the idea of a wife,' Glenn replied. Sherry laughed and he grinned. It was nice to be able to tell the truth and not pretend like with most women.

She slid upwards and accidentally jabbed Glenn in his bad knee. He swore and reared up, grabbing his leg. Sherry scuttled backwards and sat on her heels beside him, biting her lip. The sheet had fallen aside. She gasped when she saw how red and swollen his knee was. 'Glenn! Why didn't you say something?'

He didn't welcome her concern. 'Forget about my damned knee and come here.'

She did, but the sight of the swollen, damaged part of his beautiful body upset her. It changed the timbre of their lovemaking, or perhaps it was Glenn's sensitivity about his injury that did that. He became brusque and short-tempered, which Sherry didn't appreciate.

'I'm not an invalid!' he snapped.

'No, you're an idiot.'

His face darkened with anger. 'You got a problem?' He jabbed a finger at the door. 'The door is over there.'

She looked down her nose at him. 'If you think I'm going to creep into Dan and Lisa's house and risk waking my mother and getting interrogated about where I've been all night, you've got rocks in your head. Although,' she added coolly, 'that wouldn't surprise me.' She rolled on her side and pulled the sheet to her chin. 'You want to be alone? There's the door, Blitz sweetie.'

Bitch, Glenn thought savagely. He snatched at the sheet and turned to face the opposite wall, stifling a groan when his knee twisted. He punched his pillow and lay down.

They lay in silence, no longer lovers, but enemies

once again.

How did that happen? Glenn wondered.

Why did that have to happen? Sherry thought.

Glenn eventually fell asleep. He was a restless sleeper, frequently moving an arm or a leg as if he couldn't settle. When dawn lightened the curtains, Sherry slid from beneath the covers and sat on the edge of the bed. She glanced over her shoulder at Glenn. He lay on his stomach, his face half-buried in the pillow, one arm outstretched, fingers curled loosely against his palm. His ruined knee was bent at an awkward angle, even in his sleep he guarded it, and pain creased his forehead. Sherry's brow creased in sympathy — it looked so sore. His black hair was rumpled, stubble covered his jaw and he snored a little, but none of it made a dent in the odd combination of lust and tenderness that spilled through her as she watched him sleep.

She sprang to her feet, rocking the bed and making Glenn take a deep breath, shift and settle again. Sherry gazed at him in panic. Sleeping with him hadn't exorcised her attraction; if anything, it had made it worse, because now she knew just how good they were together and that beneath Glenn's cocky attitude and smart mouth there was a man she could like — a lot.

Sherry dressed quickly, keeping her eyes averted from the bed. She looked back, testing herself. She still wanted him. Angry and impatient to nip this stupidity in the bud, she pulled a twenty from her purse and tucked it under the clock on the bedside table, knowing how someone as proud as Glenn would react when he awoke and saw it, how *she* would react.

She let herself out the door, took a deep breath of the

fresh morning air and walked away. Her life was just the way she wanted it. She loved her family and her job and had great friends. Sherry Jackson had no worries.

Dan was doing an early-morning run to get diapers for Georgia. How, in a house full of adults obsessed with the care of his daughter, it was possible to run out of them baffled him. It wasn't easy finding a store with the right kind of newborn diaper this early in the morning, which meant he'd had to drive further. As he sat in his car yawning and waiting for the lights to change, he saw Sherry cross the car park of a motel opposite. Dan was about to lower the window and call her, but his finger stalled when he registered that she was leaving a motel at daybreak, carrying her shoes and with the rumpled appearance of a woman who'd just spent the previous night having sex. He watched her climb into Lisa's car — his sister-in-law's sex life was none of his business.

The lights changed and, as he took a left past the motel, Dan spotted an ice-blue BMW tucked in a corner, partly hidden by some trees. Dan slowed the car. There was only one M6 convertible in Denver painted that particular shade of ice-blue with Blitz licence plates.

Glenn awoke at six-thirty to discover he was alone — and that a twenty-dollar bill was tucked beneath the digital clock on the bedside table. He stared at the money for several moments before snatching it up and tearing it in half. He wasn't sure what offended him more: being treated like a gigolo, or the fact that she thought he was worth only twenty bucks.

He swung his good leg over the side of the bed and followed it carefully with his bad one, gritting his teeth at the angry throb in his knee. His foot brushed against something. Glenn looked down and saw a used condom on the carpet and bent to pick it up. It was the first one they'd used, the one that had gone missing. There was a small telltale stain on the carpet beneath it. It was broken.

Holy shit!

Glenn's heart hammered as he checked the condom and a tiny residue of semen seeped from a tear in the rubber onto his hand. He remembered Sherry putting it on him and blaming her clumsiness on her long purple nails. She must have snagged the latex. He needed to call her and tell her to get the morning-after pill, tell her that he was clean and check that she was, too. Glenn's eyes strayed to the two halves of the twenty-dollar bill on the carpet and his jaw hardened. Then again — maybe not. Ms Jackson had made it clear that a one-night stand was all she wanted from him. She didn't strike Glenn as the kind of woman who left things to chance. She was probably on the pill.

He threw the condom in the trash, climbed into the cramped shower, and ran cold water onto his knee. With luck, the next time he'd have to set eyes on Sherry Jackson would be at Georgia's wedding.

Chapter 6

Sherry lived and worked on Auckland's North Shore. She was part of a five-member problem-solving team in the Family Violence Unit. There were two arms to the FVU, the PST and Investigation. The PST was a relatively new unit established to work proactively with 'The Top Twenty', the families requiring the most callouts for domestic violence or those deemed as being the most at risk. It wasn't unknown for some families to be visited eighty times because of domestic violence.

There were four officers in the FVU, two men and two women, led by Detective Sergeant Dave Pomana. They worked in a long rectangular office with fluorescent lighting and no windows. Long, grey-topped counters with computers ran the length of two sides of the room, and four desks were set in pairs, back-to-back, in the middle so that the officers working at them faced one another.

Dave Pomana looked up from his computer as Sherry walked into the room and began removing her 'SRBA' vest — or Stab Resistant Body Armour — by the rack where they were stored. 'How'd it go?' he asked.

Sherry hung her dark blue vest on the rail, split her ponytail in two, and pulled on the ends. 'I waited 'til somebody from the Women's Refuge picked Stacey and the kids up.'

The police didn't visit the refuges but arranged to drop women and their families off at agreed sites. Stacey was well known to the FVU. Sherry had been working with Stacey and her partner, Vance, for months to improve things at home, but the previous night Vance punched Stacey and then their eldest son when he'd tried to stop his father hurting his mother. Stacey had waited until Vance left in the morning before calling Sherry and asking to be taken to the Women's Refuge. She'd allowed Sherry to take her son to the hospital to be checked out, but insisted she didn't need treatment herself, saying, 'It's just a black eye.' She'd had much worse. Sherry took photos anyway and got the doctor at the hospital to examine Stacey's eye so that they had a record of her injuries.

Vance had recently lost his job and become even more violent at home. As things deteriorated, Sherry had encouraged Stacey to think about moving to the Women's Refuge, but Stacey had refused to consider it — until Vance hit their son, Stan. She was stoic about her own abuse but devastated that Vance had attacked one of the children. 'He shouts at the kids, but he's never hit one of them before.' They both knew it would happen again, and that next time it might be one of the smaller kids that got 'the bash'.

'I told Stan to stay out of the way, but he wouldn't listen.'

If Vance had continued to hit Stacey instead of one of the kids, Sherry knew she'd be at home now, hobbling around the kitchen trying to put a meal together.

Sherry and a colleague had driven Stacey and the children home from the Emergency Department to collect some clothes, and then taken them to the collection point to wait for the worker from the Women's

Refuge. The family's belongings were crammed into a few black plastic bin-liners. There wasn't much, just what they'd managed to grab before they fled the house. Sherry had kept an eye on the kids so that Stacey could step out for a cigarette to calm her nerves. She'd listened to Stacey's nervous chatter, and suspected Stacey wasn't telling her all the reasons behind her decision to leave; however, each time she'd broached the subject Stacey had clammed up, so Sherry had concentrated on getting the family to the refuge.

'Did Vance get wind of what was happening?' Dave asked.

Sherry nodded. 'He started calling her. One moment he was crying and saying how much he loved her and the kids, and the next he was threatening to give her the bash if she didn't get her arse home and cook some dinner. I took the phone away and gave it to Misty from the refuge.'

The odds of Vance enticing Stacey home were better than the odds of her staying at the refuge and getting a protection order, but at least it was a step in the right direction.

Sherry checked the clock on the wall. 'I've got a doctor's appointment. It'll only take half an hour; I should be back by two.'

'OK.' Dave turned to his computer, his mind already busy with the million other things he needed to do until he suddenly remembered and called out, 'Hey! Congratulations. I heard you passed your Crim 214.'

Sherry caught the side of the doorway and swung back towards him. Crim 214 was shorthand for 'Introduction to Criminal Behaviour' and was one of two papers she needed to pass before she could apply for a sergeant's position; the other was 'Core Policing Knowledge' or 'CPK'. Sherry made no bones about one day wanting Dave's job. She smiled and raised her brows. 'First step on the path to world domination.'

Dave snorted. 'Yeah, hold that thought.' He liked Detective Constable Jackson's ambition and frankness; she had the drive and smarts to go far.

She laughed and disappeared, and he thought how well she looked.

She was positively glowing.

The nurse's name was Vicky. She had highlighted blonde hair, a warm manner, and she liked to talk. Sherry listened to Vicky apologize about keeping her waiting for twenty minutes and politely cut her short. She had reports she needed to complete so the admin staff could enter them into NIA, the police computer. 'That's OK, but I'd really like to get this done so I can get back to work. I've got a pile of reports.'

Vicky was used to these driven professional types. This one was a cop. She turned to the computer screen and clicked the mouse a few times. 'You're here for a routine cervical smear?'

Sherry nodded.

'When was your last one?'

'Three years ago. It was normal.'

'So I see.' Vicky moved the mouse across the blue pad on the desk. 'How have you been?'

'Fine.' Sherry tapped her fingers on her arm and

glanced at the clock on the wall.

'Periods regular? Any abnormal bleeding between them or after sex?'

'No, no abnormal bleeding.' She hadn't slept with anybody since Glenn; in fact, her libido had been at an all-time low. Sherry pushed the memory of that night away and added, 'They've been a little lighter than usual, but they're still regular.'

Vicky's hand paused on the mouse. 'What do you mean by "lighter"?'

She shrugged. 'Just lighter. Less.'

'How long have they been like that?'

'A couple of months or so.' Sherry tapped impatiently. 'Why?'

Vicky swiveled the chair to face her. 'Have you had any nausea?'

'No.'

'Any breast tenderness?'

Sherry's brows drew together. 'No.'

'Any weight gain?'

'A couple of kilos, but I've been spending a lot of time at my desk. I assure you, I'm not pregnant,' Sherry replied, with a touch of irritation.

Vicky's expression said she'd seen and heard it all before. 'I'd like to check before I do the smear test.'

'No!'

Sherry gazed about the room in bewilderment. It looked just the same as it had when she'd walked in, the same examination couch against the wall with the curtain rail above, the same white sink and soap and towel dispenser in the corner, the same laminated poster of — she looked away — the female reproductive system on the wall beside the desk. The same nurse, but she was wearing a different expression now, one of tolerant concern.

'It *can't* be right,' Sherry insisted. 'Do it again.'

'We've already done it twice, Sherry,' Vicky pointed out gently. 'The test is positive. You're pregnant.'

She shook her head stubbornly. 'I can't be! I haven't missed any periods; I haven't been sick … I *can't* be.'

'Some women continue to have periods and don't notice anything different for a while. They only find out when they go for a routine check like you have today. If it makes you feel any better, I've got a friend who's a lawyer who didn't find out until she was seventeen weeks pregnant.'

How was that supposed to make her feel better? Sherry pressed her fingertips against her eyelids and tried to think. She hadn't slept with anybody since Glenn in Denver. She swallowed a groan. It just got better and better.

'You've had a shock.' Vicky touched Sherry's arm and she jumped. 'Is there somebody I can call for you?' She wasn't happy when Sherry wouldn't let her call anybody and insisted on leaving the medical centre. 'Where will you go? You shouldn't be alone.'

She just wanted to escape. 'I'll go and see my brother.'

Vicky had no choice but to let her go, but not before she'd made an appointment for an ultrasound the next day. 'Because we're uncertain of your dates, we need to find out exactly how far along you are.'

Sherry wanted to cover her ears and wind the clock back to the morning — or even better, back to before that night at the motel with Glenn. How had it happened? They'd used condoms.

Vicky gave her a slip of paper with her appointment time and a book with 'Pregnancy Record' on the front. Sherry threw it in the back of the car. A part of her still functioned adequately enough to call Dave and say she was taking the rest of the day off sick.

'Nothing bad, I hope?' he asked.

'No, nothing bad.' Sherry remembered the appointment the next day. 'But I've got to get some blood tests and things done tomorrow, so I'm not sure when I'll be in. Sorry,' she ended lamely.

For a few moments, Dave didn't answer. 'That's OK. Take all the time you need. Let me ... uh ... know how you are, OK?'

Better and better and better. He'd guessed.

'I will.'

She hugged the steering wheel and rested her forehead on her arms. This couldn't be real; it had to be a mistake. Maybe the pregnancy-testing kits Vicky had used were old or out of date. Maybe it was a false positive. Tears threatened, and Sherry swiped angrily at her eyes and started the car. She didn't know where to go or what to do. So she just drove.

Ben Jackson was a builder. He was perched on the roof of a house, checking the flashing, when he saw his sister's black SUV pull up in the street below and Sherry get out. She sometimes dropped by during the day to say a quick 'Hi' if she was near wherever he was working. Ben stood astride the roof and raised his arm in greeting. Sherry looked up at him but didn't smile; her face wore the blank expression of somebody in shock.

Ben slowly lowered his arm. He ran nimbly across the roof and climbed down the wooden framing. He hit the concrete running and pounded up the newly laid driveway to Sherry. Up close, she looked even worse. Ben caught her arms. 'What is it? Has something happened to Mum or Dad?' Dread deepened his voice. 'Is it Lisa or Georgia?'

'*No!*' Sherry shook her head vigorously from side to side. 'No — no, they're fine.' She dropped her eyes to the faded black AC/DC T-shirt he wore. 'It's ... me.'

Ben felt like he'd been launched off a high building and was waiting to hit the ground. He gripped her arms. 'What's wrong?' Tears glittered in her eyes, and he grew more alarmed. Sherry *did not* cry. 'Sherry! What's wrong? Are you sick?' He gave her a little shake. 'Sherry!'

'The nurse said ...' Her pale cheeks turned rosy.

'The nurse said ...?' Ben prompted and felt her tremble. It grew like the rumblings of a volcano.

Sherry erupted. 'The nurse said I'm pregnant!' she yelled. 'I can't be! We used condoms! How can I be pregnant when I haven't missed any periods?'

Behind him, the hammers and air guns fell silent as Ben's crew stopped work and stared.

'Bloody hell ...' he whispered.

'Go pee on the stick.'

'You go pee on the stick!'

'Oh yeah, that'll work.' Ben leaned a shoulder on the doorway of Sherry's bathroom and nodded at the pregnancy-testing kit opened on the vanity. 'Go pee on the stick.'

Sherry knew she was behaving like a child, and that Ben was right and wouldn't budge until she gave in. He had an inexhaustible supply of something Sherry lacked — patience. She banged the door shut in his face.

Once he'd recovered from his shock, and knowing how obstinate Sherry could be, Ben had bought another pregnancy-testing kit and then driven her home listening to all the reasons why she couldn't be pregnant. He waited for Sherry to run out of steam and asked, 'Have you slept with anybody in the last three months?'

'He *used* a condom!'

Ben stared out the windscreen. 'Condoms can break,' he said. 'Accidents can happen.'

He looked at the bathroom door. She'd had plenty of time to do the test and read the result. The fact that Sherry hadn't opened the door told him all he needed to know. His sister was knocked-up. He was going to be an uncle again.

He didn't know what the hell to do.

The door opened. Sherry stood clutching the stick, her eyes wild and her chest heaving. Ben had read the instructions in the kit because she'd been too agitated to do it. He took the indicator from her and studied it. 'Yep, you're pregnant.'

She kicked the door so hard it slammed against the wall. *'The bastard!'*

'You mean Stuart?' Ben asked.

She stopped mid-rant and echoed in a puzzled voice, 'Stuart?'

'Stuart — your old boyfriend.'

'Er ... no ...' Her eyes slid away. 'It's not Stuart.' Thank the Lord for small mercies. Stuart would care; Glenn wouldn't. Stuart still left messages on her answering machine asking her to call him, but she erased them.

Ben shouldered his way past her and ditched the stick in the pedal bin next to the vanity. 'Has the bastard got a name?'

Sherry contemplated her heavy black work shoes. 'It's complicated.'

He didn't know any other way to ask and decided to just say it. 'Do you know who the father is?'

Her head shot up. 'Of course I know who the father is!' she cried indignantly.

Ben raised his hands in a placating gesture. 'I'm not judging you, Sher. It's just that I got the impression that you sometimes ...' He searched for the right words. 'Mix your drinks.'

Sherry wasn't nearly as sexually active as Ben, or Lisa, imagined. She gave the impression that there were plenty of men in her life to keep her family off her back, because they worried that she worked too hard and didn't balance her career with a social life. Her relationships with men tended to fizzle out when her boyfriends realized they'd always play second fiddle to Sherry's career and she didn't see herself as their wife or the future mother of their children. Knowing it was her own fault that Ben thought she was promiscuous didn't make her feel any better.

'I do not *mix my drinks*,' she said frostily. 'I sleep

with one person at a time.'

Ben stared. 'OK. So who is he?'

Imagining Glenn Brogan's reaction if he found out she was pregnant made Sherry want to buy a one-way ticket to Outer Mongolia. Leaving the twenty on the bedside table had been unspeakably rude, and Sherry had expected a phone call from Glenn to tell her so. His silence was more eloquent than words. Their agreement had been for one night, a night that had surprised and delighted them both until Glenn's hang-ups about his injury and Sherry's stubbornness had intruded to remind them how little they had in common besides shared relatives and great sex.

She looked at Ben. 'It doesn't matter. He's out of the picture.'

'You mean he doesn't know?'

'He doesn't need to,' she said stiffly.

He wouldn't let it go. 'He's got a right to know he's going to be a father.'

Sherry looked at her shoes again, and muttered, 'He's not.'

'What does that mean?' Ben demanded.

'I can't have a baby, Ben,' she said in a troubled voice.

'Yes, you can,' he insisted. 'If you're worried about money or looking after it, I'll help. Mum and Dad will love having a grandchild nearby — you know how much they miss seeing Georgia. Lisa and Dan might not be here, but you know they'll support you any way they can.'

Hearing Dan's name made Sherry wince. She liked and respected her brother-in-law and didn't want him to ever know that she'd slept with his brother and been stupid enough to get knocked-up. Sherry came as close to pleading as she was able to. 'Ben, I'm not like Lisa: I've never wanted to be a mother.'

He cupped the back of his neck and sighed. 'Do me a favour, take your time and don't make any snap decisions, Sherry. Promise me that.'

At the ultrasound appointment the next day, they discovered that Sherry couldn't take her time because the doctor estimated she was ten weeks pregnant. If she wanted to terminate the pregnancy, it'd have to be done soon.

Ben accompanied her into the scanning room.

'Are you Ms Jackson's partner?' the doctor asked.

'No, I'm her brother.'

There wasn't much of a family resemblance. They were both tall, but Ben's hair was dark brown and wavy instead of black and straight like Sherry's, and his eyes were blue-grey like Jill's. He watched the monitor, but Sherry looked away — she didn't want to see anything that might remind her of Georgia. But she made the mistake of looking at Ben's face as the doctor rolled the sensor back and forth across her tummy and his riveted expression unnerved her.

'What's that?' Ben asked.

'A heartbeat,' the doctor replied.

Sherry screwed her eyes shut. Ben's warm, work-toughened hand curved around hers, and he stopped asking questions. Sherry wanted to cry. She made an appointment to see her doctor the following day, and let Ben drive her home. They didn't speak until he stopped his truck outside her house and killed the engine.

He turned and spread his arm along the back of the seat. 'I'll pick you up tomorrow and take you to your doctor's appointment.'

'You don't have to.' Sherry flicked her thumbnails together and stared out the windscreen. 'I don't want to put you behind at work.'

'A few more hours won't hurt.'

Silence stretched between them, filled with the things they couldn't say or didn't want to hear.

You can't, Sherry. I saw it: it's got a heartbeat. You can't.

I can't, Ben. I don't know how. I can't.

'You won't tell Mum and Dad, will you?'

Her uncertainty tore at Ben. Sherry was always so sure, so confident; the only time he'd seen her like this was when they thought they'd lost Lisa.

'Of course I won't.' He cupped her shoulder. 'It's not my story to tell.'

Lexi Bartlett was a receptionist who relieved at local medical centres; currently she was standing in for a sick receptionist at the medical centre Sherry was registered with. Lexi was an inveterate gossip who had been 'let go' from her permanent job because she didn't understand the difference between chatting and breaching patient confidentiality. When she saw Sherry's name on a request for routine antenatal blood tests amongst the specimens waiting to be collected by the courier, Lexi felt a thrill of excitement. She knew Jill Jackson, who was a medical receptionist at one of the big practices in town and couldn't wait to congratulate her.

Since her appointment with Vicky, Sherry had turned into a dormouse — all she wanted to do was sleep. She kept on turning down invitations from friends to meet up for dinner or drinks, because she was too exhausted to go out and had even developed a preoccupation with strange food combinations. Sherry was convinced her body was playing a big trick on her. She could understand her tiredness — her body was undertaking a major building project — but she curled her lip at the idea of cravings. They were a crock, something thought up by pregnant women as an excuse to eat all the wrong stuff and send their husbands out at midnight to buy food nobody in their right mind kept in the pantry. Sherry ignored the cravings, but embraced sleep because it provided an escape. When she was asleep, she didn't have to think.

She awoke suddenly from a deep sleep, and at first thought she'd been disturbed by her neighbour's cat which was curled up on the bottom of the bed. The cat was a stray that Sherry's irritating, nosy neighbour had taken in and tried to domesticate. He was ugly, unsociable, had one eye and only half a tail, and for some reason liked Sherry's house better than her neighbour's. The neighbour called him Otto; on a good day, Sherry called him 'You Damned Nuisance' or 'That Damned Cat'. She prodded him with her foot and the cat hissed and leapt off the bed. 'You'd better not have fleas, you mangy pest.'

The front-door knocker rattled. It sounded like whoever was wielding the knocker had been at it a long time. Sherry rolled over and gazed groggily at the digital clock. The backlit red numbers read 18:10. She'd fallen asleep in her clothes with the bedroom curtains open. The late October evening was still bright and, thanks to daylight saving, sunset was still some time away. The knocker had fallen silent but started up again with renewed urgency.

Sherry stumbled out of bed and down the stairs to the front door to find her parents on the other side. Their faces were taut with concern. She looked from one to the other. 'What? What's wrong?'

Her motor-mouth mother stared at her as if she'd opened the door in the nude.

'Can we come inside?' her father asked.

Sherry backed up and held the door open. 'What's wrong?' she repeated. 'Has something happened to Lisa and Georgia? Or Ben? Or Dan?'

Brian followed Jill in and closed the door behind him. 'They're all fine. It's you we're worried about.'

The first alarm bell rang inside Sherry's head. 'What about?' she asked warily.

'Sherry,' Brian said heavily, 'are you pregnant?'

She felt like she'd slammed into a brick wall. 'Ben *told* you?' she cried incredulously.

Jill started. 'You mean he *knows*?' her voice rose indignantly.

Great, now they were both in the bad books.

The Jackson Family Jungle Drums beat. They boomed so loudly that the noise reverberated across the Pacific Ocean, hit the west coast of America, swooped across California, took a left at New Mexico and touched down in Denver. Unlike Chinese Whispers, the message didn't change, Sherry was pregnant and wouldn't say who the father was.

Dan was taking Georgia out of the bath when Lisa burst into the bathroom to deliver the news. He looked at their pink, squirming daughter clasped between his wet hands, her dark hair slicked against her tiny scalp and the gummy smile on her face, and asked, 'You're sure your mother hasn't made a mistake?'

'Of course she hasn't made a mistake!' Lisa cried. 'How could she make a mistake about that?'

Dan clung to the hope that his brother wasn't responsible. 'How far along is she?'

'Nearly three months, but Mum's not sure Sherry is going to go through with it. She won't say who the father is, just that he's out of the picture. I don't think it's her ex, Stuart, because she broke it off with him before she came to visit.'

He took a deep breath and blew it out slowly. Georgia watched his lips move and kicked her legs to show her appreciation for the free entertainment.

Lisa sat on the edge of the bath and said in a bewildered voice, 'I can't believe it. Sherry ... *pregnant.*'

Dan wrapped Georgia in a towel and handed her to Lisa. 'I need to go out.'

'Go out? Go out where?' She followed him onto the landing and down the stairs carrying Georgia. 'We're in the middle of a family crisis. How can you go out?'

Georgia sucked her fist and peeked at her father from beneath a corner of the towel as he searched the hallway table for his car keys.

'Dan, did you hear what I said?' Lisa narrowed her eyes. 'You *know* something!'

He went to the hallway closet and began patting the pockets of jackets.

'Daniel!'

He returned to the table to renew the search.

Lisa reached around him and shoved her hand into the front of his jeans.

'Not now, honey—'

'I'm looking for your car keys, you moron!' She dragged them from his pocket and tossed them at his chest. 'Tell me what you know.'

Dan escaped to the front door. 'I just remembered something I needed to do at the hospital.'

Lisa dogged his heels. 'You're no better at lying than you are at keeping track of your car keys. *Tell me!*'

'There's nothing to tell.' At least, he hoped not. 'Lisa?'

She cupped Georgia's bottom through the towel. 'What?'

'Better get a diaper on her before she pees,' Dan suggested and left.

'I know how to look after Georgie!' Lisa shouted through the glass in the front door as Georgia kicked her legs — and flooded her mother's palm with urine.

Glenn was surprised to see Dan, because he'd had dinner with him and Lisa at their place the previous night. He'd closed the deal on the house in Cherry Hills but couldn't be bothered to move in and was still living at his condominium. When Glenn opened the door, Dan didn't say a word, just walked past him and into the living room. A bottle of beer and the remnants of a meal were on the black lacquered table beside a couple of outsized sofas covered in nubby slate-grey fabric, and a fire had been lit in the fireplace.

Glenn followed Dan. 'What's the matter?' He joked, 'Did you and Lisa have a fight?'

Dan picked up the remote from the table, aimed it at the seventy-two-inch television screen mounted on the wall, and hit the off button. He threw the remote onto one of the sofas and turned and glared at his brother.

Glenn's brows rose. Dan seldom lost his temper, but right now he looked really pissed about something. 'What's wr—'

'Sherry is pregnant.'

The words seemed to drop into Glenn's brain one at a time.

Sherry. Is. Pregnant.

Sherry is. Pregnant.

Sherry is pregnant!

He felt as though a vortex roared through his head, blasting his mental files to kingdom come. When he hadn't heard from her, Glenn had assumed everything was OK; he'd tried to put Sherry and the night they'd spent together out of his mind. How did Dan know about it? Had Sherry told him? Had she sent him to tell Glenn? It didn't seem likely — she was too proud. Glenn tried to imagine her pregnant and failed. He tried to imagine her reaction to finding out she was pregnant and winced. She wouldn't send his brother. She'd send an assassin.

Dan's voice reclaimed his attention. 'I saw Sherry leaving a motel the morning before she flew out. I saw your car parked around the corner.'

Glenn was still grappling with the information. *Sherry is pregnant? Ice Queen Sherry?* She'd probably give birth to an ice cube. He raked a hand through his hair. 'That was nearly three months ago. It might not even be mine.'

Dan growled, 'She's nearly three months' pregnant, you asshole!'

The vortex roared again.

'If I didn't have surgery tomorrow, I'd hit you!' Dan snapped.

'Shit …' Glenn whispered. 'The broken condom …'

When one of his ex-girlfriends had claimed he was the father of her unborn child, he'd been sure he wasn't because the dates were all wrong and he was always careful about using protection — or at least he had been until the night with Sherry.

'A condom broke? Did Sherry know?' Dan demanded.

Glenn threaded his hand through his hair again but didn't speak. He felt like pond scum.

Veins stood out on Dan's forehead. 'You mean you didn't tell her?' he cried incredulously.

Glenn began to shake his head and reeled back when

his brother's fist connected with his right eye. He fell backwards onto one of the sofas, clutching his eye, and thought vaguely that it was just as well he wasn't still playing.

Dan loomed over him, cradling his hand against his chest. 'Get me some ice for my fucking hand and then get yourself on a plane to New Zealand!'

Chapter 7

Glenn walked the perimeter of the rugby fields, searching for a team wearing yellow shirts and ignoring curious stares from the people watching twilight touch rugby. October was the middle of spring in New Zealand. He'd arrived earlier that afternoon, picked up a rental car at the airport and found his way to Sherry's house in Torbay. She didn't know Glenn was coming; the only people who knew were Dan and Lisa. He was their least-favourite person at the moment. When Lisa had seen the black eye Dan had given Glenn, she'd said tartly, 'If I could reach, I'd black the other one.'

Sherry's house was built on a hill, with views across the street to the beach opposite. It was reached by a private road that serviced all the properties on the hill. Sherry's place was the first house, and, like numbers two and three, it had been built by Ben. She wasn't home when Glenn knocked. While he waited for an answer, Glenn stood on the deck outside the front door, curiously studying her house; he decided he liked it. There was a shallow flat area out front and native bush behind. It was built of wood and had three different levels, with a wide balcony on the top floor to sit and enjoy the sea views.

A cat sat beside the front door, washing its face with a paw. Sherry didn't seem like the type to have a cat, but then what would he know? The cat looked like a beaten-up old prizefighter. It growled at Glenn when he crouched down to give it a stroke. *Just like its owner*, he thought. He was contemplating booking into a hotel and returning later when Sherry's neighbour appeared carrying a watering can and shouted at the cat, 'Otto! Come here!'

Otto ignored her.

The woman waved the can at Glenn. 'I'm Nora Ditchburn. I keep an eye on the place for Sherry when she's out.' Sherry could have told Glenn that the watering can was empty, and that the reason Nora kept so many plants on her front step was because it gave her an excuse to come out and interrogate Sherry's visitors.

A few weeks after Georgia was born, Glenn had bought a copy of *Where The Wild Things Are*. 'Just what a one-month-old baby needs,' Dan observed. 'A little light reading before she turns out the light.'

Glenn read it to Georgia, anyway, ignoring her yawns and the fact she was more interested in staring at his face than the pages of the book. Sherry's neighbour reminded him of one of the Wild Things. She was tall, shaped like a barrel, and wore black polyester slacks and an outsized grey T-shirt with *Looks Good, Feels Even Better* written on the front. Her mousy brown hair was scraped back into a thin plait that accentuated her round face and double chin. She looked like a refrigerator with feet.

'Are you a friend?' Nora took in Glenn's height and black eye. 'Or family?'

Glenn accurately identified Nora as a nosy neighbour and lonely, middle-aged spinster. In his experience, the uglier the woman, the more romantic the heart. He gave her his best matinee-idol smile and drawled, 'Neither,

I'm afraid, Ma'am.'

The smile and the cowboy drawl reduced Nora to a gooey, sticky puddle. The watering can dangled in her hand. She didn't even notice that Glenn hadn't told her who he was. 'You're American?'

'Guilty, Ma'am.'

Her round face turned pink. 'Have I seen you somewhere before?'

It would be just his luck if she turned out to be a Cougars fan.

Glenn shook his head and lengthened his drawl, 'No, Ma'am.'

Nora almost dropped the can. 'I love your accent.'

He thought about throwing in an *'Aw shucks, Ma'am'*, but decided he'd keep it for another time. Charming women came as naturally to him as breathing. Sherry wasn't likely to be so accommodating when she saw him, and her neighbour might become a valuable source of information. The black eye Dan had given him was good for camouflage.

'That's real sweet of you, Ma'am.' Glenn thought about the last time he'd called a woman 'Ma'am' and his smile slipped.

Nora beamed and her eyes disappeared in the folds of her doughy face. 'What happened to your eye?' she asked.

'I'm a lumberjack back home. Tree fell badly.' It sounded better than *My brother punched me because I got his sister-in-law pregnant.*

Nora pressed a hand to her romantic heart. 'That's terrible! Can you still see?'

'The doctors are hopeful.' He was impatient to see

Sherry. 'Do you have any idea where I might find Sherry?'

'She plays touch rugby on a Thursday night.'

Rugby? She was pregnant and playing *rugby?* Glenn forced a smile. 'Do you think you could give me the directions to where she's playing? I'd like to surprise her.'

He'd had plenty of time on the flight to wonder why Sherry hadn't been in contact to tell him she was pregnant, and the only reasons he could come up with were that she was a cantankerous, contrary witch, and that she wasn't planning on keeping the baby. A cold fish like Sherry wouldn't want a child, but Glenn decided he did. Although he knew there was precious little he could do to stop her, he was prepared to beg if he had to.

Nora gave him directions to the playing fields and a detailed description of the yellow shirt Sherry's team wore.

Glenn thanked her and left without giving his name or the reason for his visit.

He continued searching for a team wearing yellow and ignoring the looks his height always drew. What Glenn knew about rugby could be written twice on the back of a postage stamp, although he'd heard of New Zealand's national rugby team, the All Blacks, because he was a fan of Jonah Lomu. Glenn was relieved to see that, as the name suggested, there was no tackling in touch rugby. Instead, the opposition tagged the player with the ball, who then passed it to another team member until somebody either crossed the try line at the end of the field or the team used up their quota of tags and the ball was turned over to the opposition. There wasn't any tackling, but there was plenty of sprinting and fancy footwork by players to avoid being tagged.

The evening was mild and still. Players sweated and ducked and dived, shouting for the ball and cheering when they scored. Glenn's concern that Sherry didn't care about the child increased as he prowled the perimeter. This wasn't the kind of exercise a pregnant woman should be involved in; she should be doing meditation or yoga or knitting or ... something.

Glenn spotted a team with yellow shirts. He watched as a figure with a familiar black ponytail and long, long legs sprinted along the sideline and caught the ball. Her legs stretched for the try line. Sherry crossed the line, leaned down, and touched the ball to the ground as the hooter sounded and Glenn reached the pitch.

An argument immediately broke out between Sherry's team and the opposition about whether the try counted.

'The hooter had already gone!'

'Try not to be an arsehole all your life, Raymond — it *counts*.'

Raymond took exception to being called an arsehole but had to back down when the referee awarded the goal and Knobs and Knockers were declared the winners. Sherry's team erupted into cheers and directed some heavy-handed back-slapping her way. Somehow, she tripped and fell, and some of the other players celebrated by diving on top of her.

Glenn bolted across the pitch, grabbed hold of the yellow shirt on top of the pile and began tossing bodies aside. 'Get off her!' he roared.

'Hey man! Who the hell—'

'Get your fucking hands off—'

Confronted by a furious man-mountain, Sherry's team-mates backed off or scrambled aside rather than be thrown off by Glenn.

'Sherry?' He brushed them aside anxiously. '*Sherry?*'

She lay at the bottom of the pile with a man huddled on top of her. Before Glenn could drag him off, the man rolled aside but kept an arm extended protectively over Sherry. He looked up at Glenn but made no move to get off her, which enraged Glenn. He hauled back a fist and yelled, 'Get off her, asshole! She's pregnant!'

The guy didn't move, just stared up at Glenn who began the downward swing.

The sight of the big, meaty fist descending towards her brother eclipsed Sherry's shock at seeing Glenn. She grabbed his arm and shouted, 'Glenn! Don't hit him! It's Ben, my brother!'

Glenn stopped mid-swing and looked from her pale, panicked face into Ben Jackson's narrowed, intent gaze. 'Ben!' He let go of Ben's shirt and lowered his arm. 'Sorry, man! I didn't recog—'

His head snapped back as Ben's fist connected with his left eye. 'Didn't you, Brogan?' Ben growled. 'Well, I recognize you, you prick. And I've got a bloody good idea why you're here.'

Nora was understandably suspicious when Glenn returned to Sherry's house with his other eye rapidly swelling closed. 'Don't tell me another tree fell badly?'

Sherry was all fingers and thumbs as she tried to unlock the front door of her house. Seeing Glenn had set her insides jangling like wind chimes, not just because she was pregnant and shocked to see him, but also because even with his face beaten up the sight of him did strange things to her equilibrium. She glanced at her nosy neighbour and muttered, 'What's she talking about?'

'I'll explain later,' Glenn said.

It was the first time she'd spoken to him since he'd announced to her team-mates that she was pregnant. If looks could kill, he'd be toast. How was he supposed to know it was a big secret? *Why* was it a secret? And if Sherry was almost three months' pregnant, shouldn't there be something to show for it? Lisa had popped out pretty fast, but Sherry looked just the same: mile-long legs, round, tight ass covered in black Lycra bike pants, and voluptuous breasts pushing at the front of her yellow shirt. Glenn remembered the night at the motel and wanted her all over again, which was inappropriate given the circumstances. It would help if Sherry looked pregnant — he was certain he wouldn't be turned on if she was leading with her belly and waddling like Lisa had in the months before Georgia was born. The yellow shirt was roomy, which made it difficult to see any changes to her waistline. She'd caught Glenn looking and given him the evil eye. He fingered the puffy flesh around his left eye — hell, he could hardly see straight anyway. Glenn doubted even his mother would recognize him at the moment.

Nora lumbered to the bottom of her steps to water a primula; it brought her into earshot. Glenn noticed she had a bigger watering can, and this time it was filled with water.

'So help me if you've been talking to her ...' Sherry muttered threateningly as she pushed open the front door.

He bent down and whispered angrily in her ear, 'What are you going to do? Black my eye?'

She stepped over the threshold and hissed, 'Get inside!'

Glenn didn't appreciate being ordered around. He loitered on the doorstep and raised his voice for Nora's benefit. 'Is this your idea of rolling out the welcome mat?'

'Just *get in!*'

He strolled inside.

Sherry looked expectantly at Ben, who was standing outside with his hands tucked beneath his armpits and a distinctly unhappy expression on his face. Glenn was offended that she'd insisted that Ben accompany them. 'You too, Ben.'

He glanced at Glenn. 'I think I should go home and give you some time to talk.'

She pushed past Glenn, grabbed Ben by his yellow shirt and hauled him inside. Ben looked different to the last time Glenn had seen him at Dan and Lisa's wedding when he'd been a couple of stone overweight. He'd lost weight since, and must have been working out, because he was six feet of solid muscle with a punch like a sledgehammer. Glenn always laughed at Dan's claim that Sherry had thrown him out of her house, but now he wasn't so sure.

Sherry slammed the front door. Glenn looked around and glimpsed a kitchen and a dining room through a couple of doorways opposite. He expected to be ushered towards one of them, but she headed left towards the black wrought-iron staircase spiralling towards the upper floors. The entrance way was flooded with coloured light. Glenn tipped back his head and saw a stained-glass skylight cut into the ceiling at the top of the house. The filtered light bathed the white walls of the staircase and the black-and-white tiled floor of the entrance in purple, rose, green and blue.

Ben gave a sigh and began to climb the stairs, but Glenn continued to stare at the stained-glass window above. It depicted a woman in a flowing pink dress riding an emerald-green horse and offering a purple flower to a blue knight. Sherry Jackson wasn't the kind of woman Glenn would expect to have a stained-glass window of a blue knight and a pink lady on a horse.

Sherry stopped with a hand on the wrought-iron balustrade and looked down at him. 'Are you coming or not?'

Glenn could tell she was pissed at the attention he was giving the window. 'Where are we going?'

'To my bedroom.' She continued up the stairs like Boadicea going into battle. 'It's the only place the Bat Woman won't hear us. She's got ears like radar dishes.'

Glenn was suddenly intensely curious to see Sherry's bedroom. He hurried up the stairs after Ben, ignoring the lingering stiffness in his knee from the long flight.

The top of the staircase ended at a big, open-plan bedroom. The carpet and walls were white, and it was sparsely furnished. There was a black dressing table with a mirror hanging above, its silver frame decorated with tulips. A mint-green chaise longue piled with striped and floral green and white pillows stood before the sliding glass doors that opened onto the deck. Outside, a white wrought-iron table and matching chairs faced the beach view. The only other furniture in the bedroom were a pair of black bedside tables and a black, wrought-iron four-poster bed draped in gauzy swags of white material.

Sherry's bedroom was as much of a surprise as the stained- glass window. It hinted at a side of her that Glenn never would have imagined existed. It wasn't a girly room; there weren't any bows or ribbons or dolls left over from childhood. Instead, there were flowered pillows, a mirror decorated with tulips — and a bed made for dreaming. It wasn't a girl's room — it was a woman's bower.

Ben pointed a thumb at the deck. 'I'll wait outside while you two talk.'

'There's no need for—' Sherry began.

'Yes, there is.' Glenn watched Ben through the slit that was his left eye; the right was already closed. 'Thanks, Ben.'

'I don't want to be—'

'Be quiet, Sherry.' Ben sent Glenn a warning look. 'If I hear or see you do anything to her, I'll be back in. I don't care how big you are: if you hurt her, I promise I'll hurt you.'

'I can look after myself, Ben,' Sherry insisted.

'Yeah, like you looked after yourself charging around playing touch rugby,' he retorted.

Glenn raised a brow. He might have an ally in Sherry's brother. 'The doctor said it was alright,' she said stiffly.

'I promise to call you if the urge to strangle her gets too much for me,' Glenn said.

Ben stepped outside.

Glenn faced Sherry with his hands on his hips and asked coldly, 'Why didn't you tell me?'

Her smile was as chilly as his voice. 'I don't know; I guess I was just so gosh-darned happy it slipped my mind.'

On closer inspection, Glenn could see that she looked tired. So why was she running around playing touch rugby? He thought about the broken condom and felt the familiar sense of guilt. She needed to know how it had happened, and that he was sorry. 'Sherry—'

Having Glenn in her bedroom made Sherry feel as jumpy as a jack-in-the-box. She blurted, 'Who blacked your eye?'

'What?'

'Who blacked your eye? The first one?'

He touched his right eye gingerly. 'Dan.'

'Dan?'

'He saw you leaving the motel that morning and guessed.'

Sherry moaned and closed her eyes. 'And I thought I couldn't feel any more humiliated.' She looked at Glenn. 'He didn't tell Lisa?'

'Of course not,' he replied. 'He wouldn't.'

No, Dan wouldn't. He'd keep it to himself unless there was a good reason not to.

'I suppose that's how you found out?' she said tightly.

Glenn nodded and retorted sarcastically, 'Yeah, it was one of those moments you want to frame and keep forever. You know the one: big brother knocks on the door, announces you've got his wife's sister pregnant, and punches you in the face.'

Sherry glowered at a framed sampler hanging on the wall beside the bed.

It was happening again; they were fighting when they needed to be talking. Glenn couldn't see a way to avoid it, and decided he might as well be hung for a sheep as a lamb. He took a deep breath. 'Sherry, there's something I need to tell you.' There was no reaction; she continued to stare at the sampler, like her batteries had suddenly drained. Glenn frowned. 'Sherry?'

She wasn't listening. It had been a mistake to bring Glenn to her bedroom, sporting stubble, black eyes and an attitude, and turning her insides to mush. She should have taken him to the living room and risked Nora overhearing. Having him here reminded Sherry of what they'd done to one another, *with* one another. It reminded her of the twenty-dollar bill she'd left sitting on the bedside table. Glenn wouldn't believe her, let alone understand if she tried to explain she'd done it because she needed to reduce that night to a one-night stand. Her feet were nailed to the carpet and her tongue glued to the roof of her mouth by a combination of misery and humiliation. She felt like an adolescent who'd made the oldest mistake in the book. Tears threatened and Sherry blinked them away. It was yet another development she didn't know how to cope with.

She dragged her attention back to Glenn, who was studying her baby sampler with a perplexed expression. It was decorated with fairies and had *Sherry Ann Jackson, January 15th, Weight 9 1b 3 oz, Daughter of Jill and Brian* embroidered in pink, and beneath that in green: *Friday's Child Is Loving And Giving.* Jill had made one for all of her children. Lisa's had angels, and

Ben's had teddy bears, which the girls teased him about.

A long, white wisp of muslin masquerading as a nightgown was tossed on the end of her bed. Sherry grabbed the nightdress and stuffed it under her pillow. She couldn't put it off. She had to tell him. Hopefully he'd understand that under the circumstances it was the only course of action.

'Glenn, I'm going to have a termination.'

His fury was palpable. 'Oh no, you're not,' he growled.

'You ...' Sherry swallowed, 'can't stop me.'

She sank onto the side of the bed and clasped her hands between her knees. Glenn moved soundlessly. Sherry started when his shoes and jeans-clad legs suddenly appeared before her. She looked up at him and flinched. The indolent, charming playboy was gone; he'd been replaced by a hard-eyed, unsmiling stranger. If she'd ever seen Glenn play, Sherry would have recognized this was his game face. She glanced uneasily at Ben leaning on the balustrade on the deck with his back to the sliding doors.

'It's too late,' Glenn insisted.

'No, it's not. There's still time.' *Just.*

'Let's ... let's get married.'

'*What?*' Marry Glenn and be swallowed up by his ego? It was Sherry's worst nightmare. '*No, thanks!*'

Plenty of women had tried to get Glenn to pop the question, so it was ironic that the one woman he finally proposed to acted as if he was handing her a death sentence. He felt as lukewarm about the prospect of marriage as she did, but under the circumstances it seemed the right thing to do; when it came to home and family, his views were fairly conservative.

'I'm loaded,' he pointed out.

'You're also a pain in the arse.'

'We're great in bed.'

She shifted uncomfortably and looked away. 'And so modest.'

Time to change the game plan. 'Don't you want the baby because it's mine?'

'No, I don't want it because it's *mine*.'

What was wrong with her? Wasn't she supposed to be awash with hormones and maternal instinct? '*I* want it.' Until then, Glenn hadn't realized how much.

She laughed hollowly. 'I doubt that.'

'What's that supposed to mean?' he demanded.

'A baby would put a serious crimp in your playboy lifestyle.'

'I don't have a playboy lifestyle.'

'Oh? You mean you just like collecting women?' She raised her brows. 'Or maybe it was another Glenn Brogan I spent the night with.'

'If I slept with all the women I'm supposed to have been with, I'd never get my pants zipped.'

Her lip curled. 'Give me a break, Glenn. You're a bona fide slut.'

'I didn't hear you complaining,' he snapped, and had the satisfaction of seeing her flush.

He was wearing a salmon-pink and burnt-orange cotton plaid shirt which should have looked terrible but didn't. Sherry felt tiny pinpricks dance across her skin. Her hibernating libido had woken up with a vengeance, and if Glenn knew he wouldn't hesitate to use it to get her to see things his way. She shrugged. 'I think you enjoy chasing a woman more than catching her.'

Glenn's eyes drifted to the little black mole high on her cheek. 'I enjoyed catching you,' he said in a low voice. Sherry tried to look bored, but Glenn wasn't buying it. He'd seen beneath that cool, haughty exterior. 'About the night at the motel—' he began again.

Petrified that he was going to bring up the money, Sherry interjected hastily: 'Some day you might want to get married, and your future wife might not be too happy to inherit a stepson or stepdaughter.' Although she felt sure the future Mrs Glenn Brogan would get over it if it meant having access to that body and all those millions.

'I'm not going to get married,' Glenn insisted.

'You just asked me,' Sherry pointed out.

'That's different.' He had to.

She'd received two other proposals of marriage, and turned them down, too; but at least the other guys had asked because they thought they loved her, not because they had to. 'You might change your mind.'

'No, I won't,' Glenn replied emphatically.

'You might meet that special someone.' Her voice dripped sarcasm, 'I'm sure she's out there somewhere, just dying to swap her bunny-girl outfit for life as Mrs Blitz.'

'That's original,' he drawled and Sherry bristled. 'I'm thirty-six years old. I've been proposed to three times, twice by the same woman.'

She smirked and opened her mouth.

'*Do not* come out with some smartass crack about memory loss.'

She closed her mouth.

Glenn struggled to keep his temper. 'I had another

girlfriend try and trap me into marriage.'

'I know — Amber.'

He scowled. 'How did you know about Amber?'

'Your proud mommy told my proud mummy.'

Thoughts of Amber still had the power to upset him. It took a certain kind of lowlife mentality to use a baby to try to make money. 'My point is,' he said curtly, 'I could have tied the knot, but I've never been tempted.'

Sherry's look was scathing. 'Who knows? When you hit seventy, you might marry a sweet young thing to push your wheelchair.'

Glenn smiled unpleasantly. 'By then the baby will be thirty-four.' Hell, two years younger than him and four years older than Sherry. They were talking about a real person.

'Of course — I forgot. You'll be able to get him or her to push your wheelchair instead.'

'Do you think you could stop behaving like an infant for a moment?'

Sherry was furious, with him for saying it, and with herself because it was true.

Ben checked through the window. Sherry was sitting on the side of the bed with her arms and legs crossed, angrily swinging one cross-trainer while Glenn stood in front of her with his hands in his pockets, presumably to keep from strangling her. There wasn't any blood or visible wounds and no broken objects littering the carpet, but it looked like they were in there for the long haul. Ben pulled out one of the wrought-iron chairs, sat down and propped his feet on the chair opposite.

Glenn was determined to make Sherry see things his way. 'I'll take care of the baby and bring it up. You won't have to do a thing.'

Sherry was equally determined not to. 'What? Just lie there and let you do all the work? I've heard that before and look where it got me.'

'That's another thing I need to talk to you—'

'How exactly do you propose to give birth? Build yourself a uterus and vagina?'

Of all the women he'd slept with, why did he have to knock up this one? 'Obviously, there are some things I *can't* do.'

'Which are exactly the things that I *don't want* to do. Can you sit down?' Sherry demanded. 'I'm getting a crick in my neck looking at you.'

Much more of this and she'd have more than a crick in her neck. Glenn grabbed the end of the chaise longue, dragged it across the carpet and sat down in front of her. 'Lots of women do it,' he began.

Her foot bounced in agitation. 'I'm not lots of women.'

Amen to that. God must have taken one look at her and headed straight back to the drawing board.

'I'll make sure you get lots of painkillers,' he promised.

Sherry regarded him incredulously. 'Being stoned is supposed to make it *attractive*?'

'It's a natural—'

'Don't say it, or I swear I will deck you!'

Glenn looked at the books on Sherry's nightstand for inspiration. One was some kind of police manual, and the other a book on pregnancy entitled *When Your Miracle Makes You Miserable*. He rubbed his bad knee absently. She had him stumped.

'What I don't understand is how I got pregnant. We used condoms.'

He paused mid-rub. 'Yeah, about that ...'

His uneasy tone alerted Sherry. 'What?' she asked sharply.

Glenn looked at her short, unvarnished nails. 'You remember you had long nails?'

Her eyes bored into him. 'Yes. What about them?'

'And how you helped me put on the first condom?'

Sherry's throat closed over. She stared mutely at Glenn.

'Well ... I think your nail caught on the rubber and ...' He trailed off.

The colour drained from her face. Her blue eyes blazed. 'You *knew* I might get pregnant?'

Glenn nodded reluctantly.

'But you didn't bother to *tell me*?'

He shook his head slowly.

Her voice rose. 'You mean I could have got the morning-after pill and wouldn't have got *pregnant*?'

Ben opened his eyes and looked through the glass in time to see Sherry's cross-trainer land in the middle of Glenn's chest and send him tumbling off the chaise longue and onto the carpet. He ran inside as Sherry jumped up and aimed another kick at Glenn that could have ruined his future chances of fatherhood. Fortunately, this time Glenn saw it coming and tucked up his knees and rolled aside.

Wild-eyed, Sherry stalked him. 'Do you realize what you've done to me? You've *trapped* me! Do you think I want to blow up like a beach ball and push *nine bloody pounds* out of *there*?' She landed a solid punch to

Glenn's shoulder as he got up and winced when she hit bone and muscle. It made her even angrier.

Ben got between them and took a whack in the back of the head that was meant for Glenn.

'Get out of the way!' Sherry yelled.

Glenn made the mistake of trying to reason with her. 'Sherry, stop it! You'll hurt yourself!'

Ben sighed.

'Hurt myself? *Hurt myself?*' she raged.

Ben grabbed Glenn's arm. 'Time to go, Glenn.'

'Sherry, calm down!' Glenn ordered.

She ran to the walk-in closet and reappeared with her arms full of shoes which she began firing at him one at a time, hitting both his eyes and narrowly missing his crotch when he hastily lifted his knee to deflect a tennis shoe.

'Sherry! Stop it!' he shouted.

She launched the other tennis shoe at his bad knee, and it glanced off his thigh. She was aiming for the place where she could do him the most damage — apart from his crotch, of course.

Ben shoved him towards the stairs. 'Move it!'

'Sherry!' Glenn roared.

'*Shut up and fucking move it!*' Ben yelled as an evening sandal with a six-inch heel whizzed past his ear and hit Glenn above one of his black eyes. They ran down the stairs with their arms wrapped around their heads, as shoes, boots and sandals rained down on them.

Sherry leaned over the balustrade on the landing, screaming: 'Instead of wasting your time making bloody commercials for sunglasses and screwing anything in a skirt, why don't you become a sperm donor? *Get Blitzed*

*by Glenn Brogan and spend nine months paying for it!
He'll even throw in a pair of sunglasses!'*

Nora was waiting when they bolted from the house.
'What's going on in there?' she cried. 'Should I call the
police?'

'Sherry *is* the police, Nora,' Ben said flatly.

Glenn stared at the house, and said in bewilderment,
'She aimed for my knee.'

'No, she didn't; if she'd aimed for your knee, she'd
have hit it.' Ben nudged Glenn down the driveway and
away from Nora's flapping ears.

'Do you think I should knock and see if she's alright?'
Nora called after them.

'Only if you want a stiletto heel in your eyeball,' Glenn
muttered.

'Leave her alone, Nora,' Ben warned.

'But—'

'Leave her alone, Nora!'

At the bottom of the drive, Ben inspected Glenn's
face. 'Can you see to drive?'

'I'll manage,' he said in a surly voice. 'Just tell me
where I can find the nearest motel.'

'What did you say to make her so mad?'

Glenn flushed and explained.

Ben looked stunned and then angry. 'You dickhead!'

'She's going to have an abortion.' His voice throbbed
with anguish. 'Why did she leave it so long?'

Ben sighed. What a mess. 'She didn't know.' He
explained Sherry's lack of symptoms.

Glenn looked at him oddly. 'You seem to know a lot
about pregnancy.'

He shrugged. 'I got some books out of the library.

Sherry won't do it, and one of us needed to know what's happening.'

Glenn thought about the book on Sherry's nightstand. 'How do I stop her?' he asked desperately. 'I told her I'd take the baby.'

Ben stared. 'Are you serious?'

'Yes!' Glenn was sick of people treating him like all he did was chase women and make commercials for sunglasses. It wasn't true. Or at least, not for the past couple of years.

'I don't think she'll go through with it.' 'Why?'

'Sherry takes her responsibilities seriously. She isn't the type to take the easy way out.' Ben raised a brow. 'Do you really mean it?'

'What? About taking the baby?'

He nodded.

'Yes!' Glenn snapped. 'I meant it — I *mean* it.'

Ben looked doubtful, and it occurred to Glenn that Sherry wasn't the only person he'd need to convince that he was serious. A baby. A Georgia. Full-time. Panic rose up and strangled him. Glenn swallowed and said hoarsely, more to himself than to Ben, 'I'll get a nanny.'

Ben didn't answer. He seemed to understand that Glenn was having one of those moments that one guy left another guy to deal with. 'You can't drive like this.' He nodded at the red late-model SUV parked in front of his truck. 'Get your stuff and throw it in the back of the truck. You'd better come home with me tonight.'

Chapter 8

Sherry retrieved her shoes and restored order to the racks in her wardrobe. Nora knocked and called out to ask if she was alright, but Sherry ignored her. The argument with Glenn had left her feeling drained and utterly furious. He'd known she might get pregnant but had deliberately not told her. If Glenn had planned to pay her back for insulting him with the money, then he'd pulled off a real doozy, but that didn't fit with the man Sherry had spent the night with. That man had been generous, funny and considerate, he'd put her pleasure ahead of his own, which was why she'd left the twenty dollars. If Glenn had been mean or vindictive, or useless in bed, he'd have been forgettable. She pressed the heels of her hands against her eyes as she remembered how she'd gone after him. She was no better than the men who lost their temper and beat their wives and kids.

Ben phoned to check that Sherry was OK. He agreed not to tell their parents that Glenn was in town but warned her it was only a matter of time before they found out from Lisa and Dan, or Molly. The two mothers had struck up a firm friendship and spoke to one another regularly.

'Glenn's not exactly easy to miss, Sherry,' Ben pointed out. 'Somebody is bound to recognize him.'

'I want him *gone*,' Sherry said.

'I wouldn't hold your breath. He's not going anywhere until you've decided how you're going to handle this.'

She closed her eyes and shook her head as she recalled the accusation in Glenn's eyes when she'd announced her intentions. 'I've got an appointment at the clinic early in the morning. I'm going to bed.'

Her bed had become her refuge — it was where she could escape into oblivion and didn't have to think about the baby, the future, or disappointing her family. But Glenn's arrival had ruined that, too, because, instead of falling asleep, Sherry lay there thinking about the afternoon she left Denver ...

She was finishing her packing when Dan appeared in the doorway of her bedroom. 'Almost done?'

He sounded so much like Glenn that for a minute Sherry thought it was him. She folded a shirt and put it in her suitcase. 'Pretty much. Why?'

'Lisa wants you.'

It was understood that Dan and Lisa's bedroom was a 'no-go' area, the one place where they got to spend time alone with Georgia and each other, so Sherry was surprised when Dan took her there. Lisa was sitting cross-legged in the centre of their wide bed, propped against pillows and with another tucked under her arm, and Georgia balanced on top of it wearing a nappy and pink bootees. The baby's dark head and one little fist were pressed against Lisa's breast as she fed. Lisa patted the bed with the side of her foot. 'Have a seat.'

Sherry sat down while Dan sprawled on the bed beside Lisa, with his head propped on one hand. He was wearing a disreputable pair of jeans and a faded T-shirt that was stretched out of shape, and his hair desperately needed a cut. Nobody would have guessed he was a highly respected paediatric surgeon who attracted patients from all over the country. Lisa said if she didn't check, Dan would leave for the hospital wearing odd socks and shoes and clothes that clashed.

Sherry curled her long legs beneath her. 'Are we hatching a plot against the mothers?'

Dan smiled wryly and reached out a long finger to stroke the soft, shiny tuft of hair on Georgia's head.

'No,' Lisa watched the baby suckle. 'It's the only way we can stop one of the grandmothers from snatching Georgie away.'

Sherry felt like she was intruding on a very private moment but was oddly touched. She'd kept her distance from Georgia, but this was her last chance to see her niece before she left. She braced a hand on the bed and leaned forward to take a cautious look at the baby.

Georgia's cheeks pumped slowly. She sighed, and her long feathery lashes fluttered on her soft cheeks like lace. Sherry was entranced. When had Georgie become so beautiful? The baby's lips parted, and Lisa's nipple popped from her mouth.

'She always looks like she should let out a good beer belch when she's finished,' Dan observed.

Georgia was asleep with her mouth open. Lisa lifted her daughter and kissed her on the forehead. 'You're too much of a lady to do that, aren't you, Georgia Brogan?'

'Doesn't get it from her mother.' Dan held up a small white pad and Lisa stretched out her arms and put the baby against Sherry's chest. 'Here.'

Sherry closed her arms cautiously around Georgia.
'Er ...'

Lisa took the pad from Dan and slipped it into her maternity bra. 'It's OK, Sher, she won't explode.'

'Maybe when she starts eating solids, but you're OK at the moment,' Dan said and changed the subject.

They talked about Sherry's work with the Family Violence Unit and Dan's at the hospital, and their plans to bring Georgia for a visit so that Brian and Ben could meet her. Dan and Lisa didn't seem concerned at how Sherry was holding their daughter. The baby's head nestled into the crook of Sherry's arm and her pink bootees rested on the palm of her hand. Sherry stopped listening to Lisa and Dan, stared at her niece — and felt her heart squeeze.

Lying in her bed, Sherry remembered. She stared into the darkness above her and willed the memory away, but she could still feel Georgia's warm, insubstantial body resting on her bare arm. The urge to clasp her belly overwhelmed her. Sherry drew up her knees, dug the heels of her hands into her eyes, and gritted her teeth. *'Go away.'* She stayed that way, trembling, until exhaustion overtook her. Her legs relaxed and her hands fell to her shoulders. She dreamed.

A man dressed all in white, with dark auburn hair and disapproving blue eyes, intruded. He clearly wasn't happy with Sherry and kept saying over and over, 'He needs you' in a cockney accent.

'*Who* needs me? Who are you talking about?' Sherry asked.

'You're a smart girl, Sherry — you know who I mean,' the man replied.

'No, I don't,' she protested. 'Who are you?'

'You know that, too.'

'I don't!' Sherry gasped and quavered. 'Omigod ... are you George the angel? The one Lisa talks about?'

George gave her a big, twinkly smile. 'That's right.'

'You can't be! You're not real!'

He returned to his original theme. 'Do the right thing, Sherry. He needs you, they both do.'

'Who needs me?' George couldn't mean Glenn; he must mean the baby. Was it a boy? 'Go away!' she cried. 'Leave me alone!'

Sherry woke up with her heart bouncing around inside her chest like a pinball. She sat up and looked around her bedroom, expecting to see George standing somewhere waiting to continue their argument but saw she was alone. She pushed the hair from her eyes and leaned her elbows on her raised knees. It was the middle of the night, her nightdress was damp with sweat, and she needed to pee. She visited the bathroom to attend to her most pressing need, and then filled the sink and splashed cold water on her face and neck. Her face in the mirror looked haggard and weary; there were bags under her eyes that she could have packed a week's grocery shopping in. Sherry sat on the side of the bath, buried her face in a towel and sobbed, '*Somebody help me. I don't know what to do ...*'

Glenn knew he wouldn't be able to sleep, and not just because he was jet-lagged. He kept thinking about the appointment Sherry had in the morning — and what he could do to stop her going through with the abortion. He'd made a complete hash of things. What if she went ahead with it just to get back at him?

'That's not Sherry's style,' Ben said. 'Why do you think she became a cop? She's got strong principles, she hates violence. She was upset that I hit you, and she'll be upset that she lost her temper and tried to hurt you.'

Glenn wasn't convinced. 'It didn't look that way to me.'

'You don't know her like I do. Sherry is tough — except when it comes to her family.'

And there was the crux of the problem. They didn't really know one another at all. He'd had relationships, most of them short-lived and superficial, with a lot of women, but he'd never had one with a pregnant woman. Glenn tried to find some answers in the pregnancy books that Ben had given him. Ben had been only too happy to hand them over. 'It doesn't seem right when it's your sister.'

Glenn went straight to the meaty stuff, colour photographs of births, and was in total agreement with Sherry, there was nothing natural about it. 'Have you seen these photos?' he asked Ben.

'Do you mean the action shots?'

'Yeah.'

'I skipped that whole chapter. I'm only interested in

blood if it's on the inside.'

Glenn closed the book. 'I asked her to marry me.'

Ben grimaced.

'I don't get it. I was trying to do the right thing, but you and Sherry act like I'm committing a cardinal sin. I got her pregnant; I should marry her.'

'Sherry isn't like most women. She means it when she says she doesn't want to get married or have kids.'

Glenn scowled and threw the book on a nearby table. 'Isn't her biological clock supposed to be ticking?'

Ben gave him a pitying look. 'Sherry's biological clock isn't ticking; it isn't even on snooze.'

He was cautiously supportive of Glenn, who seemed to have Sherry and the baby's best interests at heart, and, unlike most of the men she hooked up with, Glenn wasn't a wimp. Sherry usually led men around by the nose, and then wondered why they left and she didn't care. Ben opened a couple of beers and handed one over.

Glenn sat down and rested his elbows on his knees and the cold bottle against his forehead. 'How am I supposed to get to know her when she won't even talk to me?'

Ben sipped his beer and studied Glenn's despondent figure. He filled up the two-seater sofa like a giraffe perched on a deckchair. Ben remembered a kid in school who was almost as big as Glenn, and who was forever banging into furniture or bumping his head on the top of doorways. But there was nothing awkward or clumsy about Glenn: he moved with the confidence and grace of an athlete. Being so tall seemed to have given him an inbuilt radar system for low-hanging light fittings and doorways. He automatically dipped his head when he came through Ben's front door and trod a path around the pendulum light hanging inside the entrance. Ben's first loyalty was to his sister, but right now he didn't think Sherry was in the right frame of mind to make good decisions for herself or the baby. 'What do you need to know?' he asked cautiously.

A couple of hours ago Sherry's brother had wanted to rip his head off, now he was offering to help. Glenn decided that Ben must really love his sister. 'I'd settle for talking to her without getting a stiletto heel in my eye or nuts.'

'Can't help you with that one.' Ben put the bottle to his mouth, tipped back his head and took a long pull.

Glenn dragged his hands down his face and gazed at the ceiling in frustration. 'Tell me what makes her laugh, what she cares about. What was she like when she was little?'

When Ben was seven, he'd borrowed Sherry's brand-new blue bike with a white clip-on puncture kit and fluorescent rainbow decals, without permission. 'She really wanted that bike. To make sure she'd look after it, Mum and Dad made her save half the money and said they'd put in the other half. Sherry did jobs for the neighbours and earned the money in three months.'

Ben had ridden the bike over a hill and into a creek, where it had sunk. The bike was a wreck and so was Ben, because eleven-year-old Sherry had taken her revenge by feeding him the story that he wasn't really Ben Jackson but an alien child called Archibald and that his alien parents would be coming back to collect him on his eighth birthday. Lisa had been hoping to inherit the blue bike when Sherry outgrew it, and so corroborated the story. Ben had insisted that he knew he wasn't really an alien, but still spent the night of his eighth birthday sitting bug-eyed in his bed watching through the window for strange lights in the sky. Sherry and Lisa got into big trouble when their parents found out why.

Ben chuckled. 'She caved in and wrote on my birthday card that it wasn't true — that was how Mum and Dad found out — but I didn't believe her. She really loved that bike.'

But she'd wanted the bike and she didn't want the baby.

Glenn shared some of his own childhood memories. 'When Dan was eight, he got his first love-letter, from a girl called Deanna. I stuck it on the window of our den. It overlooked the school bus stop and just about every kid in the neighbourhood read the letter.'

'What did he do after he'd beaten you up?'

'He told me I was an amoeba. I was six and didn't know what that meant, and Dan explained it by saying if I took a bath I'd dissolve and disappear down the plughole when the water drained. I screamed the house down every night for weeks when Mom tried to make me take a bath. Dan got grounded for a month. I used to make candy runs for him on my bike.'

'You put family first; Sherry's the same,' Ben said. 'She's not against abortion, but you've given her an alternative. That's why I know she won't go through with it.'

Glenn prayed he was right. 'I do some work with underprivileged kids and their families — most professional athletes do. When you've been handed so much, it's only right that you give something back. Some of the kids I've met have been so badly screwed up by their parents that I sometimes thought it would've been kinder if they hadn't been born at all — but,' he shrugged a shoulder helplessly, 'it's different when it's yours.' Glenn stared at the green glass bottle. 'You said Sherry's eleven weeks pregnant. I read in a book that the baby is fully formed at twelve weeks. It can blink and squirms away if the mother's uterus is prodded.'

Glenn smiled when Ben snorted and asked, 'Can you see Sherry letting anybody poke her uterus?'

Ben gave him a tour of his unfinished house, including the garage where he kept his work truck and his pride and joy, a red Ducati 900SS Desmo, in a corner beside his collection of guitars and amp. Glenn remembered Ben's band had provided the music at Dan and Lisa's wedding. Ben was the lead singer and played guitar. The wedding guests had all enjoyed listening to him and the rest of the band, but Glenn had been struck by how unenthusiastic Ben seemed to be about Lisa and Dan's marriage. Later he'd discovered that Ben had reservations about Lisa's claim that she was his sister and was pissed off at her for putting a stop to his own wedding a few weeks earlier. They'd settled their differences since then.

'You still playing in the band?' Glenn asked.

'No, too busy working, but I'm OK about it. I come out here and play and write when I feel like it.'

'I never knew you were a motorbike buff.'

Ben stroked his hand across the seat of the Ducati. 'I've always wanted one of these. My first bike was a Honda 250 that I got when I was twenty. One day I'm going to take six months off and ride from Cape Reinga at the top of the North Island all the way down to Bluff at the bottom of the South.' It was a sweet dream.

Glenn understood. 'When you finish the house?'

'When I finish the house,' Ben agreed.

'How long have you been building it?'

'Two years.'

Glenn's brows rose. 'When were you planning to finish it?'

'About eighteen months ago.' Ben switched off the garage light and led the way to Glenn's bedroom. He pointed to a door opposite the bed. 'Bathroom's through there. The shower and toilet work, but don't use the bath — I haven't finished doing the plumbing.' He gestured to the curtainless window taking up most of one wall. 'I'll give Mum a call and ask her to arrange some curtains. In the meantime, get changed in the bathroom so you don't flash the neighbour. She's just moved in and she's old.'

Ben's house wasn't nearly as luxurious as Glenn's condo or his new place in Cherry Hills, but he felt at home because it was a bachelor pad. 'Thanks, Ben; I appreciate it.'

He nodded. 'Just do me a favour, will you, and try not to piss Sherry off. She's vulnerable.'

As he lay in bed squinting at the books through his swollen eyes, Glenn remembered how he'd wanted to see Sherry lose her cool. He'd certainly got his wish.

In the morning, his left eye was swollen shut but his right one was beginning to open. He could see well enough to walk a straight line but not enough to drive, and so asked Ben to take him to the clinic where Sherry had her appointment.

He refused. 'I'll go, you stay here.'

Glenn was furious. 'Like fuck I will! Would you sit by while your kid gets murdered?'

'If you go down there and start snarling shit like that, you'll only upset her. If I go down there, she'll be able to think straight and make the right choice.'

'I can't sit here and do nothing!' he protested.

'You don't have a choice.' Ben picked up the keys to his truck. 'I'll call you as soon as I know what's happening.'

Waiting was agony. Glenn roamed around the house, checking his BlackBerry every few minutes to see if Ben had left a message. He'd grabbed Ben's cellphone when he was in the shower and saved Sherry's number into his BlackBerry. Glenn kept on bringing up her number with the intention of sending her a text, then changing his mind when he thought about what Ben had said.

Dan phoned, but not Ben. The only new information Glenn could give him was that he'd asked Sherry to marry him and she'd turned him down and he had another black eye.

'Sherry?' Dan queried.

'No, Ben. Sherry tried to harpoon my eyeball with a stiletto heel.'

'Was that before or after you told her about the broken condom?'

'After. Her aim is lethal. I should tell the Cougars coach to dump McCosh and sign-up Sherry. She should be a shooting guard.' Glenn grumbled.

'What did you expect her to do? Say "Thanks, Glenn,

for getting me pregnant"?'

'I didn't expect her to turn into a female version of The Terminator.'

'You're forgetting something important; *I've* got the daughter who knows how to hand-wash woollens; *you've* got the daughter who knows how to change spark-plugs and fuses.'

Glenn wasn't in the mood for jokes. 'She's gone to get an abortion.'

'I know.'

'How did you know?' he cried hotly.

'Ben told Lisa,' Dan replied quietly. 'Lisa says she won't do it.'

Glenn's eyes felt gritty from worry and lack of sleep. He rubbed them and winced. 'Ben says the same thing, but what if she does, Dan? What if she does?'

'She won't,' he replied firmly.

'Sherry doesn't want to raise the baby, but I told her I would.'

'You?'

Dan's incredulous tone infuriated Glenn. He'd make a great father — everybody said so. 'Yes, me. Why is everybody so surprised? You said I'm great with Georgia.'

'You're great at buying her presents and pulling faces and making her laugh, but that's not the same as being a parent,' Dan said bluntly. 'Raising a child takes sacrifice and commitment.'

'You think I don't know about sacrifice and commitment? What do you think kept me at the top of my game for all those years?' Glenn demanded angrily.

'You can't compare that to bringing up a child. How

will you look after a baby?'

'I'll hire a nanny.'

'You haven't thought this through. Being a parent doesn't mean just organizing a nursery and hiring a nanny — your whole life is going to be turned upside-down. Georgia had a cold last week. She was awake crying three nights in a row. Lisa and I were dead on our feet from taking turns walking her. Do you really think you're ready for that?'

In a nutshell, no, but Glenn didn't feel he had a choice. When he'd imagined having children, he had pictured a wife who would be content to reap the benefits of being Mrs Glenn Brogan and be a stay-at-home mother, not a sharp-tongued cop who wore body armour and was intent on earning him a permanent spot in the Vienna Boys' Choir.

The next time his BlackBerry rang it was his agent, Fraser, who knew nothing about Sherry or even that Glenn was in New Zealand. Glenn had told Fraser he was spending a couple of weeks at his beach house in Malibu, although he knew he'd eventually have to come clean about his whereabouts and personal situation. Since his retirement, Fraser had become more of his business manager than a sports agent. He was used to dealing with professional athletes who screwed up their personal lives, but Glenn's transgressions had been largely minor, like disgruntled ex-girlfriends selling their stories to the tabloids, until the incident with Amber.

Glenn wasn't in the mood to talk to Fraser about endorsing a new range of sports apparel or looking at the latest designs for the next Bona Fide Blitz menswear line. The clothing range had come about when, frustrated by his inability to get a shirt in a colour and design he liked, Glenn had asked his current girlfriend, who was also a budding designer, to make him some shirts. People had started asking where he'd got them, and the Blitz shirt range was born. His relationship with Candace, the designer girlfriend, went south, but Glenn had asked her to stay on as head designer for Blitz shirts and sweetened the deal with shares in the business. Four years later Candace was still the head designer, married to the company's financial advisor, and had two kids. She'd added jackets, vests, jeans and formal wear to the range, and a significant chunk of the profits were donated to community projects and supporting small-business initiatives.

Despite his retirement, Glenn's star hadn't waned. The Blitz ads had generated a lot of interest, and Fraser regularly received enquiries from major companies interested in Glenn endorsing their products. Glenn turned down most of them.

'*Infinite* wants you on the cover of their January edition.'

Infinite was a magazine that combined fitness and fashion advice for men and women.

'It's only a couple of years since I did the last one,' Glenn replied indifferently.

'The theme is a big new year, which is why they want a big guy for the January issue.'

'Ask Chopper to do it. He's bigger than me.'

'Chopiak doesn't look as good in a tux as you do. That big forehead just isn't photogenic,' Fraser replied. 'They want to do a piece about how your life has changed since retirement and the success of the Bona Fide Blitz range. They also want to talk to some of the people who have started businesses thanks to seed money from the trust.'

'I'll think about it.'

'It's a shame you don't have kids,' Fraser continued. 'There's a real niche market for promoting sports equipment and exercise programmes that fathers can do with their kids.'

His comment was akin to a dentist shoving something sharp into a sore tooth. 'I'll think about it,' Glenn repeated flatly and ended the call.

He checked his messages, but there was still nothing from Ben. He found Sherry's number again and stared at it, his thumb hovering over the keypad. He couldn't sit around waiting to hear. He had to do something. Glenn tapped out a message and pressed send.

Sherry, please. I meant what I said. Glenn.

Sherry had already cancelled her appointment at the clinic, picked up a leaflet for antenatal classes, and was preparing to leave with Ben when she saw Glenn's message. Ben had told her that Glenn was staying at his place, and Sherry wasn't happy about it.

She stopped in the middle of the car park and stared at the message on her phone. 'Did you give Glenn my mobile number?'

'No.' Ben peered at her cell. 'Why?'

Sherry snapped it closed and stalked towards her car. 'He sent me a text. How did he get my number?'

He shrugged. 'Must've got it off my phone.'

'Just the kind of underhand thing I'd expect from him,' she fumed.

They stopped beside Sherry's black SUV.

'What did you expect him to do?' Ben said. 'Ask *you* for your number? In his shoes, I'd have done exactly the same thing. You should talk to him.'

'Whose side are you on?'

'The baby's. I'm not getting involved in your petty squabbles with Glenn.'

Sherry gaped. 'Petty squabbles!'

'You heard me.' Ben nodded at the leaflet in her hand. 'What's that?'

She shoved it impatiently in her handbag and flicked the locks on her car. 'Antenatal classes.' When Ben frowned, she jammed a hand on her hip and demanded, '*What?*'

'I'm no expert, but—'

'Really?' Sherry said cuttingly. 'I was beginning to think you'd developed ovaries.'

'If I do, I promise to let you borrow them on special occasions,' Ben replied. 'I didn't think you started those classes until you were about to hatch.'

Sherry grimaced — he made her sound like a battery hen. 'They're some kind of start-up classes.'

Ben still looked doubtful. 'Don't you think you should find a midwife first?' He knew her well, and guessed Sherry's priority was gathering information so she could dictate the best possible terms for herself when it came to the birth, which was why she was already looking at classes. 'This isn't like a police exam, taking a few classes won't make you an expert. You have to get booked with somebody — like joining a gym and getting a personal trainer.'

She produced the list of midwives Vicky had given her and thrust it at Ben. 'Here! *You* book the personal trainer.'

He tried to give it back. 'I can't. You need to choose somebody you like.'

'I don't need to like them. Just find me the one with the best track record for quick, painless births.' She shoved the list and the leaflet for the classes down the front of Ben's shirt. 'You might as well have this, too. This is the only class Vicky thought I'd be able to get a place in at short notice. The first one is next Monday so keep it free — you're my birth partner.' She climbed in the car and slammed the door.

Ben pulled the papers from his shirt. 'Like hell I am!' he yelled at her through the window. 'Ask Mum to be your birth partner! She'll jump at it!'

Her reply was muffled. 'Never in a million years — I've seen her in action. She thinks pointy heads and bitchy midwives are par for the course, whereas I know you'll be so freaked you'll question everything.'

'Ask a friend!'

Sherry shook her head stubbornly. Her best friends were Lisa and Ben.

He reached for the door handle but she snapped the locks. 'Sherry, I'm *not* going to be your birth partner! I hate the sight of blood!'

'Wear dark glasses and bring a book.'

'I'm *not* doing it.'

'How about I sweeten the deal?' she offered. 'I'll let you fix the pantry door in my kitchen.'

The sticky pantry door was an ongoing family joke.

Ben had built Sherry's house, Nora's and the one next-door, and took it personally that the pantry door had dropped and begun catching on the kitchen lino. There was a knack to opening the door which Sherry and the rest of family had mastered, and she constantly thwarted Ben's plans to fix it just to annoy him. It was a rare thorn in Ben's Teflon-coated skin.

'You can stick the pantry door up your—'

'You're missing the point, Ben, I want the door unstuck.' Sherry slipped on sunglasses and started the car. 'I can't hang around chatting; I've got to get to work.'

Ben stepped back hastily as she reversed out of the space and drove away. He looked at the black lettering at the top of the leaflet for the antenatal classes: *Getting To Know Your Body — A Foundation Class For Natural Childbirth*. He had a feeling Sherry had missed the 'natural' part.

'She's not having an abortion?'

'No.'

Glenn dragged his palms down his face and sighed heavily. 'Thank God.'

'I wouldn't get too comfy,' Ben advised. 'She's treating pregnancy like it's one of her police exams.' He slid a crumpled leaflet and sheet of paper across the kitchen counter. 'She's got herself signed up for antenatal classes, and the race is on to find the midwife with the highest percentage of short, painless births.'

It sounded like a plan to Glenn. 'Lisa and Dan went to prenatal classes. It'll be the same thing.'

Ben snorted. 'You're missing the point, Glenn. I'm betting Sherry didn't read the leaflet properly and doesn't realize she's signed herself up for *natural* childbirth classes. Does fast and painless sound like natural to you?'

Glenn studied the leaflet. 'She gave me the impression that if she has to do it at all, she wants to be either stoned or shit-faced.'

'It gets worse,' Ben grumbled. 'She wants me to be her birth coach.'

In Glenn's book, fathers out-ranked uncles, but he was about as keen to be at the birth as Ben or Sherry.

'I'm going to work,' Ben said. 'You start calling the names on the list.'

Glenn threw him a panicked look. 'What do I say?'

'How would I know? Read the books. Give them marks out of ten.'

Chapter 9

S herry requested a private meeting with Dave Pomana and told him she was pregnant.

'Thought you might be.' He hesitated. Congratulations?'

Her cheeks glowed. 'It's due in May. I'll stay operational for as long as I can.'

'You'll stay operational until you can't get into your SRBA vest. After that, you'll be driving a desk.'

Sherry's heart sank at the thought of spending the last few months chained to a desk. 'I'm coming back to work full-time after the birth.'

'OK.'

She could tell that Dave didn't believe her. 'I am,' she insisted. 'The father is going to raise the baby.'

'Who? Stuart?' He'd met Sherry's boyfriend at a retirement party for a fellow officer and been as curious as everybody else to see the kind of man she dated. She had lots of friends, but never spoke about a particular man and didn't date police officers. Stuart Sherborne had struck Dave as a handsome wimp.

'He's not the father,' Sherry said stiffly.

'I see.'

Dave had four children and three grandchildren. He was an old hand at pregnancy and births, and suspected Sherry didn't have a clue what she was talking about. She was the last person he'd have expected to get knocked-up and knew her colleagues would be shocked when they

137

heard the news. Sherry was smart, focused and ambitious. She was meticulous about her work and a good investigator, and whilst her somewhat abrupt, unsmiling manner was very effective with perpetrators, it didn't go down so well with victims. Dave had taken a gamble giving Sherry a caseload of families with a history of family violence and dysfunction. Her tough no-nonsense attitude made the women feel safe and the men wary, but the women wouldn't unload to Sherry the way they would to some of her colleagues. She was trying to loosen up, but she wasn't a person who confided in others.

'You need to see the DSS to talk about when you plan to go on maternity leave,' Dave said.

Sherry blinked. *Maternity leave*? She was going to have to take *maternity leave*?

'Keep me posted, OK?' He changed the subject. 'Stacey's partner, Vance, has been in asking for you. He's not happy because Stacey isn't answering his calls.'

Sherry was grateful for the distraction. She'd far rather be dealing with other people's problems than her own. 'She's not?'

'She left a couple of messages while you were away. She wants to see you.'

'She's still at the Women's Refuge?'

'For now.'

Sherry was pleased that Stacey hadn't caved in and returned home.

'Better go and see her,' Dave advised.

Sherry met Stacey at the community centre where Stacey had been collected by Misty the day she went to the refuge. Misty was the refuge manager. She drove Stacey and her children to the centre and met Sherry in reception when she arrived. Misty was tall with long, frizzy red hair. Sherry didn't know how old she was; she could have been anywhere between forty and sixty. Misty knew all about bruises and black eyes, about the headaches and fuzziness that came from having your head slammed against the wall or floor. She knew about inventing stories to cover up how you got the worst injuries, which the doctors and nurses didn't believe anyway, and that got you another hiding for being slow or stupid and making him lose his temper in the first place.

Sherry adjusted one of the Velcro straps on her SRBA vest to relieve the pressure on her breasts, and listened while Misty gave her an update on what was happening with Stacey. 'Vance has been hassling her. I took her phone off her again. Where have you been?'

'I was ... sick.'

Misty stared at Sherry; there was something different about her. She neither liked nor disliked Detective Constable Jackson. But Sherry was prepared to dig for evidence in the cases where the women were too scared or too jaded to speak up, and in Misty's book that got a big tick of approval. She just wished Sherry would lighten up and share a little more of herself instead of hiding behind her uniform.

'Is something wrong?' Sherry asked frostily when Misty continued to eyeball her.

'You look different.'

'I changed to a different brand of shampoo.'

Misty raised a brow. *Interesting*. She pulled a white envelope from her bag and handed it to Sherry. 'Did you get one of these?'

Sherry opened the envelope and pulled out a wedding invitation. 'Marjorie is getting *married*?'

Misty allowed herself a smile. 'Let's hope this time round she does a better job of choosing a husband.'

Marjorie was the first case of so-called 'white collar' domestic violence Sherry had encountered in her police career. Marjorie's ex-husband, Jonathan, was a well-respected businessman who owned a luxury-car dealership. They lived with their two children in a beautiful home overlooking a lake, drove leased BMWs that were upgraded every year, and sent the kids to private schools and weekly music and tennis lessons. Marjorie wore beautiful clothes and expensive jewellery, and the family went on at least two holidays a year. Majorie's job was to oversee the running of the house and take care of the family. She was always there for Jonathan and her children. She was also there for Jonathan to beat up whenever something went wrong or upset him.

Jonathan was careful to hit Marjorie in places where the bruises didn't show. He never touched her face, and in the warmer months avoided hitting her arms and legs.

Marjorie dreaded warm weather, because then Jonathan confined his punches to her torso and pelvis, which was worse.

Sherry met Marjorie when she was doing routine roadside checks for drink-driving in the lead-up to Christmas; she stopped Marjorie in her BMW. The breathalyser test was negative, but Marjorie's speech was slurred and her eyes glazed. Sherry asked her to come to the mobile unit for a blood test. Marjorie wasn't able to get out of the car, because the night before Jonathan had broken one of the vertebrae in her back. Sherry accompanied her to the hospital and met Misty for the first time when Marjorie was discharged. She had nowhere else to go but the Women's Refuge.

Her friends were all married to Jonathan's business associates, and she was an only child and her parents were elderly and frail. The only money Marjorie had was what her husband gave her. She blamed herself for her children not speaking to her, and for worrying her parents.

'I shouldn't have said anything, I should have been stronger. If I'd kept quiet—'

'You'd have been dead,' Sherry said flatly. 'Your kids definitely wouldn't have been able to talk to you then.' She couldn't understand why Marjorie was prepared to take the blame for her husband's brutish behaviour, or why she felt like she'd somehow failed.

'When you've got holes in the walls and floors and no food in the cupboards, coming to the shelter is a step-up,' Misty said. 'But when you've got a house on the lake, a leased BMW, and the kids in piano and tennis lessons, making the decision to come to the refuge isn't so easy.'

Marjorie's children wouldn't visit or talk to her on the phone. Jonathan denied that he was responsible for his wife's injuries, and even confided in a phone call to Misty that he thought she might be depressed and that he'd urged her to see a psychiatrist.

'Guys like him put the hairs up on the back of my neck,' Misty said.

Sherry kept in touch with Marjorie and convinced her to press charges. Jonathan had been charged with injuring with intent, which carried a maximum penalty of five years' imprisonment, but, because he lacked any previous record and his lawyer had eventually convinced him to plead guilty, he'd got only three years and was out in two-and-a-half. While he was in prison Marjorie moved back to the house on the lake and her children.

Misty watched Sherry jot down the name of Marjorie's husband- to-be. 'Going to check him out?'

'I might.'

'What will you do if you find out that Robert what's-his-name is no good?'

'Probably show up at the wedding and stop the ceremony,' Sherry replied. 'It won't be the first time somebody in my family has done it.'

It was the most personal information Misty had ever got from her. She decided maybe she liked DC Jackson more than she disliked her. 'Keep an eye out for an invitation. I'm sure Marjorie will want you to be there.'

'That'd be nice.' Sherry pocketed the paper. 'Where's Stacey?'

'She took the kids to the gymnasium to play while she waited for you.'

Stacey was perched on the bleachers at the side of the basketball court with her little girl, Nikita, playing at her feet while her older children threw a basketball around on the court. She was desperate for a cigarette. A look of relief flooded her face when she saw Sherry coming towards her.

Sherry noticed that Stacey was wearing a cardigan and clutched it tightly around her neck. It was a warm day — there was no reason for her to be wearing a sweater. She hadn't seen Stacey since Misty had collected her and the children and taken them to the refuge. Stan, the oldest boy, was eleven, big for his age and, like his mother, wore faint bruises on his face from Vance's fists. He was standing at the free-throw line, shooting at the basket with a look of deep concentration on his face and nailing more than he missed.

Eight-year-old Lianna and seven-year-old Storm were taking turns to dribble a second basketball down the court and fling it at the hoop. They lacked their older brother's expertise and looked bored. Nikita, the baby of the family, was three; she sat beside her mother playing with a plastic dump truck.

The children all looked up as Sherry came in; they knew her from her visits to their house. Lianna, Storm and Nikita resented being in the refuge; it had been fun to start with because there were lots of other kids to play with, but the crammed conditions and lack of freedom was beginning to pall. Stan was the only one who didn't blame Sherry and their mother for their move to the refuge. Lianna and Storm dropped the ball and came

over to join
Sherry, Stacey and Nikita.

'Are you going to take us home?' Storm asked.

'That's not a good idea at the moment, Storm,' Sherry replied.

Nikita took her fingers out of her mouth. 'Where's Daddy?'

Sherry noticed she was wearing nappies and guessed the move to the refuge had started her wetting again. She knew Stacey couldn't afford the nappies. 'I don't know, Nikita.'

Nikita threw the plastic truck onto the court. Stacey didn't seem to notice.

'I want to go home!' Lianna yelled at her mother. 'Why couldn't you just stand there and let him yell at you like you always did?'

Stacey didn't answer. She was thirty-three but looked closer to fifty. Her hair was thin on top and at the back because clumps of it had been pulled out, and she had deep lines around her lips from chain-smoking. If Vance didn't get her, lung cancer probably would. The bruises on Stan's face and the basketball he was holding reminded Sherry of Glenn. She didn't want to think of him. 'Can we go somewhere and talk, Stacey?' she asked.

They moved outside and sat in the sun at a wooden table and bench on a grassy area beside the centre. Stacey lit a cigarette. Sherry watched smoke curl from the end and thought about the baby. It was the first time she'd had to consider it, and she felt crushed by the weight of responsibility. Suddenly everywhere she looked Sherry saw a threat. *I'll go mad with worry,* she thought.

'What's the matter?' Stacey continued to hold the edges of her cardigan closed at her throat.

Sherry thought her voice sounded different. 'Nothing.' She edged away from Stacey and the smoke. 'Are you getting a cold?'

Stacey shook her head nervously. 'Tell me what's been happening.'

The first night that Stacey and the kids were at the refuge Vance had called her mobile repeatedly and tried to talk her into coming home. When Stacey refused, he started sending threatening texts, and that was when Misty had taken the phone away and contacted the Family Violence Unit.

Stacey looked at Sherry accusingly. 'Where were you?'

'I was ...' Sherry stopped. She wasn't sick, she was pregnant. 'I found out I'm pregnant.'

Stacey's cigarette hung in midair. She looked as shocked as if Sherry had just announced she'd found out she was a man. 'Do you wanna be?' she asked.

It went against Sherry's professional instincts to discuss her personal life, but she felt she owed Stacey an honest answer. 'No.'

'It was a mistake?'

'Yes,' Sherry said stiffly.

Stacey stubbed her cigarette out on the table and tossed it on the grass while she tried to get her head around the notion of Officer Jackson making *any* mistakes, let alone that one — she always looked so perfect, was always so in control. Stacey respected Sherry, but she'd never been able to warm to her. Hearing her admit she was less than perfect made her seem more human.

'People always thought Stan was a mistake, but he wasn't, Vance and me wanted to get pregnant.' Stacey watched the wisp of smoke rising from the butt on the grass and toyed with the cardigan at her throat. 'The other three were all accidents, but it doesn't make me love them any less, or Stan any more.'

Sherry's hormones ganged up on her. Tears pricked her eyes. Stacey stared at her. 'Are you going to cry?'

Sherry blinked furiously. 'I wasn't planning on it. It just keeps on happening.'

'Yeah.' Stacey let go of the cardigan and reached for her cigarettes. She opened the packet, looked at Sherry and closed it again. 'Is the guy still around?'

'Yes.'

'Are you gonna marry him?'

'No.'

'Why not? No good?'

Sherry was only half-listening; her attention was on Stacey's neck. 'Do you mean does he hit me?'

She nodded and shrugged at the same time.

'No.'

Stacey toyed with the cigarette packet. 'Sometimes they change when the babies come.' The matter-of-fact way she said it made it even sadder.

'Stacey?'

'Yeah?'

'How did you get those marks on your neck?'

Stacey had arranged to meet Vance at a park away

from the refuge. 'Just to talk,' she said. 'He wanted me to meet him at the house, but I knew not to do that. I thought I'd be safe at the park in daylight.' Her hands started shaking so badly she couldn't light her cigarette.

Sherry took the match and held it for her. 'What happened?'

She sucked on the cigarette like an asthmatic on an inhaler. 'He got really angry when I said I didn't want to come home and he ...' her voice wavered and she gestured to her neck, '... did this.' The only reason Vance had stopped was because somebody had come by walking their dog — that was how Stacey got away.

Bruising from strangulation had a lag time of twenty-four to forty-eight hours before it appeared, which was why it was so important to follow up with photographic evidence within a day or so after the incident. In Stacey's case, days had passed but the bruising was still visible. There were no telltale red spots in her eyes, she wasn't drooling, coughing or having difficulty swallowing: the only sign beside the bruises was her husky voice. Stacey was an expert at hiding her injuries; she'd even managed to fool Misty. Sherry felt like she'd failed her by not being around when the attack happened. She explained that she needed to take Stacey to a doctor, get a statement from her, and take photos of her neck.

'Don't arrest him. I don't want you to arrest him,' Stacey pleaded.

'It's not up to you, Stacey. It's a police decision to prosecute. Vance tried to kill you.'

That was another thing she'd struggled with — that the women were often reluctant to testify against the men who beat them. It was one of the reasons the

Problem Solving Team had been created: to get the men to go to anger management courses and the women counselling or to help them move out. In Sherry's experience, they only left when it became too dangerous for them or their kids to stay. Some didn't leave in time and ended up in hospital or dead.

'Has Vance done this before?' Sherry asked.

'No, this is the first time.' When Sherry looked sceptical, Stacey insisted, 'It's true.'

'What made you decide to leave? Was it really because Vance hit Stan?'

Stacey finished her cigarette and ground the butt out on the table again. 'I wasn't happy about that,' she said in a major understatement. 'Stan got hit because he stood up to Vance. He's a big boy; pretty soon he'll be too big for Vance to hit and not get walloped back, and Vance knows that. No, it's not Stan I'm worried about.'

'Why then?' Sherry probed. 'What was different this time? Did he rape you?'

'No.' Stacey reached for another cigarette, remembered Sherry was pregnant and dropped the packet on the table. She ran her thumb back and forth across the tip of one of her nails nervously. 'It was Lianna.'

Sherry steeled herself for what was coming.

'Did you hear her? When she said I should have stood there and let Vance yell at me like I usually did?'

She nodded.

'That's when I knew I had to do something.'

Chapter 10

The hunt for a midwife wasn't going well. Most were booked up and not taking on any more clients, and those that weren't took offence at the list of questions Glenn had made up with help from Ben and the pregnancy books.

'Pregnancy and birth isn't a competition, each woman's experience is different.'

'I appreciate that,' Glenn said. 'But how many of the women you've looked after have had a prolonged labour? And what are your feelings about giving pain relief? Are you for it? Or against it?'

'Is this a joke?'

'No, I'm very serious.'

'What do you want? Marks out of ten?' the midwife asked tartly.

Frankly, yes. It'd make the process a damned sight easier.

'I don't know how you arrange these things in America, Mr Brogan, but we do things differently in New Zealand. I suggest you try someone else,' the midwife said coolly. 'I'm all booked up.'

Sherry was making things worse by being as unhelpful as possible. Apart from the tiredness, she felt well and she had Vicky and her doctor to call on until Glenn found a midwife. The more he tried to enlist her help, the more Sherry dug her toes in.

'Why don't you set up face-to-face meetings at an

expensive restaurant?' she suggested. 'Once they see how gorgeous and loaded you are, they'll be begging to deliver your kid. You could throw in a pair of sunglasses to sweeten the deal.'

'Do you have to be such a bitch about this?' Glenn asked.

'Yes, I do!' Sherry snapped. 'If you'd picked up the phone and called me, I wouldn't be bloody pregnant!'

He vented his frustration to Ben. 'Sherry should be doing this, not me. I've upset every woman I've spoken to.'

'You'd better do something about that,' Ben replied, 'because Sherry and you are going to have to pay Mum and Dad a visit.'

Glenn had forgotten all about Brian and Jill. 'They know I'm the father?'

'I might have given them a hint.'

'How did they take it?' he asked uneasily.

'Hard to say, their mouths were still hanging open when I left. Have you spoken to your parents?'

Glenn had forgotten about them, too. He broke the news to them in a three-way call; Kell listened in on the bedroom extension while Molly used the phone in the kitchen.

'I never even knew you were seeing each other,' Molly said faintly.

'We weren't,' he said. 'We aren't.'

'What does that mean? You're having a baby!'

'Yes, Mom, I know. That's why I'm here in New Zealand.'

'Do Dan and Lisa know?'

'Of course they know, Molly,' Kell interrupted drily.

She gasped. 'Oh no! What about Jill and Brian? Do they know?'

'Yes. The baby is due in May.' Glenn waited for the six-million-dollar question.

'Are you getting married?' his mother asked.

'No.'

'Why not?' she demanded. 'You did ask Sherry, didn't you?'

'Molly,' Kell said sharply, 'that's none of our business.'

'I asked her, but she said no.' It hurt Glenn's pride to admit it, but he was secretly relieved — being shackled to Queen Sherry would have taken years off his life.

Molly was indignant. How dare Sherry Jackson turn down her son? He was handsome and smart and rich. 'Does she think she's too good for you?'

No, she thinks I'm an emotional lightweight.

Because he felt so guilty, Glenn wouldn't accept any criticism of Sherry. 'Back off, Mom. Sherry's got a right to be angry, it was me who messed up, not her.' He imagined his father's disappointment, and his straight-laced mother processing the new information and blushing.

Kell sighed. 'I knew that game of golf was a bad idea.'

'Is Sherry going to let you keep in touch with the baby?' Molly asked anxiously. 'She will let us see it, won't she?'

Glenn was relieved he had something positive to tell them. 'The baby is going to live with me; you'll get to see it all you want.' The ensuing silence reminded him eerily of his conversation with Dan. 'Mom? Dad? Are you still there?'

'*You're* going to bring up the baby?' his mother said cautiously.

'Yes. I'm in a much better position to take care of a child than Sherry is. She'd have to give up her career.'

Silence.

His father asked, 'Glenn, have you really thought this through?'

It rankled that even his parents had doubts about his ability to take care of his own child. 'I'm not some irresponsible, feckless bum,' Glenn said curtly. 'I'll make sure that it has the best of everything.'

'We know that,' Molly interjected quickly. 'It's just ...'

'What?'

'Ever since you retired, you've been feckless and irresponsible,' Kell said bluntly.

If Glenn was feeling hurt by his family's doubts about his ability to raise a child, Sherry was getting similar treatment from hers. Denver was nineteen hours behind Auckland, but Lisa didn't let that stop her from calling at one in the morning to voice her concerns about Sherry giving Glenn custody of the baby. Lisa knew that away from the public eye — and when he wasn't around Sherry — he was a different person to the man seen on the basketball court or portrayed by the media. Glenn had a strong sense of family, and Lisa was sure he'd put the baby before anything else, including women in string bikinis. It was Sherry's conviction that he would make a much better parent than she would that worried Lisa. She was certain that Sherry was making a mistake that she would regret for the rest of her life.

Sherry's bed was still her best friend. She was no longer a night owl who existed on very little sleep. If she wasn't on a two-to-ten shift, she was in bed by nine o'clock and didn't stir even when Otto snuck in to join her. She'd started having weird dreams, which she attributed to broken sleep because she had to keep getting up in the night to pee. When Lisa called, Sherry was sitting in an aeroplane watching Glenn's sperm line up and jump out. The sperm in charge was marching up and down yelling encouragement, but stopped when he noticed Sherry hiding in the corner.

'How did you get in here?' he demanded. 'You're supposed to be waiting in a fallopian tube.'

Sherry looked down and saw that she was a big white egg. 'I got separated from the other eggs,' she said nervously. 'Don't mind me, I'll leave.' She tried to get up, but her big, round, white body bumped against the side of the plane and she fell onto her back.

The head sperm shouted to the others, 'It's an ovum, boys! Come and get her!'

Sherry screamed and kicked as the sperm skydivers put down their heads and rushed her.

The sound of the phone ringing and Otto's indignant yowl at being booted in the bum woke her. She rolled over and groped for the phone. 'Wha— wha— what?' she panted.

'Sherry?' Lisa said anxiously. 'Are you OK?'

She shoved her hair off her sweaty forehead; her eyes darted around the darkened room. 'Sperm!' she croaked. '*Lots* of them! They had his face!'

'Ahhhh. You're having the weird dreams.'

Sherry licked her lips and babbled. 'I was in a plane. There were skydiving sperm with Glenn's face. I was an egg and they attacked me! What's wrong with me? I *never* remember my dreams!'

'I dreamed about tadpoles when I found out I was pregnant with Georgia. Dan was offended, said his sperm were much better-looking than tadpoles.'

Sherry flopped against the pillows. 'They probably are.'

When Lisa had first met Dan and was in denial about her feelings for him, Sherry tried to annoy her by making pointed comments about how attractive the big American surgeon was and what she'd like to do to him.

Lisa neatly turned the tables on her. 'I'm sure Glenn's are even prettier, but that isn't what I called about.'

'No?' Sherry squinted at the digital clock. 'What do you need to talk about at one o'clock in the morning, Lisa?' She'd avoided speaking to Lisa since the identity of the baby's father had come out. She switched on the lamp and hauled herself up the pillows. 'I guess you were shocked when you heard the news.'

'Which piece of news do you mean? That my sister spent the night in a motel with my brother-in-law and got pregnant? Or that my husband saw her sneaking out of the motel the next morning with her knickers in her hand and didn't tell me?'

'I did not have my knickers in my hand!'

'I left messages on your answering machine, why didn't you call me back?'

Because I've turned chicken.

'I've been flat-out at work and didn't have time to answer any of my messages.' Including the ones left by

Stuart asking if they could try again.

'I sent texts and you didn't answer them either.'

Ditto for Stuart.

'You've been avoiding me,' Lisa accused. 'I thought I'd catch you before you went to bed.'

'Since my egg got head-butted by Brogan's sperm, I'm tucked up by nine unless I'm on an afternoon shift.' Sherry watched Otto put his paws on the edge of the mattress and check the bedcovers for a likely spot to resume his nap. 'Go away, you damned cat,' she snarled. Otto hissed back.

'Otto, the one-eyed cat? I thought you hated him?' Lisa asked.

'I do. I don't know how he gets in, but he's there on the end of the bed every morning when I wake up. I think I kicked him when I was dreaming, so maybe he'll think twice about sneaking in uninvited.'

'Glenn told Dan that he's going to have custody of the baby when it's born.'

Sherry traced a finger around the tulip pattern on her white bedcover. 'That's right. We haven't discussed the details yet but—'

'How can you hand your baby over, Sherry?'

'Why not?' she said defensively. 'Glenn's got all the time in the world to devote to being a parent, whereas I'll have to either give up my job and stay at home to look after the baby, which I'll be terrible at and resent, or try to juggle work and shifts and study, which I know will be a disaster because I've watched other cops try to do it.'

'What if you change your mind and regret it later?'

Guilt dug sharp little talons into Sherry's conscience. 'I'll regret it more if I try and force myself into a role I'm not cut out for. Not everybody is like you, Lisa. I'm too selfish to be a mother.'

No, Lisa thought, *you're too scared.* 'Glenn's lifestyle doesn't exactly lend itself to parenthood.'

'He knows he'll have to make changes.' Surely, he did? 'Mmmm ...'

'When I was in Denver, you kept telling me what a great guy Glenn was and that he was just misunderstood. Why have you changed your mind?'

'I haven't changed my mind. I think Glenn's a very generous, very honourable man.'

Sherry snorted — *except when it comes to women.* But that didn't matter; all she cared about was how Glenn would treat a child and if he was capable of making a lifetime commitment to it. 'Do you trust him with Georgia?'

'Of course I do, he's great with her,' Lisa replied. 'Georgie loves Glenn; she just about wriggles out of our arms to get to him whenever she sees him.'

'And you'd trust him with your niece or nephew?'

Sherry was missing the point. Lisa wanted her to understand what she was giving up. She sent Glenn a silent apology and asked, 'What if he sleeps with the nanny?'

'What nanny?'

'The one he'll have to hire to take care of the baby when he's away on business.'

Sherry hadn't really thought about how Glenn would take care of a baby. She'd had a vague picture of the baby living in Denver, with Lisa and Dan and Molly and Kell all being around to help, but now she realized that this was wishful thinking. Lisa had Georgia to look after, Dan was at the hospital, and Molly and Kell lived in Boulder. Sherry tried to picture some faceless stranger left to take care of a helpless infant, and felt invisible fingers tiptoe up her spine. 'But you said he's honourable and he'll be a wonderful father,' she said weakly.

'I still do, but I also think if you gave yourself a chance, you'd make a great mother,' Lisa insisted. 'All I'm saying is make sure that you think this through properly and really talk about it before you make a decision. It's hard enough being a parent when there're two of you, but even harder when you're on your own — even if you have got time and money. *Talk to Glenn.*'

Glenn thought his family's reaction to his plan to become a solo parent was unwarranted. The physical and mental demands of playing in the NBA and making the starting line-up each week required discipline and commitment; it wasn't a game for wimps or lightweights. He knew he hadn't exactly been a model citizen in the past couple of years — since he'd retired, he'd lacked focus — but Glenn understood that bringing up a child alone would require some major changes to his lifestyle. Would he have chosen to become a father at this point in his life? No: whenever he'd imagined having children, he'd pictured having a wife alongside him who would be responsible for the day-to-day stuff while he went about the business of bringing in the money. But Sherry wasn't cut out to be anybody's stay-at-home wife, so he'd just have to get on with it and do the best he could for the baby, which included convincing its grandparents that he was the right person to raise it.

Sherry was supposed to be working a two-to-ten shift, so Glenn planned to visit her the following morning, determined that she was going to talk to him whether she felt like it or not. They needed to talk before they went to see her parents, plus at some point there was the delicate subject of getting their lawyers to draw up custody and access arrangements. Glenn didn't want any nasty surprises.

'Are police officers in New Zealand armed?' he asked Ben before he left for Sherry's.

Ben shook his head. 'Sherry wouldn't shoot you — too messy and impulsive. She'd go for something far more clever and stylish, like slow poison.'

'Thanks for that,' Glenn said drily. 'It's very reassuring.' 'Don't mention it.'

Sherry was out when Glenn got to her place; there was only Otto waiting by the door. The cat hissed when he saw Glenn.

'Keep it up, cat, and you'll wake up one morning as a coonskin cap,' Glenn promised.

Nora opened her front door and lumbered out, wearing a black visor decorated with *Nora Ditchburn For Prime Minister* in pink neon letters, navy-blue three-quarter-length slacks, bright yellow ankle socks, and pink sneakers. Glenn saw that his initial impression was right: Nora's legs were like tree trunks.

'You looking for Sherry?' she asked.

As he crossed the strip of grass that separated

Sherry's property from Nora's, he slipped off his sunglasses and hooked them in the pocket of his lilac-and-purple Bona Fide Blitz shirt. It was a beautiful, sunny spring day with a light wind, the kind of day that should be spent on a golf course. Glenn rested a foot on the bottom step and looked up at Nora. 'I thought Sherry was on a two-to-ten today.'

'She is.'

He didn't bother asking how Nora knew.

She seemed keen to boast about her insider knowledge. 'She got an invitation to a wedding. I know because I brought in her mail.'

Glenn hoped the bride and groom got a better response than he had when he'd asked Sherry to a wedding.

'Sherry's playing golf.'

That got his attention. 'What?'

'She got bitten by the bug in Colorado. She's been playing ever since she got back.'

Glenn contemplated the foot he had propped on the step. *I'll be damned*, he thought. It occurred to him that Sherry had probably asked God to do just that several times since he'd arrived.

'She's playing with some girlfriends,' Nora continued in a disgruntled tone. 'I tell her all the best courses, but she never asks me to play.'

It was unlikely Sherry would be asking him along, either. Glenn slipped his hands into the pockets of his jeans. 'I think you know why, Nora.'

'I'm head of the Neighbourhood Watch,' she said defensively.

Her talents were wasted: she should send her resume

to the New Zealand Secret Service — putting her on the payroll would instantly double national security.

Nora checked her watch; it was a man's one with a thick black leather strap. 'She won't be back for another hour-and-a-half,' she started to say, when the sound of a car coming up the driveway made her turn in surprise. 'Oh, that sounds like Sherry now. She's early.'

Annemarie Nicklin worked alongside Sherry in the Family Violence Unit, and Mary Latoa was a detective in the CIB. After Ben and Lisa, they were Sherry's closest friends, but they'd been as shocked as everybody else at the police station when they heard that Sherry was pregnant. When a colleague had asked Annemarie who was the father of Sherry's baby, she'd replied, 'I have no idea — and even if I did, I wouldn't tell you.' But that didn't mean Annemarie didn't want to know. She thought the best chance of her or Mary winkling any information out of Sherry was during their weekly game of golf.

They weren't scratch golfers — they'd all taken up the game in the past couple of months. Mary was Samoan. She had big brown eyes, wavy dark-brown hair and, in her opinion, too many curves following the birth of her son a year ago. Her husband disagreed and couldn't understand why his wife was always on a diet. Mary had taken up golf because she thought the exercise would help her lose weight.

Annemarie was nearly as tall as Sherry, and a fitness fanatic. She kept her blonde hair short, had a year-round tan, and a toned, muscular body from hours spent cycling, golfing, running and whatever else she managed to fit in when she wasn't working. When Annemarie's ex-husband was asked if there was anybody else involved in the break-up of their marriage, he replied, her racing bike, golf clubs and running shoes.

Sherry had got hooked on golf at Fossil Trace, and harboured fantasies of one day beating Glenn Brogan and rubbing his nose in it. She was the best of the three players, but today was having one of her worst-ever rounds. She'd outgrown the pants she usually wore for golf and was wearing a pair of white jeans with the zipper undone and a safety pin holding the waistband together. She had to take two unscheduled trips into the trees, once to pee and the second time to find a lost ball. She'd lost another ball, topped her tee shots, and her slice was so bad that she was sure one ball changed direction and sailed back to the clubhouse.

Annemarie and Mary waited for Sherry to bring up the subject of her pregnancy, but when she still hadn't mentioned it by the seventh tee, Mary cracked. 'So how did you get pregnant?'

Sherry pulled her driver from her golf bag. 'The usual way: penis — sperm — broken condom.'

Mary exchanged glances with Annemarie. 'Whose condom broke?' Annemarie demanded. 'Was it Stuart's?' Neither of them had liked Sherry's ex.

Sherry took a few practice swings. 'It wasn't Stuart's. It happened when I was away in Denver.'

They waited.

'Yes?' Mary prompted. 'It happened in Denver?'

'I had a one-night stand with an American guy,'

Sherry said briefly.

'You skanky ho!' Annemarie cried delightedly.

Mary glared at her. 'Annemarie!'

Annemarie shrugged. 'Who was he?' she asked.

'Just some guy; nobody you know.' Sherry thrust a golf tee into the grass so hard that she almost buried it and had to dig it out again.

Annemarie locked eyes with Mary. They were experts at reading body language, and Sherry's was telling them that whoever had got her pregnant was more than 'just some guy'. Things got more interesting when she glowered at the innocent white ball balanced on the tee and muttered, 'I almost wish it was Stuart.'

'Why?' Mary asked.

'Because Stuart was easy.'

'You mean he was a wimp?' Annemarie said.

'I *mean*,' Sherry said irritably, 'if I hadn't broken it off with Stuart before I went to Denver, I never would have slept with the other guy.'

Annemarie agreed with Sherry about not sleeping with guys you work with — having to discipline someone who'd done push-ups on you wasn't advisable — but she didn't understand why Sherry made it a rule to sleep with only one guy at a time. So long as a person took care to protect themselves and their partner from catching any social diseases and was upfront about just wanting to have fun, Annemarie didn't see what the problem was. Fortunately, Sherry's brother agreed with Annemarie. They went to the same gym, and Annemarie was a sucker for Ben's twinkling blue-grey eyes and clever builder's hands.

'If Stuart hadn't started talking about getting

married, I wouldn't have split up with him.'

'What's wrong with the man?' Mary asked. 'Why'd he have to go and fall in love with you?'

Sherry wasn't in the mood for jokes. 'He wasn't in love with me; he just liked the sex.' She yanked up her blue golf shirt to reveal her gaping white jeans and the safety pin. 'Look at this!'

Annemarie and Mary examined the evidence of the disastrous one-night stand: a small bulge just visible above the edge of Sherry's pink lacy panties.

'What did you think would happen?' Mary asked. 'That you'd go up a couple of shoe sizes?'

Sherry was a picture of dejection.

'How about we leave the golf for another day?' Annemarie suggested. 'Let's go back to your place and drink coffee and bitch about men instead.'

If Mary and Annemarie hadn't been following her in Mary's car, Sherry would have slammed on the brakes and reversed back down the driveway when she saw Glenn standing outside Nora's house. He lifted his foot from the bottom step and turned and watched as she drove past him and into the garage.

Sherry leaned forward and gripped the steering wheel, listening as Mary parked on the concrete in front of the garage. Doors slammed. The safety pin dug into her belly and forced Sherry to sit up. She clung to the faint hope that Glenn might spare her embarrassment and disappear off down the driveway. A quick check of the rear-vision mirror revealed Mary peering into the garage with a puzzled expression on her face, and Annemarie holding her sunglasses on her head and staring in Glenn's direction as if the Chippendales were lined up at the foot of Nora's steps. Sometimes Sherry thought that Annemarie had missed her calling, she was a good cop but would have made a good hooker or sex therapist as well. She was fairly sure Annemarie had slept with Ben — several times if Sherry had read the signals right; Annemarie only went back for seconds if the guy was good.

She hauled herself from the car, walked into the sunshine, and watched with resignation as Glenn strolled across the concrete towards them with his usual loose-limbed grace. He always managed to look like he had all the time in the world, whereas she was always in a hurry. A pair of silver sunglasses hung from the front pocket of one of his trademark shirts. This one was purple with a thin lilac stripe and would have looked girlie if it hadn't graced the chest and shoulders that made women watching the Blitz sunglasses adverts hit the pause button on the remote.

Glenn squinted in the sunshine and unfurled a lazy smile. 'Hello.' The two syllables instantly proclaimed him as one of Uncle Sam's.

Annemarie stretched her neck and tipped back her head to take in all six foot seven inches of him. She reminded Sherry of a meerkat that had just spotted danger — or a meal. 'Are you ...?' She looked at Sherry. 'Is he ...?'

Don't say it! Sherry flung a panicked look at Nora's porch, and sagged with relief when she saw that it was empty. Nora had gone inside to answer the phone.

'You're Blitz Brogan!' Mary shrieked.

Sherry had forgotten that Mary's husband, brothers, and most of her nephews played basketball. Glenn's bruises were no disguise for a dedicated NBA fan. She wasted no time in hustling him and his fans inside the house.

Glenn gave Mary autographs for her family and one for Annemarie, who didn't follow basketball and, if the circumstances had been different, would have liked a phone number to go with the signature. He was as charming and attentive to them as he'd been to his fans at the honky-tonk, but his eyes kept straying to Sherry, and Mary and Annemarie eventually took the hint and excused themselves.

As she left, Mary clasped Sherry's arm and murmured, 'Don't worry, we won't tell, but that man needs an alibi.'

Sherry's brow creased. 'What?'

'A reason to be down here. He's a big name in basketball; people are going to recognize him.'

She nodded wearily.

Annemarie gave Sherry a comforting pat on the shoulder. 'You did the baby a favour getting knocked-up by him. If Stewie was the father, you'd have to worry about it looking like Mrs Stewie if it was a girl.'

'Annemarie, you're not helping!' Mary cried.

No? She tried again. 'If it makes you feel any better, I'd have been a skanky ho, too.'

Like her bedroom, Sherry's living room didn't look

the way Glenn expected. It had white walls, dark wooden floorboards, a long white sofa with old-fashioned turned legs and two unmatched wing chairs upholstered in sage green. A thick, white fleecy rug lay in the middle of the room, topped by the sofa and chairs and a low black table with two drawers and silver handles. In one corner there was a black wood burner on a white marble hearth, with black cast-iron fire tools on a stand beside it. Large pillows in pale shades of rose, lavender and green were strewn on the floor in front of the fireplace. The windows were hung with gauzy white drapes, and the walls held abstract paintings in vivid colours. Glenn had glimpsed cheerful yellow walls and bleached pine cabinets in the kitchen as Sherry led him past; by contrast, the living room was cool and sparsely furnished, which made the plump sofa and floor cushions covered in luxuriant silks a surprise.

Sherry asked him to wait while she went upstairs to change. Ten minutes passed and she still hadn't returned. Glenn made his way to the foot of the stairs and frowned up at the lady on the emerald green horse. 'Sherry? Are you OK?'

Silence.

He put a foot on the bottom step. 'Sherry?'

Her voice drifted down to him. 'Not exactly.'

His fingers tightened on the balustrade. 'What d'you mean, "Not exactly"?'

'I've got a problem — *ow!*'

Glenn imagined her having a miscarriage and bolted up the stairs.

Sherry was standing by her bed with the hem of her shirt tucked beneath her chin, struggling with her jeans.

He rushed across the room and grabbed her arms. 'What's wrong? Are you bleeding?'

Her brows curled in puzzlement. 'From a safety pin? I don't think so.'

Glenn looked down at her jeans. 'What?'

'I don't fit my jeans,' Sherry muttered. 'The safety pin bent and I can't open it.'

'You said *"Ow!"* like you were in pain.'

Red flags of colour painted her cheekbones. She tried to cover her belly with her hand. 'I stuck myself with the pin. Do you mind going back downstairs and waiting like I asked you to?' she said haughtily.

Glenn took a closer look at what was going on beneath the tucked-up hem of her shirt. A silver safety pin held the waistband of her jeans together. It was open, but the prong was bent at an angle, preventing her from removing it. Queen Sherry was highly pissed off. Now that he knew she wasn't having a miscarriage, Glenn began to see the possibilities in the situation. He started flexing and wriggling his fingers, like a safe-cracker approaching a bank vault. 'Did you know I hold the Cougars' speed record for unhooking a bra one-handed?'

Sherry looked down her long nose. 'You held a competition to unhook bras?' she sniffed. 'Why am I not surprised?'

He bent to examine the safety pin more closely. 'How else does a bunch of bored, over-achieving athletes stuck in a hotel the night before a game amuse themselves? We weren't allowed to drink or—' Glenn stopped and slanted a look at Sherry.

She raised her brows. 'Help old ladies across the

road?'

'No, young ladies up to our rooms,' he drawled. 'The head coach thought it turned some of the guys' legs to spaghetti the next day. You probably won't believe me, but professional basketballers take their jobs seriously. If they don't, they get axed.'

His warm breath fanned across her bare skin. Sherry moved restlessly. 'What a proud moment that must have been, knowing you could pop the cups off some sweet young thing faster than everybody else in the team.'

'Mmm hmm. If memory serves me right, we beat the Phoenix Suns the next day.'

'Did you line up some of the groupies in their underwear and have somebody standing by with a stopwatch?' Sherry asked tartly.

'Much too time-consuming to organize,' Glenn replied. 'We sent one of the rookies downstairs to buy some lingerie and borrow a mannequin from the hotel store. I had some competition from one of the forwards, but my outstanding manual dexterity beat him into second place.'

'Outstanding manual dexterity?' she echoed.

'His hands were bigger than mine.'

Sherry studied Glenn's big hands and wondered what the forward's had been like. 'You know, I'm surprised that the women you date actually own bras. I thought strippers and pole dancers preferred pasties.'

Glenn flexed his fingers again and brushed aside her hand. 'This is a delicate operation, Sherry Ann; it's in your best interests not to upset me.' She sucked in a breath as he slid his fingers beneath the waistband of her jeans. 'Sorry. Are my hands cold?'

She shook her head. Quite the opposite, in fact.

Glenn tried to ignore the feel of her warm, silky skin and wriggled his hand deeper. 'Can you breathe in?' He jiggled her from side to side and grunted. 'They sure are tight.'

Sherry clutched his shoulder and felt lust shoot her in the groin. 'Breathing in won't make any difference, it's not me that's in the way.' The waistband parted. She bent her head and rubbed at the red marks on her abdomen. 'That feels so good,' she sighed.

Glenn studied the white parting in her inky black hair and breathed in the scent of Chanel No. 5 and melon shampoo. His gaze dipped to where the two halves of her jeans curled away to reveal the edge of lacy pink underwear and a small bulge above. He had an overwhelming urge to touch the telltale bulge.

Sherry saw where he was looking, and stepped back and wrapped her arms around her waist. Their eyes tangled.

Don't look at me like that.

But I want to look at you, and touch you, too, if you'd let me.

Glenn tried to lighten the tension. 'Is that it?'

'Is what it?' she asked in a puzzled voice.

He pointed at what she was trying to hide. 'Is that all there is to show for all my hard work?'

'All *your* hard work? What about all *my* hard work?' Sherry demanded indignantly. 'I have to get up twice in the night to pee and my boobs look like helium balloons.'

'They do? Can I see?'

'No, you bloody can't! You're supposed to fall on your knees, cup me tenderly and tell me I'm wonderful, not say "*Is that it?*"'

'If I fall to my knees and tell you that you're wonderful, can I cup the helium balloons instead?' Glenn asked hopefully.

Sherry clamped her lips together to keep from smiling. 'No, you cannot.'

'I promise I'll fall to my knees the instant you've got something worth cupping.'

She tossed her head and headed for the bathroom. 'I can hardly wait. Now, go away. I'll meet you downstairs in a few minutes.'

Glenn was stretched out on her bed with his hands tucked behind his head looking at the ceiling when she emerged from the bathroom. He still wore his shoes, but his feet hung over the edge of the mattress. Sherry couldn't be bothered kicking him out. He didn't look out of place on her white pin-tucked bedcovers; just like everything else he came in contact with, Glenn stamped his mark on it and owned it.

She was tired and wished she didn't have to go to work. She curled up on the chaise longue, tucked a hand beneath her cheek, and studied Glenn. 'Thanks for signing the autographs for Mary; her family will be thrilled.'

Glenn's gaze lingered on the tiny black mole pushed into prominence by her hand. 'I would have left when I saw you had company, but Nora was watching.'

'I hope she didn't hear Mary call you Blitz.'

Her hang-up about him being recognized was beginning to bug him. 'She was inside her house answering the phone.' Sherry relaxed, and Glenn added shortly, 'I've got to go home soon.'

'What?' She sat up. 'You haven't changed your mind, have you?'

'About taking the baby?'

She nodded anxiously.

For a moment there, Glenn had thought she was going to miss him. 'Of course I haven't; I've got to film an ad campaign.' His irritation grew when her lip curled. She probably thought he was making more advertisements for sunglasses. Glenn couldn't be bothered to tell her about the literacy campaign he'd agreed to front. 'I'll be back before Christmas. I dropped by because Ben said you'd arranged for us to meet with your mom and dad.'

'The day after tomorrow. I was going to call you.'

Glenn looked sceptical.

'I *was*,' Sherry insisted.

He shrugged, sat up on the side of the bed, and picked up a green-and-white cushion that had fallen on the floor. 'I told Mom and Dad and Dan.' He spun the pillow in his hands and caught it. 'They don't think I'm responsible enough to take care of a child.'

'Lisa does.'

Glenn sent her a look of disbelief.

'She *does*. She thinks you'll make a great father — but then,' Sherry paused and added, 'she also thinks I'll make a great mother.'

Glenn watched her closely and spun the pillow and caught it again. 'Maybe you will.'

She laughed hollowly. 'I don't think so.'

His lips tightened and he went back to his pillow-flipping.

Had he just proposed to her again? Or was she just

like Lisa and her brain was taking the slippery slide towards her uterus? 'Mary said you need an alibi.'

Glenn knew at once what she meant. 'I was thinking the same thing. I've got an idea that might work.'

Sherry worried her bottom lip with her teeth. 'Are you *sure* Nora didn't hear?'

'Don't worry about Nora. I know a perfect way to get her to keep quiet.'

'You do?'

He dropped the pillow on the bed, fisted his hands and stretched. 'Nora is being drafted to Team Brogan.'

Sherry watched him extend his arms above his head and arch his back, and decided it was time he left. 'I've got to get ready to go to work.'

Glenn took the hint. He was surprised she'd let him stay so long. She didn't look like she should be going to work, she looked tired, but it was none of his business.

'I'll let you know about Mum and Dad.'

'And I'll let you know about Nora.'

On the way out Glenn made a detour to Nora's. Her door opened before he made it up the steps. Without preamble, he asked, 'You play golf?'

'Do I play golf?' Nora scoffed. 'I used to be club captain until my hip got bad. I'm waiting for an operation for a new joint; that's why I'm bored.' She peered at Glenn. 'Do you?'

'Some. You can't play at all?'

Nora drew back as if he'd uttered a profanity. 'Of course I can! I just can't do two rounds back to back any more.'

If she was thirty years younger, a hundred pounds lighter and not so hard on the eyes, Glenn would have proposed to her on the spot. He had an idea percolating in his head that would give him a good reason to be in New Zealand. Sherry needed a reminder that he played golf, and Glenn knew he could rely on Nora to give her a hole-by-hole description of each round they played.

'How many rounds do you play a week?' he asked casually.

'I'm not supposed to do more than two until after the operation — although when that will be is anybody's guess. What about you?'

'I've got a dud knee. My therapist says no more than three rounds a week.'

Nora narrowed her eyes. 'How many?'

'Four or five a week. You?'

'Three or four.'

They measured one another. It was clearly a case of one bullshit artist trying to out-bullshit another.

Glenn folded his arms. 'You know the best local courses?'

Nora folded hers. 'And the best national courses, too.'

'Nora, darlin',' he drawled, 'I think I love you.'

Her doughy cheeks turned as pink as raspberries.

Chapter 11

They played Gulf Harbour the next day, and, in deference to Nora's bad hip, Glenn booked a cart and did a combination of walking and driving. It was a championship course with breath-taking views across the Hauraki Gulf from the back nine. Nora wore her *Nora Ditchburn For Prime Minister* visor, a pair of black and white checked golf pants that made her arse look the size of the Grand Canyon, and a hot-pink polo shirt with *Golf — Eighteen Good Reasons To Get Up In The Morning* embroidered on the front. Glenn was sure she'd missed the sexual connotation. They argued when Nora had the gall to tell Glenn that his black Stetson wasn't suitable attire for the golf course.

'What do you mean? Greg Norman used to wear a Stetson.'

'Greg Norman can play.'

His eyes narrowed, and he smiled. Glenn could trash-talk with the best. He watched Nora carefully remove leaf litter from around her ball and said, 'Nora, honey, I admire a woman who isn't a slave to fashion.'

Her head whipped around so fast that her skinny braid slapped her cheek. 'What's that supposed to mean?'

Glenn rested his hands on top of his club and said innocently, 'You have a distinctive look all of your own.'

She frowned suspiciously, straightened her visor, twitched the hem of her polo shirt — and hooked the ball into the trees.

'Damn.' Glenn shook his head in sympathy as Nora ground her teeth. 'And you said you always birdie this hole.'

'You did that on purpose!' She pointed her seven-iron at his hat. 'That is a gay hat!'

He stopped smiling. 'It is not a gay hat.'

'It's almost as bad as that gay purple shirt you were wearing the other day.'

The 'gay purple shirt' was one of the biggest sellers in the latest Bona Fide Blitz shirt range.

'There's nothing wrong with that shirt!'

'There's *plenty* wrong with that shirt!' Nora grabbed another club from her bag and lumbered towards the trees.

Playing golf with Nora was a love/hate relationship. They loved the game but hated the way each other played it. Nora was a stickler for rules. When Glenn's ball was merely inches from the cup, she refused to let him have a gimmee and made him play the shot. As he was preparing to tap it in, Nora asked if having eyes like a girl had made Glenn a gay icon. Glenn hit the ball too hard and went one over for the hole. Nora knew the course well, beat him by three shots, and cackled like the Wicked Witch from The Wizard Of Oz.

He smiled tightly. 'You'll keep, Ditchburn.'

'You owe me ten bucks, Blitz.'

He froze as he was about to return his putter to his bag. 'How long have you known?'

'Lumberjack, my Aunt Nelly! I thought I recognized you the day you arrived but wasn't sure until the swelling went down around your eyes. After golf, my favourite sport is basketball.' Nora smirked: 'I watch it all the time on Sky TV.'

Glenn slotted the putter into the bag. Nora looked smug until he started to smile. He studied the sparkling blue waters of the gulf and the smooth, velvety greens, and tipped back his Stetson. 'This has been a great day, hasn't it, Nora?'

'Yes,' she agreed cautiously.

'You've enjoyed yourself, haven't you?'

'Yes ...'

Glenn lifted the Stetson, raked his fingers through his hair and set the hat down again. 'Want to do it again, Nora, honey?'

His tone made Nora's heart skitter nervously. The Blitz had on his game face. It was thrilling. 'You can't tell me what to do, Blitz Brogan!' she cried breathlessly. 'I'm an old lady.'

Glenn played along because he knew she was lonely and bored. 'You're not old, Nora, and you're not defenceless. If the New Zealand Secret Service doesn't want you, I'm going to offer you to the CIA.'

She bristled. 'What are you going to do? Get me banned from courses I've been playing for years?'

'As if I could.' Glenn dropped into good-ol'-boy mode, which they both knew he wasn't. 'Nope, I think I'll just find somebody else to play with.'

She glowered.

He concentrated on unfastening his golf glove. 'This is the deal, Nora: you can ask anything you want about basketball and me, and I might answer you. But if you do anything to make trouble for Sherry or draw attention to my visit, you'll be sitting at home watching television and watering your plants.' He looked up at her through his lashes. 'Understood?'

Nora wasn't going down without a fight. 'You think you're so important, don't you?'

'It's a failing of mine, but I'm working on it.'

'Good!' she huffed. 'Because we're booked to play twenty-seven holes at North Shore tomorrow. And don't you dare wear that gay hat!' She stomped around for a while, but eventually came back and asked, 'I need to know something.'

'What?'

'Is Sherry pregnant?'

Glenn's indulgent expression turned to granite. 'Sherry is out of bounds. Remember?'

'I'm not being nosy,' Nora hesitated. 'It's just ...'

She thought Glenn should know about Sherry's ex-boyfriend. Glenn was a *big* improvement on Stuart. Nora wasn't surprised when Sherry dumped Stuart — she'd overheard, because Sherry had told him it was over in her living room. Stuart had made a big fuss and pleaded with Sherry to give them another try, and had kept on coming around, but Sherry wouldn't budge. Nora had a feeling Stuart could make trouble if he found out Sherry was pregnant.

'Just what?' Tomorrow Sherry was taking Glenn to see her parents. He wasn't in the mood for Nora asking difficult questions.

'Nothing,' Nora replied reluctantly. For once she'd do the right thing and keep her mouth shut. Except to Sherry — she had an idea Glenn wanted her to know they were playing golf. Nora had always been the plain, lumpy girl who was overlooked by boys; she had never been called upon to make one of the pretty girls jealous. So the first chance she got, Nora cornered Sherry and told her all about playing golf with Glenn.

'He wore a gay hat,' Nora said.

Sherry didn't know why she cared that Glenn was playing golf with Nora but knew that she didn't want Nora to see that it annoyed her. 'People are gay, Nora, not hats.'

Nora waved a hand. 'It's a big black Stetson; made me think of those cowboys in *Brokeback Mountain*.'

Glenn has brought the black Stetson with him? Sherry's stomach caroomed as she remembered what he'd been doing to her the last time she'd seen him in it. 'Nora, that is *definitely* not a gay hat.'

'Why would a man who looks like that wear a gay hat and gay shirts?'

'I like Glenn's shirts.' And now he'd know.

Nora sniffed. 'Too colourful.'

'Glenn could wear a tutu and a tiara and he'd still look hot.'

She needed a zipper on her mouth, and Glenn needed one on his pants that could only be lowered to answer calls of a non-sexual nature.

Nora's inquisitive nature and tendency to interfere drove Sherry nuts. She'd kept her distance from the older woman, but they'd started speaking more when Sherry took up golf, which was the ruling passion of Nora's narrow life. When she'd moved in, Nora had told Sherry she'd nursed her mother through a long illness before she died and intended making up for lost time on the golf course. At first, she'd been out every day, regardless of the weather, and a steady stream of grey-haired women with leathery faces and muscular knees wearing golf attire had marched up and down the driveway after leaving their cars inexpertly parked at the bottom. But then Nora's hip got bad, she couldn't play as much, and her visitors had dried up. She'd begun filling in time watching who came and went from her neighbours' houses, and because Sherry was closest, Nora gave her the most attention. She'd been offended when Sherry bluntly told her to keep her eyes, ears and nose out of Sherry's business and her opinions to herself.

'If you've got time on your hands, find something better to do than staking out my house. Take up knitting or do some voluntary work. Why don't you become a volunteer at the hospital?' Sherry suggested.

'I'm sick of sick people!' Nora snapped, and against her doctor's orders went back to playing golf.

Twice Sherry had to haul Nora and her golf clubs into the house when Nora couldn't make it up the stairs to her front door. Finally, Nora had admitted defeat, taken up knitting and retreated to a La-Z-Boy in the front window of her living room where she could watch the goings-on of the neighbourhood. She was delighted that Sherry had taken up golf and was constantly angling for an invitation to ride along in the golf cart. Sherry couldn't face eighteen holes of interrogation about her personal life, but she did let Nora give her advice on golf courses and her golf swing.

Memories of Glenn's black Stetson lingered as Sherry stepped inside her house. She couldn't imagine somebody as competitive as Glenn putting up with Nora criticizing his game for long.

Tomorrow, they were meeting with Sherry's parents.

She hoped Glenn knew how to eat humble pie without choking on it.

Sherry had arranged to pick Glenn up after she finished work but called to say she was running late. She'd spent most of the day with Stacey, who was distraught that Vance had been arrested and then released when his mother provided him with an alibi for the day of the alleged attack. Sherry had taken a description of the man walking his dog who'd disturbed Vance, but despite door-knocking in the local area they'd been unable to find him, so Vance was released. As he was leaving the station, Vance threatened to 'smack that bitch cop Jackson' for turning his wife against him and causing trouble. Dave Pomana had warned him that threats against police officers were taken seriously.

'Watch your back, Sherry,' Dave said. 'If he gives you any problems or does anything out of the ordinary, I want to know right away.'

Stacey was terrified. She'd wanted to retract her statement, and Sherry had stayed late reassuring her until she calmed down. When she'd broached the subject of getting a protection order against Vance, Stacey had got hysterical again.

'Are you trying to get me killed?' she screamed. 'He went apeshit because he thinks I talked and got him arrested. If I get a protection order, he'll murder me for sure!'

Sherry was exhausted and not in the mood to meet with her parents and talk about what she and Glenn planned to do about the baby. She called him and asked unenthusiastically, 'Can you meet me at the house instead?'

Glenn wasn't used to such offhand treatment from a woman and didn't much like it. He arrived at Jill and Brian's house and parked on the road opposite. Ten minutes passed and Sherry still hadn't arrived. Glenn drummed his fingers on the steering wheel and watched the nearby intersection for her black SUV. Waiting outside her parents' house reminded him of waiting outside the principal's office in high school. As a youngster, Dan had got up to mischief, yet had managed to fly under the radar; Glenn's exploits, however, had been like him: big and spectacular. When they'd come off, he'd been the hero of the student body; but when they hadn't, he'd paid dearly. But Glenn's saving grace had been that he'd never picked on underdogs and always admitted responsibility. There was no malice in him; he'd been a charming scamp and liked by his teachers and, to a lesser extent, the school principal. On one of Molly and Kell's frequent trips to his office, the principal told them he thought Glenn had been born a few hundred years too late.

Kell had been mystified. 'What does that mean?'

'Glenn gave professional basketball player, pirate or highwayman as his preferred occupations to the careers counsellor,' the principal explained. 'Let's hope he continues to shine at basketball.'

Glenn was considering knocking on the Jacksons' front door when a police squad car pulled up in front of him and Sherry got out. She was in full police regalia, including protective vest and personal radio, and looked nervous. He joined her and tried to lighten the atmosphere with a joke. 'Why didn't you warn me we were dressing up? I'd have worn my Batman costume.'

Sherry felt ugly and unglamorous; Glenn looked the exact opposite. He filled out his silky, mustard-yellow shirt in all the right places, and oozed charm the way other people oozed sweat on a hot day. Sherry refused to be charmed and took exception to the yellow shirt. The only time she'd ever seen Glenn wear a T-shirt was when he'd came back from a run in Denver. *He must create a mountain of laundry and ironing,* she thought, conveniently forgetting the fact that she was as much of a clothes horse as Glenn. She marched up the path in the middle of her father's beautiful front garden, muttering, 'Hurry up. I've still got to take the squad car back.'

Glenn gave up trying to be reasonable and decided to forget what he'd read about pregnant women being tired and emotional in the first trimester. He couldn't get his head around Sherry being pregnant: she didn't look pregnant; she didn't act pregnant. He dawdled behind her, knowing that it would piss her off. 'Can I get a ride in the Bat Car and play with the siren before it goes back?'

She jerked the rope on the cow bell hanging from the rafters by the front door. 'This isn't funny! My parents aren't going to understand what we've got planned.'

His smile faded. She was right.

She waited stiffly for the door to be answered, or at least Glenn thought she did — he wasn't sure if it was her posture or the thick blue body armour that made her look that way. The radio on her shoulder crackled, and she reached up to silence it. What idiot came up with the line that uniforms were sexy? There was nothing remotely sexy about a woman wearing thick-soled black shoes and body armour.

The door opened. Glenn looked across Sherry's head into Brian Jackson's accusing gaze and felt like he was back in the principal's office. His memory of Sherry's father from Lisa and Dan's wedding was of a quiet, hospitable man who loved gardening and managed the local garden centre. When Glenn had mentioned to Ben that Brian was out of luck if he wanted to take a shot at him because he'd run out of eyes, Ben laughed. 'Dad won't hit you. He isn't the type.'

Glenn looked into Brian's condemning blue gaze and wasn't so sure. His and Sherry's sense of foreboding grew when they went inside and saw that Jill had baked scones and a cake. The look of dismay on Sherry's face as she studied the best china on the dining-room table increased Glenn's uneasiness. This was not a celebration.

Jill gasped when she saw his face. 'Glenn! What happened to your eyes?'

'A tree fell on him,' Sherry said. 'In fact, two trees, one named Dan, and one named Ben.'

Glenn watched a smile of quiet satisfaction curve Brian's lips.

Not the type, my ass.

Jill gasped, 'Ben *hit* you? *My* Ben?'

Sherry pulled a chair out from the table and collapsed onto it. 'If it makes you feel any better, Dan hit him first.'

Jill sat down beside her. 'I knew about that — Lisa told me — but I didn't know about Ben.'

Glenn took the chair opposite Sherry. So it was OK if

Dan hit him, but not Ben?

Sherry frowned at the snowy white cloth, home baking and best china. 'What are we celebrating?'

'The baby, of course.' Jill put a scone on a plate and shoved it at her. 'Eat a date scone; the fruit is good for you.'

Sherry exchanged glances with Glenn. This was going to be tougher than they'd expected. 'I don't like dates,' she said.

'Is that you? Oh, I thought it was Lisa. Glenn?' Jill offered the plate to him. 'Scone?'

'Have one,' Sherry urged sarcastically. 'The fruit is good for you.'

Glenn found her foot beneath the table and applied gentle pressure. *Shut up*, his eyes telegraphed. Sherry tried to escape, but his foot was five sizes bigger than hers.

There was a pot of coffee and two pots of tea sitting on protective mats on the table.

'What you would like, Glenn?' Jill enquired. 'Coffee? English breakfast tea? Or Earl Grey, like Sherry?'

What a surprise: Queen Sherry drank Earl Grey tea — not the tea-bag stuff, but real tea leaves with purple and yellow flowers floating in it. Glenn felt like he was attending the Mad Hatter's Tea Party. Brian reminded him of the Red Queen about to shout *Off with his head!* 'Coffee will do fine thanks, Jill.'

Jill handed around the cups. 'Have you been taking folic acid?'

Glenn thought it was some kind of remedy for his black eyes. 'No.'

'Not you, stupid — *me*.' Sherry accepted a cup from

Jill and shook her head. 'It was too late.' She couldn't remember what the folic acid was for; finding out she was pregnant and the weeks after were a blur.

'Why do you need to take folic acid?' Glenn and Brian asked together.

Despite the dates, Sherry had her mouth full of scone. She was ravenous; she was *always* ravenous at the moment. The previous night she'd eaten two bags of sour cream and chives potato chips, which she usually hated as much as dates. If she kept on eating at this rate, she'd be the size of an ocean liner by May — which reminded her, she must ask Lisa to find out how much Glenn weighed when he was born. She felt the weight of his huge foot resting on hers and had to force the scone down.

'It reduces the chances of the baby having neural tube defects.' Jill liked to parade the fact that she worked in a doctor's surgery and knew medical terms.

Glenn's gaze sharpened. His brother was a doctor, so he knew some medical terms, too. 'Spina bifida?'

Sherry thought the scone might come up again. What if the baby was born with something wrong with it because she hadn't taken care of herself? One of the families she worked with had a seven-year-old boy with spina bifida, but the culture of violence in his family affected him far more than his physical disability. She put the scone down carefully on the plate. 'I didn't know.'

Brian was glaring at Jill.

'I'm sure it will be alright,' she said quickly.

Sherry fiddled with the straps on her vest to ease the pressure on her boobs. Taking it off wasn't an option, because she didn't trust her mother not to tell her she needed to buy bigger bras.

'Wouldn't you like to take that off?' Jill asked.

'No.'

'Nobody is going to shoot you.' Brian glanced at Glenn — him maybe, but not her.

'I'm cold,' Sherry said, and watched them look out the window at the sunny spring weather.

'You can understand our surprise when we heard who'd made Sherry pregnant,' Brian said sarcastically. 'We thought you hated the sight of one another.'

Jill snapped, '*Brian!*'

Sherry gazed at her father in shock. She'd never seen this side of him. Until now, she'd seen herself as the injured party, but Sherry objected to Glenn being cast as the ogre in the piece because it inferred that she was a gullible idiot.

Glenn met Brian's condemning gaze squarely. 'We had more in common than we thought.'

Brian snorted, and Sherry lost her temper. 'There were two of us in that motel room; we're both equally to blame!'

Glenn closed his eyes and pinched the brim of his nose. Did she have to mention they'd visited a motel?

Jill's jaw dropped. 'You went to a motel?'

He hadn't thought it was possible for Sherry's father's opinion of him to sink any lower; Glenn wished he could gag her.

Sherry tried to take back control. 'You've got the wrong idea about Glenn, Dad. He asked me to marry him, but I said no.'

Jill raised her eyes to the ceiling and muttered,

'*Difficult.*'

'What did you expect?' she asked. 'That we'd fall into each other's arms and live happily ever after? We wanted to sleep with each other, not get married.'

Jill busied herself sweeping non-existent crumbs off the tablecloth.

'Sherry,' Glenn said pleasantly, '*be quiet.*'

Unfortunately, she wasn't finished. 'And for the record, it was my fault this happened.'

'Oh?' Brian looked sceptical. 'You mean you got pregnant on your own?'

Glenn applied pressure to Sherry's heavy black lace-up. 'That's not true.'

She braced her heel against his instep and tried to prise him off. 'Yes, it is.'

He stared at her, his face set. 'It's only half the story.'

Sherry gave up on his foot and dug the toe of her shoe into the heavy muscle in his calf. Glenn casually dropped his shoulder and tried to grab her foot, but she was too fast for him. He returned his hand to the table and drummed his fingers.

Jill lost patience. 'For goodness' sake! Your father and I both know how you got pregnant — we've had three of our own. What we want to know is: what are you going to do about it?'

Glenn removed his foot; Sherry wished he'd put it back. 'Glenn is taking the baby back to the States.'

Jill and Brian stared at her.

'For how long?' Jill asked warily.

Sherry licked her lips. 'For good. Glenn is going to raise the baby.'

'*What?*' Jill whispered.

Brian gripped the edge of the table. '*Why?*'

Sherry hurried to explain. 'Glenn's retired. His career is over.'

Glenn clenched his jaw.

'He's got lots of time, but I'm just getting started in my career. I can't take care of a baby and study and work, too.'

'We'll help you. We'll *all* help you. Glenn can visit, and you can take the baby and visit him.' Jill turned desperately to Glenn. 'You'll help pay for the flights, won't you, Glenn?'

He couldn't meet her eyes.

'What about when you go away? Molly said you're always going away to ...' she waved a hand vaguely '... shoot your sunglasses commercials and ... things.'

She made him sound like a celebrity rent boy. 'I'll hire a nanny,' Glenn said tightly, and saw Sherry frown.

'It's all decided, Mum,' she said.

Brian and Jill began to point out all the things that could go wrong with their plan, all the things that Sherry and Glenn had thought of and not discussed. Sherry assured her parents that it was the best course of action, and Glenn promised he'd make sure they got to see the baby, but Jill and Brian remained sceptical. Glenn watched Sherry retreat into Ice Queen mode and had to bite his tongue to keep from telling her parents to back off and leave her alone, because he knew it'd only make things worse.

'Do you *really* think you'll be able to have this baby and give it away, Sherry?' Jill demanded.

'I know it won't be easy, but I think Glenn will make a good father.'

It was the nicest thing she'd ever said about him.

'Well, why don't you marry the man?' Brian asked.

'Because I also think he'd make a lousy husband.'

She had to spoil it.

Jill wailed. 'Can't we have *one* of our grandchildren living in New Zealand?'

Sherry had never seen her father look so stern. She flinched when he said, 'You haven't thought this through, Sherry.'

Glenn decided she'd had enough. He got up and reached for her hand and was relieved when she let him help her up. 'We have to go. We've got to get to a childbirth class.' He hustled her from the house.

Outside he asked, 'Are you OK?'

'I knew how Mum would react, but I never expected my father to be so ... so ...' She shook her head in bewilderment.

'Paternal?' Glenn supplied.

'He acted like I was a teenage virgin! I'm thirty years old!'

In Brian's shoes, Glenn knew he'd be a hundred times more vocal, and it occurred to him that, if the baby was a girl, one day he could be wearing those shoes. Chastity belts were outlawed, so how was the new-millennium father supposed to keep his daughter safe from spotty, testosterone-overloaded teenage boys? Or testosterone-overloaded basketball players?

Sherry raised troubled blue eyes. 'Glenn?'

'Yes?'

'What if something is wrong with it?'

He cupped her cheek. 'It'll be fine.'

She clung to his wrist. 'But if it isn't? Will you still feel the same?'

He stroked the mole beneath her eye. 'I'll love it anyway — even if it gets your snotty temper.'

His touch evoked the usual sensation of firecrackers going off under Sherry's skin but was also oddly comforting. She pulled away before she started rubbing herself against him like a cat. 'Thanks for making up an excuse for us to leave.'

'I didn't make it up.'

'What?'

'You really do have a childbirth class to go to tonight.' Glenn checked his Rolex. 'It starts in five minutes.'

<h1 style="text-align:center">Chapter 12</h1>

Ben was waiting outside the community centre when they arrived. He jogged over to the car. 'You're late!' He saw Sherry was still wearing her uniform beneath the black pea coat she'd thrown on. 'Couldn't you have changed first?'

'I didn't have time. I had to take the squad car back to the station.' She slammed the door of her car and strode into the centre.

Ben regarded Glenn quizzically. 'She's letting you come?'

He shrugged. 'Not exactly. She's pissed about being late, so I'm hoping she won't notice I tagged along.'

Yeah, it was easy to miss a man with two black eyes who was at least seven inches taller than everybody else.

'Just be grateful she ditched her body armour and radio,' Glenn advised as they headed to the glass doors at the entrance. 'And I'd be careful what you say: she's a little volatile at the moment.'

Ben cocked a brow. 'Things didn't go well with Mum and Dad?'

Glenn paused with one hand on the glass door and considered. 'It reminded me of the first time my team made the finals and we lost in the last quarter because we didn't stick to the game plan. Sherry and I were doing fine until she tried to run the defence single-handed.'

Ben grunted sympathetically.

'A defining moment was when she told your parents

she thought I'd make a lousy husband.'

He winced.

Sherry banged on the glass and mouthed impatiently, *Come on!* She spun on her heel and disappeared.

Ben grabbed Glenn's arm to stop him following her. 'I have to warn you, this class looks a little weird.'

Glenn sighed; he *did not* need this. 'Define "weird".'

'When Sherry didn't show up, I thought she might have gone in already, so I put my head in the door,' Ben explained. 'I thought I'd got the wrong room and walked into a family party. There's loads of people in there — kids, grannies, granddads, aunts, uncles.'

'Pregnant women?'

'Yeah, but way more pregnant than Sherry. I think she might have jumped the gun.'

Sherry reappeared and yanked open the door. 'Can you two girls save this for later?'

Ben hadn't exaggerated. Instead of nice orderly rows of pregnant women and their partners seated in chairs before an instructor, the room was packed with people of all ages. It looked more like the kind of gathering seen at an end-of-year school concert than a childbirth class. Glenn had a feeling they'd made a mistake.

Sherry's gaze swept the group. 'What is this? Have we got the wrong room?'

A tiny woman with waist-length brown hair and big blue eyes came over to them and smiled. 'Hello, I'm Layla. Welcome.'

Sherry checked her over. She looked about ten years

old and wore a cotton skirt and blouse that made Sherry think about pioneer women scrubbing clothes in a creek. 'Are you the instructor?' she asked uneasily. Pioneer women probably gave birth beside the creek and went straight back to scrubbing their petticoats.

'I prefer the term "facilitator".'

Glenn watched Sherry's lip curl. Yep, a *big* mistake.

Layla seemed puzzled. 'Are you pregnant?'

'That seems to be the general opinion.'

'This isn't an early-bird class,' Layla explained patiently. 'It caters for women in their eighth month.'

'So I'm a trimester or two early.' Sherry waved a hand. 'Does it really matter?'

Ben was admiring Layla's long hair and big eyes. He gave her a lazy smile that crinkled the corners of his blue-grey eyes. 'Sorry we're late.'

Layla made fluttering motions with her little hands. 'No need to apologize ...?' She looked enquiringly at Ben.

'Ben. I'm her brother.' He jerked a thumb at Glenn. 'He's the father.'

Layla tipped back her head and looked up at Glenn, while Sherry glared at Ben who was watching the way Layla's long hair brushed her buttocks beneath her pioneer woman's skirt. 'Oh my goodness!' she gasped when she reached Glenn's face. 'What happened to your poor face?'

'Ben punched him,' Sherry said with satisfaction.

'Oh.' Layla gave Ben a disapproving look and turned her attention to Sherry and her uniform. 'You're a police officer! How wonderful.'

She can read, Sherry thought. *It's a start.* Her gaze swept the room again. 'Why? Have you had some trouble?'

'Oh, no!' Layla's brows drew together. 'I mean it's wonderful to have so many different sectors of the community represented in the class.'

Ben was smarting over Sherry's comment about him punching Glenn. 'You're not here to arrest anybody, Sherry.'

'And you're not here to pick anybody up,' she shot back.

Glenn smiled — it was nice seeing Sherry fight with somebody else for a change. He decided to step in before he had to give them both time-out in the car. He'd seen Ben's teddy-bear sampler hiding behind the DVD player in his living room. 'Sherry Ann and Benjamin Brian, behave.' He grinned at the daggers looks he got from the warring sibs, then redirected his attention to Layla, whose head barely reached his chest. 'We didn't expect so many people to be here.'

Layla clasped her hands and said earnestly, 'Birth is an experience that should be shared by the entire family. I encourage my mothers to bring their extended family to classes.' She gestured towards a collection of chairs in the centre of the room. 'We're going to start now. Come and find a seat in the circle of chairs. Don't be shy ...' She drifted away.

Sherry watched her go. Being able to read wasn't going to be enough; this woman was a fruitcake.

A toddler on a red and yellow plastic ride-on was propelling himself round the room, running over people's toes and crashing into what had once been the circle of chairs. The group closest to them included both sets of grandparents. Sherry estimated her group was at least six people short. Glenn was attracting a lot of attention from the rest of the men, because he was so big and his beat-up face made him look dangerous, and from the women because he was so big and, even with a beat-up face, wafted sex appeal like he'd been marinated in it. She was worried because Ben had identified Glenn as the father of her baby and somebody might recognize him as Blitz Brogan. 'I think we should go.'

'We're staying,' Glenn said firmly.

Ben watched Layla. 'We've just got here; give it a chance.'

Sherry snagged the front of his shirt. 'If you get off with Layla, I'll kill you.'

He prised her fingers apart. 'One woman's misfortune; another man's opportunity.'

Sherry was delighted when the class started and straight away Ben lost more Brownie points with Layla when he called himself Sherry's birth coach.

Her little nose wrinkled. 'A coach belongs on the rugby field.' She fluttered her hands. 'I much prefer the term "birth partner" or "doula", which is a wonderful Ancient Greek word meaning "female servant or caregiver".'

Layla's two favourite words were 'term' and 'wonderful'. Sherry was starting to hate them both; she also wanted to cuff those fluttering hands. 'What about doofus?' she asked. 'Is doofus good?'

Glenn and some of the other men laughed, but Layla frowned. Sherry's uniform and Glenn's height and black eyes had shifted the focus from Layla. She ignored Sherry's remark and began talking about the role of the birth partner in more detail.

The man sitting behind Glenn tapped him on the back, and Glenn turned to look at him. Sherry heard the man ask, 'Do you play for the Breakers?'

Thanks to extended periods of time spent watching cable television at Ben's house, Glenn knew that the Breakers were the Auckland-based pro-basketball team that played in the National Basketball League. He shook his head. 'No.'

'Oh,' the man seemed disappointed, 'I thought you looked familiar.'

Layla's patience was wearing thin. 'Can we get on?' she cried shrilly.

Sherry wanted to leave. A combination of nerves and her black jacket was making her sweat, but if she took it off it would draw even more attention to her police uniform. She wasn't interested in the power of positive imagery or doulas. She wanted a PowerPoint presentation and graphs and was disgusted that Layla didn't even have a whiteboard or notice that the toddler was creating a racket riding around the sacred circle. Sherry slid down in the chair, crossed her arms, and tapped her fingertips on her biceps. Glenn and the doula's eyes had glazed over. She noticed the number of open handbags strewn on the floor at women's feet with wallets, car keys and mobile phones carelessly on display. Life would be a lot easier if people took better care of their possessions. Exhaustion took its toll, her eyelids drooped ... and she jerked awake.

Glenn leaned towards her. 'You OK?'

Sherry sat up. 'I'm fine.'

Layla droned on about the benefits of having the extended family present at the birth. 'Birth is a celebration of life. Some families go to extraordinary lengths to make the occasion special.'

'Clowns,' Ben murmured.

'Pony rides,' Sherry whispered.

'Bouncy castle,' Glenn added.

Ben's shoulders shook and Sherry started to giggle. They drew Layla's frowning attention again, but Glenn's innocent expression reassured her and she began to recount her favourite stories about how families had made the birth special.

The toddler was making loud *Vroom!* noises and riding round and round his father's chair. His sullen-looking mother made a half-hearted attempt to stop him, while his father sat like a statue. Sherry took a closer look at him and recognized Jerry, a local house-burglar whom she'd arrested twice. What was he doing at a childbirth class? Collecting addresses for future jobs? Jerry's brow shone with perspiration. He wore a panicked look that made Sherry's cop instincts twang like banjo strings and told her he'd spotted her long before she'd noticed him. She guessed he'd deliberately chosen a seat on the opposite side of the room, but his cover had been blown by his son. To get to the door, Jerry would have to walk past her. Sherry looked at all the goodies in the handbags and knew that the temptation would be too much for him.

Layla got out a plastic three-dimensional model of the female reproductive system and began taking it apart and describing the anatomy. Ben went pale and Sherry got annoyed. Finally, the stupid woman was talking about something useful, and her attention was being monopolized by a potential thief.

The toddler changed direction and began weaving clumsily between the chairs and working his way around the circle. Glenn watched him get closer, and casually extended a leg. Junior ground to a halt and blinked at the mile-long obstacle barring his way. He stuck a finger in his mouth and studied Glenn's battered face while the rest of the group held their breath. They'd grown tired of the child and his ride-on back when Layla was talking about positive imagery, but her strong opinions about the participation of the extended family had made them swallow their complaints. The toddler took his finger out of his mouth and pouted.

'Time to stop that now,' Glenn said in a firm, pleasant voice.

I'm right, Sherry thought. *He would make a good father and a lousy husband.*

Layla peered suspiciously in their direction again, a fallopian tube in one of her hands. 'Is anything wrong?'

Jerry's wife stood up. 'Merlin?'

Merlin? The kid was called Merlin? People gazed at her accusingly. Merlin put his bare feet on the floor and kicked his legs to propel himself backwards but ran into a handbag that a woman a couple of chairs down shoved in his way. Items spilled from the bag and she leaned down to pick them up.

'Merlin? Come here!' Jerry's wife snapped.

The woman dug around inside the bag and searched the floor beneath the chairs around her. 'I can't find my wallet and phone!'

Jerry's Adam's apple bobbed.

Sherry pulled out her cellphone. 'What's your number?'

'What?' The woman looked up at her and frowned. 'Oh! Zero-two ...'

Jerry shot to his feet a couple of seconds before his pocket started ringing. It turned out he'd stolen three wallets and two cellphones. His wife would have attacked him with Merlin's ride-on if a couple of the guys hadn't got between her and Jerry.

Sherry phoned for a squad car, and asked Glenn to stay by the door so that Jerry couldn't make a break for it.

'What do I do if he tries to get past me?' he asked loudly. 'Do I punch him? Or just body-slam him?'

Jerry's complexion turned ashen.

When he heard Glenn's accent, one of the fathers nudged another and said, 'It's Dirty Harry.' And one of the women who'd had something stolen shouted, 'Let him body-slam him! Better still, let me!'

Ben never knew childbirth classes could be so much fun. 'Now, Ma'am,' he soothed, 'we don't hold with vigilante justice in this neck of the woods.'

Merlin threw himself on the floor and started screaming because he'd lost his ride-on. His mother snatched him up and snarled at Jerry, 'I told you this was your last chance! That this time we'd do things right and go to baby classes! And what do you do? Steal fucking phones right from under the nose of a fucking cop! Why didn't you turn them off? You're a moron, Jerry! A moron! I'm leaving you! Do not come home or I swear to God I'll take those cellphones and shove them up your bum!'

She stormed out, clutching Merlin.

'Seems unfair that she gets to leave *and* keep the

house,' Ben said.

'You're forgetting that she gets to keep Merlin and the ride-on, too,' Glenn replied.

'Good point.'

Layla's positive imagery was shot to pieces. Before they left, she suggested Sherry might like to find another childbirth education class.

'That's got to be a record,' Ben said. 'Expelled before you even got a chance to enroll.'

Sherry looked down her nose at him. 'Oh, shut up!'

She swept from the room, failing to notice her old boyfriend Stuart leaving his wine appreciation class further along the corridor. But he saw Sherry and stuck his head curiously into the classroom she'd left. What he saw made him clutch the door for support.

Glenn wasn't nearly as amused as Ben by what had happened. Watching Sherry in action had brought home to him the dangers of her job. If Jerry had some backbone or she'd been alone, things could have turned nasty. She'd kept her cool and thought quickly — calling the woman's cell had been smart — but that didn't change the fact that Sherry's line of work placed her in potentially volatile situations. Glenn wanted to talk to her about it but didn't know how to bridge the distance Sherry maintained between them. On the drive to the community centre, she'd become withdrawn and aloof again, as if to emphasize that her moment of vulnerability outside her parents' house was over.

One thing was certain, they had to find a midwife to take care of Sherry, because she wasn't going to pay any attention to what Glenn or her family said. Glenn had commitments in the States which meant he had to return in a fortnight, but after that he planned to divide his time between the two countries until the baby was born in May. When he got back to New Zealand, his bruises would be gone and there would be more chance of people recognizing him. Basketball wasn't as big in New Zealand as it was in the States, but it still had a loyal fan base, like Mary and her family. Glenn remembered the 2002 FIBA World Champs in Indianapolis when the New Zealand Tall Blacks stunned the basketball world by coming fourth. For a country of only four million people, it was an extraordinary achievement.

Blitz Brogan was newsworthy. People back home would want to know what had brought him to New Zealand if — no, *when* — word got out he was here. That would inevitably lead them to Sherry. The press would be all over her. Glenn had to create a smoke screen, a reason for him to be in New Zealand that would steer attention away from her. He needed to devise a strategy to manage any publicity, and for that he needed his agent's help.

'I've been trying to get hold of you for days on your BlackBerry and at your beach house!' Fraser cried when Glenn called him. 'Have you forgotten that filming starts for the Adult Literacy Awareness campaign in a few weeks' time?' He continued heatedly, 'The producers have been asking for you to give the OK on the final script, but I haven't been able to give them any answers because I can't find my fucking star client!'

The national campaign was to combat adult illiteracy

and encourage people to take advantage of free programmes set up in their local communities. The campaign's catch-phrase was: *I can't read and write, but that doesn't mean I'm dumb.* In the past, he'd lent his support to child and adult literacy campaigns on a smaller scale, but it was his performance in the hugely successful commercials for Blitz sunglasses that had made the television and film industry sit up and take notice. That the camera loved him was no surprise; that he was a natural in front of it was. Fraser had been approached by a Hollywood producer interested in casting Glenn in a basketball movie, but Glenn turned down the offer saying he wasn't interested in pretending to play and would make a lousy actor. 'I had enough trouble sitting still for make-up and hanging around while they set up the lights and stuff for the sunglasses ads. I'd go out of my head if I had to do it for months.'

'You need to be in Los Angeles by the sixth for the Adult Literacy campaign,' Fraser reminded him.

'I haven't forgotten. Fraser, there's been some developments you need to know about ...'

Glenn gave a brief explanation of where he really was, and why.

'*You've what?*' Fraser exploded. Blitz was the last person he'd have expected to fall into the oldest trap known to mankind.

'You heard me.'

'You're in *New Zealand?*' Fraser made it sound like Pluto.

'I'm in Auckland.'

'*Where the hell is Auckland?*' Fraser searched Google for maps of New Zealand. 'And you're *pregnant?*'

'Not personally. I just helped make it happen.'

'Are you sure she isn't another Amber?' Fraser demanded.

'Sherry is *nothing* like Amber.' If she was, Glenn would have her twisted around his finger and be calling the shots by now.

Fraser located Auckland on a map. 'And you say she's a cop?'

'Yes.'

He groaned. 'Why couldn't you knock up a model or an actress like everybody else?'

Hearing his own sentiments repeated didn't help. 'Stop talking crap and start earning that big fat fee I pay you,' Glenn snapped. 'I need a reason to be down here that will draw attention away from Sherry.'

Fraser was already surfing the web for info on New Zealand. 'Agriculture — *nope,* sheep and cows aren't sexy. Kiwifruit, beaches, ski fields — this place is really pretty. Wine! Wine is good!' He began to get excited.

'Forget about kiwifruit, forget about wine. *Golf.*' Glenn said firmly.

'Golf?'

'Yeah, *golf.* The place is jam-packed with golf courses with nobody on them. I'm going to do a golfing tour of New Zealand.'

'Your physical therapist might have something to say about that.'

'I don't give a rat's ass what my physical therapist says.'

Fraser sighed. People often mistook The Blitz's easy-going smile and good-ol'-boy charm for a low IQ and indolence and got knocked on their asses when they discovered they were up against one of the sharpest business brains in the NBA. 'I'll get back to you when I've done some more research.'

Glenn was godfather to Fraser's youngest son, but Fraser couldn't picture him with a kid of his own. Glenn was the eternal Peter Pan. It would help if his lawyers got warning that he might be embroiled in a custody battle. In Fraser's experience, it was inevitable that things would get messy. 'How're things going between the two of you?' he asked carefully.

'We went to a prenatal class last night.'

'You did?' Fraser tried to imagine Blitz Brogan at a prenatal class and failed. 'I mean — that's good.'

'Sherry arrested one of the fathers.'

'She ... did? I'm sure she had a good reason,' Fraser added hastily.

'You don't know the half of it,' Glenn said flatly. 'I know you're thinking about lawyers and how much this is going to cost me. Tell the lawyers the baby is going to live with me.'

'It ... *it is?*'

'For crissakes, Fraser, you're starting to sound like that doll I bought Lucy for Christmas.'

Lucy was Fraser's five-year-old daughter. 'Sorry. Keep talking.'

'Sherry and her family will have all the access they want. I'll let you know the name of her lawyer once we've discussed the details.' Glenn was looking forward to that discussion about as much as a knee in the groin. Sherry would want every 'i' dotted and every 't' crossed, but so would he. 'Tell my lawyers I don't want any hard-ball tactics. If they've got a problem with anything, they come to me first.'

'OK,' Fraser said reluctantly. 'I'll make some calls and get back to you with ideas for a publicity campaign. Anything else you want me to do?'

'Yeah, find me a midwife who can keep Sherry under control.'

It was Lisa who found a midwife when Glenn told Dan he'd struck out. Lisa had met Starr Warrender when they'd worked at the same café and Lisa was on the run from Dan. Starr was a midwife. She was tiny with red hair and huge lavender eyes and looked like she should have a set of wings sprouting from her back and be wearing a gauzy, petal-shaped dress instead of Doc Martens and bike leathers. She'd been a staunch friend to Lisa at a difficult time, and they'd kept in touch after Dan and Lisa moved to Denver. If Georgia had been born in New Zealand, Starr would have delivered her. She was the perfect person to take care of Sherry. She was sensitive without being sappy, and totally professional. Starr wouldn't be fazed by Sherry's unconventional approach to pregnancy, because she was more than a little alternative herself.

Starr remembered Sherry from Lisa's wedding, where there'd been an awful lot of very tall guests. According to Lisa, the biggest one of all, Dan's brother, was responsible for Sherry's pregnancy. She also explained that Sherry wasn't exactly over the moon about her condition.

'Sherry's kind of in denial about being pregnant,' Lisa

said.

'How long does she plan to stay there?' Starr asked.

'Until May.'

'I see.'

'Don't let that put you off,' Lisa said hastily. 'She really needs you.' She explained briefly about Sherry's reaction to seeing Georgia born, and that Glenn planned to bring the baby back to the States and raise it.

A nice, easy case, Starr thought.

'It's not all bad. For once, Glenn is trying to do the right thing, and my brother, Ben, is keeping a close eye on him and Sherry. He's the voice of reason. You remember Ben, don't you? He was at the wedding.'

'Was he one of the tall people?'

'No.'

'Afraid not.'

'You must remember him.' Lisa insisted. 'He was the guy playing guitar and singing in the band.'

Oh him — *the overweight guy who'd dumped his fiancée at the altar. He was the voice of reason?*

'Will you do it, Starr?' Lisa cajoled.

'Get Sherry to give me a call so we can talk. It's up to her to decide if she wants me or not.'

Lisa passed on the information to Glenn. 'My friend Starr Warrender is a midwife, and she's met Sherry. She said she'd do me a favour.'

Glenn wrote down the number. 'I knew buying you those golf clubs would pay off.'

'*Don't* joke with me, Glenn. If you were closer, I'd wrap one of those golf clubs around your head. You treated Sherry abysmally.'

'I'm aware of that, Lisa,' he replied stiffly.

'Getting her pregnant is the *worst* thing you could have done to her.'

'Sherry has communicated that to me.'

'So I heard,' she snorted. 'How are your eyes? Can you see straight yet?'

'I thought you were the sweet sister?' Glenn accused. 'The one who knows how to hand-wash woollens?'

Lisa fought back laughter. In her opinion, Glenn's sense of humour was even more attractive than his Hollywood good looks. 'I wouldn't let Sherry overhear you, unless you want another black eye.'

'Don't you feel just a little bit sorry for me?' he coaxed.

'The only thing I feel sorry about is that Dan and Ben got to you before me.'

'I'm sure Dan broke medical ethics when he hit me. His hands are supposed to be instruments of healing.'

'You deserved everything you got.' Lisa paused. 'I hear you and Ben and Sherry went to a childbirth education class the other night—'

'Who needs the Internet when the Jackson and Brogan family jungle drums are so efficient?' Glenn asked drily.

'And my big sister arrested somebody,' Lisa continued.

'Not me. There wasn't a banana in sight.'

She giggled.

'Hey, Lisa?'

'What?'

'You're the only one who seems to think I'll make a good father. Thanks for that.'

'You'd better not prove me wrong.'

'I won't. Can I speak to Dan?' When Dan came on the line, Glenn demanded, 'Who's Starr?' He trusted Lisa's judgement, but still wanted to know more about the person who would be taking care of Sherry.

'Remember the little redhead at our wedding? The girl Ben kept staring at when he was singing?'

Glenn couldn't recall Ben paying attention to any particular woman, but he did remember a small girl with short, mahogany hair and purple eyes whom Dan had nicknamed the Lavender Fairy.

'Do you mean the one you called the Lavender Fairy?'

'That's her.'

'I don't remember Ben paying any special attention to her.'

'You wouldn't,' Dan replied. 'You were too busy watching Sherry.'

And look where that got me, Glenn thought. He should warn Ben about the dangers of hooking up with women he met at weddings — or who threatened to arrest a man for bringing a banana into the country in his golf bag.

'Lisa said Starr will be the perfect midwife for Sherry, because she won't give or take any bullshit.'

Glenn looked at the telephone number he'd written down and thought that was why he'd bombed-out in his search for a midwife. Instead of asking what their philosophy was on pain relief during labour, he should have asked if they gave or took any bullshit.

George the angel popped up again in Sherry's

dreams.

'You could do with being nicer to Glenn, he's doing his best,' he said.

'Go away, George. You're not real.'

He laughed. 'Aren't I?'

'I want the sperm skydivers back,' Sherry said petulantly.

'And pay attention to the little 'un. She knows what she's talking about.'

'Who?'

'You heard me.'

The next morning there was a message on her answering machine from Glenn giving her the contact details of a midwife: Lisa's diminutive friend, Starr Warrender.

According to Ben, a lack of good household staff had forced his house guest to take over most of the meal preparation.

'You don't have any household staff,' Sherry said.

'There you go — Glenn's right,' Ben replied.

They were living on a lot of healthy liquid concoctions courtesy of the blender, plus fresh meat, fish and vegetables, and some nights, expensive dinners shipped in from a local restaurant when Glenn couldn't be bothered to cook.

'When it comes to his clothes and food, he's fussier than most women I know,' Ben said. He was the opposite.

Living with Sherry's brother reminded Glenn of his

college days. Despite the nine-year age gap, they were ideal house mates and when Glenn made noises about moving to a hotel Ben told him not to bother. Ben was so laid-back he was almost horizontal, but Glenn knew that, by letting him stay, Ben could keep a close eye on how Glenn was treating his sister. In true male fashion, they skirted the issue of Sherry and the baby. The most personal conversation they had was a brief discussion about why Ben called off his wedding to his long-term girlfriend at the altar a couple of years back.

'I realized I was doing it for all the wrong reasons. We thought Lisa was dead, and Mum and Dad were basket cases. Brenda and I had been engaged forever, and I thought a wedding would make everybody happy. Just as well Lisa knew better. What about you?' Ben asked. 'Before you asked Sherry, had you ever proposed?'

Glenn shook his head. 'Maybe if I'd practised, I wouldn't have botched things up when I asked Sherry.'

Ben snorted. 'Wouldn't have made any difference. The only man Sherry might consider marrying is Perry Westgaard.'

'The New Zealand golfer?'

He nodded and Glenn looked pissed. Perry Westgaard was making a name for himself on the US PGA tour.

'She's got the hots for him, plus all that free tuition would appeal to her.'

Glenn's admiration for the lanky New Zealander's game dimmed upon hearing that Sherry would look more favourably upon becoming Mrs Westgaard than she would on becoming Mrs Brogan. So what if Westgaard was a superlative golfer? Glenn was better-looking and had way more money.

He understood that Ben's loyalties lay with Sherry. Glenn tolerated his obsession with motorbikes and understood that Ben's lackadaisical attitude to his household plumbing was because, after building houses all day, he didn't want to think about plumbing when he got home at night. Glenn arranged for the supermarket to deliver, which kept the kitchen cupboards and refrigerator stocked and meant he could usually provide something edible at dinnertime. Ben ignored Glenn's chronic untidiness (no housekeeper to pick up after him) so long as he confined it to his bedroom, his dubious cooking skills (the housekeeper also cooked), and the way Glenn hogged the phone when his BlackBerry was out of order.

They both liked horror movies, especially the ones with crappy special effects, and some of the more recent animated kids' movies. Glenn's need to keep a low profile meant that Ben had to visit the DVD store and choose the films. The first time Glenn couldn't be bothered to cook and served up something stuck to the bottom of a roasting pan, which he swore was beef flash-fry, Ben paid him back by hiring *Bridget Jones's Diary* and *Thelma and Louise*.

Glenn was momentarily speechless when Ben tossed the DVDs onto the living-room sofa beside him. 'What the hell is this?' he erupted. 'You were supposed to get *Toy Story* and *Alien Goat Coven*.'

'And you were supposed to cook beef flash-fry, not beef fuck-up. If you don't get your act together, tomorrow night it'll be *Pride and Prejudice* and the other Bridget Jones movie,' Ben warned.

The next day Glenn swapped midwife-hunting for restaurant-hunting and found a local restaurant with an excellent menu and a young, single manageress who was easily persuaded to put a three-course meal for two into a cab. A few 'Aw, shucks' and 'honey's uttered in a slow, deep voice were just as effective as slow, smouldering looks at getting women to flutter, and the fat tip Glenn added helped sweeten the deal. Being cooped up at Ben's place was making him crazy; if he was deprived of decent movies, Glenn wouldn't be held responsible for his mental meltdown.

That night, after they'd finished prawns in a soy and ginger sauce, braised rack of lamb in a port jus, and tiramisu with raspberries, they propped their feet on Ben's coffee table and watched *Alien Goat Coven*.

Ben was so full he could barely move. 'If you could get rid of the five o'clock shadow, shrink ten inches, and become a woman, I'd let you propose to me.'

Glenn balanced a bottle of beer on his stomach and replied, 'I want a man who's in touch with his sensitive side. You're not prepared to talk through our problems, and you meddled with my DVD selection.' He smiled. 'Did I mention I met Sherry's friend Annemarie the other day?'

'No.' Ben kept his eyes on the credits rolling by on the screen.

'That woman is so toned she twangs when she walks. She asked me to tell you that she sends her best, but I got the feeling you'd already had it.'

'Annemarie is one very fit woman,' Ben said. 'It's a good idea to carb-load the night before a date with her.'

Glenn's duties also included taking messages from

the women in Ben's life. 'By the way, a girl called Ashley called for you today.'

'Ashley?' Ben brightened. 'What did she say?'

'Not to call her back.'

His feet hit the floor. 'Why not?'

'I told her that you'd finally come out of the closet about the long-distance relationship we'd been having for the past five years, and that I'd almost given up on you because I thought you couldn't commit.'

'What did you do that for?' Ben bellowed.

Glenn shrugged and sucked a drop of beer from his bottom lip. 'You messed with my DVDs.'

Ben glared at him. 'You know, I *like* living alone! And if I want somebody to watch crappy horror movies with me, I can phone Sherry.'

The bottle stalled halfway to Glenn's mouth. 'Sherry likes crappy horror movies?'

'She's the one who told me about *Alien Goat Coven*.'

He was equal parts surprised and impressed. When it came to dreadful special effects, AGC was right up there. He would have picked Sherry for a foreign-movie-with-subtitles girl — when she wasn't studying police training videos, of course.

'Sherry would have made a great guy,' Ben said.

Glenn snorted softly. 'Oh no, she wouldn't.' He considered this latest piece of information — at last, some common ground. 'Let's invite her to dinner.'

Chapter 13

Recent events had caused Sherry to rethink her opinion of Glenn. He'd been supportive — protective, even — when they'd visited her parents. He didn't like what she did for a job but he'd helped out when she'd arrested Jerry, and he'd offered to marry her when they both knew he didn't want to. Sherry considered she'd done Glenn a favour by refusing, but he'd done her a bigger one by offering to raise the baby. When it came to women, he was a hopeless case: they threw themselves at him, and Glenn didn't see why he shouldn't catch one or two. He was shameless about using his looks to get what he wanted — his behaviour around Nora was a perfect example: Glenn only had to look at her a certain way and she started fluttering like a flag.

Sherry used dropping off the curtains for Glenn's bedroom as an excuse to pay a visit to Ben's house. She'd been so freaked-out by what George had said in her dream that she'd only just got around to making an appointment with Starr Warrender. Sherry refused to believe that the George in her dreams was the same George Lisa talked about; it was just a coincidence. She said nothing about it to Lisa when they spoke. Lisa mentioned Starr would want to know Glenn's family medical history, too, so Sherry decided to invite him along. He was returning to the States soon, and they needed to talk about the legal arrangements.

She stopped by her parents' house to collect the curtains and mend a few fences with her mother and father. Things had been strained between them since they'd heard the news about Glenn raising the baby. Ben had awarded his mother the job of chief-in-charge-of-curtains when he'd moved into his house, and Jill had been systematically working her way through each room putting up curtains. Glenn's bedroom was the last to be done. Ben kept forgetting to collect the curtains, and Jill had given up reminding him — or at least she had until His Highness took up residence.

'The guest bedroom overlooks the house next-door, and Ben said his new neighbour is an old lady. I bet Dan's brother is just as bad as Ben about wandering around in the altogether. What must the poor old dear think?' Jill asked as she handed over the curtains.

That she got the house really cheap? Sherry laid the plastic bag on the back seat of her car. 'I doubt that Glenn would care, he's used to people looking at him. If we hung a hoop on the bedroom door and gave him a basketball, he probably wouldn't even notice.'

'Very funny,' Jill remarked tartly. 'Ben says he's got a housekeeper in Denver to take care of things like curtains.'

Sherry pictured a buxom blonde with waist-length braids wearing a gingham mini-dress and answering to the name of Heidi. She'd have to insist there was something in their agreement about Glenn employing a kind but ugly nanny — like Nanny McPhee.

'Have you been overdoing things?' Jill asked. 'You look tired.'

Sherry had spent the morning with one of her

families, an elderly couple who'd taken protection orders out against one another but still lived in the same house. It was hardly an ideal situation, especially when one or both of them got drunk and started fighting and the neighbours called the police. When Sherry had arrived at the house, she'd discovered Ida, the old woman, stuck in the toilet, and Trigg, her husband, pounding on the door because he needed to go. Sherry managed to get the toilet door open and Ida out and into bed. Trigg calmed down once he'd used the toilet.

If she looked tired, it wasn't because of Trigg and Ida, though, it was because of nuisance ex-boyfriends. Stuart had called twice last night and woken her up. After the second call, Sherry unplugged the phone and pulled the battery out of her cell but hadn't been able get back to sleep. Nora said he'd called around a couple of times when Sherry was at work. He was becoming a royal pain in the butt, but Sherry didn't want to worry her mother. 'I'm OK,' she said.

'You'd say you were OK if you were in the middle of an earthquake,' Jill retorted.

And Sherry thought: *Isn't being pregnant the same thing?*

Sherry had a key to Ben's house. She let herself in and found Glenn sprawled on the sofa in the lounge, wearing a pair of shorts and a sports vest and looking sweaty. He was watching *Ice Age* on the television and jumped when Sherry appeared beside him carrying the curtains. 'Shit! Don't do that!'

Sherry hugged the plastic bag and smiled. 'Oh dear, did I frighten you?'

Glenn hit the pause button. 'How did you get in?'

She held up the door key. 'I thought you were in charge of catering. Why aren't you in the kitchen wearing an apron and waving a whisk?'

He stretched to his feet. 'It wasn't a choice. Somehow, I inherited the job.'

'Ben's style of management is very inclusive. He's a great believer in delegating — especially the jobs he doesn't like doing.' Sherry studied the bug-eyed squirrel grappling with an acorn, frozen on the screen. 'That's a kiddie movie.'

Glenn shook his head. 'A common mistake; it's actually a social commentary on the decaying morals of society through the ages. That's why it's called *Ice Age*.'

'It's a kids' movie, Glenn.'

'I'm not going to waste time trying to convert a non-believer.'

Sherry checked out the DVDs stacked around Ben's plasma television. *Shrek, Wallace and Gromit, Swamp Monsters from Fifth Avenue, Killer Piranhas in Paris, Bridget Jones's Diary* and *Thelma and Louise*. 'You and Ben watched *Bridget Jones's Diary* and *Thelma and Louise?*' she demanded incredulously.

'It was my punishment for ruining dinner the other night. *Thelma and Louise* was OK because it had a car chase at the end, but *Bridget Jones* didn't even make it out of the box.' Glenn watched Sherry closely. 'However, *Alien Goat Coven* was excellent.'

Especially the zombie goat-attack scene, which was so bad it deserved an Oscar, but Sherry kept that to herself. She'd seen *Bridget Jones's Diary* with Annemarie and liked that, too, but preferred something grittier. *The Shawshank Redemption* was her favourite movie, closely followed by *The Taking of Pelham 123* — the John Travolta/Denzel Washington version. 'It's nice that the baby will have somebody to go to the movies with until it outgrows kiddie flicks and leaves you behind.'

Glenn hit the off button. 'By which time it'll be ready for those training videos on organizing identity parades and fingerprinting felons. Did you call the midwife?'

'I'm seeing her on Friday. Want to come?'

For a few seconds Glenn was too surprised to answer. When he did, he was careful to adopt the same offhand tone as Sherry. 'OK.'

'Lisa said Starr will want to ask you some questions, too — like, are you human?' Sherry looked at the huge pair of blue high-performance sports shoes he wore. 'You are, aren't you?'

'Not only human,' Glenn drawled, 'but perfect, too.'

'I see that problem you have with low self-esteem is still giving you trouble.'

He smiled at the comeback and the view. Ever since he'd helped break Sherry out of her jeans, Glenn kept thinking about the little bump under her belly button and how strangely possessive he felt about it and her. It was like he'd taken a few steps backwards on the evolutionary scale and turned into a caveman. He could imagine what Sherry would say if she knew.

As usual, she looked great. Her black hair was loose on her shoulders, and instead of her uniform she wore black leggings, flat-heeled black boots with narrow toes, and a white T-shirt with thin, horizontal navy stripes beneath a man's black suit jacket. All that was missing was a beret slanted over one eye. The jacket had belonged to Sherry's grandfather and been destined for the second-hand clothing store after he died, but she had rescued it, along with a trilby hat. Glenn recognized the quality of the vintage jacket. He'd bet his house in Cherry Hills that the tailor who'd made it had never pictured it on a long-legged, full-breasted siren with a sexy black mole on her cheekbone. He wondered if Sherry was wearing one of her frilly balcony bras, or if pregnant women had to give up that kind of thing.

'I didn't think you went anywhere without your Kevlar vest and personal radio.'

'For your information, it's called a SRBA vest, short for Stab Resistant Body Armour.'

When did pregnant police officers stop wearing stab-resistant body armour and get assigned to a nice, safe desk job?

'I promise I'll stay away from the kitchen knives.' Glenn pointed at the plastic bag she was carrying. 'Are those for my room? The hotel management has been promising them ever since I got here.'

Sherry laid the bag over the back of an armchair. 'The hotel management had nothing to do with it. We've been receiving complaints at the station about a big Yank flashing the neighbours.'

'I keep telling people on the waiting list to be patient. There's only one of me to go around.'

She rolled her eyes. 'Where's Ben?'

'In the garage communing with the Ducati.'

Sherry gave Glenn's rumpled khaki shorts and faded

turquoise, yellow and white Cougars vest the same critical once-over he'd given her jacket. His Superman curl was stuck to his forehead like a fishhook. The vest showed off his chest and shoulders, and the shorts, the muscle in his legs and the shiny pink scar on his knee. It occurred to Sherry that if she had to be pregnant, she'd picked the perfect sperm donor. The baby owed her a thank-you — Glenn could supply the looks, and she'd supply the brains.

'Glenda, I hope your housewifely duties aren't turning you into a frump.'

'I was shooting baskets earlier.'

So far as Sherry knew, Ben didn't own a basketball hoop. 'Where? In your head?'

He crooked a finger. 'Follow me.'

She followed him down the hallway to his bedroom, which was a chaos of clothes, shoes, books (on pregnancy and childbirth, Sherry noted, and urban design — what was that all about?), hand weights (apparently His Highness didn't think Ben's were up to scratch), a Swiss ball, and empty coffee mugs and plates. The only tidy area was the corner where his precious BlackBerry was plugged in, recuperating on the chest of drawers.

Sherry picked it up. 'I'm surprised you didn't just throw it away and buy a new one.'

'I'm grounded, remember?' Glenn replied drily.

She replaced the BlackBerry, and tripped over a size-fourteen custom-made shoe as she made her way around the bed. 'Oops!'

Glenn's hands shot out to catch her, but she righted herself. 'Are you OK?' he asked sharply.

Sherry waved him away. 'Are there any clean dishes and mugs left in the kitchen cupboards?'

Glenn kicked the shoe and other debris under the bed to clear a path to the bi-fold doors overlooking the courtyard outside the bedroom. 'It was a minor problem until I bought two more dinner services.' He gestured expansively at the large courtyard beyond the glass. 'My new practice area.'

The concrete was wet from the rain that had been falling all afternoon. Two sides of the house and the back of the garage wrapped around the courtyard, leaving one end open to a grassed area with a clothesline and fence and the house next-door. A basketball hoop with a backboard was bolted to the back wall of the garage. Sherry rested her fingertips on the glass. 'When did that arrive?'

'The day after I did.'

'That is so sweet,' she purred. 'Most little boys have blankies, but you have a basketball hoop.'

Glenn grinned. 'And most little girls have Barbies, but you probably have an Action Man with a ball and chain strapped to one ankle.' He stared at the back of her head. 'I was going to call and ask you to dinner.'

She stiffened.

'I'll cook, and Ben said he'll tidy up.'

Glenn watched Sherry relax and reined in his frustration. She'd thought he was asking her out on a date.

'OK, I'll come so long as you promise I won't catch botulism.'

He stared across her head and said sarcastically, 'How can I promise that, Officer Jackson? I can't even spell it.'

Glenn moved away and scooped a basketball from the chaos on the floor. He spun the ball on his fingertips and watched Sherry. 'I hear you've taken up golf.'

She turned to look at him. 'I decided if you could play it, then anybody could.'

The ball spun and his eyes gleamed. 'What's your handicap?'

'Twenty-four, plus a really bad slice. What's yours?'

'Two.'

Sherry spread her fingertips against her chest and widened her eyes. 'Why, Blitz, I'm surprised. I'd have thought you'd be a scratch golfer, playing every day like you do.'

'I don't play every day, Scarlett.'

She gasped. 'You mean you take Sundays off for church?'

Glenn smiled. This was the playful side of Sherry that he'd seen the night at the motel.

Sherry's stomach broke into a tap dance. Annemarie was right about Glenn being a gorgeous hunk. He was used to women dropping their knickers like leaves in autumn, and Sherry was convinced that her main attraction for him was that she was unavailable and didn't care that he was rich and famous. He *was* still attracted to her; it was there in his eyes and in the air between them. Sherry wondered how long he'd feel that way when she began to puff up like popped corn and her ankles got thick. When Glenn started spinning the ball on the tip of his index finger, she rolled her eyes. 'You are *such* a show-off.'

He grinned. 'So where are you going to take me to

play?'

'I don't want to play with you — the repercussions are too long- term.'

'Come on,' Glenn coaxed. 'I know how much you want to beat me at something.'

'No — *with* something — I want to beat you *with* something.' She considered his offer. 'OK. We can fit in a round of golf on Friday before we see Starr, and I'll come to dinner on Saturday night.'

'I was going to spend Friday morning in the kitchen, but I'm willing to rearrange my diary.'

'More like sit on your bum in the living room and watch kiddie movies,' Sherry said. 'Come incognito — I don't want to spend the morning fighting off basketball groupies — and I get to choose the course.' One that didn't favour a big hitter. 'How many shots are you going to give me?'

Glenn grunted. 'You want me to wear a disguise *and* give you shots? What's in this for me, Sherry Ann?'

She smiled sweetly. 'The pleasure of my company.'

Ben wandered past the bedroom doorway, wiping his hands on an oily rag. He stopped when he saw Sherry smiling at Glenn and wondered what Glenn had done to earn it. Find a way to give birth for her? 'I didn't know you were here.'

'I brought the curtains over. I'm coming to dinner on Saturday night.'

'You are?' Ben's surprise grew. 'I didn't know.'

Sherry arched a brow at Glenn. She'd bet Ben didn't know he was on dishes, either. 'Can you make Saturday night a restaurant-food night? I like to chew my food.'

Glenn looked wounded. 'I find that remark

particularly hurtful considering the strides I've made in the kitchen.'

'Just make sure you don't cook your beef specialty.' Ben stared intently at Glenn's long, bare legs and the length of Sherry's beneath the black leggings.

She glanced down at herself and back at Ben. 'What are you staring at?'

He flipped the rag around his neck and gripped the ends. 'As soon as the baby is up and walking, I'm going to start training it for the Melbourne Cup.'

Titirangi Golf Course was situated in the western suburbs of Auckland near the bush-clad slopes of the Waitakere Ranges. It was a pretty course, but this Friday morning it looked even prettier because the previous night's rain had turned the bush and fairways a brilliant green. Birds dipped and flitted as the sun came out from behind the clouds and turned the drops of water clinging to the grass and leaves into diamonds. The only storm clouds were the ones on Sherry and Glenn's faces as they stood opposite one another outside the clubhouse.

'I said come *incognito*, not as Zorro,' Sherry snapped.

Glenn was dressed from head to foot in black — black pants, golf shirt and shoes, black golf glove, and Blitz Easy Rider black wraparound sunglasses. All that was missing was a black cloak and a sword. During the car ride, Sherry had been sunk in gloom because she'd had to buy a pair of golfing pants similar to the ones Nora wore. Being pregnant wasn't the same as being overweight; you couldn't breathe in and redistribute excess kilos. She'd already deprived the baby of folic acid; she didn't want to flatten it, too.

It wasn't until they exited her car that Sherry noticed Glenn's resemblance to Don Diego.

Glenn jammed his black Stetson on his head. 'You said you didn't want anybody to recognize me.'

Her eyes skittered away from the hat. 'Yes, I know. I just wish you were a little more ...'

'What?'

'Invisible.' His lips thinned, and Sherry decided to retreat to the golf shop. 'I'll pay the green fees and pick up our cards.'

'*I'll* pay the green fees,' he insisted.

She retraced her steps and looked up into the mirrored lenses of Glenn's sunglasses. His mouth was set as hard as concrete. 'I'm trying to be reasonable.'

He reached into his back pocket, pulled out his wallet and slapped several bills into her palm. 'I'm touched.'

Sherry paid the green fees and went to load her golf clubs onto the back of the golf cart, but Glenn nudged her aside and loaded her bag and his custom-made set of Callaways. The four hours it would take to get around the course stretched ahead of them like an eternity. This was supposed to be fun, not punishment.

Glenn relented when he saw the dispirited droop of Sherry's mouth. It was hard to stay angry with a woman who had such pretty, pink lips and a sexy mole on her cheekbone. Her periwinkle-blue shirt brought out the colour of her eyes, and her ponytail bounced beneath her black cap with the silver fern above the brim. Glenn watched her slip on a pair of D&G sunglasses and reach under her shirt to tug at her white pants. She'd been fiddling with them and wriggling around on the drive over like a toddler wanting to go potty.

'Have you got a safety pin in those?' Glenn asked.

She coloured. 'No! They're brand-new!'

He studied the pants. 'Nora's got a pair just like them.'

Sherry glared at him.

Glenn was on a roll. 'You're sure you don't need to use the restroom before we start? We've still got a couple of minutes before we tee off. You're sure you don't want to go potty first?'

She gritted her teeth. 'No, I do not.'

'Only asking,' he said mildly. 'I don't want you to have any excuses when you lose.'

Glenn was impressed by how much Sherry had improved since Fossil Trace. If she could lose her slice and stop rushing her shots, she'd make a decent player. Sherry was desperate to beat Glenn, but it became increasingly obvious she was still way out of her league when he drilled his tee-shots straight up the fairway while Sherry drilled hers into the rough.

'How do you do that?' she demanded after he'd hit a shot that faded gently to the right and landed on the green.

'Lots of practice.'

'Like all those baskets you used to shoot when you were playing basketball?'

'Something like that.'

The only part of Glenn's face that Sherry could see

was his nose and bad-boy mouth, which right now looked more sad than bad. 'You really miss it, don't you?'

He braced a hand on his club and stared at the green. 'More than I can say.'

They got back in the cart and went to find Sherry's ball. When they stopped again, she suddenly asked, 'Do you really think you're ready to take on a baby?'

He slipped off his glasses and stared at her. 'More ready than you.'

Sherry pulled a five-iron from her bag. 'I suppose you think I don't care.'

Glenn felt like he was walking into a minefield blindfolded. 'I don't really know you,' he hedged.

She practiced her swing. 'Because I'm a woman, people automatically expect I'll be the one who puts my career on hold and stays at home.' Glenn watched the head of the club swish through the grass. 'But I like what I do. I just passed one exam, and I'm studying for another to make sergeant.' The club swished again. 'I don't want to put my career on hold, and I've seen what happens to kids who don't have a stable home life.'

'I've seen what happens to them, too.' When Sherry remained doubtful, Glenn looked her squarely in the eyes and said, 'You don't know me either. We've done everything back-to-front.'

She looked glum. 'That's what happens when you act like a skanky ho.'

'If you were a skanky ho, then so was I.' Glenn dropped his voice. 'But you weren't,' he said quietly, 'you were wonderful.' His gaze took in her direct blue eyes, too-long nose, soft, pink lips and determined jaw line. How did such unrelenting features manage to look so feminine?

Sherry pointed her five-iron at him. 'You're trying to schmooze me.'

'No, I'm not.' One of her black brows rose at the blatant lie, and Glenn's mouth curved in a rueful smile. 'Well ... maybe a little.'

The club wavered. 'Every time you look at me like that or make a suggestive comment, I'm going to add a shot to your score card.' He reached up and deliberately altered the angle of the Stetson.

'You wore that hat on purpose, didn't you?' she accused. 'To put me off my game.'

'I don't know what it is about this hat,' Glenn said innocently. 'Nora complains when I wear it, too, but it never puts her off her game.'

Sherry took her shot and marched back to the cart. 'Come on, we're holding up play.'

'Yes ... Ma'am.'

While they played, Glenn and Sherry discussed how they wanted the baby to be raised. They both wanted it to know it had two parents, which would mean Glenn making trips to New Zealand and Sherry visiting the States.

'I'll pay for your airfares,' he said.

'There's no need: I may not have your millions, but I'm not destitute either.' She kept her eyes on the fairway. 'I know it's going to be hard ... afterwards, but I've watched colleagues try to raise a kid on their own and it doesn't work — either the job or the child suffers, usually the child, and that's not the way it's supposed to be. We both had two parents who were there for us and loved us. Better that this child has two parents who love it and one who's always there for it.' She stared at Glenn. 'Can you promise to do that?'

He nodded.

'Say it, then.'

Glenn took her hand and shook it. 'I promise I'll always be there.'

Sherry extricated her hand. 'Good.' She hit her next shot into the bush. *'Bugger!'*

Glenn laughed so hard he nearly fell out of the cart. He jumped out with his hands in the air when Sherry advanced on him waving her club. 'I swear I wasn't laughing at your shot!' Glenn protested. 'It was the way you said "bugger". It gets to Dan every time Lisa says it, too.'

He was saved from being brained with a golf club by the pressure building in Sherry's bladder. She jiggled from one foot to the other and thrust her club at him. 'Take this. I need to go.'

'What have I been trying to tell you?'

She jogged towards the bush. 'Shut up and come with me.'

'Thanks for the offer, but I don't go in for group peeing.'

'I need you to look for my ball and make sure nobody is coming.' She disappeared into the trees. Glenn rolled his eyes and followed. Sherry chose a manuka tree and pointed in the opposite direction. 'I think my ball is somewhere over there.'

The trees were so thick they met overhead and blocked out the light. Glenn removed his sunglasses and hooked them in the neck of his golf shirt. 'Forget the ball, Sherry; we're never going to find it. Play a new one.'

'It won't hurt to take a look.' She ducked behind the manuka tree. 'And whistle!'

'Why? You hate my whistling.'

'If somebody comes, stop whistling so I'll know.' There was a rustling sound. 'Glenn? Are you still there?'

He began whistling *Wet Sand* by the Red Hot Chili Peppers and kicking at the undergrowth. 'Let me know if you're having trouble getting started and I'll do *Raindrops Keep Falling On My Head*. It's a favourite of Mom's.'

Glenn continued to poke half-heartedly at the undergrowth and whistle until he saw a man coming through the trees from the opposite fairway. They stopped and eyed one another warily. Glenn wondered how he was supposed to remain incognito. Pretend he couldn't speak English? For Sherry's benefit, he called loudly, 'Hi, there! Great day for a round, isn't it?'

The man cautiously picked his way closer. He was at least thirty years older than Glenn and had a beer-gut hanging over his trousers. He took in Glenn's towering height and the breadth of his shoulders and stopped. 'Lost a ball?'

'My ...' *Girlfriend? Sister-in-law? The-woman-I-accidentally- got-pregnant?* '... partner did.' The man looked around and Glenn pointed to a different bush to the one Sherry was using. 'She's pregnant. Had to see a man about a dog.' He'd learned the phrase from Ben.

Comprehension dawned on his companion's face. 'We renamed tee shots "pee" shots when my wife was pregnant, because she had to pay a penny at every hole.' He stared hard at Glenn, who laughed politely at the joke.

Glenn had an uneasy feeling he'd been recognized and hoped that Sherry wouldn't come out yet. She wasn't the type to be embarrassed about being caught peeing behind a bush — she'd exit like a queen — but if he had been recognized it would be better if she stayed out of sight.

'I need to do the same.' The man patted his lower abdomen. 'Dodgy prostate.'

Glenn nodded and made a show of checking the area near Sherry so that the other guy would go somewhere else to relieve himself. On his way back to the fairway, the man advised, 'Wouldn't waste time on that ball, I'd play a new one if I were you.'

As soon as he'd gone, Glenn made his way over to the manuka tree. 'Sherry? Are you OK?'

Her voice was muffled. 'Not exactly,'

'What did you do this time?'

'Got my shirt stuck in my zipper.'

'Jesus, Sherry ...' Glenn rounded the bush to find her struggling with the zip. 'How do you manage to get yourself dressed in the morning?'

'It's getting more difficult by the day.'

He squatted in front of her and freed her shirt from the zipper. 'This is becoming a habit.' Glenn looked at her bump. It was bigger than when he'd last seen it. 'Would you look at that — *progress*. If you hadn't just taken a pee in here, I'd consider falling to my knees and cupping you.'

Sherry zipped her pants. 'And because I *have* just taken a pee, I'd let you.'

Glenn stood up. 'I think that guy might have recognized me.'

'He asked if you were Zorro?'

'Doesn't it bother you?'

Their discussion about the baby had gone a long way towards allaying Sherry's doubts about Glenn taking responsibility. For the first time in weeks, there seemed to be light at the end of the tunnel. 'I should have come out from behind the bush — he might have mistaken me for Catherine Zeta-Jones.'

Glenn hooked an arm around her shoulders. 'Come on, Sherry Ann, I've got to finish kicking your ass at golf.'

Chapter 14

Starr Warrender was twenty-six years old and five-foot-one-and-three-quarter-inches tall. The extra three-quarters of an inch were important, because it put her closer to five foot two than five foot one, which mattered when you had a Napoleon complex. The only thing Starr hated more than being told she was short was being told she was cute. It was one of the reasons she gelled her short mahogany-coloured hair into spikes, wore a silver stud in one nostril, dressed in bike leathers and Doc Martens, and rode a silver-and-black Kawasaki ZZR 250. There was nothing she could do, however, about her lavender-coloured eyes or the Cupid's bow in her top lip. She'd briefly considered brown contact lenses, but settled for a direct, business-like stare and never wore lipstick.

Starr parked the Kawasaki outside Sherry's garage and unpacked her laptop from one of the panniers on the bike. She removed her helmet and sunglasses and adjusted the backpack carrying the rest of her equipment. A tall, lumpy woman with a skinny braid and carrying a watering can gazed disapprovingly at her and the bike from the front steps of the house next-door. Starr could spot a hip-replacement-waiting-to-happen and a motorbike-hater when she saw one. She nodded politely and carried her laptop to the door and knocked.

Sherry Jackson didn't answer. When the door opened, Starr found herself looking up at Lisa's brother,

Ben — the voice of reason. At Lisa's wedding he'd been overweight and unhappy; now he was lean and tanned and smiling. The only thing that hadn't changed was his blue-grey eyes, which crinkled at the corners as he smiled down at her. 'I remember you. You're the Lavender Fairy.'

Starr placed her helmet and laptop at her feet and carefully removed her black leather gloves. She'd overheard the nickname Dan Brogan had given her and didn't appreciate it now any more than she had the first time she'd heard it. Keeping her hands busy gave Starr time to imagine the look on Ben Jackson's face if she used a move on him from her kick-boxing class. Starr smiled thinly. He might re-think calling her a lavender fairy when he was flat on his back and winded. 'I remember you, too,' she said politely. 'Didn't you call off your wedding at the church?'

Ben's smile faded. Women jumped to all the wrong conclusions when they heard about his aborted wedding. He'd stopped feeling the need to defend his actions or explain a long time ago, but replied stiffly, 'It was a mutual decision.'

Starr watched him with her fairy eyes. 'I'm sure it was.'

'We're still friends. Brenda's much happier than she would have been if we'd got married. She's got a new career.' *Why* was he explaining himself?

'That's nice,' she murmured. 'What does she do?'

Ben hesitated. 'She's an undertaker.'

Her brows rose.

He'd made it sound like his ex-fiancée would rather spend time with dead people than be married to him.

Starr peered around the door. 'Is Sherry here?'

Ben dug his hands into the front pockets of his work jeans. 'She's just got back from playing golf with Glenn. He went home to change, but he'll be back soon. I came by to fix the pantry door.' *And see if you're still as cute as I remembered from the wedding.*

Maybe on the outside, Ben concluded, but Ms Starr had some heavy stuff happening on the inside, including a Napoleon complex the size of the chip on her shoulder. He hoped Lisa had done the right thing recommending her. Ben noticed the Kawasaki as Starr carried her laptop and helmet across the threshold. 'Nice bike.'

'Thank you.' It was Starr's pride and joy. She waited for the usual smart comment about flying midwives, but he only asked if there was anything he could carry for her.

Starr looked up — she *always* had to look up — at Ben and considered. She loved her job, loved looking after pregnant women and their babies. It was a privilege to be invited into their homes and be part of such a special time in their lives, but along the way Starr had met some oddball husbands, brothers and grandfathers-to-be. She had a nose for sniffing out nut jobs and sleaze balls, and never put herself in a position where her safety could be compromised. Just to be on the safe side, Starr carried a can of mace in her backpack and attended regular kick-boxing classes. Ben Jackson wasn't a nut job or a sleaze ball, but he *was* trouble. She gripped the handle of her laptop bag firmly. 'I can manage, thank you.'

Ben upgraded the chip on her shoulder to a boulder. If she had such a hang-up about being small, why didn't she ditch the Doc Martens and invest in some platform boots? Although, on closer inspection, he doubted they stocked them in the children's department.

He showed Starr to the living room and went upstairs to tell Sherry the new doula had arrived.

Sherry was on the phone to Misty at the Women's Refuge. Stacey had taken the children to see her mother and Vance had turned up at the house, drunk, and threatened her. She cupped the receiver and told Ben, 'Tell Starr I'll be down in a moment; I just need to take this call. Have you got time to make her a coffee or something, or do you have to be somewhere?'

Instead of heading off to the building supplies depot like he was supposed to, Ben returned to the living room where Starr was waiting on the white sofa. 'Sherry is just taking a work call. Can I make you a tea or a coffee?'

Starr flashed what Ben was coming to think of as her professional smile. It went on again and off again like a light bulb. 'No, thank you.' He'd never heard somebody say thank you so often without meaning it. She unzipped her black leather jacket and worked her arm free. Beneath the jacket she wore a plain white T-shirt with cap sleeves that showed off her toned arms. Ben's curiosity got the better of him. The Fairy worked out *and* drove a Kawasaki ZZR. It was a small bike with big-bike pretensions — how appropriate.

He settled into the green armchair. 'How long have you had the Kawasaki?'

'About a year.'

Starr hooked her jacket over the back of the sofa, removed her laptop from the bag, and booted it up whilst unobtrusively cataloguing the changes in Ben's appearance since she'd last seen him two years ago. His double chin and love handles had been replaced by a taut jaw and lean waist. That easy smile and innocent gaze would let him slip undetected through a girl's radar and wreak havoc. Fortunately, Starr always kept her shields up. She could tell that Ben was interested in her. He probably thought she was cute. Being raised by lesbian parents had earned her a lot of teasing at school. It was more common now for kids to have same-sex parents, but when Starr was growing up people were a lot less accepting. They failed to notice that Mimi Warrender and Jocelyn Stephen's relationship had stood the test of time while parents in heterosexual relationships were getting divorced.

Ben leaned an elbow on the arm of the chair and cupped his chin. 'I've got a Ducati 900.'

Starr's hands stilled on the keyboard of her laptop and her kewpie-doll eyes glittered. 'A 900SS Desmo?'

His brows rose and fell in assent.

Beneath the white T-shirt, Starr's meagre assets rose and fell as she slowly inhaled and exhaled. The Ducati 900 Super Sport Desmo was really a road-legal racing bike. It was a raw, in-your-face superbike, the kind of bike that Starr would have owned if she'd been a foot taller and a hundred pounds heavier. She stared at Ben enviously. 'How long have you had it?'

'A couple of years.'

Her interrogation was interrupted by the arrival of Sherry, and a few moments later, Glenn. Ben was curious to see how Ms Warrender coped when confronted with a giant. She smiled and shook hands with Glenn and sat down quickly again, as if she knew how tiny she looked beside him.

The bike, the boots, the attitude — Ben was fascinated.

Glenn noticed. Starr didn't look anything like he imagined a midwife would look. Instead of a uniform, she wore black leather pants, Doc Martens, a silver star in her nose and had short, gelled red hair. He was relieved that the only decoration on the black leather jacket draped across the sofa was a white star on the back and not chains and patches. It took Glenn only seconds to decide that Ben was wasting his time. Starr wasn't giving him any encouragement; she might as well have had a 'No Trespass' sticker stuck to her forehead. It felt like payback for Glenn's unwanted role as Ben's social secretary, a job Ben had reclaimed following the debacle with Ashley.

As Ben rose to leave, he correctly interpreted the reason for the smirk on Glenn's face. 'Were you still wanting a bed at my place?' he asked pointedly. 'Or have you decided to move into that hotel?'

Glenn's smile widened. 'Your new neighbour, Cloe, offered me the spare room at her place, but I explained you'd miss me.'

Cloe was seventy and had taken a shine to The-Boys-Next-Door after Glenn helped move some furniture and Ben fixed the garage door.

Starr spoke up. 'Cloe? Do you mean Cloe Warrender?'

'I don't know her surname,' Ben answered. 'She moved next-door a couple of weeks ago.'

'What's your address?'

He told her.

'Cloe's my grandmother. She said she likes her new neighbours.' Starr paused. 'Especially the guy who doesn't have curtains on his bedroom window.'

Lisa was right, Starr did want details of Sherry's and Glenn's medical histories, and their families' medical histories as well.

'Is there any history of twins in your family, Sherry?'

Sherry looked like she wanted to wash Starr's mouth out with soap. 'No, thank God.' It occurred to her that she was only one-half of the equation. She looked at Glenn and demanded, 'You don't have any twins in your family, do you?'

He was tempted to say *only my quadruplet cousins*. 'No, the Brogans tend to come one at a time; there usually isn't enough room for more than one of us.' Glenn stopped. The quadruplet cousins remark would have been safer, because she would have known it was less likely to be true.

'What does that mean?' Sherry demanded. 'How much did you weigh at birth?'

He squinted at the ceiling as if he were trying to remember rather than think of a way to extricate himself from the crap his smart-ass mouth had dropped him in. Glenn had called his mother and knew exactly how much he and Dan had weighed when they were born, but suspected Sherry would have a heart attack if he told her. He sneaked a look at Starr and sensed that she was on to him, although how she could give the impression that she was rolling her eyes in exasperation when her expression was so composed eluded him.

'Don't look at Starr, she can't help you,' Sherry said grimly. 'You *know*. If you don't tell me, I'll call your mother.'

Glenn hadn't been threatened with that since grade school. 'Eleven pounds,' he admitted reluctantly.

Sherry turned to Starr in despair. 'I want drugs! *Lots of drugs!*'

Glenn scowled. 'It's not like I was in there asking them to super-size me.'

'We pay much more attention to the birth weight of the mother and her siblings,' Starr said smoothly.

'I weighed nine pounds three ounces when I was born,' Sherry said flatly.

Glenn tried to be positive. 'But Lisa was tiny — I remember her saying so when she was having Georgia.'

She eyed him stonily. 'Lisa was premature.'

He didn't remember that part.

'Glenn was a second baby; first babies are usually smaller,' Starr soothed.

The door knocker rattled, and Glenn nearly hurdled the armchair to answer it.

He returned tight-lipped and accompanied by a visitor in time to overhear Sherry complain bitterly, 'I thought nine pounds three ounces was bad enough.'

'Sherry?' the visitor said.

Sherry stared. It was Stuart, her ex-boyfriend. 'What are you doing here?'

'Why didn't you tell me, Sherry?' he demanded.

'Tell you what?' she asked blankly.

'That you're *pregnant*!'

Sherry's stomach felt like it had dropped into her

shoes. Stuart had to know he wasn't the father. 'How did you find out?'

'Who's this?' Glenn asked ominously.

The two men couldn't have been more different. Stuart was fair-haired, finely built and emotional; Glenn was like a huge, dark, smouldering volcano. Sherry swallowed. This was *not* good. 'Stuart is an ex-boyfriend,' she explained nervously.

Stuart didn't appreciate the description. He looked at Glenn suspiciously. 'Who are you?'

'Another ex,' Glenn replied tightly.

Starr didn't know whether to stay or go. She wished Sherry's muscle-bound brother hadn't left, and eyed the pocket on her backpack that held her can of mace.

Sherry looked embarrassed. 'I'm sorry about this,' she said. 'Perhaps you can come back later in the week?' She helped Starr pack up her things and walked her to the front door.

'Sherry, will you be alright?' Starr glanced in the direction of the living room. 'Do you want me to call anybody? Your brother?'

Sherry shook her head. 'Thank you, Starr, but I'll be fine. I know how awful this looks ...'

Starr squeezed her hand. 'Don't worry about it. Are you sure you'll be OK?'

Sherry nodded. 'I can handle Stuart.'

'And Glenn?'

'He wouldn't hurt me, Starr.'

As soon as Sherry stepped into the living room,

Stuart started on her. 'I've phoned, I've texted and I've emailed, and you've ignored every one of my messages. I've come around twice, and you've been out and your nosy neighbour wouldn't tell me when she expected you to be home, and I *knew* she *knew*,' he accused.

Perhaps Nora wasn't so bad.

Stuart designed websites and databases and lived out his life on social-networking pages. He kept staring at Glenn as if he was trying to work out where he might have seen him. Sherry was worried that if she handled this badly, he'd post something about her and Glenn and all hell would break loose. Stuart looked pale but determined; Glenn looked like a bomb about to detonate. Having her personal life hung out to dry by two of her former lovers and watched over by her midwife was even more humiliating than telling her family and work colleagues she was pregnant. Sherry was certain Stuart knew he wasn't the father and didn't understand why he was here. She didn't blame Glenn for being angry, but she could only handle one angry male at a time.

'Come back tomorrow night, Stuart, and we'll talk.'

'No.' Glenn's voice made Sherry feel like icy water was being dripped down her spine. 'Let's talk about it now.'

'Yeah, let's talk about it now,' Stuart agreed.

'You know you're not the father,' Sherry argued.

A dull stain started at his shirt collar and worked its way up his neck. 'We weren't always careful,' he said.

'Yes, we were.'

Sherry could tell a seed of doubt had been sown in Glenn's mind and knew he was thinking of Amber. She wanted to talk to her ex alone. She gave Glenn an imploring look.

Glenn wanted to know why she wanted to speak to her old boyfriend alone and why she was suddenly appealing for his help, but Molly and Kell had instilled good manners and a sense of chivalry in their sons, and Glenn couldn't ignore Sherry's silent plea. He told Stuart, 'Time for you to go.'

Stuart couldn't back down without looking like a wimp. 'I'll go when I'm ready,' he said mulishly.

'If you don't leave, I'll throw you out.'

Sherry rubbed her forehead nervously. 'Just go, Stuart!' she burst out when he seemed inclined to argue.

'Alright, I'll go,' he said petulantly. 'But you needn't think you've seen the last of me. I want some answers.'

Glenn growled and Stuart jumped. Glenn ignored his demands for blood tests and threats of legal action and showed him out.

Sherry was leaning against the kitchen sink sipping a glass of water to settle her stomach when Glenn walked in. He leaned against the wall and watched her silently. She set the glass on the draining board and swiped her mouth with the back of her hand. 'You don't believe him, do you?'

'Why did you invite him around to talk tomorrow night?'

She turned to face him and hugged herself. 'Stuart lives and dies by the Internet. I was worried that he'd recognize you and plaster the whole story all over his blog and social pages. He won't accept we're over. Seeing you just made it worse for him; I thought if I could talk to him alone, I could make him see he's being stupid.'

Glenn could have told Sherry that telling her ex he was being stupid wasn't likely to improve the situation. And what if Stuart was right and she was lying? 'A woman tried to screw me over once before by claiming I was the father of her baby. I want a blood test done when the baby is born to prove paternity.'

Sherry looked stunned. The worst thing anybody could do to her was question her integrity. 'It was *you* who came to *me!*' she reminded him. 'If I'd been after your money, I would have been on the phone the instant I knew the test was positive.'

The worst thing anybody could do to Glenn was betray his trust. 'It was *you* who put a hole in the rubber.'

She sagged against the kitchen sink. 'You think I deliberately sabotaged the condom to get pregnant? Why would I do that?'

'Money,' Glenn said succinctly.

His bruises had faded. He looked like the man she'd made love with and laughed with, but Sherry didn't recognize him — he was like a stranger. She turned her back and gripped the edge of the sink.

'For all I know, you might have already been pregnant when you came to Denver. You still got your periods — Ben told me.'

Sherry fought to stay calm. 'I wasn't pregnant when I slept with you.'

She suddenly thought about the baby, the silent victim in all of this, and imagined Glenn and Stuart waiting like vampires for it to be born so they could suck a blood sample from it and one of them could beat their chests. Her resolve hardened. *The bastards. The utter bastards.*

'I'm leaving for the States the middle of next week, but I'll only be gone a few weeks.'

Sherry tipped the rest of the water into the sink and watched it disappear down the drain. 'Don't bother to come back, Glenn.'

His voice was low and hard: 'Don't threaten me, Sherry.'

She looked over her shoulder and said coldly, 'You can't frighten me, Glenn. I'm not like Amber.'

'What do you know about her?' he asked harshly.

'Everything,' Sherry lied. 'Your life is splashed across papers and the Internet for everybody to see.' Her voice continued to drip ice. 'With you, there will always another woman. I'm amazed you haven't fathered an entire basketball team by now.'

Glenn's golden eyes were hard and cold. 'That's rich coming from a woman who doesn't know who knocked her up,' he said softly, and watched her stiffen. 'What are you going to do when it's born? Give up your precious job and be a stay-at-home mom?' Sherry clung to the sink like it was a lifeline and taunted, 'Whatever I do, I know one thing for certain — I'm the mother. Now get out of my life.'

She called Ben. He arrived soon after Glenn departed. He held Sherry, but she wouldn't cry. She was scared that if she started, she wouldn't be able to stop. 'What's happened to me, Ben?' she asked over and over again in a bewildered voice. 'How did this happen to me?'

He stayed the night in the spare bedroom, and when

he returned to his house the next morning Glenn had packed up his things and gone.

Sherry sat in the bottom of the shower and let the water stream over her. She touched the little bump Glenn had joked about and started to cry. 'I'm sorry. I messed up. From now on I promise I'll do better.'

<h1 style="text-align:center">Chapter 15</h1>

The impasse between Sherry and Glenn drove a wedge between the Jacksons and the Brogans as each family instinctively circled their wagons to support their own children.

'If Sherry would just agree to the blood test. If she weren't being so stubborn ...'

'Hasn't Glenn caused enough trouble? Sherry doesn't want his money ...'

Their lawyers racked up bills speaking to one another but kept stumbling over the same two problems: Glenn wanted Sherry to agree to a paternity test; Sherry wanted him to go away and leave her alone. One of Glenn's lawyers dangled the carrot of generous amounts of child support and got fired for his trouble. Sherry was so incensed that she went against *her* lawyer's advice and sent a letter stating that, although she didn't have Mr Brogan's millions, she wasn't destitute and could afford to raise a child, and that Mr Brogan could put his blood test the same place she'd suggested he keep his beloved BlackBerry.

'Yeeoouch!' one of Glenn's legal team cried delightedly. 'This is *good* — abuse is *good*. It casts doubts on her character and might help us make a case for Glenn to get full custody if it turns out he's the father.'

Glenn hated the way they spoke about Sherry and the baby. He was furious at her for putting him in this position, and at himself for letting her down again. He worried about the toll this was taking on her health. He worried about her trying to study and keep her career on track, and whether she was taking proper care of herself. He worried about how he'd be able to look Sherry's child in the eye when it grew up and came asking him why he hadn't been a part of its life. Letters and phone calls went back and forth across the Pacific Ocean. And nothing changed. Glenn carried out his obligations to his sponsors, did the Literacy Awareness campaign ads, spent time with Josh McCall at Cougars headquarters, and heard that Chopiak had got engaged to Desiree, the pet-shop worker from Michigan.

'She does not work in a pet shop,' Chopiak explained. 'She is an undergraduate student at Michigan State. Her friends dared her to get your telephone number.'

Glenn snorted softly. Giving out information like that was a no-no.

Chopper shrugged. 'Desiree did not know. She was on vacation and had drunk too much, and her friends were encouraging her. She is very embarrassed about rubbing herself against you and asked me to tell you she is sorry.'

Glenn hoped Desiree meant it and didn't make Leo's life a misery. 'Tell her I forgive her, provided she's given it up now she's engaged.'

Chopper's big brow furrowed. 'Truly, she is a nice girl, Blitz,' he said earnestly. 'As soon as I can, I will take her to meet my mother.' If Mama Chopiak was six foot ten inches tall like the girl from the Ukraine whom Chopper had dated, Glenn hoped Leo warned Desiree before they left for Russia.

The days dripped by like treacle from a cold spoon. He was the guest speaker at some benefit events, and he met with Fraser to consider new offers, including doing the cover of the New Year edition of *Infinite* magazine. Glenn didn't want to do it because it would mean an interview, and that meant questions about his personal life. Who was he dating? Was it serious? Was he ever going to find the right woman and tie the knot? In the past it hadn't mattered, but he didn't want some nosy journalist to go digging and find out about Sherry.

Fraser was worried about Glenn. He'd come back from New Zealand a changed man, moody and uncommunicative. Fraser reminded Glenn that the reason there'd been precious little controversy about his private life was because they'd always fed the media enough of the right information to keep them happy, and doing the interview would be a great opportunity to build on the publicity generated by the Literacy Awareness campaign, the work being done by the Bona Fide Blitz Trust, and Glenn's passion — better planning of playgrounds and youth sports facilities. Glenn used his profile to highlight the fact that recreation areas for kids were trashed and frequented by lowlife because they were placed on the fringes of communities, with lots of tall trees and bushes that allowed drug dealers and perverts to hide and made kids feel unsafe.

'I'll do it so long as there aren't any questions about my personal life.' Glenn was adamant. 'Tell them the only new woman in my life at the moment wears a diaper and likes sucking her toes.'

Fraser smiled. 'They'd like it much better if she wasn't three months old.'

Dan and Lisa were in a particularly difficult position. Dan had sympathy for Sherry's predicament, and Lisa understood why Glenn was so insistent about wanting proof of paternity. But Dan's first loyalty was to his brother, and Lisa's was to her sister. The one thing they agreed on was that what was happening between Glenn and Sherry didn't impact on Glenn's relationship with Georgia.

Despite Lisa's assurances that he was welcome, Glenn didn't feel comfortable about visiting the house anymore. Instead he saw Georgia when Dan brought her to Glenn's condo for a visit. Glenn still hadn't moved into the Italian-style villa set on four acres that he'd bought in Cherry Hills. It had cost him $6.3 million, had a 1,500-bottle wine cellar, salt-water pool, media room, seven bedrooms, eight bathrooms, eleven fireplaces, and a practice golf green — but Glenn wasn't even tempted to move in. It was a house built for a family; all those empty rooms seemed to mock him. He remained at his condo and brooded.

Georgia was turning into a real little person. She babbled and chuckled, and loved lying on the floor kicking her feet and waving her arms. She had her parents' dark hair, Lisa's nose and mouth, Dan's grey eyes, and the Brogan long legs. Glenn adored Georgia, and, judging by her excited bouncing and arm-waving when she saw him, the feeling was mutual. Uncle Glenn was fun, Uncle Glenn never got tired of pulling faces or letting her play with his fingers or bouncing her on his chest, because he was a big kid, too.

As soon as he'd returned to Denver, Glenn had contacted Nora to enlist the services of Ditchburn Surveillance. Of course Nora wanted to know why Glenn had departed so suddenly, and the truth about his relationship with Sherry.

'You're the father of her baby, aren't you?'

'I might be; I might not,' he replied honestly.

'Did you and Sherry have a fight?'

'You seem to be forgetting the terms of our earlier agreement. Sherry is off-limits as a subject — remember?'

'But you just asked me to spy on her!' Nora protested. 'How can she be off-limits?'

Glenn sighed deeply. 'Nora, you must've been spending too much time watching those James Bond DVDs I saw next to your television. I'm not asking you to *spy* on Sherry, just let me know how she's doing while I'm gone.'

'Why don't you ask her yourself?'

'Now, Nora, you know what she's like about sharing personal information. She'll tell me how many arrests she's made and the score of her last touch-rugby game.'

Nora conceded Glenn was right. Hadn't she been running into the same problem whenever she tried to winkle information out of her closest neighbour? She was thrilled to be given a mandate to snoop — by a famous athlete, no less — or at least she was until Glenn set conditions.

'The information sharing will be one-way.'

Nora was outraged. 'What do you mean it'll be one-way?'

'You give me information about Sherry, and I'll return the favour on a "need to know basis" — like, Sherry doesn't need to know about our agreement.'

'That's spying!'

'No, it's not, it's loving your neighbour. Face it, Nora, you're an expert at it.'

'Why should I help you?' she demanded.

'Because it's the only way you're going to get to use the set of Callaway golf clubs and customized bag monogrammed with your initials that I'm going to bring you.'

Nora clasped her throat as she imagined what the girls at the club would say when they saw the Callaway clubs and bag. 'I can do photos! Do you want photos?'

Glenn arranged for a computer and digital camera to be delivered to Nora's house and somebody to teach her how to use them. He wasn't sure if the reason Sherry's head was missing or her back was to the camera in the photos Nora emailed him was a sign of a bad teacher or a bad student. The photos were a disappointment, because Glenn wanted to see how Sherry looked as her pregnancy advanced, but Nora made up for her crappy photography by passing on valuable information, like Sherry had served a protection order on Stuart because he wouldn't stop badgering her.

'Is she OK?' Glenn demanded. 'Is he leaving her alone?'

'Are you kidding? Sherry was furious with him, and I think Ben paid him a visit, too.'

Nora's messages included a lot of personal opinion about Sherry's friends and acquaintances and what Sherry should or shouldn't be doing. For instance, Stuart was a wimp (Glenn agreed), that man-hungry Annemarie was always chasing Ben, and what kind of midwife rode a motorbike? She also had reservations about Sherry still playing touch rugby and jogging. *'It can't be good for the baby being shaken around like that; it'll come out like a scrambled egg. I offered to teach Sherry to knit, because it'd be a way to make her sit still, but she told me she'd rather stick the needles in her eyes than take up knitting. She still gets snotty, but she did my grocery shopping for me when my hip was bad again.'*

Glenn kept offering to pay for an operation, but Nora kept saying no. 'I paid my taxes — I'm entitled.'

Dan dropped by with Georgia one Saturday at the end of November. He'd been called into the hospital during the night to operate on a boy with a badly injured leg. Lisa hadn't got much sleep, either, because Georgia had been unsettled, so Dan had offered to take the baby out and let Lisa get some sleep, then he'd return and they'd swap.

The days were shorter and the weather colder. Dan was worried about Glenn, he was sombre and preoccupied, had been ever since his return from New Zealand. They sat in Glenn's living room, drinking coffee and watching Georgia turn herself in circles on her back on the carpet and roll onto her stomach.

Dan hated the condo's interior. Glenn had given some big-name interior designer free rein and an obscene budget to decorate. Dan thought he should ask for his money back, the neutral colour scheme was depressing, the minimalist furniture stark, and the art hanging on the walls looked like recycled junk — but

Glenn didn't seem to care. He never stayed in any of his houses long enough to get tired of them. To him, the art and condo and the rest of his properties were an investment. The closest thing he had to a home was Dan and Lisa's house and his parents' house in Boulder.

Dan tried to get comfortable on the slate-grey sectional sofa with steel legs. 'I hate this place.'

'You say that every time you visit.'

'It reminds me of an operating room.' He surveyed the matching sofa opposite. 'That looks like an OR table.'

Glenn squatted down in front of the bleached-stone fireplace, and pushed up the sleeves of the chunky oatmeal sweater he wore. 'I'll light a fire so you don't put out your hand and ask me for a scalpel. Did you know your socks don't match?'

Dan yawned and shrugged. He left the fashion statements to Glenn, and relied on Lisa to point out that navy pants shouldn't be worn with brown shoes. He gazed blearily at the piece of rusted iron hanging over the mantelpiece. 'I can't believe you paid seventy-five thousand dollars to hang a car radiator over your fireplace.'

Glenn put a match to the kindling and watched it catch. 'It's not a car radiator — at least I don't think it is — and it's doubled in value since I bought it.'

Georgia stopped turning circles on her stomach and stared at the flames. 'Throw up on the rug, Georgie — it's too clean,' Dan instructed.

Glenn braced an arm on his knee and rested his mouth against the sleeve of his sweater. He stared at the baby pensively. He loved watching Georgie discover something new. Lately, she'd fallen in love with her hands but couldn't seem to work out that they belonged to her and whacked herself in the nose whenever she tried to take a closer look at them. When she wasn't looking at them, they went straight in her mouth.

Two small vertical lines had become etched permanently between Glenn's brows since his return from New Zealand. The lines and lack of sparkle in his brother's eyes upset Dan immeasurably. 'Lisa thinks you're avoiding us,' he said. 'You never visit anymore.'

Glenn stood and picked up a mug of coffee from a low table made of glass and part of a steel girder. 'It's better if I stay away; it's too awkward for Lisa. But I enjoyed seeing her at Thanksgiving.'

Thanksgiving was always held at Molly and Kell's house. Everybody avoided mentioning Sherry, but the hug Lisa gave Glenn when he left early spoke volumes. She felt torn by the argument between Glenn and her sister.

'It's awkward for everybody.' Dan tilted back his head and studied the exposed steel beams of the condo ceiling. 'You know Sherry had a scan?'

Glenn did, because Nora had told him.

'Everything was fine. The doctor couldn't tell the sex, because the baby had its legs crossed. Jill went with Sherry and was disappointed they couldn't find out if it was a boy or girl, but Sherry didn't seem to mind.'

He knew that, too.

'The femur length is at the ninetieth percentile. It's going to be a big baby.'

The implications of Dan's remark were obvious, but Sherry also had legs up to her armpits so it might mean nothing. Glenn wished he was a better person and could call his lawyers off and tell Sherry he believed her. But he couldn't — Amber's duplicity had eroded his trust, and the doubt would always eat at him. At the same time, he knew Sherry would be petrified that the baby was going to be huge, but would try to pretend she was coping, and that ate at him, too.

There were books on pregnancy stacked on Glenn's nightstand that told him a lot of things. For instance, if it was a girl her ovaries were already at work making egg cells, and Sherry might be getting a sharp pain on one or both sides of her abdomen because her ligaments were trying to hold up her ballooning uterus. But the books didn't cover how to ask a woman you might have got pregnant and were estranged from how she was doing and if she'd let you back in her life. Glenn had tried to get Nora to pump Sherry about how she was feeling, but Nora said Sherry had pokered up and given her 'the look'. *You know the one I mean;* she'd written in her last email. Yes, he knew the one.

Glenn gazed moodily at the fire and tapped his knuckles on the coffee mug. Georgia started and looked at him, so he stopped. When she didn't hear it again, she lost interest and went back to watching the fire and babbling.

The only place Dan had ever seen Glenn look this serious was on the basketball court. 'She told Lisa she doesn't care if it's a boy or a girl as long as—'

'—it's human,' Glenn finished.

Georgia suddenly started crying. She was lying on her back, waving her arms and legs. Dan picked her up and patted her back. 'Did you see that?' he asked Glenn excitedly. 'That's the first time she's rolled from front to back. Wait 'til Lisa hears.'

Glenn pulled faces at Georgia over Dan's shoulder and was rewarded with a gummy smile. 'You're going to be a gymnast, aren't you, Georgie? Or maybe a trapeze artist?'

'As long as she isn't like you and starts walking early,' Dan said. 'Lisa and I are in no hurry.' He felt sorry for Sherry's baby. With Sherry for a mother and Glenn for a father, their kid would probably be riding a bike and have a paper round by the time it was a year old. Minus the training wheels. Dan yawned copiously.

'Why don't you go home and leave Georgia here?'

He stared at Glenn. 'With you?'

'No, I was going to leave after I'd showed her how to work the remote for the television and where to find a beer. You're supposed to be the smart one in the family — of course, with me,' Glenn retorted.

Dan needed to go back to the hospital to check on the boy on the way home, which meant taking Georgia with him. Lisa had given him two bottles of expressed breast milk. They were sitting in a cooler bag, which only left one base to cover. 'What about ...?'

Glenn was ahead of him. 'Shitty diapers? I'll cope.'

'You might change your mind when you see what she puts out. She's started solids.'

'I was lying in bed the other night thinking there must be a better way to deal with baby poop, and I think I've come up with a foolproof system.' Glenn explained it in detail.

Dan wondered why he was thinking about baby poop in the first place. 'Just for an hour, while I'm at the hospital, and you've got to promise to call me if there's anything you're not sure about.'

Glenn stuck two fingers against his head. 'Scout's honour.'

'You got kicked out of the Scouts, and that looks like you're aiming a gun at your head.'

Dan explained how to warm up the milk and arrange a nest of pillows on the bed to stop Georgia rolling onto the floor. He sniffed her butt as he handed her over. 'She's good to go.'

Glenn was unfazed when Georgia drank her milk then crapped her pants. He filled the bathroom sink with warm water and made sure a clean towel, fresh diaper and soap were at hand, and then unsnapped Georgia's sleep suit and peeled back the tapes on her disposable diaper. He held the diaper in place as he carried her to the big silver trash container in the kitchen and dangled Georgia over the opening. She beamed at him, kicked her bare legs and the diaper slipped. Glenn smiled back encouragingly. 'Give Uncle Glenn another big kick and that should do it, Georgie.' She kicked energetically and the diaper plopped neatly into the trash.

Glenn transferred her at arm's length to the bathroom, washed and dried her butt, and then gave the sink a couple of blasts with some cleaner he found in the cupboard. He got Georgia into a diaper but fell at the last hurdle when he couldn't work out the complicated closure system on her sleep suit. 'Nobody told me you needed a degree in quantum physics to close one of these things.'

Georgia yawned and set about the business of going to sleep, so Glenn left it unsnapped and covered her with a couple of fluffy baby blankets. He lay on his bed watching her sleep. He was still on the bed and reading Georgia quotes from a book on Urban Development when Dan returned an hour-and-a-half later to collect his daughter.

Glenn met him at the door with Georgia, who bounced up and down like Tigger when she saw her father.

'Sorry. It took longer than I expected,' Dan said. 'Was she OK?'

'She drank her milk, crapped her pants, and went to sleep.'

'Did your system work?'

'Like a charm. I'm going to talk to Fraser about patenting it.'

'Georgia wants shares when you do.' Dan reached for her. 'Did you have a good time with Uncle Glenn, Georgie B?'

'She had a stellar time, Dad.' Glenn handed over the baby bag and whispered in Georgia's ear, 'Not a word to your parents about the singles bar we visited, OK?'

Chapter 16

December arrived, and Down Under summer came with it. Pohutukawa trees dressed up for Christmas in their crimson finery, and the cicadas sang. Parents finished work and took kids to the beach for a swim and bought takeaways for dinner. People began talking about going camping or staying at the beach during their summer holiday. It was usually Sherry's favourite season, but this year she was carrying an in-built central heating system that meant the only way to combat the sticky humidity of an Auckland summer was regular swims at the beach across the road from her house.

'Nineteen weeks; you're nearly halfway there,' Starr announced.

Sherry wriggled the waistband of her maternity shorts over her bump. 'Do I get a special sticker in my book? Or a plaque, or something?' She sat up on the bed and turned her face into the fan humming by the window.

Starr packed away the little machine she used to hear the baby's heartbeat. 'No, but in about another twenty weeks you get a baby.'

'Really? I thought I got an all-expenses-paid trip to Fiji.'

Sherry's glib one-liners were all part of an act to give the impression she was coping, and they fooled everybody except her family and Starr. Sherry brushed aside their concerns and insisted she was fine, even when Stuart wouldn't stop ringing and visiting the house and she had to get a protection order. She suspected Stuart hadn't posted anything about her and Glenn on the Internet because his rival had left. Since Glenn's departure, Ben had taken his doula duties very seriously. Sherry didn't know that he'd told Stuart he'd have a lot more to worry about than a trip to the district court if he kept on bothering her.

Sherry treated being pregnant like everything else she'd committed to: if she had to do it, she'd do a good job — although that didn't mean she didn't hit speed bumps or have panic attacks at night when she thought about giving birth. But surprisingly, there were good points, like hearing the baby's heartbeat and watching it wave its arms and legs about on the monitor while the doctor pointed out its heart and kidneys, nose and eyes. Jill was disappointed that they couldn't find out the sex, but Sherry didn't mind.

Jill stuck the black-and-white photo the doctor had given them onto Sherry's fridge with a magnetic strawberry. 'I suppose you'll just have to paint the nursery yellow.'

Sherry hadn't even thought about a nursery. Clothes weren't a problem; things kept arriving from the most unlikely places. Stacey had knitted two little jackets, Mary Latoa had bought a Moses basket and was making covers for it, and Nora was turning out bootees in every shade possible. When she'd presented Sherry with the first pair, made from glowing orange wool, Sherry made the mistake of thanking her. Nora seemed almost disappointed that Sherry hadn't put up more of a fight about accepting them. Until then, Sherry hadn't understood that arguing with her livened up Nora's dull existence.

Blue bootees.

'What if it's a girl?'

Pink bootees.

'I can't put these on a boy — he'll look like a cross-dresser.'

White, neon-yellow, neon-green and lavender.

'It's not a centipede, Nora. How many feet do you think it has?'

A crocheted hat in a revolting shade of mustard yellow.

'My grandmother had one just like it.'

'Just tell Nora not to make a baby shawl,' Jill warned. 'I'm doing that.'

And she was, white and in the exact same pattern as the one she'd made for Georgia. Sherry's nose stung whenever she saw her mother with her lap filled with white wool and her knitting needles flashing above it.

'After Christmas, you might want to start thinking about getting a cot and things,' Brian said. 'Ben can bring his truck to pick things up, and he and I can assemble everything.'

Sherry nodded and took herself home and cried. So many people were waiting to welcome this child, and all she felt was dread. Nobody mentioned Glenn unless they had to. Sherry pictured herself like Lisa, in pain and vulnerable. Dan had kept Lisa safe. He'd calmed her, encouraged her, and told her how clever she was, and spoken up for her to the doctors and nurses when she wasn't able to. Sherry knew her mother would do the same — only it *wasn't* the same. She hadn't heard from

Glenn since he'd left, and, apart from her letter, Sherry hadn't contacted him either. They talked through their lawyers without saying the important things or getting any closer to reaching an agreement.

Stacey took out a protection order against Vance and moved out of the refuge and into a house. Vance flipped his lid when he couldn't find out where she'd gone, and called Sherry and threatened her. Dave wanted to assign Stacey's file to another member of the Problem Solving Team, but Stacey was so distraught at the idea of losing Sherry's support that she risked visiting the station to speak to Dave, and he grudgingly allowed Sherry to continue working with Stacey.

'If Vance so much as calls you, I want to know about it,' Dave growled. 'And that really will be *it*.'

Her belly stuck out like a small, hard basketball, and whatever was in there bounced around a lot. Sherry supposed that wasn't too surprising, considering Glenn was the father. She remembered his face when he saw her bump, how he'd complained that there wasn't much to show for all his hard work, and wondered what he'd say if he could see the bouncing basketball.

'Is it possible for a fetus to have attention deficit disorder?' Sherry asked Starr. 'Because I swear this kid has got it. It never stays still.'

'Some are just busier than others,' she replied. 'It'll slow down in your third trimester when it runs out of room.'

That would be when she was the size of the Sky Tower and couldn't move — Sherry could hardly wait. She'd had to give up frontline work for a desk job now she could no longer fit her SRBA vest. At least Dave Pomana had allowed her to keep in touch with the families she was responsible for.

'Do you think you can do that urine sample for me now?' Starr asked.

Sherry took the plastic container she held out to the bathroom and performed as requested. She left the sample on the vanity.

Starr returned from the bathroom and announced, 'You've got some protein in your urine.'

Sherry's muscles went rigid. Was something wrong with the baby?

'It's OK,' Starr soothed.

Sherry relaxed again. Lisa had been absolutely right when she said Starr was the best person to take care of Sherry. Starr's calm, no-nonsense manner was exactly what Sherry needed. The more she got to know her, the more Sherry admired the little midwife. 'If this is cause for celebration, I don't have a skerrick of wine in the house,' she joked. 'Doula Ben cleared out my wine rack in case I was tempted.'

Starr checked Sherry's blood pressure. 'Your blood pressure is fine and you haven't got any swelling.'

'Why is the protein important?' Sherry asked.

'Swelling, raised blood pressure, and protein in the urine are signs of pre-eclampsia,' Starr explained. 'You look tired. Perhaps you should cut back on the jogging and get some extra rest this weekend.'

'The only thing I've got planned for this weekend is a trip to the mall tomorrow to buy some new bras for the helium balloons. My next big night out won't be until January when I've got a wedding to go to.'

Starr gave Sherry one of her severe looks. 'Are you

going to buy proper maternity bras?'

'You mean the ones with flaps so I can unleash them on the poor unsuspecting child when it arrives?'

She grinned. 'Yes.'

'I wasn't intending to, but my mother is coming with me and she will put the nutritional needs of her grandchild before my selfish need to look like a woman instead of a milk tanker.'

'Are you going to the wedding on your own?' Starr didn't trust Sherry not to jog to the church or spend the night on her feet dancing.

She shook her head. 'No, my doula is coming too. He'll keep me in order and see that I'm tucked up in bed by midnight.'

Starr would prefer it if Ben Jackson also showed some self-restraint and stopped letting Sherry's friend jump him in her kitchen. She'd started to think she'd made a mistake about Ben when she saw how good he was to Sherry but changed her mind again when she was walking past Sherry's kitchen as she was leaving one day and saw Annemarie wrapped around Ben like cling-film. They were supposed to be going to a movie with Sherry when she'd finished seeing Starr. Ben had even invited Starr along, but she'd made up an excuse.

Starr ground to a halt as if she'd slammed into a wall. She gaped at Ben sprawled across one of the kitchen counters with Annemarie's bottom cupped in his hands, as if she'd leapt at him and he'd caught her.

Ben looked over Annemarie's shoulder, and his eyes

widened in dismay when he saw Starr's shocked face. Annemarie was a big girl. Ben wasn't able to speak or move because she had her tongue in his mouth and her legs wrapped around his waist. Annemarie didn't seem to notice that he wasn't participating in the kiss. Ben let go of her bottom and wrenched his mouth free and her arms from around his neck. 'Starr!'

Annemarie's head whipped around. She saw Starr and leapt off Ben as if he was on fire. 'Starr! I didn't realize ... we didn't realize ...'

Ben fumed. There was no *we* about it, she'd come flying at him like a kung fu fighter.

Starr adjusted her backpack and continued walking. He not only dumped women at the altar; he allowed them to jump him in his sister's kitchen while she was upstairs having an appointment with her midwife.

Sherry looked down her nose disdainfully. 'Is it a prerequisite that maternity bras have to be ugly and beige?'

'Not at all.' Pam, the fitter, plucked a bra from a rack. 'See? This one has got lace, it's quite pretty.'

Sherry studied the bra and Pam with equal amounts of incredulity. '*That's* pretty?'

Jill looked on. There were shops that sold pretty maternity lingerie, but Sherry was watching her money. She was sad that her daughter had to give up wearing nice underwear because Glenn Brogan was being such a pig and Sherry was too independent to let her parents buy her something nicer.

'I want to look like a woman, not a heifer.'

'Ahhh,' Pam nodded. 'I think that's where you're going wrong, dear.'

Jill watched one of Sherry's winged brows glide upwards. Sherry wasn't the kind of person anybody called 'dear'.

'While you're pregnant, you need to change the way you think about your breasts, dear,' Pam continued.

'Really, Pam?' Sherry replied coolly.

'They're no longer yours, dear. They belong to the baby.'

Sherry checked for a hidden camera, but no, it seemed Pam was serious. 'So tell me, if they're not breasts, what are they, Pam?'

'Think of them as lunchboxes, dear.'

'My boobs *are not* bloody lunchboxes!' The plastic bag containing four big, ugly, beige bras banged against Sherry's leg as she marched down the street towards her car.

Jill trailed behind, laughing.

'Be quiet, Mum!'

They stopped by the car. Sherry dropped the plastic bag on the grass verge and searched for her car keys. Jill waited behind her, still laughing. 'Wait 'til I tell Lisa.'

Sherry spun around. '*Don't* tell Lisa!'

'Why not?'

'Because she'll tell Dan and he might tell ...' She trailed off. Jill's smile faded. She'd tried not to, but she decided she hated Glenn Brogan. She reached up and cupped Sherry's cheek. 'I won't tell her ... *dear.*'

Sherry smiled. Her relationship with her mother had altered in the past weeks. Sherry wasn't sure if it was because she'd changed or her mother, or if both of them had. She just knew that Jill talked a lot of sense and was interested when Sherry told her the baby kicked up a fuss if she drank coffee and fell asleep when she swam at the beach.

Jill bent to pick up the plastic bag and gasped. 'Sherry! Look!' She pointed at the car.

'What?' Sherry turned to look.

The tyres were flat. She walked onto the road and checked. Somebody had loosened the valves, and they were all flat.

Despite the fact it was a public road, nobody had seen who'd done it. In view of Vance's previous threats and the protection order against Stuart, Sherry and Dave Pomana took the incident seriously. Vance and Stuart both had an alibi.

'Is there anybody else with a grudge against you?' Dave asked.

Sherry told him about the invitation to Marjorie's wedding. 'I gave evidence at the ex's trial. He hates me, but he hates the thought of going back to prison even more.'

Dave made a note. 'Anything more recent?'

The only other person was Glenn, but he was in America. Sherry knew that meant nothing, Glenn had money, and people could be paid to do things. She reluctantly told Dave the embarrassing details of her personal life. She didn't know he was a basketball fan.

Dave stared at her. 'Glenn Brogan?'

'Yes.'

'Blitz Brogan?'

'Yes.'

Dave was stunned. Just like everybody else, he'd wondered who the father of her baby was. 'How do you know him?'

'My sister is married to his brother,' Sherry muttered.

She'd never thought to mention that she was related by marriage to one of the greatest shooting guards in the game? Dave dropped his pen on the desk blotter and sat back. 'What else are you hiding?'

'Nothing,' Sherry insisted. 'Glenn isn't the type to do something petty like let my car tyres down. Stuart *is*.'

Glenn — she called Blitz Brogan *Glenn*. Dave picked up his pen again. 'You and I both know that with the right provocation people can act out of character. Blitz Br — I mean *Glenn* Brogan can afford to stay in America and pay somebody local to do his dirty work.' He watched Sherry's mouth set. So she still had feelings for him.

'What's his motive?'

'Scare you enough and you might turn to him for help. Hopefully, this is just a one-off, Sherry. But if it isn't, everybody is a suspect until we catch who's responsible.'

Sherry wasn't buying it. Glenn wasn't the type of person who'd do something so underhand; if he was angry, he'd say so.

All police officers' home numbers were ex-directory,

but Sherry took the added precaution of changing the details on her car registration, and power and telephone bills.

Each fortnight a meeting was held to discuss every report submitted to the FVU involving a verbal argument or major assault. The meetings were attended by the members of the Problem Solving Team and representatives from various agencies including Child, Youth & Family Services, and Victim Support. At the end of the meeting, Julia, from Victim Support, approached Sherry to say she was sorry to hear about what had happened to her and offer support.

'Thanks, Julia, I appreciate it.'

'Just because you're a cop doesn't mean you don't need somebody to talk to or help.'

The offer was meant kindly but only made Sherry feel depressed. She was officially a victim. She'd stepped over the line and into the world of the women she worked with.

A week after the tyre incident, Sherry put the rubbish out on collection day and something — or somebody — tipped the wheelie bin over and threw the contents across the road. It could have been stray dogs, it could have been kids, but Sherry's bin was the only one tipped over. It had her house number on it, which meant that, if it was the same person who'd dealt to her car, they knew where she lived.

She called Dave and was touched when he came to see if she was alright. 'It might just be stray dogs.'

Dave grunted and arranged for Sherry's neighbours to be asked if they'd noticed anything suspicious or anyone hanging around, but none of them had. He let Sherry speak to Nora.

'No. Why?' Nora asked.

'Somebody let the tyres down on my car and maybe dumped my rubbish on the road.' When Nora looked alarmed, Sherry added quickly, 'It's probably nothing.'

As soon as she'd gone, Nora called Glenn. 'Glenn! Somebody let Sherry's car tyres down and emptied her bin on the road! Do you think you're a suspect? Do you think it's that wimpy Stuart?'

Glenn managed to get hold of Sherry two nights later. 'I heard about your car and the incident with your trash. Are you alright?'

She was so surprised she had to sit down. 'Glenn?'

'Yes. Are you OK?' he repeated.

Sherry drank in the sound of his voice until her cop instincts ruined things by telling her it was strange that he was calling. 'How did you hear?' she asked warily.

'Apparently, I'm a suspect.'

Dave hadn't said anything about getting in touch with the Denver police. 'The police interviewed you?'

'They paid me a friendly visit.' He hadn't been remotely amused about it at the time, but it gave him an excuse to contact Sherry without revealing Nora was spying for him.

'Glad you find it so amusing,' Sherry said sharply. 'Did you have anything to do with it?' It was Sherry the cop speaking, not Sherry the woman who'd spent the night with him in August.

Glenn wished he hadn't bothered to call. 'No, I didn't,' he replied coldly. 'Are you going to agree to the blood test?'

Sherry felt like he'd reached through the receiver and slapped her. 'Is that why you called? Did you just need an excuse to speak to me?'

'Are you going to agree to the blood test?'

'No. I'll never agree to it.'

'I guess there's nothing more to say then.'

There was a click as the call disconnected.

Chapter 17

Sherry spent Christmas Day with her parents and Ben. They wanted her to move in with one of them, but she refused. Nothing unusual had happened since the incident with the wheelie bin. 'It's not a good idea. At my place I'll know right away if there's a stranger hanging around or if something has changed. It was probably just some kids on school break playing a prank.'

Jill tried to interest her in picking out colours for the baby's bedroom, but Sherry was feeling utterly miserable. She put her listlessness down to the weather.

In the New Year, it got even hotter. When she wasn't working, Sherry spent her time swimming, under a cool shower, or studying for her CPK exam. At night, she talked to the bump and Otto, who'd taken up permanent residence on her bed and hogged the fan. She'd given up trying to get rid of him. He had a food bowl in the kitchen, regular flea and worming treatments, and answered to 'The Damned Cat'. Sherry was glad of Otto's one-eyed, drowsy company as he stretched out upside-down on her bed, letting the breeze from the fan ripple across his fur.

She had revealing, one-sided conversations with him. 'I can't leave the father's name blank on the birth certificate. It's like saying I don't know, when I do.' She picked Otto up and lay back against the pillows with him draped across her bump. 'Shall I put your name there? What do you think, bump?' The bump kicked Otto and he slid off with a disgruntled look on his battered face.

January crept onwards in one long heat-shimmer. Alice at number three put her house on the market and moved to the South Island to be closer to her new grandchild; Sherry turned thirty-one and let Annemarie and Mary take her out to dinner to celebrate.

Nora emailed Glenn: 'Sherry went out with that awful Annemarie and nice Mary on her birthday. She's getting really big and isn't coping with the hot weather. Otto hates it, too. He won't come home, because Sherry's got a fan in her bedroom. She thinks I don't know that she's feeding him. The neighbour two houses up says Otto is chasing her pedigree Rag Doll called Custard. If you ask me, Otto isn't the problem; Custard is a tart just like that awful Annemarie. The house next-door is up for sale. Nobody has done anything else to Sherry's car or wheelie bin.'

On the day of Marjorie's wedding, Ben looked sick when he came to collect Sherry.

'What's wrong with you? Did you spend the night with Annemarie and forget to carb-load?'

How did Sherry know about him and Annemarie? Apart from the incident in the kitchen, they'd been discreet — or at least, *Ben* had. Since she'd jumped him, Ben had steered clear of Annemarie and the Lavender Fairy had steered clear of him, but apparently, she'd told her client about what she *thought* she'd seen Sherry's friend and brother doing on her kitchen counter. The idea soured Ben's attraction to Starr. His throat and head hurt. He'd had enough of hormonal pregnant women and short judgmental ones. 'There's nothing going on between me and Annemarie,' he rasped.

Ben sounded so bad that Sherry told him to go home. 'I don't mind going alone.'

'No, I'll come. I took some Panadol. Once they kick in, I'll feel better.' Sherry eyed him doubtfully. Ben straightened his tie and gave the lapels of his dark-grey suit jacket a twitch. 'I'm fine.'

It wasn't often Sherry got to see him in a suit, and she felt a thrill of pride at how handsome he looked. He'd had his hair cut and wore the cufflinks she'd bought him for his birthday the year before. Annemarie couldn't get enough of Ben. It was a shame that Starr didn't feel the same way. 'I'm always surprised at how well you scrub up.'

'Me, too,' Ben croaked.

Her dress was a dark mulberry satin tunic that tied beneath her breasts and rose above her knee to display her long legs and high- heeled black suede shoes. Her lips were painted the same shade as her dress, and her black hair fell from a side parting across one eye. Ben studied the front of the dress. 'I see you got the lunchboxes under control.'

Sherry rearranged the bodice. 'I look like a heifer.'

'No, you don't. You look like that German model married to Seal who's always pregnant.'

She beamed. 'You mean Heidi Klum on *Project Runway?*'

Ben didn't have a clue what the model's name was. 'Yeah, that's her. Shall we get going?'

As they were leaving, Nora lumbered out with her

digital camera to take a photo. Sherry had lost count of how many times she'd posed for Nora since she'd got her new camera. 'Don't you have enough photos of me already, Nora?'

Nora wasn't about to miss an opportunity to get a shot of Sherry all dressed up for a wedding. It was an excuse to get her to stand still and pose instead of pointing the camera, pressing the button and hoping. Glenn said that, thanks to Nora's photos, he could pick out Sherry's back anywhere. Nora wanted him to see how nice Sherry looked now that she was showing.

'I'm practicing.' *At taking your photo without cutting your head off.* 'Smile!'

Unfortunately, when Nora checked, she'd taken a photo of Sherry and Ben's heads but their bodies were missing from the shoulders down.

The wedding went off without a hitch. Sherry barely recognized Marjorie. She was a different woman from the one Sherry had met at the drink-driving checkpoint. That Marjorie had visited the gym and hairdresser religiously to ward off fat and grey hairs, and watched the face of whoever she was speaking to for reassurance that she was saying the right thing. The new Marjorie had grown plump, her hair was longer and was a mixture of grey and blonde, and she smiled and laughed. The new Marjorie wasn't scared to voice her opinion or disagree with her new Australian husband, Robert, who was a high-school teacher and wore the look of a man who couldn't believe his luck at finding her. They were spending their honeymoon in Queensland, and then settling in Robert's home in Brisbane.

Another person Sherry almost didn't recognize was Misty from the Women's Refuge. She was wearing a hat and dress instead of jeans and an old T-shirt.

'I only ever get to wear the hat at weddings and funerals.' Misty studied Sherry's belly beneath the satin tunic. 'Whoever knocked you up did a good job of it. Are you sure you're not having twins?'

'Are you sure you shouldn't keep the hat for funerals?' Sherry asked and introduced Ben.

They were both surprised when Marjorie's teenage son and daughter came over to say hello. When their mother had left the hospital for the refuge, they'd blamed Sherry and Misty for the break-up of their parents' marriage and Sherry for their father's imprisonment. Things had changed since then. Today, Marjorie's son was giving the bride away, and her daughter was the maid of honour; today, they kissed Misty and Sherry on the cheek and thanked them for coming, and Marjorie's daughter talked excitedly about moving to Brisbane, and her son about how he was finding his first year at Auckland university.

'Pigs do fly,' Misty remarked drily when they'd gone.

She walked down the aisle behind Sherry and Ben and watched as most of the male guests followed the progress of Sherry's lovely, long legs as she sauntered past on her spiked heels. She made pregnancy look pretty good. DC Jackson had improved since she'd got pregnant. She was much more approachable, and the women felt more comfortable around her, but Misty was glad she hadn't lost that stuck-up look she got when she was pissed off at something.

Ben sat between Misty and Sherry during the ceremony and watched them eye Marjorie's new husband critically as the couple exchanged vows.

Misty spoke across him. 'Did you check him out?'

Sherry nodded. 'Some parking tickets and a disorderly behaviour charge when his wife died of cancer.'

Ben didn't think he deserved to be sick and at a wedding with Patty and Selma. At the reception his throat felt so bad he couldn't eat anything. Every time the master of ceremonies tapped his wine glass to get people's attention, Ben felt like a fire alarm was going off inside his head, but he protested when Sherry said he needed to go home and pulled out her cellphone.

'I'm OK!'

'You're not OK. I'm calling Dad to come and get you.'

'Why don't you do the bride and groom a favour and take your bugs home?' Misty said bluntly. 'Nobody wants their wedding to be remembered because all the guests caught flu.'

Ben didn't have the energy to argue. Before he left, he caught Misty's arm and croaked, 'Keep an eye on Sherry.'

Misty shook his hand off. She didn't like being grabbed by a man, no matter how nice he looked. 'She won't be having that baby tonight.'

Sherry's brother wouldn't back down. 'She's had trouble. Watch her.'

If Ben hadn't been feeling so bad he might have noticed the white Mitsubishi Lancer tucked beneath the overhanging branches of a weeping willow on the road opposite the car park.

The sound of laughter and the throb of music drifted across the road.

Jonathan looked contemptuously at the community centre and thought how far Marjorie had fallen. There had been nearly four hundred guests at their wedding, which had been held at a private vineyard in the South Island. Marjorie had looked slim and perfect in her white wedding dress.

His stomach burned as he remembered all that he'd lost — a successful business, the beautiful home on the lake, the luxury cars and the respect of his peers. He used to drive a BMW, a new one every year. Now he drove a cheap car and worked at a used-car yard which belonged to the man who had bought Jonathan's luxury-car dealership. The man thought he was doing Jonathan a favour by giving him a job valeting and delivering cars when he got out of prison. Jonathan hated him for taking his business and giving him a job but was too smart to show it and knew the right things to say. One of his strengths was manipulating people, like he'd manipulated another valet into delivering a car to a client in Thames in exchange for covering for the other man being late to work. One of the benefits of working at a used-car yard was that having access to so many different cars made it easier for Jonathan to cover his trail.

Jonathan recalled the time he'd spent in prison like it was a bad dream; he remembered the cool blue eyes of

Constable Jackson as she'd given evidence against him in the court. It was her fault — she'd put Marjorie up to it. Constable Jackson — *Detective Constable Jackson, now* — didn't know her place. She interfered in things she didn't understand, like people's marriages and what went on behind closed doors.

Rage bubbled in his stomach and forced its way up his oesophagus. Jonathan grimaced at the pain and the sour taste in his mouth. He couldn't believe that his son had given Marjorie away at this circus of a wedding and that his daughter had been a bridesmaid. Marjorie had always been stupid. If she hadn't been so dumb, Jonathan wouldn't have lost his temper so often. At the church she'd look like a fat, white slug in her cheap white dress, and her hair was a grey, untidy mess. She'd smiled at her new husband, a penniless schoolteacher. He could never give her the life Jonathan had.

Detective Constable Jackson was a guest at the wedding. She was pregnant and accompanied by the man who'd left early. Any wife worth her salt would have left with her husband. Any husband worth his would have made her leave. Seeing DC Jackson enraged Jonathan far more than seeing his stupid ex-wife or children. He felt nothing for them but disgust. He thought of DC Jackson and his stomach hurt so much that he had to lower his brow to the steering wheel of the cheap car until he got his breath back.

Jonathan reached into the glove compartment. He took out a knife, checked there was nobody in the car park and made his way stealthily towards the black SUV.

Misty and Sherry had a surprisingly good time together. Mindful of Ben's warning, Misty walked Sherry to the car park. It was right beside the community centre and well-lit and they weren't the only ones leaving, but Misty was a firm believer in being safe instead of sorry.

'Are you in some kind of trouble?' She asked.

There was the slightest hesitation in DC Jackson's stride; if Misty hadn't been looking for a reaction, she wouldn't have noticed.

'Apart from being barefoot and pregnant? No.' Sherry stopped beside her car. 'Oh shit ...'

The tyres had been slashed.

The hair on the back of Misty's neck stood up. She scanned the car park and the shadows cast by the weeping willow across the road but there was nothing to see. 'Yeah, you got trouble.'

Once again, Stuart had an alibi and was highly indignant that he was a suspect — *so* indignant that Annemarie thought he might actually have been responsible for the first incident.

'It's possible,' Sherry agreed wearily. 'His mother thinks he should be anointed and given a feast day. Is she his alibi this time?'

'No, he says he was with his girlfriend the night of the wedding, and she backs up his story, says it was the first time Stuart spent the night.' Annemarie wrinkled her nose and shuddered.

'At last some good news — he's got a girlfriend. You're certain she wasn't made of plastic and had a valve on one end?'

'Nope, she was real.'

'Did she look sane?' Sherry asked.

'As sane as any woman dating a turd like Stuart could be.'

'I was once that woman, Annemarie.'

'I know.'

Vance had been at his cousin's birthday party in Gisborne, and Marjorie's ex-husband, Jonathan, had been out of town delivering a car to a client in Thames.

Sherry was surprised. 'He's got a job?'

'The guy who bought his dealership gave him one washing cars at a second-hand yard he owns, which if you ask me was very generous of him. Jonathan looks like a little wizened gnome and nothing like the photo on his file. He spoke so softly I could hardly hear him. I couldn't decide if he was a broken man or a good actor.'

'He wasn't like that when I met him,' Sherry recalled. 'He thought he was God's right hand and his wife was a punching bag for him to work off frustration after a bad day. Misty used to say that Jonathan was one of the guys who made the hair stand up on the back of her neck.'

'She wouldn't say that now. He gives off about as much energy as a flat battery.'

Dave told Sherry, 'I've arranged for a panic button to be installed in your house and a unit to drop by your street on a regular basis. We want whoever it is to know we're watching. You go to work. You go home. You watch your back and you report *anything* unusual. Understand?'

Sherry nodded. The panic button was reassuring, but she took a baseball bat to bed with her too, just in case.

Glenn couldn't concentrate and snapped for no reason. The only thing that had made him feel better since he'd left New Zealand was doing the *Infinite* photo shoot, because Dan and Lisa had given permission for Georgia to be in some of the photos.

At first Dan refused. 'Why do you want a baby in a photo with you?'

'Because she's cute and will help sell lots of magazines.'

Dan stared at Glenn and waited.

'And because when I get asked who's the new woman in my life, I'm going to say she's nearly six months old and likes grabbing my nose but hasn't figured out how to let go of it yet.'

Dan shook his head. 'I still don't get it, Glenn.'

'I have to go back to New Zealand, Dan; this is driving me insane. It was only luck that nobody got a photo of me and Sherry together when I was down there and sold it to a magazine or put it on the web. If I go back, I need a reason to be there that will deflect attention away from Sherry.'

'What's your reason?'

'I talked to the people I worked with on the literacy campaign and one of the sports networks about doing a televised tour of New Zealand golf courses — you know, playing with the locals, showing off the courses and scenery, having fun Down Under — that kind of thing, and they jumped at it. It'll work, I know it will. I plan to mention it in the interview I do for the magazine.'

Dan was sure Glenn was right but continued to hesitate. 'Don't you think photos of you and Georgie are a little cheesy?'

'Hell, yeah — people will love them.'

Lisa and Dan insisted that Georgie's name wasn't mentioned and there were no shots of her face, because having a wealthy, famous uncle could make her a target for kidnappers. Lisa accompanied Georgia and Glenn to the studio and fed her while the photographer took photos of Glenn and helped the stylist dress Georgia in a gauzy pink-and-silver fairy dress and matching headband.

The photographer and stylist fell in love with Georgia and were ecstatic with the result of the shoot. 'I wish we could say what she's called!' the stylist cried. 'I *love* her Georgie B nickname.'

Georgie B loved the lights and attention, chewing the silver trim on her fairy costume and headband and the pink and grey balloons clustered around Glenn's feet so much that she drooled all over the shoulder of his Lagerfeld suit.

'Oops!' Lisa exclaimed from her seat in the corner of the studio. 'At least it wasn't breast milk.'

Glenn merely laughed down into Georgia's little face, and Georgia stuck her fist in her mouth, grabbed the lapel of his jacket, and grinned back. She bounced her legs and did her Tigger impression, and the photographer took the shot. Lisa and the stylist melted.

'That man should have kids.' The stylist stared moonily at Glenn and the baby. 'I'd be happy to put my hand up for the job.'

Too late, love, Lisa thought. *Somebody beat you to it.* She wished Glenn and Sherry would come to their senses and sort out their problems.

The photographer liked the drooly look so much that he wouldn't let the stylist change Glenn's jacket and kept on taking photos. The editor chose a shot of Glenn wearing a Versace tux with the shoutline: *Let This Be The Start of Your Big Year* for the January cover, with a six-page spread of photos and the interview with Glenn inside. A whole page was devoted to the shot of Glenn standing amongst the balloons with drool on his shoulder, laughing down at Georgia. At the top of the page the words *Let This Be The Start of Your Big Year* ... were repeated; and at the bottom, ... *but don't forget the small things count too.*

People loved the photos of a big, handsome athlete holding a tiny baby girl in a pink-and-silver fairy outfit, as well as the interview describing how life had changed for Blitz Brogan and what he'd been doing since he'd retired from professional basketball. Glenn talked about the work being done by the Bona Fide Blitz trust, and his plans for a golf show in New Zealand. Men wanted to be him, and women wanted to marry him. Magazine editors and sports agents were kicking themselves for not thinking of it first.

Nora sent Glenn a photo of Sherry and Ben dressed for a wedding. Instead of cutting off their heads, she'd cut off Sherry and Ben's bodies so he couldn't see how pregnant Sherry looked. He printed the photo and kept staring at it. Sherry's features looked softer, her lips fuller, her black hair glossier — she was a picture of health. Glenn checked his emails one last time before he went to bed and found one from Nora: *'Sherry went to a wedding and somebody slashed her car tyres.'*

Glenn's phone call woke Nora up. 'Is she OK? Was she hurt?'

'She's OK, but I think she's scared. I know I am.'

'Have the police got any idea who it is?'

'Sherry said no.' Nora's voice wasn't quite steady.

Glenn had never understood the saying about feeling sick with worry until now.

'Glenn? Are you still there?'

He stared at the sculpture hanging above the fireplace without seeing it. 'I'm here. Is the house next-door still for sale?'

'Yes. Alice hasn't had any offers but—'

'Why? Is it unliveable?'

'Oh no! Alice is *very* fussy; the place is immaculate.'

That was good enough for Glenn. 'Give me the address and tell me how much she's asking for it.' He reached for a pen and jotted down Nora's answers.

'Before you go ahead, I think you should know that it's definitely what I'd call a woman's house,' Nora said nervously.

Lace curtains and plastic gnomes in the garden — nothing that couldn't be fixed. Glenn didn't care what the place looked like, only that it was next-door to Sherry's house. 'Thanks for the help, Nora. Do me a favour and don't tell Sherry, OK?'

'Alright,' she said reluctantly.

Glenn hung up and called Fraser. 'Fraser? I need you to buy another house for me.'

Sherry noticed as soon as the 'Sold' sticker was added to the real estate agent's sign advertising Alice's house. She headed straight over to Nora to find out who their new neighbour was. Whoever had bought the place either had the money to do a radical makeover before they moved in, or shared Alice's questionable taste in décor.

'Somebody bought Alice's house?' she asked Nora incredulously.

Nora busied herself watering her plants. 'Yes.'

'Who?'

She got a funny look on her face. 'I'm not sure.'

Sherry was instantly suspicious. 'Don't give me that. You know everybody's business — sometimes you know mine before I do.'

Nora jammed the knuckles of her hand against her good hip. 'I *don't* know everybody's business.'

Sherry propped her fists where her waist used to be. 'This is important, Nora. I need to run a background check.'

Nora became flustered and Sherry got more suspicious.

'I've lost Alice's new number,' Nora lied. Sherry didn't blink, and she squirmed. If that was how Sherry looked when she interviewed suspects, Nora was glad she was honest. Maybe she could give her a hint without saying anything outright. 'Have you seen the photos of your niece and Glenn?' she blurted.

Sherry drew back and frowned. What was Nora

talking about? 'What photos?'

Nora went inside the house and returned with a thick, glossy magazine which she held out to Sherry. There was a photo of Glenn on the cover wearing a tuxedo with his bow tie dangling and the top buttons of his shirt undone. He was leaning against a white background with his arms and legs crossed and his sulky bad-boy mouth tipped up in a one-cornered smile. Next to his face in blue lettering were the words *Let This Be The Start of Your Big Year*.

Sherry slowly reached for the magazine. 'Where did you get this?'

Hah! Giving Glenn the cold shoulder was a load of codswallop — Sherry was still hooked on him. Nora wasn't surprised. She folded her arms and lied some more. 'I get it sent to me from America. Take a look in the middle. Your niece is such a sweetie; she even looks a little like Glenn.'

'She looks like her father.' Sherry flipped to the middle of the magazine and the photo of Georgia in her pink-and-silver dress looking tiny and adorable in Glenn's arms. The penny dropped. Sherry's eyes snapped to Nora's. 'Glenn bought Alice's house, didn't he?'

'I'm not saying a word,' she replied.

She was furious. 'Why didn't you tell me?'

'How can I tell you something I don't know?'

'You should have told me!'

'I respect people's privacy,' Nora said loftily.

Sherry rolled up the magazine and whacked it against her thigh. 'Bullshit! I bet you've been snooping for Glenn while he's been gone!'

'I'm not staying out here to be insulted!' Nora grabbed the handrail and shuffled up the stairs to her house one foot at a time. She stopped when Sherry laughed. Nora looked over her shoulder and snapped, 'What's so funny?'

Sherry was smirking at Alice's house. 'What's wrong?'

'Has Glenn seen any photos of the décor in his new house?'

Nora pursed her lips.

'No?' Sherry gloated. 'Did you not mention that Alice's favourite colour was pink?'

'I tried to, but he wouldn't listen.'

Sherry imagined Glenn calling his agent and telling him to buy Alice's house. What was one more house when you already owned so many? The Pink Palace would be the jewel in the crown.

Nora wasn't the only person in Sherry's bad books; she wasn't too happy with her sister, either.

'Why didn't you tell me?'

'Because I knew how you'd react,' Lisa answered. 'He's going to New Zealand to play golf.'

'Lisa, is your brain still stuck in your uterus? He's moving into the house next-door!'

'Leave my brain out of this.'

'You're right, I should! *You* obviously did!'

'I'll ignore that because you're pregnant and hormonal. What else was he supposed to do? Glenn *is* the father; he wants to see you.'

'I don't want him to see me!' Sherry shouted.

'You should have thought about that when you were jumping his bones at the motel!' Lisa shouted back. 'And stop shouting at me!'

'I want to shout! You have Dan to shout at — I've got nobody!'

'And whose fault is that?' Lisa yelled.

Sherry tried to compose herself. 'Does Glenn realize my boss and Annemarie will be all over him asking questions when he gets here?' *For different reasons, of course.*

'Glenn doesn't have a problem with that. He's glad they're keeping an eye on you. He's worried.'

He was? Sherry thought he'd forgotten her.

'If he was stalking you, he'd hardly move into the house next-door, would he?' Lisa asked reasonably.

'Stranger things have happened,' Sherry replied in her cop voice.

'What do you think he's going to do? Slip notes with words cut from magazines under your front door?'

'It isn't funny, Lisa. I look at everybody sideways. I go to the supermarket and check out people in the queue next to me and wonder if they've followed me in. Or if the pimply-faced kid pumping petrol for my car is older than he looks and I arrested him once and he's got a grudge against me. I never really understood what it was like for the women I worked with, but I do now.'

An uneasy silence fell.

'I'm sorry,' Lisa said quietly. 'That was a stupid thing to say. Has anything else happened since your tyres were slashed?'

Yes. There'd been a run of phone calls at three in the

morning that had dragged Sherry from sleep and sent her stumbling from bed to answer the phone, half-expecting Stuart to be on the other end pleading for another chance because his new girlfriend-without-a-valve had met Stuart's mother and given him the elbow. But she had been met by silence — a heavy, ominous silence that made goose bumps rise on her skin like bubble wrap. 'Who is this?' Sherry had grabbed her cellphone in the other hand and tried to send a text to get the call traced, but the caller had hung up. It happened twice more. Each time the person on the other end of the line hung up, although the second time the call was traced — to a public phone booth which was out of sight of any surveillance cameras.

'No,' Sherry lied.

Lisa was scared. Ben and their parents had jobs; they couldn't always be with Sherry when she wasn't at the police station. The sooner Glenn got on the plane to New Zealand the better; Lisa only wished he was moving into Sherry's house instead of the one next- door. 'Amber really did a number on Glenn; you can't blame him for being wary. Can't you just agree to the blood test?' she pleaded.

'I needed him to trust me. I needed him to stick by me.'

She'd read the interview with Glenn in the magazine and learned more about what mattered to him and made him tick from a few pages of text than she had from spending the night with him or months of long-distance quarrelling through their lawyers. She'd found out why he was interested in urban development.

'Why put parks and outdoor sporting facilities on the

fringes of communities? It attracts bad elements. Isolation makes it easy to smash lights, sell drugs and beat people up. Tall trees and bushes provide perfect places for perverts to hide and watch. Kids get scared and stay away, and parents don't want to take them there. Building skateboarding ramps and volleyball and basketball courts in parks in the centre of the community means they get used and there's plenty of people to see and report anything unusual.'

Glenn's trust, Bona Fide Blitz, was heavily involved in seeding money to local communities to help them create safe areas where parents could take their kids to play. The profits Glenn received from Blitz sunglasses went directly to the trust. Sherry recalled him mentioning he was doing another ad campaign when he got back to the States. She'd assumed that it was for sunglasses, but she'd been wrong: the adverts were part of a campaign to publicize learning programmes for illiterate adults.

'Why didn't you tell me about the literacy campaign Glenn was doing?' Sherry asked.

'How could I when you refused to talk about Glenn and never want to hear anything good about him?'

'I admit that I might have judged him a little unfairly.'

Lisa snorted. 'That's one way of putting it.'

'Don't try and pretend Glenn's a saint. He treats women like a box of disposable tissues.'

'It's hard not to when the box keeps filling up,' Lisa sighed. 'Look, I know he isn't perfect, but please, for both your sakes, try to be nice when you see him.'

Chapter 18

Towards the end of February a removal van chugged up the driveway and men began unloading brand-new, expensive-looking furniture, including a huge super-king bed. It took several attempts before they managed to get the mattress through the door.

Sherry's checks on the purchaser had yielded a company name: GM Holdings Ltd. Lisa said that the 'GM' stood for Glenn Michael and was annoyed that Sherry hadn't contacted Glenn.

'I've been busy. Somebody keyed my car at the supermarket yesterday.'

'*What?* Did anybody see who did it?'

'Of course not,' Sherry retorted. 'And there aren't any security cameras in that car park either.' She comforted herself that at least the phone calls had stopped.

Sherry was now nearly thirty weeks pregnant. Her belly itched, her navel stuck out like an extra nose, and she had a stripe down her belly that wouldn't have looked out of place on a donkey's back. As soon as she lay down at night, the baby woke up and performed a repertoire of callisthenic moves that made Sherry feel like a washing machine set on spin cycle. The gymnastic routine, coupled with the heat and almost one hundred per cent humidity, made it impossible to sleep. And she still had ten weeks to go. Sherry wanted her body back and her stalker caught.

She watched the removal men to see if there was

anything unusual about them, but they appeared to be just what they were: men moving furniture into a house.

Nora was all aflutter about the return of her hero and had dressed for the occasion in a fluorescent pink T-shirt with *Doing It The Ditchburn Way* on the front. 'Glenn's putting me on television,' she announced.

Sherry was nervous about seeing Glenn again, and when she was nervous, she was frosty. 'Doing what? Spinning the wheel while he comperes some quiz show?'

Nora refused to let Sherry spoil her fun. 'I'm going to be playing golf with him for the television show he's making.' The doctor had prescribed some new medication and she was walking a little better, plus Glenn had promised she'd only have to get out of the cart to play a few holes; the rest of the time she was there for local flavour. Nora had never been anybody's flavour, local or otherwise. It was news to Sherry. She was trying to process the concept of Nora as a golfing pin-up girl when Nora added, 'Glenn said we might have to stay away overnight sometimes, so you'll have to
look after Otto.'

So much for Lisa's assurances that Glenn wanted to keep an eye on her; he was going to be flitting around the countryside with Nora, not watching over her. 'I'm not looking after that damned cat. I keep sending him home, but he keeps on coming back.'

'I can't go away if you don't take care of Otto.'

Otto spent most nights romancing Custard the Tart who drove the neighbourhood mad yowling her head off on the fence to advertise she was horny. He only came home to check out the contents of his food bowl and recharge his batteries sleeping on Sherry's bed before heading off for another night of carousing.

'That's your problem,' Sherry said. 'He's your cat.'

'Glenn won't like it if I can't go away with him,' Nora warned.

'Then it's his problem, too.'

'Fine!' Nora flounced towards her house and Sherry's brows rose. Nora must be feeling better or have a bigger crush on Glenn than she'd guessed if she could flounce.

'You can tell him,' Nora huffed. 'He'll be here soon.'

She froze. 'Glenn is coming *today?*'

'Yes, he just called me from the airport. He's on his way.'

Sherry's heart started doing the cardiac version of *The Macarena.*

She turned and made a dignified retreat across the baking concrete towards her house, but once inside Sherry hurried upstairs and began searching her wardrobe for an outfit that disguised her resemblance to a pregnant heifer. She settled on a green cotton maxi dress with a shirred bodice and pleated straps that hid the industrial-width straps of her maternity bra. She shoved her feet into a pair of thin-soled gold sandals with dainty ankle straps, but they drew attention to the chipped nail polish on her toes. Pre-pregnancy, Sherry would never have tolerated chipped nail polish, but now she couldn't reach her toes and couldn't be bothered getting a pedicure.

She kicked off the sandals, remembered the concrete was too hot to walk on, and put them back on again. The name of the game was to draw attention away from the bump to her best features. Her hair was looking shiny and lustrous, so she gathered it loosely on her head and wrapped a scarf the same shade as her dress around it. Sherry checked the result. She looked like Carmen Miranda minus the fruit. The hair came down and then went up again minus the scarf. She settled on long strands of blue and green beads to act as decoy instead and looked in the full-length mirror on the wardrobe wall. Her breasts looked like two helium balloons; the only thing missing was *Happy Birthday!* and a couple of strings. Sherry smoothed her hands over her belly. It looked like one of the boulders on the beach at Moeraki. Her shoulders slumped. Why was she bothering?

The purr of a car engine coming up the driveway drifted through the doors opening onto the balcony outside Sherry's bedroom. It sounded expensive.

Glenn had arrived.

Sherry cautiously approached the shiny, blue BMW convertible parked beside the removal van. Some of the removal men had stopped work to look at the car. It was the same model as the one Glenn drove in Denver but was a different shade of blue and didn't have the *Blitz* licence plates. The windows were tinted black so Sherry couldn't see if the number three was stitched into the headrest on the driver's seat like the one in Denver. The M6 retailed at NZ$275,000. Surely Glenn hadn't bought himself another one just for his stay in New Zealand?

A noise behind her made Sherry turn. She watched Glenn lift Nora off the ground, as if she weighed no more than Georgia, and hug her. Nora fluttered like a flag caught in a strong wind, and Sherry's stomach bottomed out.

It was almost four months since she'd seen him. Her appearance had changed dramatically, but he looked just the same: huge, dark and rakishly handsome, like some old-fashioned movie idol. But when Glenn's golden eyes met hers across Nora's head Sherry realized she was wrong — this cool-eyed stranger was not the Glenn she knew. Her hands rose in a self-conscious attempt to hide how ungainly she'd become.

Glenn's eyes grazed her belly and moved away again. He was overwhelmed by the difference in her, and angry that he'd walked away and missed out on watching it happen. She looked wonderful — healthy, and round as a basketball beneath the green dress. He'd dated enough models to know the reason she wore so many brightly coloured necklaces was to draw attention away from her stomach. The extra weight she was carrying out front made her throw back her shoulders and arch her back. Nora had told him about Sherry's car being keyed. She should be at home safe, not working with criminals and riding around alone getting her car keyed.

Glenn set Nora on her feet. This time he wasn't going to let Sherry get under his skin — he wasn't going to lose his temper and shoot himself in the foot. He kept an arm around Nora's shoulders. 'Hi, Sherry. How are you?'

Nora peered up at him in confusion. This wasn't the reunion she'd imagined.

Sherry felt like she'd been doused in cold water. Glenn was the fiery one; *she* was the cool one. 'Fine, thank you,' she said.

'I thought there'd been some more trouble with your car.'

More trouble? Sherry glared at Nora. 'Nothing I can't handle. You must be in your element — new house, new game show.'

'Golf show,' Glenn corrected.

'Sorry! *Golf* show. Are you taking a break from making adverts for sunglasses?' Sherry asked sweetly. She knew about the literacy campaign. She knew about the Bona Fide Blitz trust. Why was she being such a bitch? *Because you abandoned me, because you broke your promise and left me to become a single mother.*

He smiled thinly. 'I got it written into the contract that Nora and I have to wear a different pair of Blitz sunglasses each day.'

It was the first Nora had heard about it. Glenn's arm felt stiff and heavy on her shoulders.

'You lucky girl, Nora, you'll get to keep them, too.' Sherry had to get away before she took a swing at him. 'I'm sure you and Nora have lots to discuss, so I'll leave you to it. I bet you've already arranged a pot-luck dinner to introduce Glenn to the neighbours, haven't you, Nora?'

Nora nodded slowly. What was wrong with them?

I hope you choke on it, Glenn Brogan, Sherry thought savagely, and gathered up her dress and set off down the driveway.

Glenn released Nora and demanded, 'Where are you going?'

Sherry stopped and looked over her shoulder. 'I beg your pardon?' she asked haughtily.

He glared at her. 'Your car was keyed yesterday. You shouldn't be wandering around alone.'

'I'm used to being *alone*; I've been *alone* for months,'

she said, and walked away.

Glenn watched her disappear. So much for his plan to stay calm — already things were going wrong. Sherry felt abandoned and he felt out of his depth. What did he do now? He started when Nora slapped his chest, and cried, 'What did you do that for?'

'Stay out of it, Nora,' he muttered.

'I thought you came back to make it up with Sherry!'

'Will you keep your voice down?' Glenn checked to see if any of the removal men had overheard, but they'd gone back to work. 'I'm here to film a golf show, remember?'

'What about Sherry?'

He scowled. 'She just gave me the verbal equivalent of the finger. What the hell am I supposed to do? Tie her up?'

It sounded like a good idea to Nora. She was disappointed with Glenn. How else did he expect to get a pig-headed know-it-all like Sherry to listen to him? Nora relented when she saw how worried he looked. 'She's probably gone to the beach. She isn't coping with the heat, so she swims a lot. Maybe you need a swim, too, to put you in a better mood?' she suggested.

Glenn started walking down the driveway. 'There's nothing wrong with my mood.'

'Aren't you going to change first?' Nora called, but he was gone.

Sherry left her sandals on the beach and waded into the water with her dress hoicked up around her thighs, cooling her feet and her temper. The sun felt like a blowtorch burning a hole in the sky. She considered sitting down, but it meant she'd have to walk home with her dress plastered to her belly and boobs and run the risk of bumping into Glenn. She was angry. She was disappointed. She was pregnant and unhappy and scared. Sherry felt Glenn's presence before she saw heads turning and the people in the water staring at a spot behind her left shoulder.

'We need to talk.' She ignored him.

'I guess having to waddle like a duck hasn't done anything to sweeten your disposition.'

She twisted angrily towards him. 'And whose fault is that?'

Glenn's brows rose. It was the multi-million-dollar question that kept them apart.

'Oh piss off!' She waded deeper into the water.

Glenn followed her, soaking his trousers and shoes. 'Keep your voice down! There are kids around!'

Her blue eyes blazed. 'I don't want to keep my voice down! I'm angry! I have been angry ever since I found out I was nine weeks pregnant. Ever since you buggered off back to the States because you decided to believe my ex-boyfriend instead of me.'

A wave broke early and soaked them. Sherry let go of her dress and wheeled her arms to keep her balance. Glenn grabbed her to stop her from falling, and the old sizzle of awareness leapt between them. Sand swirled in his ruined shoes as he stared at her belly outlined by the drenched green fabric. He'd made such a damned mess of things. Glenn looked into her face and the tiny black mole beckoned. 'You think I'm happy about how things have turned out?'

There was plenty Sherry wanted to say about that but couldn't because they were in a public place. She plucked her dress away from her belly. 'Why did you buy a house and a car?'

'The car is leased.'

'Don't split hairs! Why are you here?'

'To see you.'

Her brows arched in disbelief.

'To film a golf show and keep an eye on my investment.'

'What do you mean your investment? As far as you're concerned, you didn't even make a deposit in the bank.'

Another wave broke and knocked her into Glenn's chest. His arms closed around her. She really was like a warm, hard basketball. Sherry clutched his arms and struggled upright, forcing him to let her go.

Glenn watched her wrap her arms around herself and back away. 'Stop trying to hide it. You look fine.'

'You said I waddled like a duck!'

'I was pissed at you.' She looked better than fine — she looked great. Glenn the charmer surfaced with a vengeance. His voice dipped: 'You're the sexiest-looking pregnant woman I've ever seen.'

He had to be joking. Sherry took a closer look. He wasn't. But if Glenn thought he could schmooze his way into her good books, he was in for a big disappointment. 'Don't waste your time trying to pull any of that crap on me. I'm immune.' She splashed awkwardly onto the beach, unaware that she'd made the mistake of throwing down the gauntlet to a man who'd made his living out of beating the opposition.

Glenn savoured the view of her long legs while he pondered how to go about defrosting Ice Queen Sherry. This time he'd rely on his own skill and instincts instead of allowing so-called professionals to screw things up. 'I'm just trying to be neighbourly.'

Sherry bent sideways and awkwardly scooped up her shoes. 'Oh yeah, I'm sure you'll be spending a lot of time in your new kitchen, baking.' She thought of Alice's pink kitchen and smirked.

'I'd be happy to let you sample the goods,' Glenn drawled.

A hot bolt of lust made her toes curl into the sand. She had to make a stand or she'd end up acting as dippy as Nora. Sherry scooped her hair behind her ear. 'Have you been inside your new house yet?'

He looked wary. 'No. Why? What's wrong with it?'

'Nothing at all. In fact, it's *lovely* — the kind of place where a man can get in touch with his feminine side.'

'Or a woman can get in touch with hers?'

Sherry gripped her sandals and looked down her nose. 'In a Stetson?'

She stiffened. 'Ma'am?'

She fled.

Glenn strode up the driveway. Something was wrong with the house, something Sherry knew he wouldn't like. She was nowhere in sight, but Nora was standing guard by his car while a small contingent of men from the street looked it over. Instead of checking out his house, Glenn had to wait while Nora proudly oversaw the introductions to his new neighbours. She seemed disappointed when they were more interested in Glenn's car than him, but that suited Glenn just fine. He'd rather answer questions about the M6's top speed than explain why a famous ex-pro basketball player had chosen to move into a small house on Auckland's North Shore instead of a mansion overlooking the harbour with round-the-clock security. He also didn't want to explain why he was drenched in sea water, but the BMW deflected attention from its owner for only so long.

Roger, a guy with a squashed nose and close-set eyes, studied Glenn's soaked trousers and waterlogged shoes. 'Took a dip?'

'Went to take a look at the beach and got hit by a rogue wave.'

Named Sherry.

Roger had heard about eccentric millionaires, but never actually met one before. 'Why'd you decide to move in here?'

Glenn was ready for him. 'To be closer to Nora. I'd appreciate it if people didn't mention I was here so I could have some privacy. It'd be hell if the shared driveway got blocked by paparazzi.'

Roger nodded sagely, as if photographers camped at the bottom of the drive were a regular occurrence. 'I'll tell the others.'

Nora had seen Sherry come flapping by like a wet hen with a fox on its tail, disappear into her house, come out again wearing dry clothes that didn't match, and drive away. Nora had never seen Sherry wear mismatched clothes. She looked at Glenn's soaked trousers and waterlogged shoes, and accurately guessed the name of the fox. She dragged him aside.

'What did you do to Sherry? She blazed up here like a skyrocket, threw on some clothes that *didn't go together* and roared away in her car.'

'Where's she gone?'

'That's what I'm asking you, stupid.' Glenn scowled and Nora's disappointment deepened. How was he going to woo Sherry if he kept upsetting her? 'Why are you all wet?'

'I took a swim,' he replied shortly.

'In your clothes?'

'It was hot.'

Nora was sure Glenn wasn't talking about the weather and felt more hopeful.

Glenn wasn't exactly upset that he'd rattled Sherry. But he was upset about her accusation that he'd abandoned her, and that she'd taken off alone. He checked his watch — he'd set it to New Zealand time on the plane — to see what time Sherry had left. Where the hell had she gone? What if the lowlife who'd been bothering her had been watching on the beach and followed her?

'Did she say where she was going?' he asked uneasily.

'From the look on her face, to buy a gun. How would I know?' Nora replied. 'Try not to worry; she's good at taking care of herself.'

If she wasn't home in an hour, he'd call Ben; and if she wasn't there, he'd call her parents. And then Annemarie and her other friend, Mary — Ben would have Annemarie's number. Glenn reconciled himself to the fact that he'd be doing a lot of waiting around and worrying until the stalker gave up or was caught, or he could persuade Sherry to give up her job. He tried to comfort himself with the thought that Nora was right, Sherry was a cop and knew what she was doing. Moving next-door to her might put Glenn on the fast-track to a stomach ulcer, but it was better than sitting in his condo in Denver waiting for news and worrying. He'd rather have Sherry abusing him first-hand instead of via her lawyer.

Glenn signed an autograph for one of the neighbour's kids, and assessed the progress made by the removal men. He didn't get involved in boring details like unloading furniture and unpacking household contents when he moved house. Fraser took care of hiring the movers and getting an interior designer to decorate and arrange the contents of the house, but there was no sign of a designer. For once, his über-efficient agent must have forgotten to book one. In lieu of a designer or his mother, that left ... Glenn's eyes settled on Nora. He gave her his best matinee-idol smile. 'Thanks for supervising things; you're a real sweetheart.'

Nora preened. 'If I hadn't been here, they would've put your kitchen things in the bathroom.'

'What would I do without you? I'm hopeless at this kind of thing. Thank you, darlin'.'

Two men walked past carrying a long, flat brown box with a picture of an exercise treadmill on the side. 'Where do you want us to put this, mate? In the pink bedroom? Or the pink garage?'

Nora pushed past Glenn. 'Why would he want a treadmill in his bedroom? Put it in the garage.' She ushered the men towards it like Big Bo Peep shepherding a couple of unruly rams.

'*Pink?*' Glenn repeated. 'Did he say a *pink* garage?'

'Yeah,' said a man carrying one end of the headboard of Glenn's custom-made bed. 'Didn't you know? The whole house — it's pink.'

Glenn ran around the front of the removal van and ground to a halt in front of the double garage. The walls and door were cotton-candy pink. There was even a pink tinge to the concrete. 'Fuck!'

The man carrying the headboard nodded as he came past. 'That's what we all said when we saw it. Seems wrong to put a car like that in a pink garage.'

Sherry fled all the way to Ben's house. He roared up on the Ducati just as she pulled into the driveway in her SUV. She climbed out of the car and waited for him to shut off the bike. 'Glenn is back!'

Ben sat astride the bike and removed his helmet, sunglasses and gloves. He put the glasses and gloves inside the helmet, placed it on the seat between his thighs, and folded his arms. His cool, confident, clothes-horse sister looked nothing like her usual self: she wore no make-up, and her black hair was stiff with saltwater; there was sand on her feet and ankles, and her red peasant top clashed with her baggy blue shorts. The last time Ben had seen Sherry look this agitated was the day she found out she was pregnant.

'He's moved in?'

She nodded. 'He's even got a car like the one he drives in Denver.'

The news momentarily distracted Ben from the main

issue. 'What kind of car?'

'A BMW M6.'

His eyes glazed over with car lust.

'Forget the car!' Sherry howled. 'What about me?'

He started. 'Sorry — what did he say when he saw you?' 'That I waddled like a duck.'

Ben winced. 'What did you say?'

'I told him to piss off.'

He unzipped his leather jacket. 'That's a good start.'

'He's going to make my life hell! I don't want him living next- door to me!' she wailed.

Ben shrugged out of the jacket. Underneath it he wore a black T-shirt with the sleeves hacked off, not because he was trying to make a fashion statement — he left those to Sherry — but because it was one he wore for work and the only thing he had clean. 'If it bothers you that much, move in here.' He'd been trying to get her to do that ever since the air had been let out of her car tyres.

'And let him drive me out of my house? I don't think so!'

Ben studied her closely. 'What else did he say?' He watched her poker up and guessed. Sherry couldn't get her head around the idea that a pregnant woman could be sexy, particularly to the man who'd got her that way. Under normal circumstances, Ben wouldn't dream of discussing Sherry's sex life, but these weren't normal circumstances. 'There's nothing wrong with Glenn wanting to take you to bed, Sher.' He wished he'd kept his mouth shut when her face turned as red as her top.

'Yes, there is.' Sherry looked at Ben wretchedly, 'Starr is talking about getting another scan done. What if I got it wrong and Glenn isn't the father? What if it turns out

I'm further along than I thought and Stuart—' Her voice broke.

Ben got off the bike and hugged her. 'Why does Starr want you to have another scan?'

She buried her face in his shoulder and sobbed, 'B-because I'm so b-big ...'

He felt the solid shape of his future niece or nephew between them. 'Didn't the doctor say at your last scan that the baby was big?'

'Long ... long ... femur.' Sherry's shoulders jerked. 'But my ... my belly is about three w-weeks ahead of sched-dule.'

Ben felt her ahead-of-schedule-belly change shape as a tremor like a mini earthquake rolled across it. He leaned back and looked down. 'What was that?'

She sniffed and swiped her nose with the back of her hand. 'It rolled over.'

'Doesn't it make you feel sick?' he asked incredulously.

'No.'

'It felt like a sumo wrestler warming up for a bout.' Ben rubbed Sherry's shoulders. 'Forget about the scan and listen to me instead: that kid is super-sized — Stuart ain't responsible.'

Sherry gave a watery laugh. 'What a doula. Can you convince Starr of that?'

Ben went one better. The next day, when he returned from surfing, he noticed Starr's motorbike parked outside her grandmother's house and knocked. Cloe

Warrender beamed when she saw who her visitor was. 'Benjamin! How are you?'

There was a family tradition of naming Warrender girls after flowers or plants. Cloe's real name was Clover, and her daughter Mimi was Mimosa. Mimi had followed the tradition by naming her daughter Starflower, but Starr would admit to that only under pain of death. Cloe was tiny with a soft, wrinkled face, faded red hair, and lavender eyes. She called people she liked *'love'* and ramped it up to *'my love'* for those she loved. Ben had been introduced to Mimi and Mimi's partner, Jocelyn, when they'd visited, and had soon worked out that Starr had inherited her grandmother's looks, but it was Mimi who had inherited her disposition.

Ben smiled down at Cloe. 'I'm good. How's the garage door?'

She clutched the edge of the door in her soft, white hands. 'It's perfect since you fixed it, love. Starr and I have been baking — you've met Starr, haven't you?' Cloe rushed on before Ben could nod. 'Of course you have! She's looking after your sister, the police officer. Shelley, is it?'

'Sherry.'

'Sherry! That's it!' Cloe touched Ben's arm and leaned closer. 'Tell her I think she's very tall and very beautiful.'

'I will,' he promised. 'Would you mind asking Starr if I could have a word?'

'I can do better than that, love. Come and have a cup of tea and a melting moment.'

'I'm covered in sand from the beach.'

'That's alright!' She was already tripping away on her little feet, so Ben had no choice but to brush off the worst of the sand, close the door and follow her.

His interest in Starr had waned after the incident with Annemarie in the kitchen. He didn't like people who were narrow-minded and judgmental and Starr seemed to tick the boxes on both counts. Since the day at Sherry's house, he'd seen her twice across the fence when she came to mow the lawn for her grandmother. Ben nodded, said hello, and then ignored her. Once he'd been working on his motorbike in the courtyard behind the garage, had sensed somebody watching and, from the corner of his eye, seen Starr staring at the Ducati as she emptied the grass-catcher from the mower. She didn't like him, but she definitely liked his motorbike.

Cloe led the way to the kitchen at the back of the house. 'Do you like melting moments, Ben?'

He eyed the back of her softly permed head. Cloe had a way of saying things that made him think she hadn't always been sweet and innocent. 'I think so. They're those little cakes stuck together with jam, aren't they?'

'I suppose that's one way to describe them.'

He grinned. They turned into the kitchen and his smile faded. The windows and back door were thrown open to the sunshine, and the room smelled of home baking and freshly mown grass. Starr leaned on her elbows on one of the kitchen counters, stroking the short hair at her nape and reading a page from New Zealand's cooking bible, the *Edmonds Cookery Book*. Ben had only ever seen her in bike leathers or the raggedy jeans, outsized T-shirt and battered black cap she wore when she mowed the lawn, but today she was wearing a dress.

It was bright yellow, tied in bows on her shoulders, and fell loosely to the middle of her thighs. There were dimples in the back of her knees and her small feet were bare. Her toenails were painted coral, a silver ring glinted on one of her toes, and a fine silver chain with three hearts hung from one narrow ankle. Ben watched Starr's pert bottom sway slowly from side to side beneath the dress as she bent over the cookbook. And Cloe watched him watch Starr.

'Who was it, Cloe?' Starr asked. 'Shall we make some butterfly cakes?'

'If you like,' Cloe replied serenely. 'Do you like butterfly cakes, Benjamin?'

Starr spun around so fast that the cookbook skated along the counter and landed in the kitchen sink. Ben enjoyed her wide-eyed, open-mouthed astonishment, and the way her little breasts pushed at the front of the yellow dress as she leaned back against the counter.

'I'm more of a melting moments man,' he confessed.

Starr recovered quickly when she noticed where his eyes had briefly landed and the laughter lurking in their depths. She gave the straps of her dress a twitch and straightened. Without the protection of her bike leathers and laptop, she felt exposed. Ben Jackson's interest in her had cooled after she'd caught him with Sherry's friend. On the two occasions their paths had crossed, he'd barely spoken, and Starr had sensed disapproval in his manner — as if *she* had done something wrong.

He looked like he'd just come from the beach. His feet were bare and dusted with sand, a pair of blue-and-orange board shorts rode low on his hips, and a dark-blue cap shaded his eyes. He was lean and tanned and had muscles in his shoulders and arms and chest — and on either side of the thin line of black hair running from his navel and into the waistband of his shorts. He was very ... healthy-looking.

Ever since she'd moved in, Cloe had been going on about how nice Ben was and wanted to know why Starr didn't approve of him. Starr told her about him dumping his fiancée at the altar, and how she'd seen him in the kitchen with his hands full of Annemarie's bum. Cloe listened carefully and remarked, 'It's good that he knows which ones to let go of and which ones to catch then, isn't it, my love?'

Cloe began making the tea. 'Ben wanted to speak to you, so I asked him in for a cup of tea and one of your melting moments.' She smiled at Ben. 'Starr made two kinds. Which would you like? One with icing? Or one with jam?'

Ben managed to keep a straight face. 'Definitely jam.'

Starr's lips worked as if she'd tasted something nasty.

'How's your friend Glenn?' Cloe asked. 'Is he coming back?'

'He's here.' Starr looked at Ben sharply, and he explained, 'That's what I came to talk to you about.'

She led him to an old wooden seat at the back of the garden. 'How is Sherry?'

'Pretty upset.' Ben rested one elbow on his knee and plucked at the grass between his bare feet, giving Starr a perfect view of smooth brown shoulders and the long indentation of his spine. 'She's worried that, if her dates are wrong, Stuart is the father.' He looked across at Starr perched primly on the other end of the seat.

'Thanks for letting me know.' She seemed sincere.

'Do you really think Sherry's further along than she thought? I thought the doctor said at the last scan that the baby was big.'

Starr explained that scans performed later in pregnancy weren't done for the purpose of checking dates but to assess fetal growth and estimate the baby's weight. They were useful in cases of gestational diabetes or, in a case like Sherry's, when the size of the uterus was bigger than expected for gestational age and there was a concern about shoulder dystocia: in laymen's terms, the baby being too big for the mother to deliver naturally. Sherry was tall, but Glenn Brogan's size and the chances of Sherry having a ten-pound baby were good enough reasons for Starr to want another scan.

Starr appreciated Ben's concern for his sister, but she couldn't discuss Sherry's case. 'I can't discuss Sherry's case with you; I'd be breaching patient confidentiality.'

'If I wasn't worried about my sister, I wouldn't be here,' he said curtly. 'I know you don't like me, and, frankly, I don't like you either.'

She was stung. '*You* don't like *me*? Why?'

He looked her squarely in her Lavender Fairy eyes. 'I don't like people who are narrow-minded and judgmental and jump to conclusions. You've decided I'm a Lothario who jilts women at the altar and likes to have sex with my sister's friends on her kitchen counter.'

Starr opened and closed her mouth several times. 'I am *not* judgmental and narrow-minded! My grandmother walked out on her husband when he wouldn't accept my mother was gay! My parents are gay!'

'I've met your mother,' Ben retorted. 'I've met *both* your mothers and liked them. I think your grandmother is lovely, too, but you ...' His voice cooled. 'You've got a chip on your shoulder the size of Mount Cook about being short and God knows what else. If you're gay just come out and say you are and stop taking it out on a man for showing he's attracted to you.'

He didn't understand. She'd been surrounded by strong, positive female role models all her life, but had dipped out when it came to the male variety. Her father, Emlyn, was Mimi's cousin. He was weak and ineffectual, and under the thumb of his wife and Cloe's ex-husband, Royce. Starr wasn't about to air her family secrets, and focused instead on something she could talk about.

'I'm *not* gay.'

Ben shrugged; he didn't care. 'Whatever. You're good at your job and Sherry likes you; that's all I care about.' He set his hands on the edge of the seat and boosted himself to his feet. 'I'm going to have that tea and one of your melting moments, and then I'm going home to check the counters in the kitchen for any sharp edges. And if I ever decide to get married, I'll be sure to tell Cloe so you can turn up at the church and watch me dump the bride.'

'Ben! Starr!' Cloe called. 'Your tea is ready!'

It was the first time Starr had felt small *inside*. She watched Ben cross the sun-browned grass towards the back door, watched the up-down slide of his buttocks beneath the board shorts and the glide of the muscles in his shoulders and back, and tried to work up a head of steam. How dare he say she jumped to conclusions and in the very next breath accuse her of being gay? Because

Ben probably expected her to remain in the garden and sulk, Starr joined Cloe and him for tea and cake and managed to make a contribution to the conversation. It wasn't as if Ben or Cloe needed any help from her, they acted like they'd known one another for years. He really did like her grandmother.

Before he left, Ben promised to come by the following weekend and trim some branches off a tree in the garden.

'I can do that, Cloe,' Starr insisted.

Cloe shook her head. 'It's the big tree in the corner at the back.

The branches are too high for you to reach safely, my love.' Starr hoped she imagined that Ben winked at her.

'He's a nice-looking young man,' Cloe remarked after she'd shown him out.

'He used to be fat.'

'He's not fat now.'

'He's twenty-seven, Cloe, too young for you.'

'I know. Isn't it a shame?' She began rinsing the teacups. 'I saw a surfboard propped against the side of his truck when I let him in. You both love surfing and motorbikes, isn't that nice?'

This needed nipping in the bud — *pronto*. 'It would be if it weren't for something else we have in common.'

Cloe said brightly, 'What's that?'

'We *have* nothing in common.'

A vee appeared in the soft skin between Cloe's eyes. 'What a shame. I'm certain Ben could help you with that problem.'

'Having an intact hymen isn't a problem.'

'It is if you're twenty-six and you haven't got a

boyfriend to help you get rid of it. You don't have to talk to him. It was always my experience that there wasn't a lot of talking done during the actual event.'

Starr held out the plate of cakes. 'Have another melting moment.'

'Surely you must like the look of Ben? I think he's hot. Don't you think he's hot?' Cloe asked hopefully.

Starr sighed. None of her friends had a grandmother like hers.

'I just don't like to think of you missing out. Sex is wonderful with the right man.'

'Or woman,' they chorused together, out of respect for Mimi and Joss.

'Sherry is my client,' Starr replied. 'It would be unprofessional for me to get involved with her brother.'

And Sherry needed her.

Ben certainly didn't.

Chapter 19

G lenn hated parking his car in the pink garage.

Ben shared his pain. 'It's sacrilege. You can leave it at my place if you want.'

'I might be stupid when it comes to dealing with pregnant women, but it doesn't apply to their car-crazy builder brothers.'

'OK, but don't blame me if the V10 engine dies of shame,' Ben warned.

His feelings about Glenn's return were mixed. He was glad that Sherry had Glenn to call on, but worried his presence next-door would continue to upset her. Ben stopped by Glenn's place to warn him that Sherry was fragile and didn't need more aggravation in her life.

Glenn regretted the loss of their previous easy-going relation- ship. 'That's not why I'm here.'

'Good. Keep it that way.'

They were standing in the pink garage. Every morning before Glenn went to get in his car, he told himself that the walls and concrete weren't really pink. And every morning when he opened the door to the garage, he winced when he saw that they were. The pink bathroom, living room, kitchen and his pink bedroom offended him too, but not nearly as much as the garage.

Glenn looked at Ben accusingly. 'Did you build this house too?'

He nodded. 'It's not my fault Alice liked pink. The guys who work for me almost threw a fit when they saw the colour of the garage door.'

'Sherry has a smirk on her face every time she looks over here,' Glenn said sourly.

'You really should thank me — it could have been worse.'

'You put fucking pink concrete in my garage and you expect me to thank you?'

'If it wasn't for me, you'd have a pink flamingo weathervane on the roof as well.' Ben stroked the M6's gleaming blue chassis. 'You can thank me by letting me take your car for a drive.'

They took the motorway north so that Ben could open up the V10 engine. At Orewa they stopped and bought fish and chips and ate them on the beach.

'How's Starr?' Glenn asked as he finished off the last pieces of battered tarakihi.

Ben stretched out on the sand with his hands tucked under his head and his ankles crossed and closed his eyes. 'Like she always is, uptight and anal.'

'Last time I was here you couldn't get enough of her.' Glenn took a sip from a can of coke. 'Or was that any of her?'

'You're in no position to talk. All you do is upset Sherry.'

Glenn frowned at the waves curling onto the sand. 'I don't mean to.'

'Maybe not, but it's what happens when you two get together. Sherry's not as tough as you think. You can walk away; she can't.'

Brian Jackson hadn't been nearly so diplomatic when he'd spoken to Glenn. 'Go home. We'll take care of Sherry and the baby. She needs somebody who'll stand by her, not baulk at the first hurdle.'

Glenn's hackles rose. 'I'm staying. Until the nut who's stalking her is caught, she needs as many people watching out for her as possible.'

'How do we know you're not the nut?' Brian asked.

Nora was in heaven. Filming for the golf show took place during the week, and she and Glenn got to play a couple of courses providing the weather didn't break. They usually travelled by helicopter to the best courses in the country, where Nora played for free using the new set of Callaways Glenn had bought her. Tony, the director, loved her T-shirts, neon-coloured ankle socks and *Nora Ditchburn For Prime Minister* visor. Nora quickly forgot about the camera and sound man when she got to the first tee. Playing golf and beating Glenn was all that mattered.

The crew looked askance at Tony the first time they heard Nora and Glenn arguing about the best choice of club or who'd made the worst shot, but Tony just smiled and signalled for filming to continue. Later when they saw the uncut footage, the crew realized why; Nora was screamingly funny and had no idea about it, and Glenn knew just what to say to keep her going. She was also very knowledgeable about golf and the courses they played, which Glenn and Tony knew the golf aficionados would love. Everybody made sure that Nora didn't overdo things and hurt her hip. She loved being fussed over and felt glamorous and important.

'When we've finished filming, you're getting that damned hip done, Nora — no arguments,' Glenn grunted when he had to carry her inside her house one night. 'If you don't, I'm going to need more surgery on my knee from hauling you up these stairs.'

She hung over his shoulder, cackling. 'It'll make it even easier to beat you.'

If only it were as easy to take care of Sherry. Glenn barely saw her, because he left early each morning for the golf course and got home late, and Sherry worked shifts. Each night when he got home, Glenn checked to see if the lights were shining in Sherry's house. If they weren't, and Nora hadn't said Sherry was doing an afternoon shift, Glenn called and asked Ben where Sherry was, and didn't sleep until she came home.

The golf show gave Glenn a perfect reason to be in New Zealand, which was just as well, because he'd been recognized several times since his return. But Glenn was an old hand at manipulating media attention. He got Fraser to engage a local PR company and met with members of the New Zealand Tourism Board, who were keen for some of the local talent to have a guest spot on some of the shows. Glenn was all for involving the locals until Fraser explained that the NZTB weren't thinking of local amateur players.

'Who then?' Glenn asked.

'You'll never believe it — Perry Westgaard!' Fraser exclaimed and was surprised at Glenn's lukewarm response.

He kicked things off by doing an interview for the six o'clock evening news slot and followed it up with a guest spot on a national sports quiz television show, where he got nearly every rugby question wrong but made up for it with his basketball and golf knowledge and sense of humour. More women watched the show that night than ever before, and the producers asked if Glenn would like to do another show.

The PR people were under strict instructions to keep the location of where Glenn lived a secret, and accepted his explanation that he wanted to live in an ordinary house in an ordinary community while he was in the country, and that it made sense to stay near Nora. The only other people Glenn needed to get onside were his neighbours. Sherry was right; Nora had arranged a pot-luck dinner to introduce Glenn to the neighbours, but it didn't take place until a couple of weeks after he'd moved in because of the filming schedule.

'I'm sure the neighbours understand. We wouldn't want to interfere in the making of a great epic,' Sherry said when Nora knocked to give her the invitation.

'If you're going to get snotty about it, don't come.' Nora still had on the clothes she'd worn to play Wairakei Golf Course. 'We flew down to Wairakei Golf Course by helicopter today.'

Sherry was jealous. Wairakei was a wonderful course near Taupo that she'd only managed to play once.

Nora wasn't finished. 'Perry Westgaard played with us.'

'*Perry Westgaard?*' Sherry gasped. 'You played golf with *Perry Westgaard*?'

'And his caddy, Mozart Morris,' Nora said airily.

Sherry thought she might start hyperventilating. Perry Westgaard had won the New Zealand Open twice and was making a name for himself on the US PGA tour. His flamboyant caddy, Mozart Morris, was almost as famous as his boss. When Westgaard was playing in a televised tournament nobody bothered inviting Sherry to anything, because they knew she'd be glued to the television watching Perry work his magic on the golf course. Sherry admitted she was fifty per cent a fan of Westgaard's swing, and fifty per cent his blue eyes and lanky six-foot-three-inch frame. If she'd been nicer to Glenn, she might have been invited along.

Wairakei's fourteenth hole, known as 'The Rogue', was notoriously difficult thanks to a huge tree in the middle of the fairway. 'How did Perry do at The Rogue?' Sherry asked eagerly.

'He eagled it,' Nora said. 'I almost cried.'

'How did Glenn do?'

'He went one over.' She looked smug. 'I parred it — Glenn wasn't happy.' The message on the front of Nora's turquoise-blue T-shirt read: *Blitz and Ditch — A Winning Team.*

Sherry eyed the shirt. 'What does Glenn think of your T-shirt?'

'He says it's even worse than my *Nora The Scorer* shirt, but Tony and the crew love it. Tony said the producers think my T-shirts will be a big hit in the States. They think there might be a market for them.'

When Jill was a teenager, there'd been a market for loud tartan pants with cuffs, but nobody had looked good in them, either. Sherry knew, because she'd seen photos of her mother wearing three-quarter-length tartan pants during what Jill called her 'Bay City Rollers stage'.

'Who's Tony?'

'The director,' Nora said grandly.

Sherry was still smarting at missing an opportunity to meet her favourite golfer. 'I've got an idea for a T-shirt: how about *The Diva and The Doula?*'

'Are you trying to be smart?' Nora asked.

No, throwing a tantrum. 'What night is the pot-luck dinner?'

'Next Wednesday.' She studied her list. 'Can I put you down for a potato salad?'

How had they skipped the part where Sherry said she wasn't coming? 'I thought pot-luck meant you brought whatever you wanted to? That's why it's called pot-luck.'

'If people bring what they want, we'll have too many green salads and garlic bread.' Nora waited with her pencil poised.

'Why do I have to come? I've already met him.'

'Glenn will be hurt if you don't.'

Sherry doubted that. On the few occasions they'd met, Glenn had alternated between voicing his displeasure that Sherry was still working and trying to flambé her with his eyes. He'd flirted with her on the beach because he'd flirt with any female that was conscious — Nora was proof of that. Pregnancy might have done wonders for Sherry's hair and skin, but she still looked like a beach ball.

'Alright, I'll come for a while when I finish work. Put me down for a dessert — raspberry crumble.'

Nora was about to write it down but stopped. 'Won't

that be pink?'

'It might.'

Her brows lowered. 'No.'

'Pink lamingtons?'

'No.'

'Watermelon?'

'No!'

'Beetroot — it's not pink, it's red.'

'You're just trying to pick a fight!' Nora scrubbed at her list with the pencil. 'Hayley at number nine wanted to make a lasagna, but she can do the potato salad instead. Yours is much nicer; Hayley's always gets stuck under my dentures.'

Sherry grimaced.

'Do you think you could make a pavlova as well? With whipped cream and kiwifruit? But no strawberries,' Nora added hastily.

'I won't be home until late most of the week, Nora.'

'You can make everything the night before and leave it with me in the morning.'

Oh yeah, she felt like chopping herbs and beating egg whites after a long day at work. 'Are people bringing gifts?'

'What do you mean?'

'Gifts? You know, house-warming presents?' Sherry asked innocently.

Nora eyed her warily. 'No. Why?'

'No reason.' She'd arranged for something special for Glenn that he would absolutely hate.

'No presents,' Nora said firmly, and handed Sherry a piece of paper. 'Here's the invitation.'

Since she'd got her new computer and laser printer,

Nora had been churning out leaflets for garage sales and community meetings and posting them all over the street. The wording on the invitation was no better than what was on her T-shirt: *Pot-Luck Dinner To Welcome Our New Neighbour, Blitz Brogan, basketball legend.*

'Has Glenn seen this?' Sherry asked dubiously.

Nora was busy counting salads on her list. 'No, he said he was happy to leave everything in my capable hands.'

More like happy to let Nora do all the work so that all Glenn had to do was turn up to charm the locals at the appointed date and time. He was used to his agent organizing his public appearances, and had apparently forgotten that Nora was a bored, sixtyish woman with a bad hip and high-powered Apple computer.

'Is something wrong with the invitation?' Nora demanded when Sherry continued to stare at it.

'Do you really think he'll want to be introduced as a basketball legend? Don't you think he'd rather people got to know him as Glenn Brogan, rather than The Blitz?'

'There's quite a few basketball fans living in the street,' Nora said huffily. 'You'd know that if you bothered to come along to things.'

It wasn't Sherry's problem; Glenn should have paid more attention. She pointed to some round shapes on the invitation. 'What are those? Balloons?'

'They're basketballs!' Nora snatched it back. 'I'm putting you down for pavlova as well.'

On Wednesday morning, Sherry delivered the

lasagna, pavlova and a gift-wrapped package to Nora's house before she went to work.

Nora's face fell when she saw the pavlova. 'Did you have to do that?'

'What do you mean? I went to a lot of trouble to make that.'

'More like you want to make trouble,' Nora grumbled.

'What are you doing today? Playing Kauri Cliffs with Tiger?' Sherry asked sardonically.

Nora folded her arms. 'I'm putting that pavlova at the back of the table where Glenn won't see it.'

Sherry was late finishing work because she'd agreed to catch up with Stacey. Dave Pomana kept Sherry tied to a desk working for the investigation arm of the FVU, but he occasionally let her out, provided the women weren't from a 'hot' family and Sherry met them somewhere safe. Vance hadn't shown up at Stacey's new house, which meant he either hadn't worked out where his family was living or was paying attention to the protection order — Sherry tended to think the former. Driving her own car and not wearing uniform meant that the neighbours wouldn't know Stacey was being visited by a cop. Annemarie would be taking over Sherry's families while she was on maternity leave and had come along to meet Stacey and the children.

Stacey's house was a rental in a poor area, but it was in reasonable condition and the street wasn't known to police for drug-dealing or gang activity. Stacey didn't care that her new home was a little shabby; it was a haven of peace for her and the children because she didn't have to share it with Vance. She liked that the house was set at the top of a sloping section and overlooked the street below, because it made her feel like she'd be able to see Vance coming if he suddenly arrived to make good on his threats.

Her eyes went round when she saw Sherry. 'Hell! Are you sure it isn't twins?'

'That's what we keep asking at the station,' Annemarie said.

Sherry couldn't answer, because she was out of breath after trudging up the two flights of concrete steps from the street. She leaned against the worn metal handrail and puffed, 'It's not twins, but I am having a scan to check how big it is.' Or at least, Starr arranged dates for scans and Sherry kept on making excuses and changing them. If her dates were wrong, it meant Stuart was the father; and if her dates were right, it meant she really was going to give birth to a whale.

Stacey ushered Sherry and Annemarie into the kitchen and offered them a cup of tea. Lianna and Storm were watching television in the living room next to the kitchen. Sherry introduced Annemarie to them and left her talking to the kids while she returned to Stacey in the kitchen.

Nikita was lying on the floor between the kitchen and living room, with her bare, grubby feet stretched out behind her, drawing on pieces of newspaper with a red crayon. Sherry was pleased to see that she wasn't wearing a nappy beneath her pink-and-lime Lycra shorts. Since she'd been pregnant, she kept noticing details like that. 'Hi, Nikita.'

There were red marks on the faded linoleum where Nikita had missed the paper. She stared at Sherry. 'You're fat.'

'Thanks,' Sherry said drily.

Stacey got milk from the fridge. 'She's not fat; she's got a baby in her tummy like Auntie Crystal.'

Nikita studied Sherry for a few more moments before returning to her drawing. 'A *big* baby.'

Why bother with a scan when even a three-year-old could tell she was carrying Moby Dick?

'Sit down.' Stacey nodded sideways at the old-fashioned Formica table in the corner of the kitchen and dropped tea bags into some mugs. 'How long have you got to go?'

'If my dates are right, seven weeks.' Sherry lowered herself onto a chair covered in tatty red plastic and sucked in a breath as her belly went rock hard.

'You OK?'

She released the breath. 'Braxton Hicks contractions.'

'Oh, them. Have you had restless leg syndrome? I got that with Nikita.'

'No, but I've got everything else.' Sherry rubbed her rib to try and dislodge a foot and nodded when Stacey held up the milk. 'It likes to play hang-ten with my ribs.'

Stacey smiled and stuck her head into the living room to ask Annemarie if she wanted milk and sugar. Sherry thought how much better she looked now than when she'd been living with Vance. He'd stopped turning up at the station and threatening Sherry and whoever was in the watch-house; in fact, he'd been almost too quiet, and

Stacey was worried he was planning something bad and the effect it was having on Stan. She gave Annemarie her tea, then carried two mugs to the table and sat down with Sherry.

'So how's it going?' Sherry asked.

Stacey looked at Nikita. 'Kita, take your drawing into the lounge with Storm and Lianna and the other lady and close the door.'

'Can't draw on carpet.'

'Do as you're told! Go and watch TV.'

Nikita retreated carrying her paper and crayon and slammed the door.

Stacey's lips tightened. 'She's as bad as Lianna and Storm.'

Lianna and Storm had always been a handful. Sherry hoped Nikita didn't follow in their footsteps. 'Where's Stan? You said you were worried about him.'

'In the bedroom. He won't go out, not even to shoot baskets with his friends, and he hates it if Lianna and Storm go to their friends' houses. He's eleven years old but acts like an old man.' Stacey leaned on the table. 'Can you talk to him? He likes you.'

It was news to Sherry. 'Have you talked to Misty and the other workers at the refuge? The ones who helped you put a plan together?'

'Yeah, and they've been great. Me and Stan, we just don't feel ...' Stacey floundered '... safe.'

Vance had a lot to answer for. Domestic abuse was an under- statement — domestic terrorism was a better description.

'Stan takes his cue from you, Stacey. If you're uptight, then he'll be uptight. Apart from moving, what's changed to make you so scared?'

She shrugged and sipped her tea. 'Nothing, it all just seems too good to be true. Sure, money is a problem — a *big* problem. Vance won't hand over any money for food, but he can afford to buy himself another car,' Stacey said bitterly.

'How do you know he's got a new car?'

'Vance has got a big mouth, and I made it my business to know what he's driving. Every time a blue Holden goes past the house or pulls up at the kerb when I'm walking Nikita to kindy I shit a brick.' Stacey reached for her cigarettes, then remembered Sherry and put them back on the table. 'At least I don't have to worry about being woken up to cook a feed at two in the morning and getting beaten up because there's no food in the house, or him coming to bed drunk and—' She stopped.

It was easier to say yes to sex than risk getting the bash. Yet many women put up with their partner's violent behaviour, or went back, because losing their man meant financial hardship.

'I'm too scared to believe it won't all go wrong, that there isn't something bad waiting around the corner and I'll end up having to go back,' Stacey said.

Sherry wished Vance and his ilk were consigned to hell. 'No, you won't. Misty and the refuge workers showed you that you've got choices. If things get rocky, you know people who will help you get through it,' she insisted. 'You're stronger now.'

Stacey gazed at the orange and yellow mug between her hands. 'Yeah, I guess.' She watched Sherry rub her ribs again. 'Better get you to talk to Stan before you pop.'

Stan was on his bed in the room he shared with Storm. He looked up when his mother rapped on the open door. 'Hey, Stan, you've got a visitor,' she said, and walked away.

He rolled over and looked at Sherry standing in the doorway. His surprise at seeing her was quickly replaced by a frown. 'Hell, you're—'

'I'm not fat.' Sherry sat on Storm's bed. 'I'm pregnant — like Auntie Crystal.'

Stan swung his legs over the side of the bed. His black hair stood up at the back like a rooster's comb. He put his elbows on his knees and cupped his chin in his hands. 'I wasn't going to say you were fat. Auntie Crystal is fat — you've just got a really big stomach.'

Sherry didn't pursue the subject. 'Why are you inside? I thought you'd be practicing your free throws.'

He shrugged one shoulder and stared at the carpet. Sherry felt his misery as acutely as if it were her own. She tried to think of what she should say to him. Stacey said Stan had been seeing the counsellor at his school until he started truanting. He'd been referred to a child psychiatrist but wasn't acute enough to jump the queue and had to wait for an appointment. He was eleven years old, and he was depressed. He should be having fun, not seeing counsellors and psychiatrists. Sherry understood how helpless Stacey felt, because she did, too.

Stan waited for Constable Sherry to tell him things were getting better, that his mother had a protection order against his father, and the police would come if his dad ever showed up at their new house. But what if he showed up when Mum sent Lianna or Storm to the shop to buy milk? What if he grabbed Nikita outside kindy so his mum had to go and get her and his father hurt her again? Bad things happened. People were liars.

Sherry shifted her weight and knocked her foot against something under Storm's bed. A basketball rolled out and stopped in the middle of the worn brown carpet. Stan stared at the ball indifferently.

'Do you know a basketball player called Blitz Brogan?' Sherry said slowly.

He looked up at her and frowned. It wasn't what he'd been expecting Constable Sherry to say. 'What?'

It was too late to take it back now.

'Do you know a basketball player called Blitz Brogan? He used to play for the Colorado Cougars.'

Stan looked at Sherry as if she was stupid. '*Everybody* has heard of The Blitz.' He went to the closet and pulled out a yellow, blue and white Cougars singlet with a big yellow three and *Brogan* written in blue beneath it. 'I got this for my birthday last year.' Stan returned the singlet carefully to the closet. 'Mum was going to get me a Chopper Chopiak shirt for my birthday this year, but she can't afford it.'

Sherry didn't have a clue who Chopper Chopiak was — she'd have to ask Glenn. Actually, she'd have to ask him about a few things. 'When's your birthday?'

'In a few weeks.'

She checked her watch and saw that she was cutting it fine if she was going to make it back in time for the pot-luck dinner. And mend a few bridges with Glenn. Sherry hoped he hadn't got around to opening any house-warming presents. He might not see the funny side of the one she'd given him, but assured herself that Glenn wouldn't let his feelings for her get in the way of making a vulnerable, unhappy boy feel better.

'I'll make a deal with you, Stan.'

He sat down on his bed. 'What kind of deal?'

'If you go back to school and stay there all day for the whole week, I'll introduce you to Blitz Brogan.'

Stan snorted.

'You don't believe me?'

He shrugged.

'I know him.'

A flicker of interest stirred in Stan's soft, brown eyes. 'You *know* him?'

'His brother is married to my sister.' The whale baby chose that moment to try to straighten its legs, and Sherry arched her back in protest. 'Can you keep a secret?'

Stan nodded. It was a dumb question; he'd been keeping the secret of what his father was doing to his mother for years.

'Blitz Brogan is in New Zealand filming a golf show.'

He sat up. 'Really?'

Sherry rubbed her side and nodded. 'I can arrange for you and your brother and sisters to meet him, but you've got to keep it quiet, because he's trying to have a holiday while he's here. If people found out, he wouldn't be able to go to the beach or come and see you or do anything without a big fuss being made about it. Do you understand?'

Stan nodded so hard that his rooster's comb bounced. 'I won't tell anybody. Not my friends, not

Storm and Lianna or Nikita. Not Mum. *Not anybody!*'

'Good.' They bumped fists, and Sherry added, 'It's OK to tell Mum.'

As Sherry and Annemarie were leaving, Nikita handed Sherry a piece of newspaper with a drawing of a red stick-figure with a huge round body and lines for arms and legs. 'Custabil Sherry.'

'Gee. Thanks, Nikita.'

On the way home Sherry thought she was being followed by a blue Holden. To check, she made a detour and doubled back. The Holden stayed two cars behind her all the way. She couldn't see the licence plate, and when she tried to double back a second time it hung a right into a side street and sped off. Her cellphone had gone off several times while she was driving, so she pulled over and
checked her messages. There was one from Annemarie, two from Ben, and four from Glenn. *Four*. What was that about?

Sherry called Ben first to say she'd got delayed at work but didn't mention that she thought she'd been followed — she'd save that for Annemarie.

'Give Glenn a call to tell him you're OK,' Ben advised. 'And get home, you're in deep shit.'

Glenn checked his watch again. Where was Sherry? She should have been home from work an hour ago. He'd called Ben, but she wasn't there; and Ben called

Annemarie, who said that she and Sherry had gone to visit one of the families she looked after and that Sherry should be home by now. Glenn kept imagining her unconscious and bleeding somewhere after being beaten up by an angry husband or the stalker. He left messages on her cellphone, but she didn't answer them. He paced up and down the driveway and tried to hold a conversation with his new neighbours, while repeatedly checking his BlackBerry to see if Sherry or Ben had sent him a text.

For the past week, Otto the cat had been climbing in Glenn's bedroom window to spend the night on his bed, and Glenn was covered in flea bites. They'd only managed an hour of filming that day because he couldn't stop scratching, and Tony said the bites on his face made him look like the Elephant Man. The last time Glenn had felt this itchy was when he'd caught measles off Dan when he was five.

Earlier that afternoon, Nora had shown him the invitation she'd sent out. It was a sure-fire way of making every man on the street not interested in basketball hate his guts.

Nora was in a huff because Glenn had criticized her invitation and told her to flea her damned cat. 'If he's got fleas, it's Sherry's fault. He moved in with her; she can't have been looking after him properly.'

Glenn didn't care about the cat. He wanted Sherry home. He scratched and paced and paced and scratched. Glenn could tell that the neighbours thought he was nuts. The women looked at him, and the men who weren't basketball fans looked at his car and his pink house.

'Seems wrong to put a car like that in a pink garage,' Roger of the squashed nose observed.

Glenn was over the jokes about his car and his garage. Sherry was the worst. Her house-warming present was a rustic wooden sign with *The Pink Palace* burned into it with a hot poker.

Nobody blamed him for the basketball legend intro — they were familiar with Nora's tendency to exaggerate, and most of them had seen the sports quiz show and heard Glenn introduced the same way. Everybody knew Otto, the itinerant cat who climbed in windows and cleaned out the food bowls of the resident cat population and sympathized with Glenn's plight. Watching him scratch made him seem more approachable.

'That cat is a menace,' Custard's owner complained. 'He won't leave my pedigree Rag Doll alone. I've told Nora that she'll be getting the vet bill if Custard gets scratched and I can't take her to shows.'

Roger snorted. 'Your cat's been getting more than scratched — she sits on the fence all night screeching her head off trying to get laid.'

Custard's yowling and Otto's comings and goings through the bedroom window to answer her calls kept Glenn awake most nights. It was a shame Sherry didn't yowl instead of giving him daggers looks; he'd rather spend the night beside her, horny and frustrated, than lying alone worrying.

Custard's owner snapped at Roger, 'That is *not* Custard! I keep her inside at night. The cat making all the noise is wild.'

Glenn kept one hand on his BlackBerry, hoping

Sherry would call or text, and one eye on the driveway for her car. *Where was she?* Not everyone was pleased he'd moved in. The paparazzi had made a nuisance of themselves for a week until Glenn had the PR company organize a photo shoot on the beach, where he had introduced Nora and bored everybody to death talking about golf courses. When the paps realized Nora really was a sixtyish woman with a bad hip, and not Glenn's latest love interest, they packed up and left. The most excitement they'd had the entire week was dodging the attempts of the old man at number six, who'd knocked on Glenn's door to warn him he'd *'run the bastards over'* if they got in his way. There was a time or two when Amber was at her worst that Glenn had been tempted to do the same thing.

'Have we seen the back of those photographers?' Roger asked.

'Hope so.' Glenn scratched his side. 'But if anybody asks where I live, I'd appreciate it if you didn't tell them.'

Hayley of the bad lasagna hung on his every word. 'We can do that.'

'Of course, if it causes any problems, I'll consider moving out.' He had no intention of leaving until he was good and ready but was banking on them feeling outraged that he could be driven out.

'No need for that,' Hayley said quickly. 'We can keep a secret.'

'If they start blocking the driveway again, I'll run the bastards over,' Number Six added.

The BlackBerry suddenly vibrated in Glenn's pocket. It was a message from Sherry: *Home in five.* The tension drained from his neck and shoulders. *Home in five.*

Glenn bristled. He'd been sick with worry and all she could manage was *home in five?*

Roger asked, 'Where's Sherry? You know, the cop at number one.'

'She won't put up with anybody blocking the driveway,' Number Six warned Glenn.

'She hardly ever comes to things like this,' Custard the Tart's owner said.

Hayley sniffed. 'She made lasagna — I told Nora I could make it.' She pointed to the food on the table outside Nora's house. 'And *that*.'

Glenn glanced indifferently at the table and noticed a large, round hot-pink creation topped in pink cream and strawberries at the back of the table. His eyes narrowed. Damn Sherry and her 'home in five' and pink freakin' desserts. 'What is that?'

'Pavlova. It's our national dessert.' Custard the Tart's owner lived further up the hill and had never seen the inside of number three. 'Doesn't it look pretty tinted pink?'

'It's usually white,' Hayley whispered. She had seen the inside of number three and wanted Glenn to know she was sensitive and available. 'I'm sure I've got something in the bathroom cabinet that would help with those bites.'

Roger and Number Six snorted. Glenn pretended not to hear.

The sound of a car engine coming up the drive in low gear made them turn their heads. Headlights crested the rise, and Sherry's garage door began to open as her black SUV swept past them. Glenn strangled the can in his hand. It crumpled and spewed beer down his shirt and pants. He stared grimly at the light flooding the concrete outside Sherry's garage. *Home in five. Home in fucking five!* He'd been halfway to a heart attack all night.

Hayley grabbed a paper napkin from the table and began scrubbing at Glenn's shirt. He eased her hand away before she could start on his pants. 'I think I'll head home and change.'

Hayley looked disappointed.

Glenn walked into his garage and lowered the door to put an end to the steady stream of visitors stopping by to admire his car. He marched to the back door, flicking on lights as he went to make it look like he was home, stalked into the back garden and vaulted over the fence onto the patio area outside Sherry's living room. He grunted as his knee jarred on landing. Keeping to the shadows, he made his way round the side of Sherry's house to her garage and slipped inside.

The driver's door of the SUV was open. Sherry was leaning inside collecting her things.

Glenn loomed behind her and barked, 'Where the hell have you been?'

She dropped her handbag and spun towards him with a hand pressed to her chest. 'Don't *do* that!'

There were red marks on his face and a white ring around his mouth. 'Why did it take you so long to answer my messages?'

'I was at work! Some of us have real jobs.' She stared at his face. 'What happened to your face?'

Glenn ignored her. 'You should have been home hours ago!' He saw something flicker in Sherry's eyes and demanded, 'What happened?'

'I'm a big girl, Glenn. I don't have to report to you.'

Sherry used the armrest on the car door to lower herself to her knees so she could gather up the contents of her bag from the concrete floor.

Glenn dropped to his heels, muttering, 'I'll do it.' He scooped up pens, a lipstick, her wallet, cellphone, and study notes for a police exam. 'Tell me what happened. I know something did.'

Sherry saw the look he gave her study notes before he shoved them in her bag. If he had his way, she'd be sitting at home with her feet up and a crochet hook in her hand. 'Nothing happened.'

Nora limped into the garage. 'You forgot to flea Otto!'

Given a choice between arguing with Nora and arguing with Glenn, Sherry chose Nora. 'I did him at the beginning of the month.' Or was it the beginning of last month? Keeping track of details like that were becoming increasingly difficult unless she wrote things down.

Glenn hooked the bag over his shoulder, caught Sherry beneath her arms, and lifted her to her feet.

'That bag suits you, Glenda. It comes in pink, you know.'

'Shut up.'

'Poor Glenn is covered in flea bites,' Nora said indignantly.

She'd just played cat-and-mouse with somebody who might be stalking her. Her neighbour was throwing a hissy fit because the cat had missed his flea treatment, and the man who'd omitted to mention a broken condom and walked away at the first sign of trouble had the gall to be angry at her. Sherry's frazzled nerves unwound so fast there was a whirring noise in her head. She slammed the car door and shouted at Nora, 'Poor

340

Glenn? I feel sorry for the fleas!' She ripped her bag from his shoulder and pointed at the garage door. 'Both of you — get out of my garage!' Sherry hit the remote and stalked to the door that led to the hallway.

The garage door began to lower; Nora scurried outside. Glenn followed Sherry.

Chapter 20

Being pregnant *and* stalked was not a good mix. At night alone in the dark, Sherry listened to the sound of the house settling and imagined somebody trying the back door or scouting for an open window. She usually got up twice to check that the doors were locked and all the windows were closed and talked to the baby until it got bored and fell asleep. Things had been better since Glenn had arrived — Sherry felt safer knowing he was next door. But tonight would be worse than usual because she'd keep imagining the driver of the blue Holden forcing the back door or a window.

She was angry with Glenn. She'd hardly seen him since his arrival. He was out most days visiting golf courses with Nora and the film crew, and, according to Nora, when he wasn't doing that, he was meeting with a publicist to arrange press conferences and television appearances or looking at the new footage. On the few occasions Sherry had seen him, they'd have the same conversation: he'd ask how she was feeling, and she'd lie and say she was fine. Then he would say if there was anything he could do she only had to ask, and she'd lose her temper and reply he'd already done it. Nora would chip in that Sherry's remark was uncalled for, and Sherry would snap that Nora should stick to her knitting and golf. Glenn would tell Nora to butt out and Sherry to grow up, and about then Sherry would erupt and Glenn would get in his car and drive away. She couldn't be nice to him; all her 'nice' was used up. Nice was safe and tepid. Her feelings for Glenn had never been safe and tepid.

Sherry hauled herself upstairs and sat on the end of her bed. What gave him the right to keep tabs on her and yell if she was late home? She braced her hands on the mattress and tried to arch the kinks out of her back while she thought about her promise to Stan. How was she going to keep it?

Sherry jumped when Glenn suddenly appeared in the bedroom doorway. 'What are you doing here?'

He braced an arm on the top of the doorframe next to his head and studied her silently. She was jumpier than one of Otto's fleas. 'I can't go home. My house is crawling with vermin.'

'Just tell the groupies to leave.'

'Whose fault is that?'

'Don't look at me — I attract stalkers, not groupies.'

'Sherry ...' he said warningly.

She arched her back. 'Otto isn't my cat.'

Glenn watched her bump bulge and settle into her lap again. If she got much bigger, he didn't know how she'd stand up without falling flat on her face. She'd given up wearing high heels, but Glenn liked her black bondage sandals. 'Otto isn't anybody's cat. What happened to upset you? Apart from me, of course.'

Sherry looked at her sandals and frowned.

Glenn sat on the chaise longue and rubbed at a spot on his chest. 'I'm not going until you tell me.'

It would be so much easier if he were less observant and more self-centred. 'I think somebody tried to follow me home.'

He stopped scratching. 'You're sure?'

'I doubled back to check. The second time I did, whoever it was seemed to click I was on to them and took off.'

'Did you get the licence-plate number?'

Sherry shook her head. 'It was a blue Holden. Stacey said Vance has got a blue Holden.'

'Who's Vance?' Glenn asked sharply.

'A mean little prick who likes to beat his wife and son. I'm top of his shit list because I helped her and the kids get away.'

'For crissakes, Sherry, give it up before something serious happens!'

'I don't *want* to give it up!' she cried hotly. 'If somebody had told you not to go out on court because you might get hurt, would that have stopped you?'

Glenn's hand stole to his knee. 'It's not the same thing.'

'You're right. What I do is a damned sight more important than playing basketball.'

The sound of people calling good-night drifted up to them as the party broke up. Nora must have made an excuse for the guest-of-honour's disappearance.

'That's not what I meant,' Glenn growled. 'And you know it.'

'I don't care what you meant,' Sherry replied wearily. 'Go back to your pink house and leave me alone.'

Thanks to Custard's yowling, Glenn slept badly most nights, and tonight promised to be worse than usual — he'd be lying awake imagining the driver of the blue car coming after Sherry. He sat back on the chaise and linked his hands across his stomach. 'No.'

Sherry had managed to evict Dan once, but only because she'd taken him by surprise, and he'd been standing right beside the front door. The odds of her manhandling Glenn down the stairs weren't good. 'If you don't go, I'll call the station,' she threatened.

Glenn rubbed his shoulders against the chaise. 'Go right ahead. You should have time to think up a reason for me being in your bedroom by the time the squad car gets here. All it takes is one photo on the Internet ...'

Sherry glared at him. 'Remind me to buy Otto something nice to eat.' She winced and dug her hand in her side as the baby rearranged its feet on her ribs.

Glenn stopped scratching. 'What are you doing?'

'Gestating.'

A lingerie model — a lingerie model would have been so much easier.

She suddenly brightened. 'Did you close the windows so that Otto couldn't get in? No? Oh dear, he's probably curled up fast asleep on your super-king-sized bed in your pink bedroom providing room service to the next generation.'

Maybe she would let him stay; it seemed only right that she got to enjoy his discomfort. Sherry boosted herself off the bed. 'You're in luck, calamine lotion probably works just as well on flea bites as it does on itchy pregnant bellies.'

Glenn considered her bed. 'I can't remember if you like the left or the right side. I know you like motel doors.'

Sherry stiffened. 'You're *not* staying the night.' She stalked into the bathroom and returned with a plastic bag full of cotton-wool balls and a bottle of calamine lotion.

Glenn was standing at the foot of the bed with his shirt off, unbuckling his belt. 'Thanks.' He unzipped his pants and nodded at the table beside the chaise. 'Put it over there.' The pants slid down his legs.

'Put your trousers back on!' Sherry cried indignantly.

He kicked them aside; the only thing keeping him decent now was a pair of stretchy, dark-green Blitz Undercovers.

'You're not staying.' Her voice lacked conviction.

Glenn made one last play for the sympathy vote. 'I'm covered in flea bites because you forgot to flea the damned cat. I jarred my knee jumping over the back fence to check if you were alright, and, according to you, my house is a no-go area because Otto and his pals are partying in my bedroom. The least you can do is offer me a bed for the night and a hand to paint that crap on my back.' He pulled back the bedcovers and lay down on his belly. His feet and calves hung off the end of the bed.

'Get off my bed!'

'If it makes you any happier, I'll take care of the front.'

Sherry's feet were taking her across the carpet towards him before she realized she was moving. She dropped the bag of cotton wool on Glenn's back and dumped the bottle of lotion on the nightstand. 'Given a choice between fleaing Otto or painting calamine lotion on you, Otto would definitely win.'

'I understand it can be a little overwhelming,' Glenn agreed modestly.

She picked up the lotion and dropped it on his head and he cursed.

'I'm taking a shower. When I get out, you'd better be in the guest bedroom.'

He wasn't in the guest bedroom. He was face-down asleep on her bed with his knee buried in a bag of frozen peas, and there were cotton-wool balls soaked with calamine lotion littering the nightstand and bedroom carpet. One foot and the bottom half of the other leg hung off the end of the bed and his left hand was buried under the opposite pillow.

It looked like she'd be the one sleeping in the guest room tonight. If the stalker turned up Sherry planned to offer him Glenn. *He's rich. He's famous. He's all yours.* She looked at the red marks on his shoulders. He wanted his back done. She'd do his back.

Sherry drew the curtains, switched on the bedside lamps, and as a final touch lit some jasmine-scented candles on her dressing table. Glenn slept through it all. She uncapped the lotion, loaded a cotton-wool ball with pale-pink liquid and poked him hard in the ribs.

He jerked awake. 'What—'

She jabbed him in the side again. 'Move.'

Glenn squinted irritably at the candles. 'Are those candles?' 'Yes, jasmine-scented. I thought it added to the romance. Me, huge and irritable; you, huge and looking like the Elephant Man.'

He moved sideways, taking his bag of peas with him. 'I can't believe I proposed to you.'

'You weren't the first.'

'I can't believe anybody proposed to you.'

She stared at the pale-pink stripes he'd left behind on the white bed linen. 'Look at what you've done to my duvet cover!'

Glenn curved his arms around the pillow and mumbled, 'I'll buy you a new one.'

Sherry looked at his naked back. If she weren't careful, she'd start yowling like Custard. 'That's your answer to everything, isn't it? Throw some money at it.' She began jabbing at the bites like a librarian stamping books.

'Ouch! Did the word *gently* somehow get missed from your vocabulary? And that's not true.'

'It is true.' *Stamp! Stamp!* 'It's what you did when I wouldn't cave in to your lawyer's demands.'

The bump jostled his side. 'I made a mistake.' He suddenly got a poke from his other mistake. Glenn turned his head on the pillow to take a closer look at it. Sherry continued to stab at his back, stopping once to slap him on the arm when he tried to scratch his chest. He grabbed her hand. 'That's enough, Sherry Ann.'

She snatched her hand back. 'Don't you *Sherry Ann* me.' She yanked down the elastic band on Glenn's Undercovers to get at a bite on his waist.

'You might want to keep going down there. I've got a couple on my ass.'

The elastic band snapped back into place. 'Congratulations.'

Glenn plucked a cotton-wool ball from amongst the mess he'd left on the nightstand and sniffed at it. 'You really use this stuff on your stomach?'

'Yes.'

'I'm amazed.'

'I would spread yak dung on my belly if it would make it stop itching, and tarantula spit on my back if it'd make it stop aching.'

Jasmine scented the air. Sherry's black hair was loose on her shoulders. Her sleeveless white cotton nightgown had lace panels and buttoned down the front. Glenn stared at the little black mole on her cheekbone. Sherry ignored him. Unlike Custard, she knew to steer clear of horny males.

She recapped the bottle.

Glenn pulled back the duvet, slid under the sheet and drew it to his waist. He gave Sherry a look designed to take her thoughts off his flea bites. Thank goodness he hadn't brought the black Stetson with him. She really should get her pillows and take herself off to the guest bedroom.

His knee and the bag of peas poked from the sheet.

'The peas are a nice touch,' Sherry observed. 'Although maybe not such a good idea if you ever get asked to do a centrefold for *Playgirl*.'

'I'll bear it in mind next time they ask.'

She snorted, but he didn't smile. Her mouth fell open. 'You never!'

'Of course not, my body is a temple,' Glenn replied solemnly. 'And we couldn't reach agreement on the number of strategically placed basketballs.'

Sherry struggled up from the bed. 'It's a waste of time talking to you.'

He reached up and curved his hands around her belly. 'There's definitely something worth cupping now.'

She grabbed his wrists. 'This isn't a good idea.'

He smoothed his palms downwards, learning the

shape of her. She was warm and round and as resilient as a basketball. 'You feel wonderful,' Glenn murmured.

Sherry's grip on his wrists slackened. She slowly sank back onto the bed.

Glenn slid his hands from her stomach to her breasts. Inside the cups of the ugly beige bra, Sherry's nipples tightened. She bet if she took off her sensible nightdress, unhooked her bra, and let Glenn see her naked and clumsy the tent pole in the middle of the sheet would disappear.

He appeared puzzled. 'Why are you wearing a bra under your nightdress?'

Brutal honesty seemed the best policy. 'Because my boobs are huge, and I'm scared if I lay on my back without them strapped down, they might suffocate me.'

Her heart thudded against Glenn's thumbs. He lifted her breasts gently. 'You think these aren't sexy?'

Sherry licked her lips. 'I'm not like I was. I'm awkward and clumsy and ...'

He stroked her. 'Let me be the judge of that.' She closed her eyes and arched into his hands. 'Let me see, Sherry,' Glenn coaxed.

She fumbled with the buttons on her nightdress. 'Don't blame me if you need counselling after this.'

'You're doing it again.'

She cracked one eye open. 'What?'

'Rushing — slow down.'

The creamy, satiny skin of her cleavage and stomach slowly appeared between the placket of her nightdress. For an awful moment Glenn thought that he was going to embarrass himself when Sherry tried to touch him through his underwear. He grabbed her wrist. 'I wouldn't. It might go off.' He sat up and pulled her arms around his waist and cupped her face in his hands. He stroked the mole with his thumb, dipped his head and touched it with his tongue.

'What is it with you and that mole?' Sherry asked raggedly.

'It isn't a mole, it's a beauty mark.' He gave her bottom lip the same careful attention he'd given the beauty mark.

Sherry parted her lips and drank him in. Her arms climbed his back and curled over his shoulders. She'd forgotten how good he was at this. When Glenn tried to brush the nightdress from her shoulders, she grabbed his hands. 'I look different.'

'I noticed. I do, too.'

She leaned back and frowned at him. 'What?'

He pointed to his face. 'Tony would only film me from the back today.'

She smiled and let him pull her nightdress over her head. Glenn stared at her beige bra. 'What the hell—'

Sherry crossed her arms. 'I was on an economy drive. If you want to get me naked, you'll have to turn out the lamps and blow out the candles.'

He tossed her nightdress amongst the cotton-wool balls. 'You're going to be difficult about this, aren't you?'

'Spark-plugs and fuses, remember?' She clutched her shoulders. 'There's too much light.'

'How much is too much?'

'Any.'

Glenn stretched left and right to turn off the lamps. 'The candles stay.' He leaned forward to gather her in again and made short work of her bra and his underwear. The candlelight flickered on her strong shoulders, dark-tipped breasts, and the line running down the length of her abdomen. He followed it with the tip of his finger. 'You feel like a basketball.'

She clasped his biceps. 'Flea bites, calamine lotion, and poetry, too.'

Glenn knew she was nervous. So was he — this was new territory for him.

The lack of light was no longer a problem. Glenn knew the way. He cupped her breast and heard Sherry's breathing quicken as he slipped a hand between her legs. She groped for his shoulders and gulped. 'Glenn? Have you ever had sex with a pregnant woman before?'

He stopped what he was doing. Why did women have to ask questions at moments like this? How could they even think? 'No.' Now she'd got him thinking. 'What about you? Have you had sex since you got pregnant?'

'Of course I haven't!'

'Why not?'

'Because ...' *Because you weren't here.* 'Because it seemed like taking in a boarder when you don't own the house.'

Glenn shook with laughter. He reached for Sherry and pulled her onto his lap. 'So you're willing to break house rules for me?'

She slid her fingers down the length of his spine; her arm wasn't long enough to reach the end. Glenn found her nipple with his mouth and touched her again. Sherry exploded. They were both a little freaked when her belly went hard.

'They're Braxton Hicks contractions; the books say it's normal to have them after an orgasm,' Glenn said when they finally stopped.

'I know what they are, doula. I've had them before. But I didn't know they could happen during sex — I skipped that chapter.'

He leaned back against the headboard. 'Lucky for you I never skip chapters.'

Sherry braced her palms against his chest. 'Are you sure you know how to do this with the basketball in the way?'

Glenn guided her knees either side of his hips. 'Honey, when it comes to basketballs, I'm an expert — wherever they are.'

The basketball booted him round the bed most of the night, but Glenn had expected that, because Dan had liked to complain about it when Lisa was pregnant. Last night had been the same and yet different to the night at the motel. The same, because it'd been so good; and different, because Sherry only managed one time and they spent most of the time talking. Afterwards, Glenn rubbed her back, and Sherry felt guilty because she wasn't up to a repeat performance. 'You don't have to do that,' she protested half-heartedly.

'Every man worth his salt knows that back-rubs are part of the deal when you nail a pregnant woman,' Glenn insisted. 'Remind me to order in some yak dung and tarantula spit.'

'You've got an answer for everything, haven't you, Glenn Michael?' Sherry luxuriated in the feel of his big hands pressing against the small of her back. 'Oh yes —

right there!' she moaned. 'Remind me to tip you later.'

Glenn's hands stilled. He leaned over her shoulder. 'That reminds me — about the money you left at the motel ...'

Her eyes snapped open. 'I shouldn't have done that.'

'Damned right you shouldn't have. I was good for more than a twenty.'

'I don't believe it — you were offended by the *amount?*'

'You should have left at least a hundred.'

Sherry rolled her eyes.

Glenn lay back down but shot up again as something new occurred to him. 'What about that sign you gave me? *The Pink Palace.*'

'Ah, yes ... that.' She smiled. 'I thought it was a nice touch.'

'Then nail it up next to your front door.'

'Can't you go to sleep?' Sherry complained.

'I'm not finished yet. How did you know my middle name was Michael?'

She yawned. 'I ran a check on who bought Alice's house and found out about GM Holdings. Lisa told me what it stands for.'

'I'll have to talk to my sister-in-law about passing on insider knowledge.'

Sherry cuddled her pillow and said drowsily, 'Yeah, good luck with that. She said you were named after your loony Great-uncle Michael.'

'I take issue with the description *loony*. I prefer *alternative.*'

'Who was he?'

'Mom's only uncle. He lived out in the middle of

nowhere and kept a whisky distillery in a shed behind the house, which wouldn't have been a problem if he'd kept what he made for his own personal consumption and hadn't sold it to the locals.'

'Moonshine? My poor baby — it's going to be torn between upholding the law and breaking it to turn a quick buck.'

Glenn traced the indentation of Sherry's spine. 'He was mine and Dan's favourite uncle—'

She opened her eyes. 'There's a surprise.'

'Get your mind out of the gutter. I was about to add *when we were little.*'

'It's the company I keep outside of work hours.'

Glenn shook his head and tutted. 'Mom thought if she named me after Uncle Michael, it might give him an interest besides making hooch.'

'Did it work?' she mumbled.

'No, but he threw a helluva party when I got drafted to the Boston Celtics.' He cupped the curve of her bottom and leaned forward to look at her. She was asleep. Glenn pressed his lips against Sherry's shoulder and lay down behind her with his arm around the basketball.

When the dawn came, he was able to peel back the sheet and take a proper look at her. She lay facing him, not exactly snoring but definitely snuffling (pregnancy stuffiness according to the books), with a pillow tucked between her legs. Rolling over had been a major undertaking, requiring assistance from Glenn and the repositioning of her pillows. The instant she was settled,

Sherry dropped back into sleep like a stone thrown into deep water.

Glenn watched her belly change shape from round with knobbly bits to full-blown Loch Ness Monster. Sherry slept right through it. Perhaps they'd overdone things. He looked up, saw she was watching him, and said in an early morning rasp, 'Morning.'

She drew the sheet over her nakedness, and Glenn felt a prickle of unease. 'Morning. How's your knee?'

'Fine. Are you OK?' he asked.

She nodded. 'It's the best sleep I've had in ages.'

He knew he was going to hear something he wouldn't like. 'Glenn?'

'Yes?'

'There's something you should know.' He waited.

'I'm booked to have a scan to check the size of the baby. I'm a few weeks bigger than I should be.' Sherry paused. 'I still think I'm right, but I thought you should know.'

Glenn didn't know what to say — there was nothing he could say. But as the daylight grew brighter, it seemed to highlight all that was wrong between them. Sherry tucked the bedcovers under her chin while Glenn got up and dressed.

'It's not your fault.' It wasn't but saying it didn't change things. 'I shouldn't have walked out on you.' But he had.

Her reply was cool and reasonable. 'You can call off your lawyers. I'll agree to the paternity test. I need to know whose name to put on the birth certificate.'

Glenn stared at the sampler on the wall beside her bed. *Daughter of Jill and Brian.*

'Can you do something for me?' she asked.

He looked back at her. 'Anything.' Anything that would make him feel less of a bastard.

Sherry explained about Stan. Glenn wished it was something bigger, like a couple of million dollars. 'Sure, I can do that. We just need to organize a time and date to fit in with the filming schedule.' The phone beside the bed rang. It was Nora calling to remind him they were playing Kelvin Heights in Queenstown and had to make an early start.

'How does she know I'm here?' Glenn demanded irritably.

'She probably had night-vision goggles trained on the house to see if you left.'

He lingered at the foot of the bed. 'I have to go.'

Sherry nodded. 'Glenn?'

'Yes?'

'We can't do this again. Nora isn't the only nosy-parker in the neighbourhood, and I don't want to become the focus of your photographer friends.'

His expression hardened. 'They've gone, Sherry.'

She shrugged. 'For now, but it wouldn't take much to bring them back again. I can see the headlines now.' She framed an invisible headline in the air: '*Blitz Brogan gets cop pregnant*. That's your world, not mine.'

'You want to know one of the good things about my world, Sherry?' Glenn asked grimly. 'Round-the-clock bodyguards and home-security systems to keep stalkers and lowlife away.'

'My idea of hell.'

'What about the panic button next to your bed?' he demanded. 'You think that's normal?'

'It's not the same thing,' she insisted stubbornly.

Glenn put his palms on the mattress and leaned closer. '*My idea of hell. Not my world.* Can't you hear yourself? Did it ever occur to you that what you're doing might not be good for the baby? What are you going to do if he comes after you and you're alone? Make a run for it? Fight back? It's not just about you, Sherry.'

Her blue eyes frosted.

He straightened and said sarcastically, 'Don't worry, Your Majesty — I'm leaving.'

Chapter 21

S tan stared. 'You're real.'

'I'm real,' Glenn agreed. 'You're really Blitz Brogan.'

'I'm really Blitz Brogan. Happy Birthday, Stan.'

Sherry sat in the stands beside the basketball court at the community centre with Stacey and Nikita, and watched Glenn shoot baskets with Stan, Storm and Lianna. After their argument, Sherry hadn't been sure whether Glenn would still meet Stan, but he'd remembered the date of his birthday and asked for directions to the community centre.

'I can come and get you,' Sherry offered.

'No, I'll meet you there.'

His distant tone made her feel awkward. 'Thanks for doing this, Glenn.'

He shrugged. 'It's no problem; I do it all the time.'

She looked at him now, towering over the children while they practiced free throws. Stan was wearing his number three shirt with Glenn's surname. Glenn had given each of the kids a Cougars hat and a shirt signed by the players. Stan's face glowed when he saw he'd received Chopiak's number twenty-four shirt.

Glenn wore an old Cougars shirt, navy blue shorts, and a lot of tape around his knee. Nikita was entranced by his size and the way he effortlessly put the ball through the hoop again and again. She clapped her hands and cried, 'Magic!'

He smiled wryly. 'Not exactly, but I'm very flattered.'

When she decided to join in, her sister and brothers tried to send her back to Stacey, but Glenn overruled them and lifted Nikita up so she could put the ball through the hoop. The expression of amazement on her face at being so far off the ground made the older kids laugh and brought Nikita rushing back to tell her mother what had happened.

'He seems alright,' Stacey said.

'He's good with kids,' Sherry admitted.

'Now I know why you look like you're having twins.'

Sherry didn't answer.

A small crowd of kids had gathered at the doorway to the court. Some carried basketballs under their arms; they were all staring at Glenn. One boy waved to catch Stan's attention, and he waved back self-consciously.

Glenn bounced the ball a couple of times and launched it at the hoop. 'Friends of yours?'

'They didn't believe it when I said you were coming, so I told them they could come and look at you.' Stan looked at Glenn uncertainly. His face was like a page in a book constantly being rewritten. *Is that OK? Did I do the wrong thing? Are you angry at me for telling them?*

Glenn had seen the same expression on other kids' faces when the Cougars visited schools. He hated it. Kids should be eager and noisy and goof around, not worried and old before their time. He retrieved the ball and dribbled it back to the free-throw line. 'If they want, we could have a game.'

Stan's brown eyes widened. *'Really?'*

'Yeah.' He sailed the ball through the hoop again. 'Tell them to come in.'

There was a stampede as the kids flooded onto the

court and screeched to a halt in front of Glenn. Under cover of the noise and chaos, he saw a woman slip through the double doors, pushing a baby in a battered stroller, and make her way towards where Sherry and Stan's mother sat. Sherry had explained briefly about Stacey's situation — again, Glenn had heard it before. The woman with the baby stroller was like a shadow. She kept her head down, but Glenn felt her eyes touch him and slip away. She didn't want him to notice her. She didn't want anybody to notice her.

Glenn looked at Stan expectantly. Stan looked back.

'You going to introduce us?' he asked.

Stan looked around the ring of faces. 'They all know who you are.'

There were nods of agreement from the newcomers. A kid wearing a faded T-shirt with a ripped neck spoke up. 'Yeah, we know who you are. You're Blitz Brogan.'

Glenn's attention remained on Stan. 'But I'm your guest.'

Stan looked at his friends and grew a couple of inches. 'This is Blitz Brogan,' his smile stretched from ear to ear, 'but you can call him Glenn too if you want.'

'Sherry, this is Crystal,' Stacey said. 'My sister who just had a baby. Crystal, this is Constable Sherry.'

Crystal set the brake on the stroller and slipped onto the bench beside Stacey. She glanced at Sherry's midriff and looked back at the court. Her kids were amongst the crowd gathered around Blitz Brogan. Lots of things happened at the community centre, but it was the first time they'd had an ex-NBA basketball star visit. It made sense for Crystal to bring her kids to see him — nobody could get angry about that. Her gaze roved nervously about the gymnasium, and, before she started to speak, Sherry knew what she was going to hear.

Glenn had a good idea of what was happening on the sidelines.

'This is what I do,' Sherry had told him.

The woman doing all the talking didn't look at Sherry; she watched Glenn and the kids and appeared to be talking to Stan's mother, while Sherry's attention seemed to be focused on the court, and any remarks she made looked like they were directed at Stacey.

Glenn bounced the ball and called out, 'Before you play, you warm up!'

For the next hour the kids were too busy to notice what was happening on the sidelines. Glenn put them into groups on the baseline and got them to run to the free-throw line, the midcourt line and the next free-throw line. On the way back they had to include a forward/reverse pivot on first one foot and then the other before they could run to the next line. Finally, he paired them up on the sidelines and got them to dribble the ball across the width of the court to each other and swap. He praised the clumsy ones and gave pointers to the better players.

'Dribble with your fingertips, not your palm. That way you'll keep control of the ball.'

When the time came to play a game, Glenn swapped

sides and added points if one team got too far behind. Gradually, the women stopped talking and watched him. He didn't run so much as glide, and he defied the laws of gravity by hanging in the air and shooting from deep in the court, sending the ball sailing through the hoop. The kids whooped with excitement each time Glenn made a basket and tried to copy him. They followed him like a bunch of over-eager puppies, once almost tangling with his legs. Sherry rose from the bench, convinced he was going to fall and hurt his knee, but before she could blink Glenn pivoted and was gone.

'You sure are good,' one awestruck girl said, and got a shove in the back from her brother for saying something so lame to one of the best shooting guards in the game. Glenn saw the shove and made the boy run exercises again as punishment.

'Slam dunk, Blitz! Do a slam dunk!' the boy with the ripped T-shirt shouted.

The rest of the kids took up the cry. '*Slam dunk! Slam dunk!*'

That's how Glenn finished the session, powering up to the hoop, leaping to dunk the ball, and hanging from the rim for a few seconds while the kids yelled with excitement. Sherry watched him flinch as he landed and knew that he would spend the night with his knee packed in ice. The kids clustered around for autographs and photos. Nikita planted herself on one of Glenn's size-fourteen feet and clung to his leg shouting, 'Up! Up!' and got to put the ball in the hoop one last time.

And Sherry realized how much she wanted her child to know its father.

On the way out to their cars, Glenn asked, 'Is that woman going to the refuge?'

She stopped. 'You knew?'

He hit the remote to unlock the M6. 'I guessed.'

I have made a mess of it again, baby, haven't I? Sherry thought miserably. *Your father is no emotional lightweight, but your mother is an idiot. Even worse, she's fallen for your father and doesn't know what to do about it.*

Sherry said sadly, 'She won't go to the refuge but at least now she knows there's an alternative.'

'Don't be so hard on yourself,' Glenn said. 'It's a step in the right direction.'

They continued towards their cars. But this time Glenn limped, and Sherry let herself waddle.

'We're bringing Georgia for a visit at the end of April,' Lisa announced. 'I'm going to stay on until the baby is born, but Dan has to go home on the first of May.'

The end of April wasn't far away. Tears pricked Sherry's eyes. 'That's great, Lees. I can't wait to see you. How's Georgia?'

'She says "Mama" and "Dada" and shouts if she doesn't get enough attention. Dan is the first one up most mornings, and Georgia sits in her cot yelling until he comes to get her. He says he wants to enter her in a yodelling contest.'

Sherry could imagine her big, quiet brother-in-law

scooping Georgie out of her cot each morning and murmuring nonsense about yodelling competitions.

'You knew she was crawling, didn't you?' Lisa asked.

'No.' Already? 'When did that happen?'

'About a month ago; I'm sure I told you.'

'Probably,' Sherry said vaguely. Her brain wasn't so much out to lunch — it had gone on holiday. 'I thought they didn't crawl for ages.'

'She's seven months old, Sher. Dan sat on his bum for the first year-and-a-half and talked, but Molly keeps saying Georgia's just like Glenn, he crawled at the same age and then got up and walked. Molly said chasing after him turned her into an Olympic athlete.'

Stop talking about Glenn, Sherry thought.

'So, how are you?' Lisa asked.

Sherry didn't know what to say, she was too mixed-up, so she started with the easiest thing first.

'Starr is very happy with me. If I had a wall chart, I'd have lots of stickers with *Well Done* and *Great Effort* written on them. The hang-ten specialist has stopped bungee-jumping off my ribs because it's run out of room. Starr assures me that head-down is good. She thinks all babies should be equipped with a compass, calendar and watch, so they know which way to head, the day to make their move, and to do it between the hours of nine and five.'

'I'm with Starr on that. Georgia could have done with a watch.'

'I'd include something about steering clear of mirrors for the first couple of days until the point on their head has gone down.'

'Was Georgia's head really that pointy?' Lisa asked.

'It wasn't only pointy; it was lopsided *and* pointy.'

'I can't remember. I thought she looked beautiful.'

'Hormones are wonderful things,' Sherry said drily.

'Just wait until it's your turn. How's Glenn?'

Constantly surprising me.

'According to Nora, well on his way to becoming a golfing legend, but of course it's all thanks to her.' Sherry wished she could still play golf, but the baby got in the way of her swing.

In a moment of weakness she had spilled the beans about Glenn staying the night. Lisa kept hoping things would improve between them, but Sherry was as stubborn as an ox and Glenn ... well, trying to get a handle on her mercurial brother-in-law was impossible.

Thanks to Special Agent Ditchburn, Ben also knew that Glenn had spent the night at Sherry's. Nora had reported the incident, and her disappointment that it hadn't happened again. Ben kept telling Lisa to be patient, and Dan kept telling her to keep out of Glenn and Sherry's business.

'Did they have any luck finding out who owned the car that followed you?' Lisa asked.

'No. Vance had an alibi.'

But he was the only one with a blue Holden; Stuart owned an Audi, and Jonathan drove a Mitsubishi Lancer.

'Has anything else happened? Have you seen the car again?'

'No, it's been quiet for the last couple of weeks. I haven't even had a phone call.'

'You were getting phone calls, too?' Lisa cried.

Sherry had forgotten she hadn't mentioned it. 'A few,

but they stopped.'

'Perhaps whoever it is has given up?'

'Yes,' Sherry reassured her sister — but she didn't really believe it. There was no discernible pattern to the stalker's behaviour; the incidents were random, as if something happened to set him or her off. Since the night of Marjorie's wedding, Sherry had kept a diary of where she went and who she saw, to see if it was anything she was doing, but had come up with nothing.

Trying to find a safe subject for discussion was becoming harder each time Lisa phoned. 'When are you going for the scan?'

'I'm waiting for a letter with a date and time.'

'Are you going to find out the sex?'

'No.'

'Why not?' Lisa demanded.

'I want it to be a surprise.'

'What about Glenn? He might want to know.'

'He isn't coming.'

Glenn knew better than to expect an invitation to Sherry's scan. He'd sensed a softening in her attitude since the day at the community centre but put it down to hormones. Nora was still collecting Sherry's mail. Glenn was surprised that Sherry hadn't put a stop to it and decided that she was either too tired or too preoccupied by the situation with the stalker to care about a nosy-parker neighbour. Glenn benefitted from the arrangement when Nora showed him a white envelope addressed to Sherry with the logo of a medical company stamped on the bottom left-hand corner.

'I think it's the appointment for the scan,' she said. 'If only we could steam the envelope open.'

Glenn took the envelope and picked up the gold letter-opener that Nora kept by the telephone in her living room.

Nora watched him insert the tip of the letter-opener beneath the sealed flap. 'What are you doing?'

He carefully eased the two surfaces apart. 'What does it look like I'm doing?'

'That's illegal!'

'Only if I get caught.' Glenn looked at her through his lashes. 'You won't tell on me, will you?'

'You think you can sweet-talk your way out of anything,' she accused.

Pretty much.

'If I stand by and watch, it makes me an accomplice.'

'Go stand in the kitchen, then.'

Instead, Nora came closer. 'It's too late, I'm already a witness.'

'My lips are sealed. It's a shame this damned envelope is, too.'

The flap on the envelope popped open and Glenn eased out the sheet of white paper inside.

'Don't touch it! You'll leave fingerprints!'

'It's OK, Nora, I've watched *Criminal Intent*.'

'You enjoy breaking rules,' she huffed.

'Only if I don't get caught.' Glenn placed the letter on a table and used his thumbnail and the letter-opener to unfold it.

Nora hung over his shoulder while he scanned the contents. 'What does it say? I'm long-sighted, I can't see without my glasses.'

'The night-vision goggles don't help?'

'What?'

Glenn folded the sheet of paper and gently inserted it into the envelope, making sure the corners didn't bend. He whizzed through the diary he kept in his head. Glenn gave the impression he didn't know what was happening from one day to the next, but he did; he just preferred to let Fraser and the PR people sort out the details.

Nora demanded, 'When is it? Are you going to find out if it's a boy or a girl? They couldn't tell last time because it had its legs crossed.'

Glenn assumed Sherry still didn't want to know. 'I'll be sure to tell you all about it afterwards,' he promised. 'Got any glue?'

'You can't glue it! Sherry will know it's been tampered with. What if they dust the envelope for fingerprints? They'll think you're the stalker and throw you in prison.'

'Sometimes that imagination of yours runs wild, doesn't it, Nora honey?' Glenn mused. 'It's got my fingerprints on it because you asked me to get Sherry's mail out of her mailbox, and as for the police thinking I'm the stalker, her boss as good as admitted he knows it's not me.' He smiled and kissed her cheek. 'And if I do end up in prison, you'll come visit me, won't you?'

Nora limped away muttering, 'She'll know that it's been glued. She's a cop.'

Which was why Glenn hand-delivered the freshly sealed envelope and the rest of Sherry's mail to her back door later that day, along with several sets of expensive maternity lingerie.

The nights and mornings were getting cooler, but the days were still warm — hot, even, for a woman who was eight months pregnant. Sherry wore an orange sarong decorated with red hibiscus flowers and her hair in a ponytail. As soon as she heard the knock on the back door, she knew that it was Glenn. Sleeping with him again had been a bad idea. She should be losing interest in sex, but Sherry felt like taking a leaf out of Custard's book and yowling outside Glenn's window.

She took the pink-and-white bag containing the lingerie in one hand and her mail in the other — and immediately spotted that one of her letters had been tampered with.

'It's not the stalker,' Glenn said quickly. Each time he saw Sherry, she seemed to have grown bigger. The top of her belly had risen to the middle of her breasts and she really did waddle.

It took Sherry longer than usual to understand what had happened. 'You opened my mail?'

She wasn't nearly as quick off the mark as she used to be, which should have worked in Glenn's favour but only made him worry about her more. 'Only the one with the date and time of your scan.'

'That's illegal!'

'Is it?' he said innocently.

'You bloody well know it is!'

Glenn smiled winningly. 'Can I come?'

'No, you can't.'

He sighed. 'Guess I'll have to gate-crash.'

'You can't gate-crash an appointment for a scan!' Sherry cried.

'What else can I do if you won't invite me?' Glenn

braced his hands on the walls beside the back door and leaned closer. 'Can I come? Please?'

Nature had screwed up. Those sultry, golden eyes belonged on a high-class hooker, not an athlete.

Sherry backed up like a freight train suddenly thrown into reverse. He was doing it again: she was being schmoozed. 'Do what you want! Just go away!' she snapped and slammed the door.

When Glenn arrived for Sherry's appointment, she was already inside the scanning room.

He smiled at the receptionist. 'Hi. I'm late — my girlfriend will kill me.' Well, it was a possibility if Sherry was pissed at him and Glenn was in range of her throwing arm. Cool, collected Sherry had disappeared along with slender, graceful Sherry.

The receptionist was dazzled by Glenn's size and looks, but not too dazzled to do her job properly. 'Who is your girlfriend?'

'Sherry Jackson. She had a one o'clock appointment.' It was ten past. Glenn had deliberately squandered ten precious minutes so that the scan had already started. He still believed gate-crashing was his best chance of success.

The receptionist walked around the desk. 'I'll let her know you're here.' Glenn followed her to the door of the scanning room. She popped her head around the door. 'Ms Jackson, your boyfriend is here.'

Glenn slipped around the receptionist as easily as he'd slipped around the opposition on court. 'Sorry, I'm late, sweetheart.' He crossed the room and planted a kiss on Sherry's open mouth before she had a chance to speak and smiled at the female doctor standing beside the couch with her hand on Sherry's gel-covered abdomen.

'Hi,' Glenn sat down in the chair beside the exam couch and took Sherry's hand. 'I'm sorry, honey, something came up.' He saw she was wearing one of the sets of lingerie he'd bought.

Sherry's hand lay limply in Glenn's grasp. 'Where were you? On the golf course?'

'Is everything alright?' the doctor asked.

'Perfect.' Glenn looked at the screen. 'Is that its head?'

'No, that's the baby's bottom — I'm taking a crown/rump measurement.' She studied him. 'Weren't you on the six o'clock news?'

He gazed at the screen and nodded absently. 'A few weeks back.'

'You're a professional basketball player, aren't you?'

'Used to be, I'm retired now.' Funny how saying it didn't bother him anymore.

'Bruce — no — *Blaze* Brogan?'

'That's right. Like the stripper.'

'The stripper?' The doctor repeated.

'Blaze Starr,' Glenn explained. Then he added, 'I'm a friend of Sherry's.'

Sherry's face clouded. She pulled her hand from his grasp. Glenn wished she'd make up her mind about whether she wanted people to know about him or not. He thought the bullshit about being her friend would make her happy. Judging by the look on the doctor's face, it hadn't fooled her. She went back to doing the scan, and Glenn watched the screen and listened as she explained what they were seeing.

The basketball was no longer a basketball. It had fingers, toes, and a white necklace of vertebrae outlining a tiny spine. It had ears, a nose, eyes closed in sleep and a thumb in its mouth. *It was sucking its thumb!* Glenn stared at the little alien creature floating in its private ocean and felt like a chink had appeared in the universe and he was being given a glimpse of the reason they were all here. He cleared his throat and glanced at Sherry. She was staring intently at the baby. How must she feel knowing that was inside her?

'It's a big baby,' the doctor said. 'I'd estimate about three-point-nine kay-gees.'

'What's that in American?'

'About eight pounds ten ounces.'

'I've still got five weeks to go,' Sherry said in a subdued voice. 'How big do you think it will be at term?'

The doctor made a few additions to the information showing alongside the black and white image. 'About four and a half kilos.'

Sherry blanched. Glenn caught her hand and looked at the doctor.

'Ten pounds,' she explained. 'It's not surprising, given your height.' She avoided looking at Glenn, so she couldn't be accused of assuming he was the other culprit in the big-baby saga and asked Sherry, 'Do you want to know the sex?'

'Yes,' Glenn said.

Sherry shook her head. 'No.'

She still looked pale, so Glenn didn't argue; he helped

her off the couch. While Sherry was outside getting an envelope with the images from the scan, he hung back to talk to the doctor. 'Is she really doing OK?'

She straightened the cover on the exam couch. 'Apart from the baby being bigger than average, everything seems perfectly normal. It might pay to talk to Sherry's midwife, though,' she advised. 'She seemed a little upset.'

That was an understatement. Having a baby wasn't a team event, when the time came Sherry would be on her own. There was something to be said for getting men to boil water or stay in the waiting room during the labour, but Glenn figured watching Sherry in pain would be his penance. And there was also the yet-to-be-resolved issue of gaining admission to the delivery room, which was going to be a lot tougher than gate-crashing a scan.

He looked at the doctor and smiled. 'One other thing, is it a boy or a girl?'

Jonathan watched Detective Constable Jackson and the retired basketball player leave the radiology rooms. DC Jackson didn't see him sitting in the pale-green Honda parked on the roadside. Jonathan changed cars like other people changed clothes. He'd driven a blue Holden the night he'd followed DC Jackson home. It had given him a nasty fright when he'd discovered somebody else was also following her, but Jonathan had quickly realized that he could use this latest development to his advantage.

The other man was an idiot. He'd made no attempt

to conceal his true feelings and shown his hand by storming into the police station where Jackson worked and making threats.

Jonathan was clever. It had been easy to borrow a blue Holden from the lot. He relished the way DC Jackson had looked over her shoulder each time she stepped out of her house or the police station, and how she hurried to her car and locked the doors. He had felt in control and happy — until the basketball player had arrived. Glenn Brogan had millions of dollars, expensive homes, and the thing Jonathan craved most: respect. He even drove a BMW just like Jonathan used to. If DC Jackson hadn't made Marjorie betray him, Glenn Brogan would probably have leased his BMW from Jonathan, and Jonathan would have shaken his hand and invited Brogan to his house on the lake for dinner. Brogan had Jonathan's *old life*. And if he was the father of DC Jackson's baby, she would have that life, too. The injustice ate at Jonathan. He couldn't eat, and the pain in his side was getting worse. DC Jackson was a liar and a thief. She had robbed Jonathan of his money and position in society, his family and friends, and now his health was deteriorating while she bloomed and looked forward to a bright future with Brogan.

She'd stolen his life. It was intolerable.

Chapter 22

Otto the cat had started life as the offspring of a feral queen. He was territorial about his three homes and the steep area of native bush that climbed the hill. The unfortunate flea infestation had resulted in Glenn's house being flea-bombed and Glenn catching Otto by the scruff of the neck and handing him over to Nora for an unwanted and deeply embarrassing apple-scented bath and flea treatment. Otto refused to speak to Glenn or Nora, and hid in the bush until the apple smell faded and he was looking

more like his usual scruffy, one-eyed self.

Custard the Tart loved the way Otto smelled, but after impregnating her he'd lost interest. Her owner had mistakenly believed Custard was pregnant to the pedigree Rag Doll tom she'd paid to service Custard, but when Custard gave birth to four striped kittens with suspiciously flat ears the game was up. Custard's owner wanted financial reparation and vengeance for Custard's fall from grace. She tracked Otto down at Glenn's house and demanded Otto be castrated.

'He's not my cat. Talk to Nora,' Glenn replied, and went upstairs to close the bedroom windows so Otto couldn't escape. He looked at the big striped tom-cat lounging on his bed in the pink bedroom and scratched him under the chin. 'Guess your condom broke too, huh, Otto?'

Otto was strolling around his houses in the darkness

debating who to spend the night with when he heard the heavy crash of human feet landing in Sherry's garden and muttered curses. A man had climbed over the fence from the bush. The fence was coming loose and the man had got a fright when it wobbled beneath him. He thought he was being quiet, but to sensitive cat ears his footfalls sounded like thunderclaps.

Otto slunk along the top of the fence separating Sherry and Glenn's back gardens, and watched the man fumble his way to Sherry's back door. He flattened his ragged ears against his head and growled when the man smashed a pane of glass in the door and tried the handle.

The kitchen light and security lights came on together. The man panicked and let go of the door handle. He bolted back the way he'd come, passing Otto on the way. Otto wrinkled his nose at the smell of alcohol on the man's breath and took a meaty swipe as he stumbled past. His claws sunk into the man's face and left a bloody trail in his cheek.

The man bellowed, clapped a hand to his face and rushed the fence. Otto swished his tail angrily and watched him bound up the wobbly section and fall over the top and heard him crash down the hill to the street below. He heard the bang of Sherry's front door as it hit the wall, and the slap of her bare feet on the concrete as she ran across the driveway to Glenn's house. He heard her pounding on Glenn's pink front door.

So did Glenn.

He was in the living room sipping a finger of whisky

when the hammering started and he heard Sherry
calling his name. Glenn didn't usually drink hard liquor,
but it had been the kind of day that called for something
stronger than beer. He dropped the whisky glass on a
side table and ran to open the door.

Sherry fell into his arms babbling, 'B-back door!
Some- some body tried to ... to ...'

Glenn closed his arms around her. 'What? What did
they try to do? Are you hurt?'

Her face was white and her eyes huge. 'N-no ... no!'

Glenn hooked an arm beneath her knees and picked
her up as Nora hobbled onto her front porch, fastening
the belt of her robe.

'Glenn!' she cried. 'What's wrong?'

He peered into Sherry's face and said urgently, 'Tell
me what happened.'

She buried her face in his neck. 'Somebody ... sma-
smashed the ba-back door—'

Glenn lifted his head and shouted, 'Nora! Call the
police!'

The police checked the back garden and the bush.
The stalker had left a path of destruction in his wake as
he fled to the road. The area was taped off and the door
handle was dusted for fingerprints, but Sherry knew
they'd include hers, and those of her family and friends
who'd visited. In the morning a search would be done to
see if there were any fibres from torn clothing on the
fence or in the bush, or any footprints in the dirt.

Glenn called Ben, and Sherry's parents. They arrived

at his house at the same time as Dave Pomana, and listened as she told him what had happened.

'I went to the kitchen to get a glass of water. The glass smashed in the door just as I turned on the light.'

'Did you see who it was?' Dave asked.

She shook her head. 'I panicked ... I ran.'

Dave was deeply concerned; the stalker was getting bolder. The squad car had paid its nightly visit twenty-three minutes before Nora called 111, but the officers hadn't noticed anything unusual. Sherry was due to start maternity leave next week. She looked tired and was wound tight as a spring. Her parents sat either side of her, their faces haggard with worry, while her brother remained close by, looking tight-lipped and angry. They'd closed ranks to protect her, but Dave noticed it was Glenn Brogan who Sherry looked to, that when he left the room, she kept glancing at the door until he returned. Brogan was still a suspect, but he'd slipped way down the list.

Dave followed him to the kitchen. Under different circumstances, he'd have been asking for Glenn Brogan's autograph. 'Where were you when you first heard Sherry knocking on the door?' he asked.

Glenn banged cupboard doors as he pulled out coffee and mugs. 'In the living room having a scotch.' *Stop asking me stupid questions and get out there and find this bastard.* 'I'd just poured it when I heard Sherry banging on the door. And no, I don't drink every night, I just felt like it tonight.'

'What was different about tonight?'

'I went with Sherry to her scan,' Glenn replied. 'She was upset.'

And that upset Brogan.

'How much do you weigh?' Dave asked.

'About two-twenty. Why?'

'No particular reason.'

'Are you going to catch this prick?' Glenn demanded. 'Don't you have *any* idea who it is?'

'Whoever he is, he's getting sloppy.' Dave said. 'He's getting sloppy, because he's getting angrier.'

Glenn stared at him. 'You know who it is.'

'No, I don't.' He didn't want Brogan or the Jacksons getting any ideas about hiring a private detective and screwing up the police investigation. 'So far our suspects have had alibis for every other incident, but we might get lucky about tonight.'

'You *must* have some idea who it is.'

Brogan radiated hostility. Dave was an avid Cougars fan and believed the team hadn't been the same since The Blitz's retirement. He'd followed Glenn's NBA career, and once even managed to get tickets to a Cougars game when he was in the States on holiday. He'd seen The Blitz in action, but he hadn't looked nearly as aggressive and wired on the court as he did now.

'Sherry is a cop. She's arrested lots of criminals. There's no shortage of suspects.'

Glenn slammed a plastic container of milk on the kitchen counter. The water boiled and he threw tea and coffee together. 'I'm going to hire private security for Sherry.'

Good luck, Dave thought. He couldn't see Sherry agreeing to a bodyguard dogging her steps. 'Leave the investigating to us. The best way you can help is to keep

Sherry close until we catch whoever is responsible. Don't let her out of your sight.'

Back in the living room Dave told Sherry, 'Forget about coming into work for the rest of the week. Finish up now.'

Brian looked relieved. 'Mum and I can pack some of your things and you can come home with us.'

Sherry shook her head. 'It's better if I stay here.'

Her mother and father missed the slight emphasis she placed on *here*. Glenn didn't. Neither did Dave.

'You can't stay here!' Jill cried. 'What if they don't catch him? What if he comes back?'

'He — or she — won't come back tonight, Mum, half the cops from the station are camped on my doorstep. I'll be safer staying here than at your place.'

'*How* can you be safer here?'

'I have explained this.' Sherry gestured wearily to Dave. 'You tell them.'

'Sherry knows this environment,' he explained. 'She'll know instantly if a stranger arrives or something changes.'

Sherry tried to reassure her parents. 'I've got the panic button beside my bed.'

'I'll move in,' Ben offered.

Glenn finally spoke up. 'No need,' he said firmly. 'She's staying here.'

Jill stared. 'Is she?'

Brian frowned. 'Sherry?'

Some of the tension left her face. 'I'm staying here.'

Dave accompanied Brian and Jill when they went next-door to collect Sherry's things, to make sure they didn't touch anything in the kitchen. He took the opportunity to speak with Sherry's father. 'You don't like Brogan?'

'Of course I don't. He's caused her nothing but grief. Do you?' he asked meaningfully.

It was what Dave would expect a father to say about the man who'd knocked-up his daughter. 'He's no longer a suspect.'

'Why not?'

'Because he'd have to be Superman to have made it back to his living room and change out of his muddy clothes in time to answer the door to Sherry, plus the back fence is rickety and Brogan weighs two hundred and twenty pounds. If he'd tried climbing over it, he'd have flattened it.' Dave paused. 'And there's another reason why I don't think he's responsible.' 'Why?'

'He cares too much about your daughter.'

Glenn and Sherry went to bed for what was left of the night. He helped her arrange her nest of pillows and get comfortable. Sherry fell asleep in a matter of seconds, but Glenn lay against her back feeling angry and worried.

Come and bother me, you cowardly bastard. Please come and bother me …

Glenn's BlackBerry woke them early. It was Dave Pomana. 'We got him. It was Vance. His mother is in hospital so she couldn't give him an alibi this time, and we found electrical goods in his car from a nearby house that was burgled last night. He's admitted to everything except slashing Sherry's car tyres.'

Sherry couldn't believe it was over. 'Are they sure it's Vance?'

Glenn put his arms around her. She was shaking. 'Your boss said he was covered in dirt from falling down the hill, and they found fibres from his clothes on some of the bushes. He said he was angry when he'd heard you'd arranged for me to meet Stan for his birthday.' Glenn stroked the hair back from her pale, strained face. 'Sorry about that.'

Sherry leaned against him. 'Don't apologize. You flushed him out for me. Everybody has a breaking point and you were it for Vance.' She gave a wobbly laugh. 'He's probably a big fan.'

Glenn was relieved the stalker had been caught but felt cheated because he hadn't been the one to do it. 'I wish I could have five minutes alone with the prick,' he muttered.

A scrabbling sound at the bedroom window made them both jump, and Otto slunk in.

Glenn greeted him like a returning hero. 'Otto! My man!'

Otto blinked his one good eye and jumped onto the bed. Glenn swept him up like a baby and stroked him under his chin. The feline scourge of the neighbourhood lay on his back with his legs in the air, purring like an outboard motor.

'What self-respecting cat lies like that?' Sherry stroked the fur on his belly, and Otto's purr went from outboard motor to jumbo jet.

Glenn rubbed the cat's ears. 'Don't knock it — he's a

hero.'

Sherry leaned against him, grateful for his solid presence. 'Why? What did he do?'

'Vance got mauled by a cat. His face is all torn up.'

She stopped stroking Otto and stared at Glenn. '*No!*'

'Can you think of another cat that might be responsible? He beats the crap out of any tom that shows its face on his patch.'

'My hero!' Sherry kissed Otto's dangling front paws. She swept the cat from Glenn's arms and took him to the bed, crooning nonsense about superheroes.

Glenn felt things click into place inside him. He was so proud of her. The last few months had been tough for her — last night had been terrible — but she'd stayed strong. He sat down next to Sherry, cupped her chin and kissed her, and then caught Otto's grizzled face and looked him in his eye.

'Are you going to kiss him, too?'

Glenn ignored her and told Otto, 'If you have to testify, I'll buy you a new suit and get Fraser to negotiate the advance for the book deal.'

'Nora promised Custard's owner she'd get him castrated.'

Glenn took Otto and settled him against his chest. 'Custard's owner can go screw herself.' He put his other arm around Sherry. 'My boy isn't getting the chop; he's getting the fillet steak.'

Glenn waited for Sherry to say she wanted to move back to her own place, but she seemed content to stay at the pink house. Glenn loved it, having her live with him meant he could hear first-hand how she and the baby were doing, thanks to Starr's weekly visits. Starr tried to talk Sherry into going to childbirth classes, but she wasn't interested.

'I'll understand if you want to go without me,' Glenn said.

'What do I need classes for? You don't miss chapters, remember?' she replied. 'I'd rather sit at home in bed and watch bad horror movies and you ice your knee.'

'Does that mean you're going to let me be at the birth?'

She wrinkled her nose. 'I'll think about it.'

Living with Glenn gave Sherry an opportunity to steal his shirts and listen into his life. It impressed upon her how different his world was to hers — for instance, she'd had no idea how adroitly Glenn used the media and paparazzi to keep her out of the public eye.

'It's like a game of chess. If I give them something every now and then, they're less likely to go digging. There's nothing more conspicuous than somebody trying to be inconspicuous,' Glenn explained. 'Fraser and I came up with the idea of the golf show as a reason for me to be down here. When I got down here, I held the press conference on the beach and bored everybody to death talking about golf. I heard one of the journos say he never knew Blitz Brogan was such a boring bastard.'

'What would have happened if you hadn't done that?'

'The paps would have been camped on your doorstep with telephoto lenses and knocking on your mom and dad's door and bugging your neighbours. And if that hadn't worked, they'd have gone through your garbage looking for anything that might link you to me.' Glenn watched Sherry shudder and felt his heart sink. So far, he'd managed to keep a relatively low profile in New Zealand, but it was only a matter of time before his luck ran out.

'What about the people who take your photo on their cellphone and put it on the Internet?' she asked pensively.

He shrugged. 'I've learned not to sweat the small stuff. If somebody wants to take my photo on the beach or in a supermarket, then I don't make a big deal about it, but I don't give out many autographs.'

'Why not? You gave Stan your autograph, and Mary.'

'Stan and Mary are different. There are people who collect the autographs of celebrities and professional athletes just to sell them. It's a money-making scam.'

Sherry saw one of them in action during an early-morning walk on the beach a couple of days later. A man approached Glenn and asked for his autograph. Glenn gave the man a long look before taking the pen and paper he held out. 'Sure. What's your name?'

'No need to personalize it,' the stranger said quickly. 'Just your autograph will do.'

Glenn scrawled on the paper and passed it and the pen back with a nonchalant 'There you go'.

The man looked at the paper and threw it in the sand and stalked away.

'Hey!' Sherry shouted. 'Don't litter our beaches!' She dropped to her knees beside the piece of paper.

'Leave it, Sher.'

Sherry smoothed the paper flat on her thigh and

started to laugh. 'I. P. Knightly.' She looked up at Glenn. 'Tacky, Blitz, *very* tacky.'

He shrugged. 'Chopiak uses Iva Begun.'

From then on, whenever they ventured out together Sherry hid behind her biggest pair of sunglasses and wore her grandfather's trilby hat pulled down around her ears. Glenn thought she'd adjust to the situation with time, but knew he was fooling himself when Sherry lost her temper at a woman who tried to snap their picture on her cellphone at a gas station.

He bundled Sherry into her SUV — she insisted on driving her car because the M6 attracted too much attention. 'You're making it worse. *Chill out.*'

'I will *never* get used to it!' Sherry cried unhappily.

If you stay with me, you'll have to, Glenn thought bleakly.

The closest they got to talking about the future beyond the baby's birth was when Glenn mentioned the Bona Fide Blitz Trust in bed one night. 'There's a lot of work being done with battered women and their families. They're always looking for experienced people to help with that.'

'I'm sure they are,' Sherry replied distantly.

Glenn stared in frustration at the credits rolling by on the television in the corner. 'Have you thought about decorating the room and buying baby furniture?'

'Hmmm?'

'Baby furniture — you know, like a cot — that kind of thing. Or were you planning on letting it sleep in a drawer?'

'I ordered a cot and a pushchair off the Internet; they're in boxes in the garage with the paint for the bedroom. As soon as Ben gets a chance to paint the room, Dad is going to put the cot together.'

Glenn was damned if he was letting somebody else paint the room and put the furniture together. He clicked the off button on the remote and tried to remember what Dan and Lisa had bought for Georgia. 'You're going to need more than a cot. What about a change table and a baby seat?'

'I'll hire the seat,' Sherry said sleepily. 'It's all arranged.'

She was drifting off when he demanded, 'What colour paint?'

'Mmmm?'

'What colour are you going to paint the room?'

'Yellow and there's a border with ducks to go around the walls ...'

'Ducks?'

'Ducks are fine for a boy or a girl ...' Sherry fell asleep.

Screw the ducks. Boys had racing cars or spacemen. And little girls had ballerinas and fairies.

The next day, after he and Nora returned from playing Paraparaumu Golf Course in Wellington, Glenn visited a shop specializing in baby furniture and clothing to check out their selection of wallpaper borders. He couldn't see anything he liked, so he called Fraser.

'A customized wallpaper border for the baby's room?' Fraser repeated. 'I don't know that they'll go for it, Glenn.'

'Of course they will, it's got huge market potential. I'll

pay whatever they want and they can take photos of the room.' Glenn figured he'd work on Sherry about the photos when the time came.

The baby furniture got put together and the room got painted, but Glenn wouldn't let Ben or Brian put up the duck border. 'Why not?' Sherry asked.

'I've got something better.'

'I like ducks.'

'Only because you've started walking like one. Trust me,' Glenn said, 'the baby will like this more.'

Sherry forgot about the ducks as she grew more uncomfortable and grumpier, and her yowling got more half-hearted.

'That's it, Custard,' Glenn announced when she climbed in the shower for one last hurrah and their lovemaking made her cry out in pain. He shut off the water. 'Your yowling days are over. I'm hanging up the Stetson. From now on, we're sticking to tarantula spit and yak dung.'

'But I like the Stetson,' Sherry said plaintively.

'I'm flattered you do, honey,' Glenn soothed. 'I like to think I've done some of my best work when I was wearing it.'

She rubbed her side and grumbled, 'I bet you've never refused to have sex with a woman before.'

'Only the mad and ugly ones.' He wrapped a towel around her and grabbed one for himself.

Sherry sat on the lid of the toilet and watched him dry off. She gazed regretfully at the gorgeous body that could be hers if she could only contort herself into the shape of a pretzel. 'I wish I'd taken up yoga. If I knew how to do Down Dog, we'd be fine.' She was sick of being pregnant, sick of having to share her living quarters with a boarder who never went out.

Glenn wound the towel around his waist and rested his hands on his hips. 'Not much longer.' He'd managed to coax Sherry out of her hang-up about him seeing her naked; now there must be a way to break through the brick wall she'd erected about their future.

'When the hang-ten specialist gets here—' Glenn began.

Sherry stiffened. 'Ow! I've got cramp in my leg again!'

He picked her up and carried her into the bedroom.

'I can't wait for this baby to get here!' she moaned.

'I can't wait for it to get here either,' Glenn grunted. 'You weigh a ton.'

Chapter 23

Lisa, Dan and Georgia arrived at the end of April. Sherry gladly gave up being the centre of attention, and Brian and Ben got to meet the new addition to the family.

Georgie B was a velvet-eyed moppet with a mass of dark curls who'd just started cruising her way around the furniture.

'When did that happen?' Jill cried.

'Just before we left,' Lisa said. 'We wanted to surprise you.'

'It doesn't look right seeing someone so short upright,' Ben observed uneasily.

Glenn crouched down and whispered in Georgia's ear, 'You go for it, Georgie B.'

Georgia stared intently at a spot above his shoulder and yelled, 'Yoll! Yoll! Yoll!'

'What's she staring at?' Brian asked.

'We have no idea,' Dan answered. 'That's her other trick. She suddenly stops what she's doing, stares into space and starts yodelling — especially first thing in the morning.'

Georgia clung to the sofa and continued to yell at the spot over Glenn's shoulder.

'Sometimes I think she's looking at someone,' Lisa said. 'Sometimes, I wonder ...' she trailed off.

'What?' Sherry asked.

She shrugged. 'Nothing.'

Georgia suddenly stopped yelling and grabbed handfuls of Uncle Glenn's shirt to sidestep her way around him.

'Want to take her for the night?' Dan asked Glenn and Sherry. 'To get some practice in?'

They both stared at the baby. Sherry panicked. *Omigod, I'm really going to have one of those.* Glenn smiled at Georgia.

Brian fired up the barbecue for the last time before next summer, and Georgia held onto Ben's fingers and wobbled around the deck between his feet.

'You'll want to give up a lot sooner than she will,' Dan warned, and went to drink beer on the seat under the five-finger tree with Glenn. 'So? Have you made any progress?'

Glenn leaned against the tree. 'If you call Sherry stealing all my shirts progress, then yeah, I've made plenty.'

'The Jackson women seem to have a thing about Brogan shirts — when I first knew Lisa she kept stealing my T-shirts for nightdresses.' Dan stretched out his legs. 'Sherry looks really good.'

'I keep telling her that, but she doesn't believe me.' Glenn paused then muttered, 'We've done everything back-to-front; we've never even been on a date.'

'Sounds just like Lisa and me,' Dan replied. 'I wound up married to her without even meeting her.'

'Let's not go there — it's too weird.'

Dan raised his beer. 'Amen to that.' He took a sip and considered. 'What about the night at the honky-tonk? Wasn't that a date?'

Glenn looked uncomfortable. 'That was more an

assignation than a date. Sherry went with some friends; I went with some friends. We agreed to meet up later for a specific purpose.'

'You *planned* to go to bed together?'

He didn't answer.

Dan's brows rose. 'That was some assignation.'

Glenn picked a leaf off the ground and began shredding it. 'I try talking to Sherry, but it's like she's in a bubble and I'm speaking to her long-distance.'

'Lisa was like that at the end.'

He tossed away the leaf and picked up another. 'I don't think it's because she's pregnant, more that she doesn't want to hear. Our expectations are very different.'

'What do you mean?'

Glenn pitched the stalk of the leaf at his shoes. 'I've got expectations and Sherry hasn't.'

'What about the baby?' Dan asked.

He frowned. 'What do you mean, "What about the baby?"'

'Last I heard, you weren't even sure it was yours.'

'It's mine,' Glenn said firmly.

Dan stared. 'You're sure about that?'

'Ninety per cent sure, and one hundred per cent don't care.'

This was a different man from the one who'd returned from New Zealand bitter and angry because he thought he'd been duped again. 'Have you told Sherry that?'

'No.'

'Why not?'

Glenn took a quick, impatient gulp of beer. 'Like I

said, she won't listen.'

Dan felt like smacking his brother in the head with his beer bottle. 'The first time I met Sherry we argued.'

'I'm shocked,' Glenn replied sardonically.

'Sherry told me I wasn't taking care of Lisa properly and I needed to up my game. So do you.'

Glenn was stung by the criticism. 'What's that supposed to mean?'

'You're supposed to be the expert when it comes to women. You've had enough girlfriends to start up a dating agency, so why the hell are you being so stupid?' Dan asked. 'I didn't tell Lisa how I felt about her because I thought it was obvious, but Lisa didn't and I almost lost her.'

Glenn remembered. He'd called, and Dan was drunk and swearing a blue streak. 'You got the sister who knows how to hand-wash woollens; I got the one who knows how to change spark-plugs, remember? Sherry isn't like Lisa; she needs action not words,' he argued.

'Take her to a motel for the night, then, and see if it helps,' Dan retorted.

Ben strolled over with Georgia in his arms and sat down between the brothers. He bounced Georgia on his knee and said, 'Yoll, yoll, yoll.'

She pulled a dribbly fist from her mouth and stared at him. 'You can't have stage-fright if we're going to enter you in *New Zealand Idol*, Georgie B,' Ben told her.

'Is that before or after you enter the hang-ten specialist in the Melbourne Cup?' Glenn asked.

'Depends if Georgie or the basketball peaks first.'

'Do Lisa and I get a say in any of this?' Dan asked.

'Just make sure she practices her yodelling,' Ben

replied.

'Don't worry about it,' Glenn told Dan. 'I'll get Fraser to negotiate their contracts.'

Inside the house, Lisa handed Sherry a glass of grape juice and picked up her wine glass.

'One of the nicest things about being pregnant is not being able to drink wine,' Sherry grumbled. 'And being too fat and uncomfortable to make love.'

'You'll eventually be able to climb back in the saddle again,' Lisa soothed. *You just might be too damned tired to put your foot in the stirrup for the first few months, but you will eventually ride again.* 'I like the shirt.'

'Thank you,' Sherry replied. 'One of the benefits of getting knocked-up by Glenn Brogan is having access to an endless supply of outsized Bona Fide Blitz shirts.'

'Lord knows, you need them outsized at the moment,' Lisa murmured.

'If you say anything about it being twins, I'll empty that bottle of wine over your head.'

'I was *knocked-up,* as you so nicely put it, by the other Brogan, remember? I know exactly how you're feeling at the moment.' Lisa spread some pâté on a cracker. 'What are you going to do when the baby is born?'

'Learn how to do Down Dog.'

She paused with the cracker halfway to her mouth. 'What?'

'Study for my exams.'

'Is that all?'

'Breast-feed and study for my exams.'

'Why can't you admit you care about Glenn?'

'Of course, I care about Glenn; he gives a great back rub.'

Lisa shoved the cracker in her mouth and munched. 'Are you still worried about the birth?'

'No,' Sherry said emphatically, 'because I'm going to be stoned at the birth.'

Lisa changed track. 'If you imagine you'll feel like studying when the baby gets here, then you're in for a big shock.'

'And if Jillian sees you talking with your mouth full, you're in for a big shock, too.'

'Georgia was three months old before I managed to get out of my pyjamas before lunchtime, and I had Dan helping me.' Lisa continued. 'I meant it when I said Glenn will make a great father.'

'I know he will.' Sherry dipped a knife in the pâté and picked up a cracker. 'But he's a great big fake, too.'

Lisa was shocked. 'What do you mean?'

Sherry slapped pâté onto the cracker. 'All the schmoozing, all the jokes at his own expense! Glenn is like an emotional aid agency. He lends money to friends that he obviously isn't going to get back, and pays attention to the ugliest, plainest women to make them feel good. Nora is a case in point.' Sherry dropped the cracker upside-down on a plate and shoved it across the table. 'He always sits down when he talks to Starr, because he knows she's uncomfortable around tall people.'

Lisa looked bewildered. 'What's wrong with that?'

'He's *kind* — I'm not. He's *traditional*, and I'm not. Glenn wants his wife and children safe at home enjoying the benefits of the life he provides for them. He won't be happy with his kids in daycare and a wife who drops by to breast-feed in between following up leads on suspects. Glenn and I aren't like you and Dan, Lisa,' Sherry said miserably. 'We're not suited.'

Lisa stared at her with her mouth open. 'You think Dan and I are *suited?* We're like chalk and cheese! Dan thinks things out to the *nth* degree. He's got so much going on inside his head that he goes days without stringing more than a few sentences together. He thinks I'm too impetuous, and I think he's too cautious. When we argue, we argue *big.'*

'So why are you so happy?'

'We were lucky to find one another. It was a mistake that we did, and we don't ever forget that.'

'You mean George?' Lisa nodded.

Sherry remembered her dream. She hesitated. 'What does George look like?'

'He was big, with twinkly blue eyes and dark-red hair. He had a big laugh. Why?' Her eyes widened. *'Have you seen George?'*

Sherry shifted uncomfortably. 'No! I don't know! I might have, I had a weird dream — but I have lots of those at the moment.'

'Whatever he said — pay attention, Sherry!'

'Can we change the subject? I can't handle this at the moment.'

Lisa scraped pâté off the plate with another cracker. 'You want to know another reason Dan and I are happy?' She leaned closer and whispered, 'Glenn's not the only Brogan who's good at back rubs.'

After the barbecue, they decided to take Georgia to

the beach so she could play in the sand before bedtime.

Dan insisted Glenn get some practice in pushing the baby buggy. It was bright green, covered in yellow chickens, and had handles that could be adjusted for Brogans. 'It's got two gears — forward and reverse,' Dan explained. 'Four-wheel-drive, and one careless owner.'

'What is it with babies and poultry?' Glenn asked as Georgia was being loaded into the buggy.

Ben crouched in front of it. 'Don't listen to your Uncle Glenn. He lives in a pink house.'

Georgia showed her appreciation by slapping his cheeks with her drooly palms.

'What's he talking about?' Dan asked Glenn.

Glenn didn't answer. 'Don't listen to your Uncle Ben,' he told Georgia. 'He's really an alien called Archibald.' He sauntered away in his Blitz sunglasses and Huffer T-shirt, making buggy-pushing look glamorous.

'Who the hell is Archibald?' Dan demanded.

Jill muttered to Brian, 'Other families aren't like this.'

'Yes, they are. Why do you think Dan and Glenn have fitted in so well?' Brian replied.

On the beach, a visitor from the States recognized Glenn and the baby from the *Infinite* photo shoot. He took a photo of Glenn, Georgia and Sherry on his cellphone, and sent it to his family back home. They got it the same night that one of the golf shows Glenn and Nora had taped was aired early because of a problem with the scheduled programme. Visits to Glenn's website tripled, and the next morning a handful of paparazzi were circling the bottom of the driveway leading to Sherry and her neighbours' houses like sharks.

Glenn's charmed existence living a quiet life in an

ordinary suburb had ended.

Sherry felt like she'd fallen down the rabbit hole. An early-morning call from Ditchburn Security alerted them to the presence of the paparazzi. Sherry stood at the balcony window in Glenn's bedroom in her night clothes and stared at the circus at the bottom of the driveway. Glenn had been on his BlackBerry ever since Nora had woken them. He pulled the BlackBerry from his ear and barked, 'Stay away from the window! You're giving them a clear shot!'

Sherry blinked at him through the cotton-wool haze of late pregnancy, and Glenn's fierce expression softened. 'Come away, honey.' He went and gently tugged her away from the window, giving the paps a clear shot of them both, and made her sit on the end of the bed. 'I'll fix this,' he promised, and returned to his call.

Glenn felt terrible. Vance's arrest had meant that Sherry could move around freely again, but now she was back to square one.

The bedroom phone rang. 'Don't!' he exclaimed, but Sherry had already picked it up.

Fortunately, it was only the man at number six ranting, 'I'll run the bastards over!'

'You do that.' She hung up, and the phone immediately began to ring again.

'Don't pick it up.' Glenn yanked the telephone cable from the wall. 'They've found the number.'

Sherry was silent. Glenn wished she'd rave and rant.

He pulled her as close as he could and repeated, 'I promise I'll fix this.'

She leaned into him. He probably would *fix this*. He'd probably fixed lots of *this* in the past. *This* was part and parcel of his life. And whoever shared it. She pulled away. 'I'm going to make a cup of tea.'

Glenn thumbed another number into his cell. 'Stay away from the windows.'

'I will.'

At the bottom of the stairs, she heard the sound of piteous screams coming through the front door. Sherry stared at the door and called, 'Glenn?'

He appeared on the landing above with the phone clamped to his ear. 'Yes?'

She pointed. 'There's something at the door.'

He tucked the phone against his neck. 'Don't open it.'

The screams grew louder. 'There's something on the doorstep.' She reached for the door handle. 'It sounds like kittens!'

'Don't open the door!' Glenn yelled.

Custard's owner had decided to demonstrate her feelings about the rugby scrum blocking the driveway by offloading Otto's unwanted offspring. Four screaming kittens were in a plastic laundry basket on Glenn's doorstep. One was trying to abseil its way down the towels draped over the edge of the basket, one staggered around a pink gnome left behind by Alice, and a third was taking a pee on Glenn's morning paper. The smallest was huddled in the bottom of the basket, screaming and shaking.

On the road below, shutters clicked and whirred as the paps rushed to get a shot of Sherry wearing a black silk robe knotted high above her belly and Glenn in jeans and not much else. He scooped the kittens and soggy newspaper into the laundry basket and hauled it and Sherry inside.

They put the kittens in the garage and tried to keep them in the basket, but they kept climbing out to search for their mother. The noise of their squealing and the sight of them wobbling around the wheels of the M6 reminded Sherry of Georgia. Her blue eyes swam. 'They're too young to be away from their mother. They need Custard. *Glenn! Do something!'*

Glenn cradled a bundle of fur in each hand. Would he ever understand this woman? She'd only just stopped calling Otto 'The Damned Cat'.

He ignored the calls from the road as he climbed the hill to Custard's house and rattled the door knocker shaped like a cat. Custard's owner took a step back when she recognized her visitor, and another step back when she saw how angry he was. The sound of Custard wailing for her kittens somewhere in the house made Glenn even more furious.

'Call yourself a cat-lover?' He stabbed a finger into the house. 'She wants her kittens!'

'They were ready to be weaned,' Mrs Custard replied nervously.

'They can hardly stand up!' It was true about the little one; the other three looked like budding mountain climbers. 'How much do you want for Custard?' Glenn snarled.

She clutched her cardigan. 'She's not for sale.'

Glenn only ever made use of his size on the basketball court, but he was willing to make an exception for Mrs Custard. He leaned forward and growled, *'How much?'*

A few minutes later he stalked back down the hill with a two-thousand-dollar cat wailing and scratching at his neck.

Photographs of Sherry and Glenn on the doorstep with the kittens were posted on the web with the captions she'd dreaded: *Glenn Brogan's Baby Blitz* and *Blitz Brogan Knocks Up Kiwi Cop*. The phone stayed disconnected, but the door knocker rattled. They couldn't visit Dan and Lisa or the rest of the family, and the family couldn't visit them. Starr was almost knocked off her Kawasaki when she made her weekly visit to see Sherry.

Glenn hired security guards and asked the local publicist to look for a secluded property with a good security system. She found them a six-bedroom country house set in fifteen acres about thirty minutes' drive away. Sherry listened to Glenn make arrangements and he mistook her silence for assent.

He found her in the bedroom standing by the laundry basket watching Custard feed her kittens. Glenn had wanted to name them after basketball players, but Sherry put her foot down when he wanted to call one of the females Chopper, and said they had to have Māori names because they were New Zealand cats. The males were Tahi and Toru — or 'one' and 'three' in Māori — and the girls Rua and Rima, or 'two' and 'five'.

'What happened to four?' Glenn had asked.

'Four is "wha" and that sounds like a boy's name.'

'I still think Chopper, Kobe, Magic and Larry were good names.'

Glenn joined Sherry beside the basket. 'It's all settled, we can move in tomorrow.'

She stared at Custard stretched out on her side nursing her babies contentedly. 'I'm not going anywhere.'

'You have to. You can't stay here.'

She shook her head. 'I'm not going. I'm not like you, I can't live like this. You treat it like a game — you thrive on it.'

Glenn tried to be patient. 'I don't thrive on it. I've just learned to live with it.'

She finally looked up at him. 'I don't want to learn to live with it.'

He walked away from her and back again. He didn't want to have this conversation, had hoped that he would never have to have it, but had known it would eventually have to happen. 'My life *isn't* always like this, but you're right, if you stay with me people will believe they have the right to know your personal business and have an opinion about it. They won't always respect your privacy.'

'Why do you want me to stay with you when you don't even know for sure that the baby is yours?' Sherry asked.

Glenn thought they'd buried that problem weeks ago, but it seemed Dan was right and Sherry needed to hear him say it.

'I don't care if I'm the father or not,' he told her. 'It's

only a damned sperm. And I understand about your job. *Yes,* it bothers me that you wear stab-resistant body armour to work instead of a blouse, and that you spend your time talking to criminals instead of customers, but I understand why you do it. I saw you with Stacey and her kids and know how you helped her. I know you're not cut out to stay at home with kids all day.'

Sherry's brows shot up. 'Kids?'

Glenn clutched his head. 'I'm spilling my guts, and all you hear is that! It was a slip of the tongue — I meant *kid*. I don't mind sharing the day-to-day stuff with you, but I'm not doing it all. I've got plans, too.'

She leaned against the pink-and-white wallpaper. 'What plans?'

'I want to go back to college and study urban planning and development.'

Sherry was almost as shocked to hear that as she'd been when he said he didn't care whether he was the baby's father. 'Are you sure?'

'Of course, I'm sure! You're not the only one with a degree.'

'So it's not the thought of going back to university that's making you look so nervous?'

'What does that mean?'

Sherry let it go. He wasn't the only one who was scared by what he was proposing. 'Where do you plan to go to university?'

'This may come as a shock to you, Sherry Ann,' Glenn said with exaggerated patience, 'but there are universities everywhere — there's even a couple in Auckland. Stan and the kids told me that they have the same problems finding somewhere safe to play that kids back home do.'

Sherry thought that Glenn had only talked basketball with the kids. 'You're prepared to stay here? You're making a lot of compromises.'

'They don't feel like compromises,' he insisted.

She was silent for a moment. 'If you weren't in this situation, where would you choose to live? Be honest.'

'America, because my family is there,' Glenn admitted. 'But I'd still want to go back to college.'

'So why do you want to stay in New Zealand?'

Wasn't it obvious? 'Because you and the baby are here.'

It wasn't exactly the wrong answer, but it wasn't the right one either.

Sherry rubbed her forehead. 'I need to think.'

Glenn headed for the wardrobe. 'Great, you think and I'll pack your stuff.'

'I need a few days to think. Alone.'

He stopped. 'Jesus, Sherry! You're so full of that baby you're about ready to pop. *Now* isn't the time to be alone. I'll take you to the new house and promise to leave you alone and give you all the time you want to think.'

Her mouth set stubbornly. 'I'm *not* coming. So you'd better figure out a way to remove yourself and those morons at the end of the driveway before I *pop* this baby.'

Annemarie was called in to play the decoy Sherry and accompany Glenn to the new house.

'If they think you're still here, they won't leave,'

Glenn explained curtly.

With the aid of a black wig, a couple of pillows beneath one of Sherry's maxi dresses, her grandfather's trilby hat, and a pair of dark glasses, Annemarie made a passable Sherry.

Glenn still wasn't happy about leaving her behind, but short of tying her up and dragging her to the car, he didn't have much choice. As usual, he'd made contingency plans, and, as he moved out, Lisa, Dan and Georgia moved in.

'What on earth …?' Sherry spluttered as she watched a portable cot and highchair go past.

'You didn't really think we were going to leave you alone?' Lisa asked.

'There must be gypsy blood in both the families,' Sherry muttered.

A loud *Reoouw!* in the garage and an even louder wail from Georgia announced that the littlest gypsy had just tipped Custard and her kittens out of the laundry basket. Dan had Georgia under one arm and was chasing Custard's babies around the wheels of Glenn's BMW while Custard took angry swipes at his ankles. 'Help me grab these damned cats!'

Lisa took Georgia from him. 'You mean the two-thousand-dollar damned cat?'

Dan stopped. 'The *what?*'

'Didn't you hear? Glenn paid two thousand dollars for her.' Dan looked at Glenn and laughed.

Glenn reddened.

Lisa gazed accusingly at Sherry. 'He did it for Sherry.'

Sherry pokered up.

Annemarie adjusted her pillows. 'It was a nice

thought.

Although, personally, I'd rather have a rowing machine.'

'Don't smile so much,' Glenn advised her rudely as he loaded suitcases into his car. 'Try and look like you've got a poker stuck up your ass.' He gave the bags a final shove with his foot.

Dan muttered in disbelief, 'This floor is *pink*.'

Sherry studied the occupants of the laundry basket. 'Glenn?'

'Yes?' he asked curtly.

She pointed at the basket. 'You've forgotten something.' Tahi's fluffy, flat-nosed kitten face appeared over the edge of the basket. 'You can't expect me to look after them; I'm about ready to pop.'

Glenn added the basket to the collection on the back seat. Maybe they both needed some time apart to think. He was glad Dan and Lisa had agreed to stay with her. And glad the stalker had been caught.

The paparazzi followed Glenn to the new house and moved on when a story about a politician's secret love-child broke. Sherry missed Glenn most at night. The bed felt cold and empty without him. *She* felt cold and empty without him. She watched Dan and Lisa. She played with Georgia and heard that Ben was helping Glenn paint a bedroom at the new house for the baby.

'Is it yellow?'

'Yeah, but Glenn says he's going to customize it.'

'What does that mean?'

'I don't know yet. Come and see for yourself,' Ben

said. 'The house is easy to find, it's just past the Bonking Bush.'

George popped into Sherry's dreams again, but instead of chastising her for not going with Glenn, he said sternly, 'Call Glenn. Make sure he comes to get you.'

Sherry awoke on the last Friday in April and found that the baby had finally unhooked itself from her ribs. She felt lighter and was able to take a deep breath for the first time in weeks. She'd had a backache all night but blamed it on not having Glenn to act as a bolster and rub her back.

'Are you sure you're not in labour?' Lisa asked.

'My water hasn't broken, and I haven't got any pains — just my usual back ache.'

'It isn't any worse?' Dan queried.

'No, I feel great. I'm going to see Glenn.'

'We'll come with you.'

'Thank you, but I want to go alone.'

Sherry packed some clothes, and at the last moment threw the baby's bag and the Moses basket Mary had given her in the back of her car.

'I'm going to call Glenn and let her know she's coming,' Dan told Lisa as they watched Sherry drive away.

'I'm going to let Ben know, too,' she replied. 'He's at the house helping Glenn finish the baby's room.'

Ben watched Glenn smooth the last piece of border into place on the yellow walls of the baby's bedroom. He crossed his arms and nodded appreciatively. 'That is very cool.'

Glenn stepped back to survey the end result. 'Not a word to Sherry.'

'I'm not going to give the game away.' Ben sounded mildly offended.

'Sorry, man. I just ...' He held up his palms: '... don't understand her.'

'Join the club,' Ben replied drily.

Glenn smoothed a tiny bubble of air from beneath the wallpaper border. 'You mean Starr?'

He shook his head and muttered, 'She's a screwball.'

'She's going to deliver the baby.'

'You know I don't mean professionally. I told you what happened.'

Ben had bumped into Starr and some of her friends at a bar in Takapuna and was shocked to see her not only wearing a dress again, but drunk, too. It was clear Starr wasn't used to the nightclub circuit or drinking. Ben would have walked away and left her and her tipsy friends to it, if it hadn't been for a couple of unsavoury-looking types hanging around them — and if he hadn't had to catch Starr when she fell off her bar stool.

She seemed delighted to see him. '*Ben!* You are sooo good at catchin' women.'

He was angry at her for getting into such a state and putting herself at risk, and angry with himself for being angry.

'Time to go, Starr,' Ben said grimly. He attempted to stand her up on her little blue stilettos, but she tipped sideways off them and fell against the bar.

'You are absolutely stonkered!' he snapped and yanked her upright.

'Don't ... be ... boring!' She punctuated each word with a finger in his chest, swayed on her heels and smiled up at him.

One of the flimsy straps of her blue dress slid down her arm.

Ben caught the strap and hooked it over her shoulder. 'What would your grandmother think if she saw you like this?' he demanded. 'You're shit-faced!'

'She wudden mine. She wants me to ... meet a ...' Starr frowned as if she couldn't remember who or what Cloe wanted her to meet, then her face cleared. 'A ... man.'

It was then that Ben grabbed her arm and marched her from the bar.

'Don't rush me!' Starr protested. 'You're goin' too fast!'

It was a three-minute walk to where he'd parked his motorbike at a friend's apartment. Luckily, Ben's friend was in and could loan them a spare helmet.

Starr knelt on the concrete beside the Ducati and tried to hug it. 'Sooo beautiful.'

Ben pulled her to her feet. 'Get up and put this helmet on.'

She tried to do as he asked, and nearly fell over again.

'We're going for a ride?'

Ben grabbed the helmet from her and shoved it none too gently on her head. He followed that up by threading her arms into the sleeves of a cardigan that belonged to his friend's girlfriend. The girlfriend was much bigger than Starr, and the sleeves hung way past her hands, which was what Ben had been hoping for. He got her on the bike behind him and used the ends of the sleeves to tie her arms around his waist. 'Don't you dare be sick on me!'

'OK!'

Starr sang tunelessly in his ear on the fifteen-minute drive to Cloe's house. 'Have I ever tol' you that you're nice?' Ben ignored her, but she hadn't finished. 'There's nothin' wrong with bein' twenty-six and still havin' a hymen.'

His eyes popped open and his brows disappeared into his helmet.

Starr wriggled her arms inside the sleeves of the cardigan. 'What have you done to me?' She tugged harder and the bike swayed.

Ben shouted over his shoulder. 'Stop that!'

'You've tied me up!' she exclaimed indignantly.

'Yeah, I bet your grandmother will be proud when she hears about it.'

Starr stayed quiet until Ben handed her over to Cloe, who was alarmed by her granddaughter's drunken state. 'Starr! What have you done?'

She hugged her grandmother. 'He tied me up, Cloe!'

Cloe's lavender eyes grew even bigger. She looked sharply at Ben who shook his head emphatically. *Not that.* He made his escape soon after.

Glenn smoothed the border with the pasting brush. 'Just as well it was you who found her and took her home. And if Sherry doesn't find her way here soon, I'm going to take a leaf out of your book and tie her up and kidnap her,' he added grimly.

Chapter 24

Apart from a white sedan behind her, Sherry had the road to herself on the journey to Glenn's house. The sun was shining. She knew exactly what she wanted to say to him: that she'd messed up, but she no longer regretted meeting him or getting pregnant.

It only took about twenty-five minutes to get to the Bonking Bush and, according to Ben, the house was just a five-minute drive from there. The bush got its name because it was a popular place to park up. Sherry and Lisa liked to remind Ben about the time he was seventeen and had borrowed their father's car to take a girl to the movies. He'd taken her to the bush afterwards, but the car broke down and Ben had to call his father for help. After that, Brian would only let Ben borrow the car if he promised he
wasn't taking it *off road*.

Fifteen minutes into the drive, Sherry's back ache began to work its way around her abdomen. The pressure was uncomfortable, but not bad enough to stop her driving. Glenn's house was only fifteen minutes away now. She didn't want to stop at a stranger's house; she wanted Glenn. Sherry told herself not to panic, and slowed down so she could concentrate on the road.

The gap between her SUV and the white car had closed. She kept to the left so the man driving could overtake, but he didn't. The country road had lots of tight turns, and she assumed the other driver didn't overtake because he couldn't see far enough ahead to pass safely.

The squeezing feeling came and went. Sherry suddenly had an overwhelming urge to pee. She bit her lip and clamped her knees together. A yellow sign pointing the way to a picnic area and toilets appeared on the left of the road, and she heaved a sigh of relief. She turned off and drove across the clearing to a concrete toilet-block next to the bush, and hurried into the women's side, praying she would make it in time. She'd just made it into a cubicle when a torrent of warm fluid gushed from her and drenched her maternity jeans and shoes.

Sherry braced her hands on the concrete walls of the cubicle and stared at the puddle on the floor. Her legs shook and her heart hammered. She took deep breaths and tried to stay calm. *Don't panic — don't panic — Glenn is only a few minutes away — go to the car and call him — call him and he'll come.*

She made her way shakily outside and back to the car.

The door was open. Sherry looked inside. Her handbag and cellphone were gone. She looked at the ground, thinking she might have knocked it from the car when she jumped out ... and saw that the car tyres were slashed. Her breathing became short and choppy. She looked wildly about the clearing and saw that a white car like the one that had been following her was parked under the trees, out of sight from the road. Sherry couldn't see the driver.

The pressure in her abdomen began to build again. It felt as though a rubber band was being tightened around her back and abdomen. Her car meant safety. If she got in the car, locked the doors and honked the horn, a passing motorist might hear her. The rubber band grew tighter. Sherry pressed her palms on the hood of the SUV and waited it out.

'Good morning, Officer Jackson.'

She looked over her shoulder and was reminded of what Misty had said about Marjorie's husband, Jonathan — that he made the hairs stand up on the back of her neck.

'Start walking.' Jonathan pointed into the bush. 'That way.'

Sherry barely recognized him. He'd never been a handsome man, but prison had ruined what looks he'd had. He looked small and wizened, and there was a yellow tinge to his skin and the whites of his eyes. A part of Sherry wasn't surprised to see him; the part that had known Vance didn't have the patience to keep up the silent phone calls or a reason to slash her car tyres at Marjorie's wedding. Vance was a vicious fool; Jonathan was just vicious. His expression was baleful, gloating.

Glenn, I'm sorry. George, I should have listened.

Sherry's palms felt damp against the hood of the car. Under normal circumstances she would never turn her back on an assailant, but it was the best way to protect the baby. 'I can't walk,' she said breathlessly, 'I'm in labour.' The pain had gone, but Jonathan didn't know that.

Jonathan looked at DC Jackson's wet jeans. She was trying to thwart him again. He needed to get her out of the clearing and into the bush before somebody saw them. His face contorted with fury. He stepped closer and punched her as hard as he could in the back.

Sherry wrapped her arms around the baby and sprawled across the car. She heard Marjorie's voice: *When he's angry he shouts and slaps, but when he's furious he hardly speaks and he uses his fist.*

She started shaking again. She needed to keep Jonathan talking and either find a phone or get the keys to his car. Under no circumstances was she walking into the bush and away from help. Sherry licked her lips. 'Why did you wait so long?' She was relying on Jonathan needing to tell her what he thought of her and what he was going to do to her.

'Do you think I don't know what you're trying to do? I'm not like that idiot.'

The rubber band began to tighten again. 'What idiot?'

'I don't care what his name is,' Jonathan said indifferently. 'I planned to wash my hands of you, just like Marjorie, but then I saw you with that basketball player. He has millions of dollars. He owns nice homes and drives the kind of car I used to drive. He has *my* life. You were going to have *my* life. The one you ruined.'

A truck roared past, and Sherry's head came up. Jonathan panicked and punched her hard in the small of her back, right where the pain was building. She groaned and fell across the car again, holding her belly. He grabbed her arm and tried to drag her towards the bush, but Sherry was taller than him and immobilized by a contraction.

'I told you to move!'

Pink fluid gushed from her and onto Jonathan's

shoes. He let go of her and jumped back in disgust.

The pain abated. Sherry shook. She tried to focus. She couldn't out-run Jonathan; she had to out-think him. Calm down and think!

She heard the sound of a cellphone vibrating at the same time she noticed a small branch lying next to one of the SUV's front wheels. Sherry watched Jonathan touch the right pocket of his blazer. He saw her watching him and drew back his fist to punch her again. Sherry ducked and fell to her knees. She groped for the piece of wood as Jonathan raised his leg and tried to kick her in the face. She caught the branch in both hands and swung it upwards between Jonathan's legs as hard as she could. He dropped like a stone in front of her.

Sherry gripped the branch and watched Jonathan curl into a fetal position and clamp his hands between his legs. He was glassy-eyed and his mouth hung open in a silent howl of agony. She had to restrain him and call Glenn before another contraction hit. For a moment her brain wouldn't work, and she couldn't decide which to do first. Sherry groped in Jonathan's blazer pocket for the phone, but panicked when she realized Glenn wouldn't recognize Jonathan's number. Jonathan groaned and she dropped the phone. The pressure was building again. She didn't have much time. How could she make sure Glenn knew it was her? *Think, Sherry!* Her hands shook so badly she could barely send the message to Glenn's BlackBerry: *Glenda Bonking Bush.*

She snatched up the branch again, and Jonathan let out a howl. Sherry dropped the branch and groaned.

Hurry! Hurry ...

Glenn rested his brow on his forearm and stared out the window at the driveway. Dan had called to say Sherry was on her way nearly forty-five minutes ago. Even allowing for the fact that this was her first visit, she should have been here by now.

Ben was at the next window. He looked every bit as worried as Glenn. They both started when Glenn's BlackBerry went off. He wrenched it from the pocket of his paint-spattered jeans. There was a text message from a number he didn't recognize. Glenn opened it and felt his gut clench.

'Ben! Where's the bonking bush?'

Glenn drove into the clearing so fast that their seat belts were all that stopped him and Ben from smashing their heads on the windscreen when he slammed on the brakes next to Sherry's car. She was sitting in the driver's seat, not moving and with her eyes closed. Glenn went hot and cold as he flung himself from the M6 and ran around the back of the SUV to her door, but she'd locked it.

Ben took a route around the front of Sherry's car and shouted in alarm when he almost fell over something on the ground.

Sherry opened her eyes and screamed when Glenn shook the door handle and banged on the window. 'Sherry, open the door!'

She popped the locks and scrabbled at the door.

Glenn wrenched it open and caught her as she reached for him and panted, 'Jonathan ... stalker ... came ... came ... after me ... tied him ... tied him ... up ...'

Did she say *stalker?*

Glenn cupped her face. '*Slow down*. Take a deep breath and *slow down—*'

Ben shouted, 'Glenn! There's a guy tied to the front of the car with a couple of bras! And the tyres have been slashed!'

Did he say *bras?*

Sherry suddenly grabbed handfuls of Glenn's shirt, crouched forward and groaned.

'What's wrong?' He peered into her face. Her mouth and eyes were screwed shut and her nostrils flared like a racehorse's. 'What are you doing?' Glenn cried.

She hauled in a breath and grunted.

'Oh shit!!'

'Glenn! Come here!' Ben shouted.

'No! Sherry's having the baby! *You* come *here!*'

There was thud and a curse as Ben banged his head on the front bumper. '*What* did you say?'

'She's having the baby! We've got to get her to the hospital!'

Ben arrived at the driver's door clutching his head as Sherry slumped back against the seat. 'Waters broke,' she panted. 'Called the police.'

'You did *what?*' His police-officer sister went into labour, and what did she do? Called the police to collect the cretin tied to her front bumper with bras and forgot about an ambulance to take her to the hospital.

Glenn cupped Sherry's face. 'Did you call an ambulance?'

'No — called you.'

Ben couldn't believe what he was hearing. 'You're having a baby, and you called the police but didn't ask for an ambulance?!'

'Shut up!' Glenn snapped. 'She's not thinking straight.'

Ben grabbed his cellphone and dialled 111.

Glenn lifted Sherry's chin and looked into her glazed eyes. 'Honey? Where are the keys to your car? We need to get you to the hospital.'

'How far do you think you'll get with the tyres slashed and a stalker tied to the bumper?' Ben demanded. 'I'm calling an ambulance.'

'Then help me get her into my car instead!'

He lifted Sherry carefully and followed Ben around the front of the SUV to the BMW, pausing when he saw Jonathan tied to the front bumper with two of the maternity bras he'd bought Sherry. Either Sherry was a master at tying knots or Jonathan was gutless, because by now most men would have either torn free or chewed their way through the bras.

Glenn gently lowered Sherry into the passenger seat of his car, but then couldn't resist going back to Jonathan. 'You piece of shit!' he snarled and gave Jonathan a kick.

They'd had to stop when Sherry had another contraction on the way to the M6, and Glenn had only just returned to the car when she was hit by another. He knew they were in real trouble when she grabbed his collar, lifted her knees and started growling like a Doberman. Glenn heard stitches pop in his shirt and tried not to panic.

Ben threw open the driver's door. 'The ambulance is on its way! Start driving and you can meet it halfway!'

Sherry plucked frantically at her soaked jeans and panted, 'Gle- Gle-Glenn!'

Oh Jesus! Where were the police? They knew how to deliver babies. Glenn turned her sideways on the seat so her legs were facing him and dropped to his knees in the dirt beside the car. 'Get in the seat behind her,' he ordered Ben.

'Huh?'

Glenn tried to speak soothingly to Sherry, but his mouth was so dry his tongue felt like it was glued to the roof of his mouth. He pulled her shoes off. 'We're too late — he's coming.'

Ben looked like he was going to lose his breakfast. 'Here? Now?' he swallowed. 'Oh shit—'

'Stop saying that and get behind her!'

Removing Sherry's wet jeans and underwear was made more difficult because she couldn't stay still, and Ben had to hold her so Glenn could complete the job. She screwed up her face and started pushing again, and Glenn saw the top of a wet, wrinkled scalp. He winced — she looked so swollen and sore. She should be in a hospital with nurses and doctors, not in the middle of the bush with Ben and him. Glenn was terrified. *Where was the fucking police car?*

Sherry's feet slipped on the leather seat as she bore down. Glenn caught her ankles and placed one foot against his shoulder and the other against the side of the car. He tried to remember what he'd read in the books, but his mind kept going blank. It was the coach's job to keep the players focused. 'You're doing a great job, sweetheart,' he said hoarsely. 'Just stick to the game plan and you'll be fine.'

'*Glennn!!*' Sherry wailed and pushed. A gush of pink fluid trickled from her and the baby's head emerged.

'Keep it coming, honey!'

Glenn heard a moan and glanced up to see Ben staring at the baby's head. His face was the colour of putty. He reached across Sherry and smacked Ben on the side of the head. 'Don't you fucking faint on me!'

Ben jerked his eyes up.

'Do *not* look down!'

'*Gle— Gle—*' Sherry grunted.

'He's almost here, darling. I love you.'

The baby's head rotated. Sherry pushed and first one shoulder and then the other emerged.

Glenn held out his hands and caught the slippery basketball that was Jackson Brogan.

The ambulance took Sherry and Jack to the hospital where Starr met them. Ben drove the M6, while Glenn called their families to tell them the news.

Apart from some bruising on her back from Jonathan's fists, Sherry was fine. Jack slept through the ride in the ambulance, and only woke up to protest when Starr unwrapped his blankets so the paediatrician could check him over.

'You did a wonderful job,' she told the two doulas.

For once Glenn had run out of words. He picked Starr up and hugged her. She hung several feet off the floor and patted his shoulder understandingly. 'Why don't you take Sherry's things into her room?'

Glenn looked at the bags and Moses basket he'd rescued from the back of Sherry's car. 'Yeah ... yeah, I'll do that,' he said and headed off.

Ben swiped his hand down his face, and asked Starr, 'Is there somewhere I can get a coffee?'

'Come with me and I'll show you.'

She led the way to a drinks machine opposite the elevators and made him a coffee.

'Thanks.' He took a big gulp of coffee.

Starr took a big gulp of air. 'About the other night ...' she began.

The coffee revived Ben. He brushed a drop from the corner of his mouth with a knuckle and raised his brows. 'You mean the night you were bombed to the soles of your Doc Martens?' He found it difficult to reconcile that Starr with the one standing in front of him wearing a neat white shirt and navy-blue trousers. She had been *so* stupid.

Starr said stiffly, 'Thank you for seeing me home. I don't usually drink like that.'

'Yeah, I guessed that,' Ben replied with heavy irony.

She reddened. 'I don't even know why I went out in the first place. I don't like nightclubs *or* drinking. I don't remember much about what happened.' Starr swallowed. 'Did I say anything unusual?'

It was tempting — it was so, so tempting — but it wouldn't hurt to keep her wondering or to have something tucked up his sleeve if she ever started accusing him again of dumping women at the altar. 'Most of what you said didn't make any sense.'

Her face looked like it was going to burst into flames.

There was so much blood in her cheeks that Ben wondered how her brain still worked. 'If you can't hold your booze, do your drinking at home. Your friends weren't in any better shape than you. You could have been robbed, raped or beaten up.'

Starr's humiliation was complete. 'Thank you again. I've got to … do something.' she mumbled and walked blindly towards the delivery suite.

Dan and Lisa were Sherry and Jack's first visitors.

'Mum and Dad are on their way.' Lisa smiled at her new nephew. 'He's beautiful.'

'Yes, he is,' Sherry agreed.

'Even if he has got a pointy head.'

Sherry fluffed the black hair on top of Jack's head. 'His head is fine.'

'No doubts about who fathered him. He looks so much like Glenn I'm surprised he isn't wearing basketball shoes.'

'You'd think he'd look a little bit like me considering I did all the hard work,' Sherry grumbled.

Lisa placed a package on the bed next to Sherry. 'I brought you a present.'

Sherry looked at the lumpy object wrapped in baby paper making a dent in the bedcovers. 'Take it away, you slapper, I don't want it.'

Glenn and Dan entered the room just in time to hear Sherry call her sister a slapper and reject her gift. Dan laughed, but Glenn was horrified. 'Sherry!'

'We don't want it back,' Dan insisted. 'It's your turn

to have it.'

'We don't want it either — nobody does.' Sherry looked at Glenn. 'It's great-aunt Violet's ashtray. Lisa is just paying me back for giving it to her and Dan as a wedding present.'

Lisa put the package on the locker beside the bed and directed Georgia's attention to the baby. 'That's your new cousin.'

Georgia gave Jack a cursory glance and returned her gaze to the more interesting array of suction tubing and oxygen masks dangling from the wall behind the bed.

Apart from being tired, Sherry looked none the worse for her ordeal. Lisa adjusted Georgia on her hip. 'Ten pounds, two ounces; no drugs, no stitches — you're like a baby machine.'

Sherry felt embarrassed when she remembered how Lisa had looked after she'd had Georgia. 'I'm not really.'

'In the middle of the bush like a pioneer woman,' Lisa teased.

'Yeah, I'm sure a lot of pioneer women had their babies in a BMW.'

'I'm so proud of you, Sher.' Lisa leaned closer and murmured, 'Anybody would think Glenn had the baby — he looks much worse than you.'

Sherry looked at Glenn talking to Dan. Lisa was right, Glenn looked tired and haggard. His hair stood on end, and he was wearing a pair of paint-spattered jeans and shirt. 'He was wonderful — both the doulas were.'

She caught Glenn's eye. They shared a smile, and Sherry gulped to swallow the lump in her throat. He had put up with her when she was cantankerous and miserable, spun stories to shield her from the media, protected her when she was being stalked, and kept his head and delivered Jack.

Jack slipped off her nipple. Sherry called out, 'Starr — he's fallen off again.'

Starr came over to help her latch Jack back on.

There was a tap on the door, and Ben's head popped around it. 'Mum and Dad are here.' He looked at Starr. 'Is it OK if they come in?'

She turned beetroot-red and nodded. 'In a minute.'

Georgia tried to launch herself at the oxygen tubing, and Lisa just managed to keep her from landing on Sherry's head.

Dan walked over and took her. 'Let's take her outside before she starts wrecking the place.'

It took a few tries before Starr got Jack to latch on to Sherry's breast. 'Your parents have arrived. I'm just going to write up your notes. Do you want me to tell them to come in?' she asked.

'Can you ask them to wait a few more minutes?' Sherry replied.

She hadn't had a chance to be alone with Glenn yet.

Starr smiled her understanding. 'Ten minutes?' she suggested.

'That'd be good,' Glenn said.

'I'll get Lisa to guard the door,' Starr promised, and left.

Glenn pulled a chair up alongside the bed. He sat down and rested his arms on the mattress. 'Promise me you'll never do that again. I aged twenty years today.'

Sherry smoothed a finger over the lines at the corners of his beautiful golden eyes and beside his bad-boy mouth. 'You do look a bit worse for wear — I'm sorry.'

She added quietly, 'Are you angry at me?'

He stared in surprise. 'Angry at you? Why would I be angry at you?'

'I put Jack in danger.'

'Not deliberately — and you were both in danger. I just wish I'd had more time alone with that sonofabitch. How on earth did you manage to tie him up while you were in labour, Sherry?'

'I hit him in the crotch with a branch. The first time he fell under the bumper so it was easy to tie one of his wrists. I jabbed him in the nuts again when I felt the next contraction coming, to keep him down, and tied up his other hand when it was over. I was shaking so much I barely managed to tie the knots.' Sherry caught Glenn's hand. 'When Jonathan was hitting me, I understood why women like Stacey put up with what they do. I felt so helpless, but it hurt less if he hit me than if he'd hurt Jack.'

Glenn squeezed her hand and cleared his throat. 'I'm so proud of you.'

'I'm proud of you, too. You were amazing today. I would have lost it if you hadn't stayed so calm.'

'I wasn't calm, I was scared shitless. When the ambulance arrived, I went and threw up in the bush.'

Sherry cupped his cheek. 'Oh, sweetheart ... I do love you.'

'Do you really?' Glenn asked. 'Or is it the hormones talking?'

She stroked his face. 'I do — really. I heard you say it when I was pushing. Did you really mean it, or was it just the hormones talking?'

'No, I meant it.'

'Is that the best you can do?' Sherry asked.

Glenn kissed her gently on the mouth. 'I'll make it up to you by taking you out on a proper date as soon as you feel up to it. We've got plenty of babysitters for Jack.'

'We can't leave him at home — he's breast-fed.' Jack fell off the nipple again. Sherry frowned. 'You never have this trouble; what's wrong with him?'

Glenn took the sleeping baby from her and kissed the point on his head. 'He's working on his technique, don't rush him.'

Sherry pointed an accusing finger at him. 'That's another thing! You knew he was a boy! I heard you say "he's coming" just before he was born. You even had his name picked out!'

'I might have asked the doctor.' Glenn rocked his son. 'You'll thank me when you see his room. He's got something much better than ducks to look at.'

'Like what?'

'A customized border of M6 convertibles, which you have to admit is only right considering he was born in one.'

Sherry started laughing. 'I'm still waiting.'

'What? Oh, that,' he said. 'Don't hold it against me if it lacks a little of my usual finesse, I just had a baby and I'm tired and hormonal.' Glenn picked up Sherry's hand, pressed his lips against her palm, and said gravely, 'I love you, Sherry Ann. I even love you when you look down your nose and act like you've got a poker stuck up your ass.'

She traced his bad-boy mouth with her thumb. 'That's good enough for me, Glenda. Better let Mum and Dad in before Jill breaks down the door.'

Georgia cruised her way around the tables in the waiting room while her parents and Uncle Ben talked. She suddenly stopped and looked up at George. She liked George. He came to see her a lot.

George beamed. 'Who's the most beautiful girl in the world with the most beautiful name?' he asked.

Georgia bounced her knees with excitement.

'You're going to have to be patient with your cousin. Jack isn't like you and your Uncle Glenn; he's going to like sitting and talking like your father used to.'

She beamed.

'Uncle Ben wants to put you in a singing competition. Let's try it again, shall we? *Diddly-diddly-diddly-dum*,' George sang. '*Diddly- dum-diddly-dum ...*'

Georgia banged the top of the table and yelled, 'Yoll! Yoll! Yoll! Yoll! Yoll!'

Acknowledgements

After Bonkers was released, I got asked by readers what happened to Lisa and Dan and the Jacksons and Brogans afterwards. I always intended that the story of the Jackson family would continue and thought Sherry's story was a few books away. I settled down to write something else, but Glenn and Sherry had other ideas: they 'talked down' the characters in the book I was working on until I gave in and wrote their story instead. A lot of people helped me with Barefoot, and I apologize in advance if I've left anybody out. Any mistakes or inconsistencies are down to me. Thank you to Detective Sergeant Kelly Farrant-Alofa from the family violence team at Henderson Police Station in Auckland. I met Kelly the day she was going on maternity leave, and she continued to patiently answer my questions on police procedure, exams, and Sherry's career pathway, even after she gave birth. Thank you to Rob Neish, physiotherapist, for advice on the injuries and rehabilitation of professional basketball players, and to Sacha Halpin for letting me borrow her hilarious 'lunchboxes' story. I'm indebted to midwife Kelly Falconer for finding time between delivering babies to discuss midwifery, pregnancy, birth and anything else I threw at her. Thank you also to Piers Scott of BMW, Auckland, for choosing the perfect car for Glenn and customizing it — The Blitz and I are very grateful. I know nothing about motorbikes, but fortunately my brother Wayne does. He chose Ben and Starr's motorbikes and filled in the gaps in my knowledge. I 'met' American author Cher Gorman via email after I sent out an SOS to the writing world asking for info on Denver. Thank you, Cher, for providing great feedback on life in the Mile High City, local golf courses, and where Lisa and Dan, and Glenn would live. Dedicated NBA fans will realize the Colorado 'Cougars' do not exist, but I had lots of fun creating the team and the players.

Finally, thank you to Dixie and Ammie at Indie Experts Publishing and Katie Fisher for the funky cover.

I love hearing from readers. You can follow me on my Facebook page and sign up for my newsletter on my website for progress and release dates on my next books. (Links on following page)

Best wishes,
Michelle

About the Author

Introducing Michelle Holman, the witty wordsmith from the lush landscapes of New Zealand, whose enchanting tales of romance and laughter have captured the hearts of readers worldwide. With a pen as her compass and humour as her guide, Michelle weaves stories that transport readers to a world where love conquers all.

From her debut novel, "Bonkers," to her latest masterpiece, Michelle's writing sparkles with warmth and charm, inviting readers on a journey filled with unforgettable characters and heartwarming moments. Her novels are a celebration of love, friendship, and the joy of finding laughter in life's unexpected twists and turns.

As a nurse turned author, Michelle infuses her writing with the same compassion and empathy that defined her career in healthcare. Her characters leap off the page with authenticity, their struggles and triumphs reflecting the universal experiences of the human heart.

For details about all Michelle's books, including upcoming titles and work in progress, please visit:

@michelleholmanauthor

www.michelleholman.com

www.ingramcontent.com/pod-product-compliance
Lightning Source LLC
Chambersburg PA
CBHW020639120726
47906CB00001B/40